PRAISE FOR
LUANNE RICE
AND *WHAT MATTERS MOST*

"None of Luanne Rice's characters love half-heartedly.... The story of these far-flung family members, their connections and how they find one another, makes for a good page-turner. The author's love of the ocean, the shore, and her native Ireland breaks through each page like a wave.... Sister Bernadette is a refreshingly real character.... Rice writes unabashedly for women, imbuing her tales with romance and rock-strong relationships. However, the stories she crafts lift themselves above the typical escapist romance novels. Rice's characters grapple with the weighty issues that come with loving other people. *What Matters Most* is something each character struggles to identify within the circle of family and relationships. Fans of Rice's work will not be disappointed. Her stories are for women who face trying relationships with their own husbands, daughters, or paramours." —*Chicago Sun-Times*

"True love never dies—but it may need the helping hand of the Virgin Mary and the luck o' the Irish to survive in Rice's latest.... There's guilt, redemption and three-hankie moments aplenty." —*Publishers Weekly*

"Emotions run deep and hard in *What Matters Most*.... Grab a hankie and experience the emotion of reading a Luanne Rice novel. The characters are real, the situations intense." —Romance Reviews Today

"Rice skillfully weaves together the stories of these two apparently doomed romances, shifting across time and continents.... Rice's characters are engaging, compelling the reader to keep those pages turning until all loose threads are tied." —*Booklist*

"What Rice is a master of is emotional intensity: I defy any woman who loves anyone (a parent, a child, a husband, a dog) to get through this book without using up at least a purse pack of disposable tissues." —CinCHouse.com

AND MORE CRITICAL ACCLAIM FOR LUANNE RICE

"A rare combination of realism and romance."
—The New York Times Book Review

"Luanne Rice proves herself a nimble virtuoso."
—The Washington Post Book World

"Few writers evoke summer's translucent days so effortlessly, or better capture the bittersweet ties of family love."   *—Publishers Weekly*

"Ms. Rice shares Anne Tyler's ability to portray offbeat, fey characters winningly."   *—The Atlanta Journal-Constitution*

"Rice has an elegant style, a sharp eye, and a real warmth. In her hands, families, and their values...seem worth cherishing."
—San Francisco Chronicle

"Luanne Rice has enticed millions of readers by enveloping them in stories that are wrapped in the hot, sultry weather of summer....She does it so well."   *—USA Today*

"What a lovely writer Luanne Rice is."   —DOMINICK DUNNE

"[Luanne Rice's] characters break readers' hearts....True-to-life characters dealing with real issues—people following journeys that will either break them or heal them."   *—The Columbus Dispatch*

"A joy to read."   *—The Atlanta Journal-Constitution*

"Addictive...irresistible."   *—People*

"Rice writes as naturally as she breathes."   —BRENDAN GILL

"Few...authors are able to portray the complex and contradictory emotions that bind family members as effortlessly as Rice."

—*Publishers Weekly*

"Full of all the things families are made of: love, secrets, traditions, and memories."

—*Providence Journal*

"Luanne Rice handles with marvelous insight and sensitivity the complex chemistry of a family that might be the one next door."

—EILEEN GOUDGE

"Rice, a terrific storyteller and a poetic stylist, takes on a difficult and brutal subject and transforms it into a source of light and hope."

—*Booklist*

"Irresistible...fast-paced...moving...vivid storytelling. Readers can almost smell the sea air. Rice has a gift for creating realistic characters, and the pages fly by as those characters explore the bonds of family."

—*Orlando Sentinel*

"What the author does best: heartfelt family drama, gracefully written and poignant."

—*Kirkus Reviews*

"Rice, always skilled at drafting complex stories...reveals her special strength in character development."

—*The Star-Ledger*

"Rice's ability to evoke the lyricism of the seaside lifestyle without over-sentimentalizing contemporary issues...is just one of...many gifts that make...a perfect summer read."

—*Publishers Weekly* (starred review)

"Rice, as always, provides her readers with a delightful love story filled with the subtle nuances of the human heart."

—*Booklist*

"Luanne Rice touches the deepest, most tender corners of the heart."

—TAMI HOAG

"Pure gold."

—*Library Journal*

Novels by Luanne Rice

LUANNE RICE

What Matters Most

A Novel

Bantam Books Trade Paperbacks
New York

What Matters Most is a work of fiction. Names, characters, and incidents either are the product of the author's imagination or are used fictitiously. Any resemblance to actual persons, living or dead, events, or locales is entirely coincidental.

2010 Bantam Books Trade Paperback Edition

Published in the United States by Bantam Books, an imprint of The Random House Publishing Group, a division of Random House, Inc., New York.

BANTAM BOOKS and the rooster colophon are registered trademarks of Random House, Inc.

Originally published in hardcover in the United States by Bantam Books, a division of Random House, Inc., in 2006.

Title page photo: "The Irish Coast," by Rachel Gilmore
Part title photos: "Child on a Beach" by Jason Conlon
"Cottage Window" by Henriette Hansen
"Sea at Sunset" by Yucel Tellici

Library of Congress Cataloging-in-Publication Data

Rice, Luanne.
What matters most / Luanne Rice.
p. cm.
ISBN 978-0-553-38686-8
1. Nuns—Fiction. 2. Connecticut—Fiction. 3. Couples—Fiction.
I. Title.
PS3568.I289W47 2007
813'.54—dc22 2006102142

Printed in the United States of America

www.bantamdell.com

2 4 6 8 9 7 5 3

Book design by Virginia Norey

To Irwyn Applebaum,
With love and gratitude

Acknowledgments

I'm grateful to everyone at Bantam Books, starting with my publisher, Irwyn Applebaum; my beloved editors—deputy publisher Nita Taublib and Tracy Devine; and Kerri Buckley. Thank you to Betsy Hulsebosch and Carolyn Schwartz for everything, including the *What Matters Most* website, and to Cynthia Lasky, Barb Burg, Gina Wachtel, Melissa Lord, Christian Waters, Sarah Elliott, Kenneth Wohlrob, Quinne Rogers, Sarah Smith, Jordana Schlisser, Stacey Levitt, Igor Aronov, Mark Brower, Kathleen Baldonado, Ruth Toda, Deb Dwyer, George Fisher, Phil Canterbury, Lane Rider, and all the sales reps. I'm grateful to Paolo Pepe for the luminous book cover, and to Virginia Norey for the poetic interior art. I'd like to single out and thank Susan Corcoran, my publicist, because I've been with her since day one.

Love and gratitude to my agent and close friend Andrea Cirillo, and everyone at the Jane Rotrosen Agency: Jane Berkey, Don Cleary, Meg Ruley, Peggy Gordijn, Annelise Robey, Kelly Harms, Kelli Fillingim, Christina Hogrebe, Trinity Boscardin, Lindsay Klemas, Kathy Lee Hart, and Penelope Bussolino.

Much gratitude to Blair Brown for reading this novel, and to Sherry Huber, producer at Random House Audio.

I am thankful beyond words for my sisters and their families: Rosemary, Roger, Kate, Molly, and Emily Goettsche; and Maureen, Olivier, and Amelia Onorato. Also, I send love to my parents and Mim.

Thank you to Robert and Joan Arrigan, for the news from Ireland and Rhode Island.

Mia and the BDG forever.

Maggie, Mae-Mae, and Maisie always.

My ancestors, my friends, my beloveds, the ghosts, my saints, the ones who guide me, thank you for letting me see what matters most.

Prologue

The annual Children's Home summer beach picnic was on everyone's mind, and the kitchen was bustling. A ham roasting, to be sliced and served cold; Dublin Bay prawns, a gift from one of St. Augustine's benefactors, chilling in the huge refrigerator; fresh-baked bread cooling on the rack; cookies already packed into baskets.

Kathleen Murphy, thirteen, stood at the long stainless-steel work table, peeling potatoes for potato salad. Her fingers worked so fast, a total blur to anyone who might be watching. Her long dark hair was held back in a ponytail, and her clothes were protected by a stiff green apron. She kept one eye on her work, another on the side door. Sister Anastasia would be back in five minutes, and if James Sullivan wasn't here by then, there'd be hell to pay.

She occupied her mind by imagining the elegant meal she wished she were preparing instead of the one she actually was. While her work as kitchen apprentice to Sister Theresa had taught her how to prepare institutional food as well as any other student, Kathleen dreamed of making gourmet meals—the kind she read about in Sister's fancy cookbooks: artichoke and arugula salad, Marseilles bouillabaisse, rack of lamb, seared tuna, mushroom risotto...

When the door finally opened and James came tearing in as if running down the football field, Kathleen finally let out a breath—along with the scolding he so desperately needed.

"For the love of God, what're you trying to do? Get us all in trouble? You want to ruin the picnic? You know if she gets mad she's liable to cancel the whole thing! Here it is, our summer outing, and you're trying to destroy our fun. That's just like you, James. Just exactly, completely—"

"Oh, stop it, Kathleen," he said, grinning as he caught the towel she threw him. "You know Sister's not canceling anything. She's as excited as you are."

"Where were you, anyway?" Kathleen asked, suspicious. James had been late to his dishwashing job every day this week. Usually he told her everything. They lived in separate quarters, of course—him with the boys, her with the girls—but they had always arranged to be in the same classes, at the same recreation periods, and in the same general vicinity for jobs.

"Could you possibly have used more dishes, cooking today?" he asked, viewing the pile in the sink.

"Don't give me any trouble," she warned him. "I covered for you with Sister. She asked what you were doing, and I told her you were unloading the grocer's truck out back. When she sees that sunburn and all those new freckles, she'll know I was lying, that you've been out in the sun somewhere. Where were you? Tell me, James."

"I will," he said, attacking the dishes. "I promise. But first, let me put a dent in this mountain." He glanced over, gave her a devilish smile, making her melt. He always did. His hair was too red, and he had too many freckles, and his ears stood out, but the sight of him made Kathleen's heart beat just right: nice and steady, safe and happy.

She worked twice as fast, now that he was here, slicing up potatoes into perfect cubes, tossing them into the big stainless-steel bowl. She and James had met as babies. They had been born in the same hospital, three weeks apart, and their mothers—for reasons known only to God, the nuns, and their mothers themselves—had decided to drop them off at St. Augustine's Children's Home, a red-brick institution on a quiet side street in a residential Dublin neighborhood. Bye-bye, babies.

Kathleen remembered being in the nursery with James. She did— no lie, and when people tried to suggest she didn't really remember that far back, she'd been known to fight them. This was her oldest, strongest memory, and she safeguarded it with a vengeance. Their cribs had been side by side. When she'd cry at night, she'd turn over and see his big blue eyes staring at her. No matter what time it was, he'd be wide awake, keeping watch over her. Always there, right there.

The nuns kept infants and toddlers together until the age of four, not worrying about whether they were boys or girls. The cuter the baby, the faster the adoption. Perhaps it was James's reputation for not sleeping that kept him at St. Augustine's that first year; probably it was Kathleen's propensity to wail her head off day and night that had thwarted her departure. Whatever the reason neither of them had been adopted, they made it through that first year together.

Even before they learned to talk, they whispered and laughed in their own language. They chased each other around the nursery— first crawling, then toddling. James's favorite toy was a corduroy lamb, and Kathleen's was a baby doll with red hair.

When he was two, a family took James for a tryout. Kathleen remembered, as clearly as if it were yesterday, the feeling that her right arm had been cut off. Instead of crying about it, she had stopped crying altogether—stopped babbling, gurgling, eating, and sleeping, too. She slept with her red-haired doll clutched to her heart.

One night she reached through the bars of her crib to pull James's crib—even though he was no longer in it, and it was now occupied by a pudgy bald toddler named Bartholomew—close to her. All she'd wanted was to touch the mattress on which James used to sleep, to grasp a corner of his pillow in her little fingers. But poor Bartholomew had been terrified, not knowing what she was doing, and he broke his arm trying to climb over the bars to get away.

The test adoption of James hadn't worked very well.

He came back to St. Augustine's. Although the official reason given had been that he kept everyone up at night with his startling imitation of Dublin's crows, Kathleen knew otherwise. "Caw!" he'd cry. "Caw, Caw!" To some, the noise he made sounded like the huge birds roosting in the trees along the serpentine of St. Stephen's Green. But "Caw" was actually James's way of saying "Kathleen." It was his first word.

When they were three, Kathleen was taken by a couple who lived in Dun Laoghaire, in a house near the harbor. They were older, disappointed by life and their inability to conceive a child of their own. They admitted to the administrator that their parish priest had suggested the adoption as a way to save their marriage. They smelled of cabbage and tobacco. Their house was small and cramped, unlike the sprawling, drafty Children's Home.

Kathleen's heart constricted with grief, missing James. At night, she would sob silently in her bed, holding her red-haired doll close to her face. If she concentrated very hard, she could feel James with her, see his blue eyes through her crib's bars. Her heartache was so deep she developed a fever, soaking the sheets with sweat and tears.

"It has *germs*," the couple told her, pulling the worn little doll from her arms. "There are diseases in that place, and this has to go." Then they threw it in the trash.

That night, after the couple went to bed, Kathleen climbed over the bars of her crib, toddled down the dark, narrow hall, and climbed backwards down the steep stairs. Her heart was broken, and even at three she knew she had nothing left to lose. Opening the cupboard under the sink, she found the overflowing kitchen garbage pail. Choking on sobs, she reached up, trying to get her little hand inside, where she'd seen them discard her doll.

Tugging the pail over, she was suddenly covered with buttered noodles, cabbage leaves, tea bags, and cigarette butts. But she had her doll, and she held it to her thrashing heart. Awakened by the clatter, the couple came running downstairs. Kathleen heard them shrieking with dismay, felt them trying to pry her doll from her fingers. She wasn't sure which one she bit—as hard as she could, sinking her teeth into his or her hand—and she honestly didn't care. "James!" she cried. "James!"

She was covered with garbage, but they didn't even bathe her before driving her back to the Children's Home.

By the time they were four, James was moved into the boys' wing, and Kathleen to the girls'. The adjustment was difficult, but they found many ways to be together. The Children's Home was shaped like a big U, and every night before bed, they would stand in their respective windows and wave. When Kathleen couldn't sleep, she would go to the window, and as often as not, James would be standing there, watching from his room across the courtyard for her.

Years went by. When she hated doing math and science homework, he did it for her. When they had a Christmas pageant, he helped her rehearse to be Mary. When she got lice and the nuns made her cut off her long dark hair, he held her while she shook and shuddered, telling her she was the prettiest girl in the world. When Sister Anastasia gave Kathleen the much-coveted kitchen apprentice job, James took the conversely loathed and always-avoided dishwashing position.

And sometimes, when the east wind blew and the smell of the sea wafted over the Dublin rooftops, they would stand in the tar courtyard and talk about going to the beach. The nuns took them once a year, during the summer, and to both Kathleen and James, those were the happiest times. Their feet in the sand, swimming in the water, playing all day and feeling as happy as anyone in the world.

While workers at the Children's Home said that James and Kathleen were like brother and sister, Kathleen knew that wasn't true. What she felt for James was so much deeper than that. He was her family, yes, but not in the simple, innocent way kids felt for their siblings. Kathleen had seen brothers and sisters—orphaned by car crashes, or abandoned by alcoholics, or left homeless by fire—arrive at the Home. She had seen them stick together, protect one another, tease each other. Kathleen had watched how comfortable they seemed together, but also, sometimes, capable of indifference, sharp cruelty, and intense rivalry with each other.

Kathleen had never felt those ways about James. She loved him down to her bones. There were moments of comfort together, but as time went on, they gave way to such deep, nameless longing, she felt it along every inch of her skin.

Sometimes the nuns rented videos for them, and when Kathleen saw love scenes, a girl kissing a boy, she thought of James. Lying in bed at night, she used to imagine him kissing her like those kids in the movies. Last winter, on a cold night when everyone else was snuggled in their beds, they had made it come true. They had kissed in the warm furnace room, and in that moment when Kathleen had felt his shy arms around her, she had known the meaning of true, utter happiness; pure closeness with another human being.

"How long are we going to live at the Home?" she asked him one day last spring, on a group excursion to Glencree, in the Wicklow Hills, shortly after a visit from the nun James called Sister Nemesis. Walking along a stream, they found a shady spot under a weeping willow tree, and sat down.

"Until we grow up," he said. "I guess. How long do other kids stay in their homes?"

By then they'd both given up hoping and fearing they'd be adopted. The Children's Home was where they belonged. The nuns were kind to them, and made special allowances for the kids who had been there longest—Kathleen and James, as well as five or six other older children. James had the attention of one nun in particular.

She didn't live at St. Augustine's, but was a member of the same order as the Sisters who ran it. Sometimes she came alone, other times with a very heavy nun by her side. Stern and odd, she would ask James questions, give him IQ tests, things like that. Whenever she came, Kathleen would panic, thinking the Sister was going to tell him she'd found him a home. But she never did.

"Do you ever think about where you came from?" Kathleen asked, shredding a willow leaf and staring at the water.

"What do you mean?"

"Your mother and father," she said. "Your parents. Do you ever think of them?"

He shook his head. She stared at him, scared of the look in his eyes.

"Never," he said. "They didn't want me. Gave me away. Why should I think of them?"

"I don't know. Just seems natural," she said. "You could ask Sister," she continued. "The one who always comes to check on you."

"Sister Nemesis?" he asked. "Or Sister Tub-o-Lard? What do they know?"

"Well, they're interested in you for some reason. Maybe they know where you came from, and they'd tell you if you asked—tell you your parents' names!"

"Why, so I could thank them personally for leaving me in this place?"

"So you don't think of your parents?"

"Think of lousy rotten people who didn't even want their own son? Ha! No way, Kat. Don't tell me you think about your parents?"

Kathleen shrugged, not wanting to admit to him that she thought of them often, sometimes had fantasies of them showing up together at the Children's Home in a great big car, with fancy silver wheels. They would walk up the steps, her mother in a beautiful fur coat and her father in a striped suit—like the adoption lawyers who sometimes showed up to haggle over paperwork—and ask to see Kathleen Murphy.

They would love her on sight, of course. She would tumble into their arms, and they would tell her it had all been a terrible mistake. They had never meant to give her to the nuns...on this her fantasy stumbled, but she figured it had something to do with amnesia, financial reversals, or a near-fatal disease. They would tell her they wanted her to return home with them, and she would ask if she could bring James. Because her parents loved her so much and could deny her nothing, they would agree instantly.

"No, I never think of them," she said to James, unable to admit the truth, knowing that he would take it as a betrayal.

"Good," he said, taking her hand. "We're alone in the world, Kat, and don't forget it."

"But what..." she began slowly, wishing she could win him over to the idea that maybe their parents were really wonderful people so he'd be more willing to join her when hers finally arrived. "What if they're really good? What if they really loved us, but just couldn't raise us?"

"Kathleen," he said, bringing his face close to hers, looking hard into her eyes, the way he used to when they were babies and their cribs side by side. And now, since that kiss in the furnace room, creating a rush of grown-up longing all through her body. "They don't care about us. They threw us away. We're *unwanted*."

"I want you," she said, squeezing his hand, not really knowing what she meant, or why the words made her throat ache.

"And I want you," he said, squeezing back. "You're mine, and I'm yours. That's just the way it is, the way it will be forever. That's why we've never gotten adopted—because we're meant to be together."

"What will happen after we grow up and leave the Children's Home?"

He shook his head. "Don't worry about that. I'll take care of you, Kathleen. Haven't I always?"

"Yes," she said. "You have."

"You're mine, and I'm yours," James said, and the way he moved his hand to her wrist and slowly up her bare arm, making her whole body tingle, the way he looked into her eyes, reminded Kathleen of the way love looked in the movies, the way she and James had started making it come true in their kiss that December night, and she nearly fainted with yearning.

But then Sister Lucia called for everyone to return to the van, and the moment was over. Kathleen had been thinking about that winter kiss, wanting more, ever since. James had had many other chances to kiss her at the Home, but he wouldn't. Not because it would be breaking the rules—he didn't care about that—but because it wouldn't be romantic. Kathleen knew that James would want their first summer kiss, especially, to be magically romantic.

Somehow she knew that he was waiting for the trip to the beach. That's when he'd kiss her. Her dream would come true on that white strand, with the blue sea sparkling all around. As she lay awake in the girls' wing, her fantasies about her real parents coming to claim her gave way, completely, to the moment James would take her in his arms.

It kept her going, it did. These were trying times. It wasn't easy being thirteen. Especially going to school with "normal" kids, ones who had real families, parents who could buy them nice clothes and drive them places, to football games and movies and parties. Not that Kathleen, James, and the other Children's Home kids weren't invited, and not that the nuns didn't try to make sure they had what they needed—but it was hard. Kathleen was actually wearing hand-me-downs from Sister Clare Joseph, a novice who had joined the order last fall and no longer had any need of jeans, sweaters, and the rattiest T-shirts Kathleen had ever seen.

The day of the picnic everyone was in a good mood. Sister Anastasia hurried into the kitchen, praising Kathleen's cooking, helping her pack everything into coolers and baskets, ignoring James's sunburn and the fact he'd been missing for the past hour.

"Kathleen, you're a wonder," she said, tasting the ham Kathleen had seasoned according to the recipe in the Julia Child cookbook. "We're blessed to have such a talented chef, aren't we, James?"

"Indeed," he said, scrubbing pans.

"Perhaps you'll go to a cooking academy one day. And open a restaurant! We'll all be sure to go, if that ever happens."

"Thank you, Sister," Kathleen said, shimmering with pride.

"A restaurant," James said, when Sister headed out to the van carrying a load of provisions for the picnic. "How about that?"

"Maybe I'll just cook for my family," she said. They'd stared at each other across the soapy water, and she'd felt a funny shiver run down her back. Did James know she was talking about him?

"Yeah," he said, his eyes shining, letting her know he did.

"To the beach!" Sister called, ringing the bell. All the kids rushed down from their rooms, the older ones carrying the youngest, some of them already wearing their bathing suits, so eager were they to enter into the day, regardless of the nuns' admonitions to change once they got there.

The ride to Courtown, County Wexford, was long and seemed to take forever. The girls sat in one van and the boys in the other. Sister Lucia drove the girls, playing the radio and all of them singing along. Kathleen sat in back, turning in her seat to look out the rear window, trying to see James.

When they got to North Beach, everyone piled out. Blankets were spread on the hot sand, and beach balls inflated, and right away a bunch of kids ran into the water. Kathleen took off her shirt and shorts, and she saw the way James looked at her blue bathing suit. It made her blush, and she hoped he wouldn't notice, would think that it was just the heat of the sun.

"Are you going to tell me?" she asked as they walked toward the edge of the water, wondering when he would reach for her hand, pull her behind the sand dunes to be kissed. "Why you were late in the kitchen? You promised."

"I did," he said, looking around, to make sure the nuns weren't listening.

"What is it?" she asked, feeling excited, but also a little scared by the look in his eyes.

"I heard something," he said. "When I was outside Mother Superior's office."

"What, James?" she asked.

"I heard that your parents called. Your real parents, Kathleen. They want to take you home."

"They what?" she asked, stopping dead in her tracks.

"It's true," he said, taking her hand. "I didn't want to tell you back at the Home, because I knew it would shock you. Listen, Kathleen. I won't let them take you. No matter what—you can count on me."

"But James..."

"It's what I was doing, when I wasn't at work," he said. "I was out back of the Home, getting some things out of chapel and the shed, hiding them in a bush. Things we can take when we escape, Kathleen!"

"Escape?"

"Yes," he said, nodding vigorously. "Some food, money, things we can sell."

"Sell? What are you talking about?" she asked, backing away. Her head was spinning—a combination of the heat that had built up from wanting James to kiss her, the fantasy of her real parents, and James talking about escape. "Did you steal something?"

"Never mind that, Kathleen," he said. "We have to survive! If they're talking about sending you back to your real parents, Jesus! I'll do anything to keep you from that. Don't you know I'd do anything for you?"

"But maybe they're wonderful," she said, grabbing his hand. "Maybe they'll let you come live with them, too!"

"Listen to yourself," James said, shaking her. "They didn't want you! It's been thirteen years—where have they been? Kathleen! Forget about them. I snuck the stuff I got for us onto the van. It's in my bag. We can wait till after lunch, when everyone is resting, and we'll slip off. You can cook, just like Sister said. I'll wash dishes. We can open a restaurant! Jesus, I nearly died when you said you could cook for your family."

"I was thinking of you," she whispered.

"I know," he said. "That's why we have to run away."

Kathleen was horrified. Run away from the nuns? From the Home? And just as her real parents were finally coming to get her? Tears scalded her eyes, and she wriggled out of James's grasp. "No," she said. "I'm not running away."

"Kathleen..."

"And you're not, either. We have to put the stuff back. I don't care what it is, but you're not a thief, you're not going to start that now. Put it back, James. Where is it?"

He stood there, arms folded across his skinny bare chest, staring at her. His eyes were hard, shocked, hurt, and as blue as the sea just over his shoulder.

"If the nuns find out..." she said, panic rising. "You know that's the one thing they don't tolerate. Stealing. We have to pray they don't discover what you've done."

"You'd go with them?" James asked. "Your real parents?"

It was as if he hadn't even heard what she said, wasn't even thinking about his stolen goods, the fact the nuns could turn him over to the police, send him to a juvenile facility, depending on what he took. She thought of an older boy from a few years back, who'd stolen a gold chalice to sell for drugs. He'd been arrested.

"Tell me, Kathleen. If you had to choose them or me, who would you choose?"

Her heart was pounding so hard, she thought he could see it through her bathing suit. It made her feel dizzy, and her mouth was dry. She wanted to lie to him, just to make him feel better, but she loved him too much for that. She owed James everything, especially the truth.

"They're my parents," she whispered. She didn't even know what she meant; they were people she didn't know, but didn't she have to give them a chance? That's all she meant—or, at least, thinking back, that's what she thought she meant. The truth was, even now, she wasn't sure whom she would have chosen. If they were standing right there before her, her real parents and James, she couldn't let herself imagine taking a step toward one, leaving the other behind.

But it was enough for James. In that instant, she saw his heart break. His blue eyes filled with tears. She had never seen him cry before, and it turned her to jelly. She reached for his hand, wanting to take it back.

"You're mine," she said. "And I'm yours."

But he turned from her and began striding away down the beach. She started to run after him, but then she heard Sister Anastasia call his name in a voice so stern, Kathleen knew even before turning around.

When she looked over her shoulder, she saw the nun coming toward them, black veil and skirt blowing in the sea breeze, holding James's blue duffel bag against her chest.

"James!" Sister called. "Come here! I want to talk to you!"

But James just kept walking. He didn't run, didn't look back. Perhaps he expected, or wished for, Kathleen to go flying after him, catch up with him, run away with him, or try to convince him to come back.

She didn't.

And her real parents were waiting when they returned from the beach that day, and they took her home, and she never saw James again.

PART ONE

One

Sister Bernadette Ignatius and Tom Kelly sat in the back seat of a black cab, driving from Dublin's airport through the city. She felt jet-lagged from their flight from Boston and all the weather delays, but full of anticipation about what she was about to find out. Although she hadn't been here in over twenty years, Dublin looked so familiar: the lovely Georgian townhouses with their fanlights and brightly painted doors, stone bridges arching over the River Liffey, the columned facades of imposing government buildings.

"Well, look at that," Tom said, leaning across the seat to point at the cozy brick bar with hot pink petunias spilling from glossy black window boxes. "O'Malley's Pub. It's still here. Remember? Our own personal *Tir na Nog*. That's where..."

"Some things never change," she said quickly, to stop his words. "I wonder if Mr. O'Malley is still behind the bar."

"I wonder what he'd think to see Bernie Sullivan in a nun's habit."

"With the convent right around the corner, I doubt he's shocked by the sight of a nun."

"No," Tom said. "But then, you're not just any nun."

"Tom Kelly," she said sternly. "We're either going to do this the hard way or the easy way. I'm voting for the easy way."

"You're the boss, Sister Bernadette," he said. "You always have been."

She nodded once, hard. He was right about that: she was his employer. Tom was the foreman and groundskeeper at Star of the Sea Academy in Black Hall, Connecticut, where Bernadette was Superior. He and his crew kept the lawns manicured, the gardens blooming, the vineyard producing, and the old stone walls and buildings from falling apart. He had quite a vested interest in the place; it had once been the mansion and grounds of his paternal great-grandfather, the well-known industrialist and philanthropist Francis X. Kelly.

Bernadette slid a glance across the seat, saw Tom staring out the cab window. She tried to read his expression. She had known him forever, or at least most of their lives. They had met at Star of the Sea, at summer picnics when his family would invite hers down to the beach for the day. Francis X. Kelly had employed her great-grandfather, Cormac Sullivan, to build all the walls on the property. Their families had long histories, and so did Bernadette and Tom.

Tom had thrown away his family riches to work the land. He was passionate about social causes and justice, caught up in the legacy of his ancestors' poverty, hunger, and fighting spirit. He had gone to private schools, then turned his back on a life of luxury and ease. He liked to keep his hands dirty and his feet planted solidly on the ground. Bernie loved him for it. She doubted she could have a better foreman and knew she could never have a better friend.

He looked tired, she thought. This trip was possibly more challenging for him than it was for her, and that was saying something. She knew that he had very strong hopes, in terms of the outcome. And she knew, even before they really set forth on their quest, that he would be disappointed.

"Here we are," the driver said in his bright Irish accent. "The Convent of Notre Dame des Victoires."

"Guess which one of us is staying here," Tom asked him.

"Very funny," Bernadette said as the driver chuckled.

Although the driver started to help her with her bags, Tom took over. She saw him reach into the trunk, pull out her suitcase. She rarely used it, hardly ever leaving Star of the Sea, except for the occasional monastic conference or retreat. Since her family—her brother

John, his wife, Honor, and their three daughters—lived on the Academy grounds, she usually spent her week's vacation right there at home.

She had applied for a sabbatical last year, hoping to go to Florence to study her beloved Fra Angelico, but had never found the time to take it. The Academy always needed her—to run the school, make decisions in the convent, keep the vineyard operating.

This trip to Dublin fell under the category of "personal time." As Superior, she had granted time away to Sisters with sick siblings or parents, funerals to attend, family emergencies. For her own leave of absence, she had made arrangements very quickly, left Sister Ursula in charge of everything, including the hectic start of the school year. None of her nuns had ever needed to deal with anything like what she herself was about to face, and the thought of it sent chills through her body.

"Are you cold, Bernie?" Tom asked, seeing her shiver, standing on the curb.

"No," she said. "I'm fine."

"Coming down with something?"

She shook her head, gazing past him at the convent's curtained windows. She thought she saw the fabric move and a shadow pass behind the glass.

"Well, I'll be at the house," he said. "You have my number if you need me. If they don't have orange juice, or you need some aspirin or something, you know who to call."

"I'm sure they'll have everything I need," she said dryly, slipping her hands into her sleeves.

"And if they don't, you'll get it," he said. "You do know how to take care of things, I'll give you that." He squinted up at the convent, as if assessing the brickwork. "There's some crumbling mortar there, needs repointing," he said, pointing at the front steps. It was probably a very effective way to block out his memory of the last time he'd dropped her off at this address.

"Not every convent can be lucky enough to have you on staff," she said.

He gazed down at her, the squint not letting up one bit. She waited for a smile, but it didn't come. What did she expect? For him to thank her for the compliment? Not likely, not Tom Kelly. Under the circumstances, it probably sounded to him meager at best.

"At least, most likely, they don't have a resident vandal," he said, giving her a quick, mischievous smile. "What was that message, carved in the stone?" He paused, seeming to think, even though she was sure he knew the words by heart. She felt the heat in her neck and face, and she shook her head. She never would have expected Tom to be so mean. "Tell me the words, Bernie. The ones that appeared first, early in the summer..."

" 'I was sleeping, but my heart kept vigil,' " she murmured.

He nodded. "That's right," he said, lifting her bag, carrying it up the sidewalk. "How could I forget?"

"You didn't," she said coolly, unlatching the wrought-iron gate at the foot of the front steps.

As they climbed the steps, she felt years falling away, almost as if she were coming to the convent for the first time, preparing to join the order. Her mouth was dry, and she was filled with a sense of trepidation, fear that she might be making the wrong choice.

"You sure you want to do this?" Tom asked, the same question he'd put to her twenty-three years earlier.

"The choice has already been made," Bernie said, echoing her own response.

Just then the door opened, and a nun stood there smiling widely, gazing at Bernie with warm green-gold eyes. She was tall and thin, and looked exactly as Bernie remembered her, all those years ago, when they were novices together.

"Sister Bernadette Ignatius!" the nun said in her Kerry brogue.

"Sister Anne-Marie," Bernie said.

Tom slid the bag into the front hall, standing back as the old friends embraced and Bernie wiped away tears.

"Is that you, Tom Kelly?" Sister Anne-Marie asked, beaming.

"It sure is," he said. "How're you doing, Annie?"

"I'm fine," she said, throwing herself against him in a big hug.

Bernie watched the affection in both their faces, and she fought to keep her own expression as blank as possible. She knew this wasn't going to be simple, and she had to maintain as much control as she could.

"Okay, I'm off," Tom said. "You have my number, Sister Bernadette. I'll see you tomorrow morning. Take good care of her, Sister Anne-Marie."

"You know I will," she said with mock sternness, locking arms with Bernie, and pulling her into the inner sanctum, closing the door behind her.

Bernie's heart was pounding. She looked around the hall, saw the delicate marble statue of the Blessed Mother standing in the alcove. The aroma of good cooking wafted down the hall, and she also smelled hints of incense from the chapel just off the front hall. Memories were flooding back, making her feel almost faint. She heard the car door slam, and when she glanced past the curtain, she saw Tom watching out the car window as the driver pulled away.

"Feels like it's happening all over again," she said in a low voice.

"It's not, though," Sister Anne-Marie replied, standing just behind her.

"I'm not sure why I came," Bernie said. "This story has already been written. Right down to 'The End.' "

"A kinder way to look at it," Sister Anne-Marie said gently, her tone bringing hot tears to Bernie's eyes as she eased her around, taking her hand, "is that the story is just beginning. 'Once upon a time…' "

Bernie opened her mouth to reply, but just then she heard heavy footsteps coming through the parlor—the room where she had seen the shadow behind the curtain. And she knew without turning around that this was the person she dreaded seeing more than anyone in this world.

Merrion Square was one of Dublin's finest addresses, hands down, and it was there that Tom Kelly directed the driver to take him. The large Georgian square was surrounded by museums and brick townhouses with wrought-iron balconies, ivy growing up the brick, bright front doors crowned by segmented fanlight windows, and commanding brass door knockers. Prosperous Dubliners had lived here since John Ensor laid out the square in 1762; the Kellys had moved in a quarter-century later.

Three townhouses along the north side formed Dublin's Kelly stronghold. They all had sea serpent door knockers—the same image engraved on Tom's gold crest ring, that of the legendary sea monster said to have risen from the deep to protect Tadhg Mor O'Kelly, Tom's fierce kinsman who fell "fighting like a wolf dog," defending Ireland against the Vikings in the Battle of Clontarf in 1014.

Tom shook his head. One hour in Dublin and he was already lost in the ancient history of another millennium. Or, more to the point, another decade. Climbing the stairs of the middle house, the one with the bright red door, he felt exhausted by his journey. His knock was answered by a maid as Elizabeth Kelly, his cousin William's wife, came charging down the stairs.

"Tommy, you've arrived already!" she exclaimed. "Billy'll be beside himself. Why didn't you tell us your flight so we could've sent a car?"

"Liza, hello. I didn't want to put you to any trouble," he said, hugging her.

"Your first visit here in twenty-three years, and you think we wouldn't want to welcome you in Kelly style?"

"Oh, you know me," he said, smiling at her warmth, happy to see her again. "I like things simple."

"That's right," she said. "I remember. No fancy airs about you, not like your cousins Billy and Sixtus and Niall and Chris and the rest of them. You've spared yourself hearing about the latest Mercedes, but not for long. Billy'll be home soon enough, and he'll show you his toys. Clara, take Tom's bag up to his room now."

Tom gave the young maid a glance, shook his head to let her know he'd carry it himself. Liza either didn't notice or decided not to care.

"Where's Bernie, now?" she asked.

"She's staying with the Sisters."

"No," Liza said, her face falling. "Even on a vacation, they force her to stay in the convent?"

Tom nodded, not really having the heart to explain that Bernie didn't take vacations, and that in any case this was far from a vacation.

"Darn it," Liza said. "I was counting on spoiling her the way she spoiled us the last time we visited Star of the Sea. I still dream of that bed, with its view over the vineyard to the Sound. And the fresh flowers she brought every day . . . She's certainly kept it a showplace; your great-grandfather would be so pleased with her."

"Yes, he would," Tom said, although he wasn't sure of that at all.

"Well, I must tell you," Liza said, her eyes sparkling, "when we heard the two of you were coming, we couldn't have been more pleased. All of us. Sixtus and Emer, Niall and Isobel, as well as Billy and myself. Emer, though . . . she was a little confused."

"About what?" Tom asked.

"Well, the part about you traveling together. She said nuns weren't allowed to go places with men, but we all assumed that since you've known each other so long, and you work for her and all, that would be the special exception to the rule. Which is why we thought Bernie would be staying here."

"Ah," he said. He should have known that the family gossip mill would be churning. He shook his head, hoping the dim hall light would hide the flush he felt spreading up his neck.

"Well, Emer had it wrong. That's all. Tommy, you must be dead on your feet. Clara, where'd you go?" She stared down at his bag, sitting in the middle of the floor, then looked around for the maid with no small degree of panic. But Tom put his hand on her wrist, stopped her.

"It's okay, Liza," he said. "Let me get that. Is it the same guest room? On the second floor?"

"Yes, Tom. The Blue Room, we still call it."

He kissed her cheek, and started up the stairs before she could offer the lift. These narrow townhouses were tall and steep, with just two rooms on each floor. The flights were different than in the States. Here in Ireland, he had to remember that the first floor was called the ground floor, and the second floor was called the first floor, and the third floor was called the second, and so on. In any case, by the time he reached the third flight, his thighs burned from climbing so many stairs, and he relished the feeling. His body felt ready to explode with pent-up energy.

When he passed the laundry room, he smiled to see a treadmill in there beside the ironing board. Tom and his cousins were at that age when they had to start taking care of the Kelly heart—especially with all the fine dining and drinking his cousins probably did. Living at the Academy, tending the grounds, gave Tom a constant workout.

Closing the Blue Room's door behind him, he stood at the window, gazing out at the square. The Convent of Notre Dame des Victoires wasn't visible. It was blocks away, but Tom saw it in his mind's eye. He wondered what Bernie was doing, whether she had decided to confide in Sister Anne-Marie or not. He wondered whether she had encountered the Mother Superior yet, and if so, whether she had managed to keep her emotions in check.

He closed his eyes, pressed his forehead against the cool glass windowpane. If he stood very still, he could block out Dublin and almost see the words scratched into the stone of the Blue Grotto back at home, on the Academy grounds. *I was sleeping, but my heart kept vigil.*

He sighed, shaking his head.

"Bernie," he said.

And then, because he was worn out from his flight and everything else, he kicked off his shoes and lay down on top of the blue bedspread, and tried to sleep.

Two

From an administrator's point of view, staying in an urban convent was interestingly different from Star of the Sea. The narrow house was much smaller, for one thing, three floors to house twenty-five nuns. There were no grounds to speak of, or maintain: only a small dark garden in back, with two benches and a gravel path among thick shrubbery, and a small shrine against the wall, overgrown with ivy.

At home in Connecticut, Bernie often started her day with a long walk through the vineyard to the beach, praying as she walked, gathering the night's sorrows and dreams, offering them to the sea and the setting stars.

Here she had heard Dublin's night sounds—trucks rumbling along the quays, people laughing and talking on their way home from somewhere. In the middle of the night, she was awakened by a couple fighting on the street, the woman sobbing noisily and the man saying roughly, "Stop that. I've heard enough about that now. Stop it."

She was awake after that, and didn't even try to get back to sleep. Her cell was in the front of the house—very similar in layout to her one at home: a narrow bed, a desk and chair, a bureau, a cross on the wall. She pulled the desk chair close to the window, sat in the dark staring out at Dublin.

The city at night was alive and electric, in a different way than the grounds at Star of the Sea. Back home there were hunting foxes, owls, raccoon, deer, even the occasional coyote. At night the bay was still, but beneath the surface swam blues, stripers, fluke, crabs, and the rare shark. Stars wheeled through the sky, and the moon trickled its golden light over the sea, beach, and acres of grapevines. When Bernie woke up from a dream, or because an owl had cried in the night, she would look out the window and find his star. And say a prayer for him.

Here, he was everywhere. She couldn't find his star, because the city lights obscured the night sky. And she couldn't say a prayer for him, because it seemed inadequate. A prayer said at night into the abyss—for what, after all this time? Back home, he was an idea. A distant memory, a fervent hope, a star in the sky's cradle.

Here, he was in her bloodstream. He was in every breath. Each voice she heard on the street was his. He was the man yelling at the woman, and the woman crying in anguish.

Bernie's skin hurt. She sat in the straight-backed chair, gazing onto the dark street, her insides quivering. Her body ached, especially her skin. Suddenly she felt as if she had been living on the surface all this time. Running a convent and school took all her energy and effort, kept her too busy and occupied to think much. Her skin had become her armor, keeping danger out and keeping herself in.

The bell rang for Vigils—a quick electric trill. At home, Sister Gabrielle rang an old brass bell by hand. This was a city convenience—bells rang at the push of a button. Bernie glanced at the clock: three-fifteen. She dressed in the dark, something she was very good at. Underwear, stockings, habit, veil.

Back home her cell was at the far end of the convent—Tom's great-grandfather's sprawling pile of a mansion—and it took her ten minutes to get to chapel. But here, all she had to do was step into the hall and descend a flight of stairs. She took the extra time to stand by the window and stare down at the street.

Any single person passing by...

She saw a couple walking past—they looked about the right age.

They laughed, and the girl stumbled. In the streetlight's glow, Bernie saw him catch her in his arms. He steadied her with a kiss, and they kept going. Bernie watched as long as she could, until they disappeared out of the light, rounding the corner of the side street.

A soft knock sounded on her door. She opened it, saw Anne-Marie standing in the hall, and let her in.

"Good morning, Sister," Bernie said.

"Good morning to you. Did you sleep well?"

"I'm not used to city life," Bernie said.

"Ah, yes," Anne-Marie said. "We're right smack in the midst of a well-worn path between Temple Bar and Parnell College."

"Temple Bar?"

"You know, that section along the river where the kids go at night," Anne-Marie said. "Bars and clubs—don't you remember from once-upon-a-time? I hope they didn't keep you awake all night." She gave her old friend a long, searching look, as if she knew the noise wouldn't have been the main reason for her sleeplessness.

"I'll be fine," Bernie said, giving her hand a quick squeeze.

"I couldn't help notice that Sister Eleanor didn't come down for supper or compline last night," Anne-Marie said. "Did she find you?"

Bernie shook her head. "When I saw Sister Theodore at supper, I was sure Eleanor would make an appearance. Are they still the Notre Dame mafia?"

Anne-Marie chuckled. "Absolutely. Sister Eleanor is so busy running the convent, she never seems to have time for choir. That's why you didn't see her last night. Sister Theodore is Eleanor's consigliere, that's for sure. She'll make you an offer you can't refuse."

"She made me one," Bernie said quietly.

"Well, I'm sure Eleanor will want to see you today."

Bernie nodded, stood straight in spite of the shiver running down her spine. "I'm sure," she agreed.

They went into chapel, joining the other sisters at silent prayer. Bernie knelt in the choir stall they'd assigned her last night. She bowed her head, picturing his star, saying the prayer she would have said at home. A moment later, all gathered, they began to chant the psalmody. Bernie hadn't lost her place—they were on the same sequence as Star of the Sea.

The Irish voices were so beautiful and melodic, they lifted her heart, and it needed lifting. She had come to Ireland for an impossible reason. Anyone with a brain would try to talk her out of it. She believed in the Holy Spirit, in deep mysteries, in the ways life had of taking care of people, leading them to their own solutions and comforts. For so many years, she had given him to God—Father, Son, and Holy Ghost. She'd given him to Mary, because of her special connection.

All these years, she had trusted in God's love to protect him. Why then, if her faith was so strong, was she here now? Why had she come all this way, now that he was all grown-up, with a life all his own? What reason could there possibly be?

This summer had been filled with powerful gifts. Her brother John had returned home to his family in Connecticut, her sister-in-law Honor had opened her heart to forgive and understand and take him back. Her nieces—eccentric, troubled, daring angels, all three of them—had each found private healings. And Brendan McCarthy— her niece Agnes's red-haired nurse—had somehow unlocked a chamber of Bernie's heart that had for so long been darkly asleep.

Heavy thumping sounded in the hall. *Ba-boom, ba-boom.* Sister Theodore's footsteps were unmistakable, and her voice, chanting the psalm as she approached, was stentorian; the combined effect somewhere between the Second Coming and Hannibal crossing the Alps by elephant. And where Sister Theodore was, Sister Eleanor Marie could not be far behind.

Sister Theodore stood in the chapel door. Folds of skin protruded over the white wimple enveloping her face. Her breathing was labored, but she still had the voice of an opera singer. It harmonized with the other nuns' sweet, gentle tones, somehow elevating them to the level of angels and art. Her eyes were blank, as if she had only enough beauty in her soul for one thing—it all went to her voice.

A shadow fell across the door as Sister Theodore stepped aside for the Mother Superior of Notre Dame des Victoires.

Entering chapel, the Superior looked left and right, derision in her bright eyes, as if she could see straight into each nun's soul, only to find it sorely wanting. She was five-eight, rail thin, and filled with kinetic energy. She didn't sing. Her mouth was a thin line. Her gaze swept the choir stalls, found its mark. And for the first time in twenty-three years, Sister Eleanor Marie locked eyes with Sister Bernadette Ignatius.

Eleanor walked straight over, passed her a note. Bernie nodded, continuing her chants, not looking at the paper until Eleanor had marched out the chapel's back door. No one knew better than Bernie how much effort it took to keep a convent running smoothly, but even so, she made a point to never miss choir.

It calmed and centered her, reminded her of her connection with this earth as well as her longing for heaven. The psalms were filled with joy and grief, passion and longing, deep sorrow for roads taken and untaken. They were songs of love and despair, asking for help. Bernie had always known that she needed help.

More than most people, she suspected.

In a way, she felt sorry for Eleanor, depriving herself of this time, this chance to sing and chant her heart out. But then, maybe Eleanor hadn't made the mistakes Bernie had.

Unfolding the note, she read: *See me in my office after breakfast.*

Bernie stared at the words for a few seconds. The words reminded her of something a stern nun would write a misbehaving pupil. That was probably how Eleanor still saw her. Bernie had been summoned. But, in a way, wasn't that what she had come for? Sticking the note into her prayer book, she sang.

The Greencastle Hotel was located on Bannondale Road, in Dublin's Ballsbridge section. All the powerful people from the States, as well as from Europe and the U.K., came to stay here. They hustled into the bright brick hotel, stopping by the concierge desk to inquire about tickets to the Abbey or Gate theaters, or excursions to Glendalough or Powerscourt—even across Ireland to the Dingle Peninsula or the

Cliffs of Moher. That's where Seamus came in. Dressed in his black suit, standing by the silver Mercedes, he was ready to whisk the rich people anywhere their hearts desired. Even if it was just the airport.

Today, for example. Although it was just past seven a.m., he had already taken a fare to the airport for a London flight, and now he was back at the hotel, waiting for his next assignment. The morning air was crisp and bright. He knew he could be assigned to a businessman who'd want to be driven to Four Courts, and then to lunch on Dawson Street, and then to offices downtown, and then back to the hotel. But he sorely hoped that wouldn't be the case. On a day like this, he really hoped he'd get a couple, or a family, or someone wanting to be taken to see the sights.

Just then a brand-new black Mercedes S-Class sedan pulled up, and the doormen flocked to open all doors. Seamus knew instantly—it was the Kellys. Very few locals rated that sort of attention here, short of Bono or the Edge or Enya or Mary Robinson or football stars like Dessie Farrell and Colin Moran.

Sixtus Kelly was a prominent barrister, Niall was a judge, and William was a politician. Seamus had dreams of entering King's Inns one day, to become a barrister himself, so the Kellys were of great interest to him. He hoped someday to be working for the likes of them; that's what this job was all about. Earning enough money, and making connections.

Watching the three Kelly brothers standing under the portico, laughing and talking, he noticed they had someone with them. The man was tall and thin, but didn't look anything like the Kellys. He wore country clothes, nice enough, but on the shabby side. A tweed jacket, black jeans, scuffed boots. He looked like a farmer, in all honesty. What the Kellys were doing with him here was beyond Seamus. The man looked as if he belonged in the stables of one of their country houses.

As the Kelly clan disappeared into the hotel, John, the chief valet, came over to introduce Seamus to his fare: an American woman, late forties, wanting to go on a tour of Wicklow. Seamus's mind was already clicking: he'd show her Dalkey on the way, then Powerscourt, Enniskerry, the military road, and wind the morning up at Glendalough.

"Good morning, madam," he said, holding the door for her.

As they drove away from Bannondale Road, he started his tour by taking her down the street lined with Dublin's biggest houses, many of them embassies, but some still reserved for private families. He knew a few Kellys lived here, the ones who didn't reside on Merrion Square.

"This is Post Code Dublin 4," he said, glancing around with pride, knowing that someday, when he became a barrister and found his true love, they would return here to live. "The best. Very aspirational. When you make it in the world, you want to live on Shrewsbury Road...."

"I can see why," the woman said. "Lovely houses."

"A superb place to live," Seamus said, driving along, heading south, wondering how long it would take to find her, what she looked like, whether they'd recognize each other. His dream was that one day she would come to the Greencastle, climb into his car. Or maybe, at some point in one of his drives, he would spot her walking along the road.

If that ever happened, he would pick her up. His fare would be out of luck, have to find another way back to Ballsbridge. Seamus would just drive her away, and they'd never stop.

He'd never let her go again, never.

Dublin Bay sparkled on their left, and his passenger opened her window, flooding the car with the scent of salt air. The smell of the sea filled Seamus with longing—so deep, bottomless, reminding him as it always did of the beach where he'd thrown away everything that mattered.

But he drove the American woman along, pointing out the yacht harbor at Dun Laoghaire, the Martello tower at Sandycove where James Joyce wrote part of *Ulysses,* the Forty Foot where men used to swim nude but now open to all, and the sea air blew through the car, and pieces of his heart rattled in his chest.

*

At the Greencastle, the generous breakfast buffet was laid out in the dining room. Long tables overflowed with egg dishes, French toast, bacon, sausage, smoked salmon, raspberries, pineapple, pastries, croissants, Irish soda bread, and pitchers of juice, and Tom went down the line filling his plate and wondering what kind of breakfast Bernie was having at the convent.

When he returned to the table—right in the center of the elegant room, the best table in the place—a waiter pulled back his chair and handed him his linen napkin. He asked for coffee, even though all his cousins were drinking tea, and the waiter filled his fine china cup.

Sixtus, Niall, and Billy were all in their seats, dressed for work in dark suits, smiling at him and reminding him of how all Kelly men looked alike—blue-eyed, troublemaking, fun-loving devils. Some had dark hair, others red, but the family resemblance was all in their bright, lively eyes.

"Jesus," he said, looking around, "haven't you ever seen anyone eat breakfast before?"

"Don't they feed you in America?" Sixtus asked, nodding at Tom's plate.

"Hey," Tom said, "your hands are so soft, you've forgotten what it's like to work. Gives you an appetite, you know?"

"Are we going to hear about this again?" Niall asked, pretending to be exasperated. "How we've sold our souls to work in offices, and you're the one true heir to Tadhg Mor O'Kelly?"

"Tough guy," Sixtus said, shoveling bacon and eggs onto a slice of buttered toast. "That's what we've got here."

"Oh, he's not so tough," Billy said. "I did see him cast a glance down the square toward the Rutland Fountain."

Tom reddened, surprised Billy would have noticed. It was true that the part of Merrion Square history that interested him most was that the fountain had been installed in 1791 to be used by Dublin's poor.

"Jesus," Sixtus said. "The boy with the big heart, that's what Bernie said of you once. She's a romantic, never mind the fact she's a nun. For the rest of us, you're just a bit nuts."

"A big heart is one thing," Billy said. "I just hope he's avoided the Kelly heart."

"Oh, enough with that," Sixtus said. "Your bypass was a hundred percent successful. Tom, see to it Billy does his treadmill every morning while you're visiting, will you?"

"Seriously, are you okay, Bill?" Tom asked.

"Other than being brokenhearted over having such cruel brothers, I'm fine."

Tom laughed, shaking his head. He avoided his Irish cousins' ribbing, living in the United States. Although they visited only every few years, to see him and Chris Kelly and the rest of the American contingent, when they got together, the jokes and laughs came back strong—Hibernian humor with an edge.

"What brings you over here, anyway?" Niall asked. "You and Sister Bernadette."

"Does she need a bodyguard now?" Billy asked. "That's the only explanation that makes sense. What's the nunnery coming to, that they let a Sister cross the Atlantic with the likes of you?"

"Or any man, for that matter," Niall said. "In our day, there was no fraternizing whatsoever."

Sixtus signaled for the waiter to pour his tea, and looked over at Tom, eyes glinting. "I'm thinking Bernie's after congratulating me on the job I did for Regis. It was a thing of beauty, my argument. You should have seen me before the judge—"

"Who was up?" Niall asked.

"Hanrahan," Sixtus said, and Niall rolled his eyes. "Anyway, it was poetic, the way I presented Regis Sullivan's case. She's no murderer, her father's no murderer, Ireland ought to be ashamed for what they put that family through. If only John and Honor had asked for Kelly help six years ago, none of it would have happened. But the good news is, Regis is off the hook, and they're all home safe."

"Thank you for that, Sixtus," Tom said, on behalf of Bernie's family. It was hard to believe that just the day before yesterday he and Bernie had seen John, Honor, and the girls at the Dublin airport, their paths crossing only briefly. He knew that it was John's home-coming, after six years in prison, that had sparked so many events this summer, including Regis's memories about the killing, and leading Tom and Bernie to travel here now.

Sixtus nodded regally, sipping tea. His chest was all puffed out; like Tom, he took pride in his work. It was just that Tom did a different kind of work; he'd turned his back on Kelly riches, feeling they got in the way of his deep roots to a family of fighters and farmers.

"Now, seriously," Sixtus said. "You're staying at Billy and Liza's, so they've probably already heard it. But tell me and Niall: what're you doing here?"

"Sister Bernadette has some business to attend to," Tom said, giving his cousins the line he and Bernie had agreed upon. "And I decided it had been too long since my feet had touched Dublin soil."

He tried not to look at his watch. Bernie had called him an hour ago, saying her meeting with Sister Eleanor Marie was right after breakfast; she hoped to get the information she needed for them to get started, and he'd told her he would meet her at O'Malley's Pub, by the serpentine in St. Stephen's Green—one of their favorite meeting places from long ago—at eleven, giving them both enough time to get free.

"What kind of business?" Sixtus asked, eyes narrowing.

"Something to do with the convent, the order?" Niall asked.

"Or," Sixtus said, squinting even more, "something to do with Great-Grandfather Kelly's land?"

"It's not Kelly land anymore," Tom said. "It belongs to the Sisters of Notre Dame des Victoires and Star of the Sea Academy."

"A waste," Sixtus said, shaking his head. "Giving a beautiful mansion like that to a bunch of religious ascetics who can't appreciate the stone carvings, or the Italian marble, or the parquet floors, or the French doors, or the bronzes, or the brass hardware, or that exquisite library..."

"I think the young ladies who attend school there appreciate it," Tom said. "And don't be so sure the nuns don't as well."

"Acreage like that on Long Island Sound would fetch quite a nice sum," Niall mused. "If we could sell it, divide it up and build luxury homes—with a golf course."

"Divide it, nothing!" Sixtus said. "I'd keep it for myself. I can just imagine our cousin Chrysogonus gnashing his teeth every time he pulls in the drive to do legal work for the order, wishing Francis X. had had the foresight to keep it for his family. That must burn Chris right up. What's the point of becoming the most successful family in Connecticut if you can't own the best piece of property in the state?"

"Religious orders don't pay taxes," Billy said glumly. "You should see my annual tax bill."

"Maybe you and Liza can start a sect of your own," Sixtus suggested. "You with a collar and her and the girls with black veils. It would solve your tax problem."

Billy waved him off, but Niall laughed at the image. For Sixtus, the moment of humor passed.

"So, Tom. If it's not land business, what brings Sister Bernadette to Dublin? She was here as a young woman, wasn't she? That was the year you came over, too; researching family roots, wasn't it?"

"That's right," Billy said. "I'd forgotten about that. The year you lived across the Liffey in an apartment you wouldn't let anyone visit. We all thought you were here to join the IRA."

"We don't know for sure he didn't," Sixtus said. "Our American cousin, the biggest revolutionary among us. So caught up in the myth of our family suffering and the poverty we came from, the Great Hunger, fighting the establishment, wasn't that it, Tom?"

"Something like that," Tom said.

"All I know is, you kept to yourself. You and Bernie Sullivan. The family all thought you were living together—but my mother couldn't bring herself to think it. 'He wouldn't live in sin, not Tom Kelly.'"

"Isobel thought you'd eloped and were secretly married," Niall said.

"Nope," Tom said. "She wouldn't marry me."

"Were you living together?" Billy asked. "Come on, you can tell us after all this time. You certainly never invited any of us over, and it couldn't have been because you were afraid we'd see your bachelor quarters. We were all living the single lives ourselves then!"

"On the other hand, we never saw you two together after a certain point," Niall mused. "Did she break up with you earlier than we thought? Christ, we never saw Bernie at all! Mother invited her to have holidays with us, but she chose the nuns instead. Guess she already knew she wanted to join the convent."

"Another waste," Sixtus said. "What a pretty girl she was. You lost out, Tom. And you made us Kelly men look bad. The day a Kelly can't convince a girl to marry him instead of taking religious vows is a sad day indeed."

"I'll agree with you there," Tom said.

"So. Once and for all. What's her business here in Dublin?" Sixtus asked, signaling the waiter to pour him more tea.

Tom's heart kicked over. He was certainly not going to tell his cousins Bernie's reasons for being here, and he wished they'd just stop asking. So he decided to join them at their own game, the sort of teasing that kept them from talking about anything real.

"Give me that," Tom said, grabbing the silver teapot, burning his hand on the hot handle. "You need a servant to pour yourself some morning tea? Don't tell me you make poor Emer wait on you this way.... Jesus, Six. You're getting too soft. What would Tadhg Mor O'Kelly have to say about that?"

"He got you good there," Niall chuckled, peering over at Sixtus.

And then Tom's cousins spun off into family myth, legend, and one-upmanship, and Tom knew that he had just bought himself and Bernie a little more time.

Three

The meeting with Sister Eleanor Marie had been postponed twice that day: first until after lunch, and then until mid-afternoon. Both times Sister Bernadette had come to Eleanor's office, waiting in the chair outside, only to have Sister Theodore clump heavily into the hall to tell her Sister Eleanor Marie was on the phone and to please come back at the next appointed time.

The worst part was that Tom was waiting for her; they had arranged to meet at O'Malley's Pub. But then Bernie's meeting was postponed, and she couldn't get hold of him. U.S. cell phones didn't work here in Ireland, but she didn't know that until she had dialed his number ten times, imagining him waiting there, just off St. Stephen's Green, alone and impatient.

She had felt a slow burn start, or rekindle, after the first dismissal, and it deepened now. Sitting in the armchair, staring at the closed door, she had a sense of déjà vu. A statue of Mary stood in a small, delicate alcove cut into the wall. Bernie turned toward it, praying to know what to do, what to say, when the time came. She had always felt Mary's love and guidance, but right now her own emotions were churning so hard, they blocked her from hearing any answers.

Hearing footsteps from inside the office, she straightened up. The door swung open. Sister Eleanor Marie stood there, tall and thin, her dark eyes glowing behind silver wire-rimmed glasses. She stared at

Bernie, and through her; Bernie had the sense of being read up and down, inside out. Rising, she was grateful that Eleanor Marie didn't attempt to hug her.

"Welcome back to Dublin, Sister Bernadette Ignatius," Sister Eleanor Marie said in her Boston accent. "Won't you come in?"

They sat across the desk from each other. Bernie took in the office with a quick glance: books in rows of glass-fronted bookcases; a simple mahogany desk, its surface clear of everything but blotter, pen, writing pad, and a loudly ticking brass clock; a cross on one wall; an icon of Our Lady on another; wooden file cabinets visible through an arched and wrought-iron gated door behind the desk.

The sight of those file cabinets made Bernie tingle. She knew, from her own experience as Superior at Star of the Sea, that the secrets of every nun's life were contained in a file. Bernie considered them precious—the biographies of her Sisters' lives, the families they had left behind, the secular hopes and dreams they'd traded so mindfully for a life of prayer, adoration, and hard work.

"Well, Sister," Sister Eleanor Marie said, sitting erect at her desk, "what brings you back to Ireland?"

"I'm here for a very personal reason," Bernie said.

Sister Eleanor Marie's eyes glinted behind her glasses, and she flashed a smile. "You were always very attached to your 'personal life,'" she said. "To your family. Even after all these years, haven't you learned that human bonds are purified through separation?"

"I live it every day," Bernie said, simmering.

Again, the quick, hard smile. "Do you? At a convent where you have so much history as a young woman? With your brother and his family living on the grounds? You must be stronger than I. I had to banish my own illusions of self, Sister. Joining the order here in Dublin, far from my native Boston. *Ex umbris et imaginibus in veritatem.*"

"'From shadows and images to the truth,'" Bernie translated. "My truth has always been love."

"To your undoing, I dare to say."

Bernie stared across the desk. "Dare to say whatever you want,

Eleanor. You and I are equals now. When I first met you, you were the Novice Mistress. You led me through my first year. Now we're both Sister Superiors. I'm not here as a supplicant. I'm here as a colleague."

Eleanor Marie stared, and Bernie felt a shiver go through her bones. What was it about this nun that had always reminded her of a devil? She had such rage in her, simmering just below the surface. Bernie remembered her first year in the order, surrendering each day to grief. While her fellow novices had comforted her, helped her travel from shadow to light, Eleanor Marie had seemed to savor Bernie's pain.

"You make yourself clear, Sister," she said now, giving a clenched smile. "What can I do for you?"

"I want to know where he is."

"He?"

"My son," Bernie said.

"You have no son."

"How dare you?" Bernie asked.

Eleanor Marie's glasses reflected the lamplight, her eyes were like dark coals in the grate of a stove, banked and burning steadily. "You made your choice," she said. "You gave him up. No one twisted your arm. No one forced you to hand him over. As a matter of fact, I recall that you were very eager. You had had a *vision*."

Bernie fought to keep from clawing her face. She wouldn't give her the satisfaction of seeing her look at the icon of Mary. The details of Bernie's vision were well known to everyone in the order; it had been investigated by no less than the "Miracle Investigator," an expert in Marian apparitions from Rome.

"From the moment you gave your child to adoption services, you relinquished all rights to him." Eleanor Marie paused, her smile becoming harder and wider. "I must say, I've been expecting this visit for two decades. I never expected you to weather the years without this happening."

"This?"

"Your weakening. I knew from the time I met you that you were not strong enough for this life. Of all the nuns I have overseen through their eight years as novices and postulants, the endurance and surrender and letting go of earthly bonds, you were the one who held on most tightly. Frankly, from the time you left Ireland to join the order in Connecticut, I have been expecting you to walk through the door and ask this question."

"Is that why you've kept me waiting all day?"

"All day?" Eleanor Marie asked coldly. "What is 'all day'? You and I live a life of the eternal. Ashes to ashes, dust to dust. The ordeal of our daily trials is meant to bring us closer to Him, and to eternity."

"Don't lecture me," Bernie said. "My spiritual life is between me and God. Not you. Give me my son's name."

"His name is Baby Boy X."

"I want my file."

"Your file is church property. You have no rights to it. Not just for your own protection, but for that of the order—and even more seriously, and your ego is so great you're unable to see this—but for the sake of the child."

"What do you mean?"

"Have you thought about him at *all*?" Eleanor Marie asked. "This young man you gave up one day after his birth? Walked away from his life and didn't look back for twenty-three years? I am the guardian of his life."

"Guardian of his life..." Bernie trailed off. For a moment she took the words literally. Had Sister Eleanor Marie somehow become her child's guardian? She knew that the order maintained an orphanage and several Children's Homes throughout Ireland. After she gave birth, she'd spent the next twenty-four hours in torment, trying to discern what to do.

First Eleanor Marie and then—more reassuringly—a different nun from the hospital, one of the nursing Sisters of their order, had promised Bernie that if she decided to give him up, the Sisters would take care of him personally. He would be cared for as if he were their own, and he would be placed with a wonderful family right away, within days. There was a long waiting list of good Catholic couples, desperate for a baby. He would be loved and adored by a family, raised and nurtured as if he were their own son.

"You can't be," Bernie stammered. "He has a family, not a guardian. They—*you*—promised me, at the hospital. He would go to a good family, be loved by them, taken in and cherished...."

"I mean that I am the guardian of his privacy," Sister Eleanor Marie said sharply. "Your records are sealed, and so are his. I have his best interests at heart here, Sister. Even if you do not."

"I have nothing but his best interests at heart!" Bernie said, slamming her hands onto the desk. "He's twenty-three now. I've given him the chance to grow up, be raised by his family, loved by his parents. *They* are his parents—that is how I view the people who adopted him. I haven't even decided whether or not to reveal myself to him. I want only to know who he is, and that he has a good life."

"*You* decide, *you* want," Eleanor Marie said derisively. "Listen to yourself, Sister. What about God? What does the Lord want for this young man? To have you sweep in at this late hour, create havoc in a life you gave away? Can you imagine the confusion and anguish you might cause him? It could turn him against the church!"

"What are you talking about?" Bernie cried.

"He could be filled with hatred and resentment for you—a nun! And that could spread deeply and quickly; it could poison his faith. I cannot and will not risk that. I am the guardian of his soul."

"You are not!"

"Have you come here to Dublin with Thomas Kelly?" Eleanor Marie asked. "Sister Theodore told me she saw him dropping you off yesterday. I know that he works as your groundskeeper. There's something unholy in your bond, Sister. I believe that it is fueling you now, not concern for the child."

Bernie started violently at the mention of Tom's name. Of all the things Sister Eleanor Marie had said to her, this felt the most vicious. She stared, seeing evil in the other nun's eyes. She tried to remind herself that Eleanor was human, that she had her own difficult history, that she had known pain.

Sister Eleanor Marie was accusing her of ego, but Bernie knew that this was personal, dating back to their early days, when Bernie had first come to this convent. She remembered their first meeting, and in spite of her desire to have compassion for Eleanor, felt her blood turn to ice. The shift in consciousness made her feel calm, because she suddenly realized what she was up against.

"I'll go over your head," Bernie said. "I'll petition your Superior for my records, and she'll give them to me."

Visibly shaken, Eleanor Marie leaned forward. "You're threatening me?"

"She's kind and compassionate," Bernie said. "Our order was founded on great love, Sister. I've been taught to replace fear with hope and love. I'm sure your Superior abides by the same credo. She would know that I intend no harm to my son. I feel only love for him. I'll tell her that, and she'll give me my file."

Sister Eleanor Marie stared at her with dead eyes. But slowly, the coals began to heat up again, and to glow. She opened her desk drawer, removed a set of keys on a ring. Fingering them slowly, she gazed at Bernie. Then she threw the keys down on the blotter.

"Go ahead," she said. "Look."

Bernie grabbed the key ring and started to walk behind the desk, to the ornate wrought-iron gate. There, in the inner sanctum, were rows of file cabinets, clearly alphabetized. Fumbling with the keys, trying to find the right one, she finally fit it into the gate's lock. Turned it open, rushed inside.

There, the cabinet marked S, for Sullivan; she had been Bernadette Sullivan before her vows, and she knew that the order kept records based on the nuns' original names. The S drawer was lowest of all, so Bernie knelt as she tried one key after another. Sister Eleanor Marie might have helped, but instead just sat in her chair, watching.

The last key worked, and Bernie's heart was racing as she clicked the lock open. Her hands were so sweaty, she almost couldn't open the drawer. But finally it slid open, and she quickly leafed through the manila folders. Stephens, Stevens, Stires, Strand, Sullivan. She tore it from the drawer, began rifling through the documents.

Copies of her birth and baptismal certificates, proof of confirmation, details of her life before coming to the convent, a thick sheaf cataloguing Rome's investigation of her vision, including one envelope sealed with a thick blot of red wax, reports of her progress as a novice that first year, even notes and clippings from the order's newsletter, detailing her rise at Star of the Sea. But nothing, not one paper, dealing with the birth of her son.

"Where is it?" she asked, turning around, unable to disguise the panic she felt rising up inside.

Sister Eleanor Marie sat there staring, a smug look behind her glasses.

"What have you done with it?" Bernie asked, jumping up, grabbing the arms of her chair, pressing her face into Eleanor Marie's. In that moment, she wanted to beat the truth out of her, but the other nun just smiled.

"I've destroyed it," she said.

"What?" Bernie asked, feeling the blood drain from her face.

"As I told you," Sister Eleanor Marie said, her expression rigid in a frozen smile, "I've been expecting this day for many years. To protect the boy, I burned his file. There is no record here of his ever having existed. I wanted you to see for yourself. He is dead to you, Sister Bernadette Ignatius."

"Oh God," Bernie said.

"So that he may have life in Christ. Away from your grasping. It's not healthy for him, nor for you. And certainly not for the order. I suggest you return to the States," Eleanor Marie said evenly. "Perhaps you'll have another vision. The Blessed Virgin Mary will help heal these wounds you've kept open all these years, Sister Bernadette Ignatius."

Bernie turned and left the room. She walked straight past Sister Theodore, hovering in the outer office, looking shocked by Bernie's obvious grief and rage, ready to fly to the protection of her Superior. Bernie's hands were shaking, and her heart past breaking. Her chest ready to explode, she hurried past the statue of Mary in the alcove, arms outstretched. Bernie didn't even look.

She strode through the center hall, past Sister Anne-Marie, waiting to hear what had happened, eyes wide with caring and compassion for her old friend. Bernie barely saw her. Her heart was tattered, and all her hope was gone. She opened the convent's front door, walked onto the street.

Dublin's sky had turned gray, low clouds seeming to touch the cross on the convent's roof. The thick, dark clouds raced above the trees, and the slate roofs, the brick chimneys, the statues in the park. She passed O'Malley's—looked past the bright flower boxes, almost hoping to see Tom still waiting inside. Of course he had long since left. She strode down Grafton Street, past all the shops and cafés, toward the bridges arching over the Liffey. Bernie walked toward the river. It flowed through the city, past the buildings where innumerable people lived, and under the bridges countless people had crossed.

Her son walked these streets, crossed these bridges, perhaps lived in one of those buildings. If only she could find the right window, she could look through it and see his face. He was somewhere, waiting for her.

And waiting for Tom.

At that thought, Bernie's eyes flooded with hot tears. She was going to have to tell Tom that their son was lost. And they'd never be able to find him. Walking through Dublin, she saw the clouds darken and felt rain begin to fall. She felt tears spilling down her cheeks, falling and falling, as she haunted this city of shadows, where their child had come to life.

Four

"Look," Billy said as Tom pulled on his jacket just before dinner, preparing to head out. "You're borrowing a car. That's all there is to it."

"I can take a cab," Tom said. "Or walk."

"You're in a hurry, it's obvious. Whatever that phone call was about, it's got you looking worried. Is there anything I can do?" Billy asked.

Tom hesitated. But Bernie had finally called; she had bought a phone card and dialed him from a pay phone near Trinity College. She needed him, and the fastest way to get to her was by taking Billy up on his offer.

"If you're sure," Tom said, "I'll take the car."

Billy handed him the keys. "It's in the car park, and it's yours while you're here."

"Just this time," Tom said.

"Listen, Tom," Billy said, meeting his eyes, "I don't know why you're here, but it's obvious you have something going on. None of us knows what to do to help you. You never ask. Keep the car while you're here, will you? It will make *me* feel better."

"Okay, Billy. Thanks," Tom said, and let himself out the front door.

He found the car, a sleek silver BMW 6-Series coupe, brand new, and a far cry from the old truck he drove in Connecticut. It started up with a purr, and he pulled into traffic. A horn blared, reminding him to drive on the left. Driving such a new, fancy car made him uncomfortable, for more reasons than he could count. But at the same time, he felt a deep stirring of emotion.

One of the great things about having a big, extended family was that they were really there for one another. But Tom wasn't very good at leaning on people. He was best at telling them he was fine; that he didn't need help, that he could do it on his own. As he drove along he thought of his son. Tom, who turned down help whenever he could, found himself thinking of all these Kelly relatives.

Their own father had died at forty—suddenly, so young, of a heart attack. They'd learned the need to stick together, becoming a tribe who looked after one another. Sixtus, the oldest, had been almost like a father to his younger brothers. Tom knew that all his Kelly cousins would have reached out to Tom and Bernie's son—would have loved to guide his son through life here in Dublin, any way they could.

Tom swore he'd never blame Bernie. She couldn't do what she couldn't do. She couldn't marry him, she couldn't let them be a family. Her vocation had called to her too strongly; she'd gotten the summons from Mary herself, back home in the Blue Grotto. Tom, whenever he worked on the stonework there, replacing loose stones or scrubbing moss off the walls, was sorely tempted to brick the place over.

Because that was the spot of Bernie's "miracle." He had long had his own private thoughts about what had happened in that shady stone chamber on the southwest corner of Academy land, over the hill and beyond the vineyards, between the chapel and the beach. He was Irish Catholic enough to believe that Bernie saw what she said she saw, but he interpreted the message differently.

Now, driving through Dublin to meet her, his heart was racing. He'd never heard her voice like that, trembling and full of fear. Something terrible had happened in her meeting with the she-wolf nun, and Bernie couldn't tell him over the phone.

Tom was used to seeing Bernie as a rock. She ran Star of the Sea with a gloved fist. Caring and benevolent, but cross her at your own peril. She worked nonstop, before dawn until after dark, running the whole operation like a type-A CEO. Sister Bernadette Ignatius was a workaholic of the first degree, and she'd found ways to hide her feelings, bury them so deep, Tom had sometimes wondered if she even had them.

Now, pulling into a parking lot, he handed the keys to the attendant and got his bearings. He walked through the main entrance of Trinity College, toward the Campanile in the central square. He glanced around, not seeing her. Memories flooded back. Bernie had brought him here during her pregnancy. They had gone to the Long Room of the Old Library—the inspiration for his great-grandfather's library at Star of the Sea—and Tom had imagined their son growing up to study here.

Suddenly he saw her, thin and dark in her black habit, standing behind the Campanile. She was gazing at the Henry Moore sculpture, the smooth stone depiction of two people holding each other. The lines were soft and round, the bodies melting into each other. He held back, wondering what the message was here. Getting his heart under control, he walked over.

Bernie didn't hear him coming. He took his time, taking her in. She was five-five, very thin, but pure power. Even in her black habit and veil, she usually looked ready to take on the world, a force to be reckoned with. Not today. Her shoulders were shaking, her cheeks streaked with tears.

"Sister Bernadette," he said.

She looked up, her eyes wide with grief. "We can leave now," she said.

"What are you talking about?" he asked.

"Let's go home, Tom," she said. "Back to Connecticut."

"Jesus, Bernie," he said, panicking. Had she changed her mind so quickly? He had wanted to do this ever since they'd left Dublin before; his body ached with restricted emotion and energy, kept inside all these years and finally about to be let loose. "We're here for a reason, and we're not going home until we find him. I don't care what you say, Bernie. You're not allowed to chicken out, have a change of heart. We're doing this. We're going to look for him."

"No, we're not!" she said, voice rising with despair. "You don't understand!"

"Damn right," he said, frantic at the look in her eyes. "Tell me what you're talking about!"

"He won't be found," she said, covering her eyes with her hands. "They've hidden him."

"Hidden him?" he asked, feeling a punch in the stomach.

"She destroyed his records, Sister Eleanor Marie," Bernie choked out. "So we can't find him. We can't."

Tom's pulse went into overdrive. He saw the witch's face: he remembered back to their fight on the convent steps, twenty-three years ago, when she'd called the police on him, the pleasure and triumph in her black eyes as they roughed him up and took him away.

"She can't do that," he said. "It's impossible."

"They're gone, Tom."

"He's a person, a living, breathing human being; he was born, Bernie. We had him! She can't destroy the records of his birth!"

"But they're not there," Bernie cried. "She gave me the key, let me see for myself. It doesn't mean he doesn't exist—it just means she's done away with any paperwork that could help us find him."

"Done away with it?"

"She said she burned it."

"To keep us from finding him?" Tom shouted.

"Yes! That's exactly why she did it," she yelled back.

"I told you we should have come sooner," he said. "We never should have left him in the first place. Jesus Christ almighty, Bernie!" He shook her by the shoulders, locking into her gaze with pure fury. Bernie shrank back, as if she was afraid of him. Students passing by stopped and stared. He grabbed her, walked her away from the sculpture, past the Campanile, through the square and out onto the street. Crowds stared at him, strong-arming a nun.

She shook herself free and walked ahead to the river. The edge of her black veil fluttered over her shoulder. He wanted to reach for her, but he restrained himself. They walked along the Liffey, and Tom stared into the water to calm down. Rain was holding off, but the clouds reflected in dark ripples. He imagined the river flowing into Dublin Bay, merging with the sea.

They got to the cast-iron footbridge and walked across. Period lanterns flickered on. His anger burned, but he held it in. When she finally looked at him, he saw that she was turned inside out. Her blue eyes beseeched him—for kindness, forgiveness, he wasn't sure—but they softened him. He stood staring at her, his heart thumping. A few strands of red hair had slipped from under her veil, and he absently tucked them underneath.

"What are we going to do?" he asked.

"We could try the hospital," she said. "They'll have his birth records."

His jaw clenched; did she really consider this a solution? He wanted to start shouting again, but her troubled blue eyes kept him in check. He held the explosion inside. Didn't she remember the fights they had had during her ninth month? She had insisted on the adoption; he had battled her, but losing badly, had tried to convince her they should go through one of the Kelly law firms.

They could have had control over choosing the family their son went to, and kept track of his whereabouts all these years. But Bernie had kept him from telling his relatives anything, and had made all the arrangements through the church—guided by the Novice Mistress of the order she was about to join.

"Bernie," he said, trying to sound calm and in control, "you had him at Gethsemani. Don't you think Eleanor Marie would manage to take care of the records there, too?"

"We can't know until we try," she said, chin tilting up. A flash of her feistiness returned, her way of drawing a line in the sand—*any* sand. Normally, it drove him crazy, but right now he was glad to see it.

"You're right," he said, staring into her clear blue eyes, fighting the urge to tuck back those renegade red strands again.

"So that's what we're going to do," she said, checking her watch.

Streetlamps had come on up and down the Liffey, and house lights started to glow warmly all over town. "It's too late today, though."

"I'll pick you up tomorrow morning," he said. "First thing, right after breakfast. We'll get an early start."

"And we'll find him, Tom," she said.

He nodded, although he had his own private doubts. His mind was racing, thinking like a Kelly. All he'd have to do was explain this to Chris or Sixtus, get Niall to issue a warrant and force Bernie's order to open their records.

But Sister Bernadette Ignatius had made her choice when she made her vows—and even before that. She had been led to this place in her life by events that some deemed miraculous. And she had risen high in the Sisters of Notre Dame des Victoires, becoming Superior at Star of the Sea. Tom had to respect that, and tormented as they both felt right now, he couldn't take actions to jeopardize her position.

"Let me ask you one thing," he said. "Why are we doing this?"

She stared at him blankly, as if mystified by the question.

"You're a nun. You're not going to marry me. Yes, I've figured that out by now," he said, and her mouth twitched with a smile. His heart opened to see it, but his own face remained stone-hard. "He's grown up. He's past needing us, if he ever did at all. So seriously, Sister. What difference does it make whether we find him or not?"

Bernie gazed up at him. Somehow the last hours had stripped away her customary veneer, her edge of command and control. She looked so soft, washed by tears and the rain. She looked so young.

"I don't know," she said.

"Really?" he asked.

"I just want to see him," she whispered. "Is that so terrible? Just lay eyes on him, see what he looks like, make sure he's okay."

"How will we know he's okay, Bernie?"

"We'll talk to him."

"Will we tell him who we are?"

She gazed up at him with sadness in her eyes, as if she'd finally accepted the fact that he was very slow. They had discussed this back at Star of the Sea, as well as on the plane.

"We'll play it by ear," she said. "We'll take our cues from him. If we ever find him."

"We'll find him," Tom said.

"You asked me before why it matters after all this time. It matters because he's our son," she said, reaching up to touch Tom's cheek. "And because we have to know."

Tom nodded. He closed his eyes for one moment, leaning into her hand. Then she took it away. They crossed the bridge and walked along the river, the dark water swirling with reflected lights. He found the parking lot, and they climbed into the car. Driving through the city, he had to concentrate on staying left. It kept him from drifting someplace he knew he shouldn't go.

When they got to the convent, he pulled over. Glancing at the front window, he saw the curtains move and a shadow fall. They were waiting for her. She saw the expression in his eyes; he didn't even try to hide how he felt.

"See you tomorrow morning," she said.

"Okay," he said.

"Till then," she said, hand on the door handle, hesitating. He had the feeling she didn't want to get out. But of course she did.

He waited at the curb, to make sure she got into the house okay. She turned to wave. He didn't wave back, but just sat there until the door opened and closed behind her.

The car felt so empty, and so did Tom. He knew this feeling well, although he had kept it at bay for many years. It had started the instant she'd touched his face. The warmth of her hand and its light pressure had radiated through his whole body, through his heart, each bone, and every inch of skin. So that, when she took it away, the cold returned. The emptiness he had always felt, whenever Bernie gave him something, and whenever she took it away.

After supper and compline, Bernie went upstairs. Theodore and Eleanor Marie kept close watch over her, but she was past caring. Anne-Marie gave her questioning looks, and a great hug, as if she knew that Bernie needed it, which she did. But what she mainly needed, right now, was to be alone.

In the cozy peace of her cell, she pulled the blanket from her bed and bundled up, sitting in her chair by the window. A strange obsession had taken hold of her; she was convinced that if she kept looking outside, she would see her son and recognize him. Records could be burned, but she felt his existence shining out.

It had all started during the summer back home in Connecticut, with Brendan McCarthy. Seeing one red-haired blue-eyed boy had unlocked her deep need and longing and love for another. Tom's, too. They had taken one look at Brendan—Bernie's niece's friend—and the moment was like a wrecking ball.

She had felt it smashing the walls she had built around the birth of their child. The walls were high and thick; she had thought them impenetrable, indestructible. But she was wrong. Even now, huddled in the chair, she felt the wrecking ball crashing, breaking the walls down. After twenty-three years of bricking off her feelings, building herself into a solid fortress, the destruction was just that much greater.

She wondered how it was for Tom. Had he always felt this, the way she felt now? She knew how badly he had wanted to raise the child. She knew that he blamed everything on the vision she had had in the Blue Grotto—and on her subsequent burning desire to follow Mary's instruction and become a nun.

But there were parts of the story that Tom didn't know. Bernie, never comfortable with confusion, had kept them from him. There was one detail of her decision to give their baby up for adoption known to only two people on earth—and Tom wasn't one of them.

She sat at the window, watching people pass by on the street below. Wrought-iron lamps illuminated the sidewalk, but tall trees cast shadows, blurring people's features. Every time someone with red or reddish hair, or who looked as if he might have freckles, walked by, her heart skipped. She hadn't always been this way. Over the years, she had encountered innumerable red-haired boys, had never experienced emotional tumult, had never wanted to intrude on his life in any way.

Why was this happening now? Bernie prayed to know. As adamant as Tom had been that she had made a terrible mistake, she had never questioned her vows. One gift of having a vision was its indisputability. Once she had accepted the truth of it, the reality of what she had seen, then her actions seemed almost predetermined.

She clutched the blanket tighter. Why had she never thought about the fact that she had had the vision *before* she conceived the baby?

If Mary had really wanted her to become a nun, why had Bernie gotten pregnant? Now, turning from the window, she gazed at the small ceramic statue of Mary standing on the top of the plain bureau.

"Did you want me to be a mother?" she asked, and suddenly the question seemed absurd.

Because she *was* a mother. She had come to Ireland that first time with Tom to help him trace his family's history. They'd visited the West in May, the Cliffs of Moher, the most inspiring place she'd ever been. Nearly nine months later, one cold January day, she had given birth right here in a Dublin hospital. The rest of her life suddenly seemed to collapse around her, through the prism of that single fact.

Gethsemani Hospital. It was administered by the nuns about to become her beloved sisters, and she couldn't have imagined giving birth anywhere else. She remembered how Tom had begged her to let him tell his aunts and cousins about her pregnancy, saying that the Kellys would know where to get the best health care for both her and the baby.

But she hadn't wanted them involved—or maybe it was just that she hadn't trusted him enough. She'd been so young, and the shame had been terrible. Getting pregnant was the worst thing imaginable for a good Catholic girl. What would his family think of her if they knew? What would *hers*?

So she had gone to Gethsemani. He had been with her. She never, never let herself remember that day. It had happened, and she had relegated the memories behind the thick wall that was crumbling now. In her spiritual life, she managed by "giving it to God." Every day her prayers included gratitude for her son's birth, for Tom Kelly's friendship, for the love she felt for both of them.

The details were another story. The contractions starting nearly a month ahead of schedule, her water breaking, the searing pain she'd felt as her baby prepared to be born, the pressure of Tom's hand squeezing hers, the cracking sensation in her chest, her heart breaking-breaking-breaking, the gray winter light slanting through the hospital windows, the sense of time standing still, a feeling of swelling panic as she realized she could still change her mind, she could marry Tom and keep the baby, it still wasn't too late.

It wasn't too late....

And then it was.

That's how she felt now, holding the blanket around her shoulders, rocking in the straight-backed chair, gazing at all those anonymous faces passing on the street below. Another face filled her mind, the one that had come to the hospital the day after her son's birth, with burning eyes behind silver wire-rim glasses.

"Don't let it be too late," she whispered now, feeling half mad as she stared down at the street, shivering in the blanket, wondering whether this was how it felt to lose her faith.

Five

P arked at the curb, Tom felt like a rude man waiting for his date instead of going to the door. But he didn't want to stress Bernie more than she already was, or cause trouble with the wolf-nun by knocking on the convent door. He kept Billy's silver BMW idling while he stared at the parlor window; Eleanor Marie's fat tub of a henchman was peering from behind the white curtain. He felt dangerous, and although it wasn't yet nine in the morning, he had the feeling he knew how the day would end. There would be violence, he was pretty sure.

He'd planned it all night. Unable to sleep, staring at the ceiling, he had thought it through—Plan A wouldn't work, so they'd need a Plan B. He hoped it wouldn't land him in jail, but he honestly didn't much care. Jet lag, lack of sleep, and burning anger had left him feeling explosive. By the time Bernie came down the sidewalk, his heart was in overdrive.

"Good morning, Tom," she said, climbing in.

"Good morning, Sister," he said.

Her face was pale, and she had violet circles under her blue eyes. She had such thin skin, literally; when she was a young girl, her moods had always shown through. He stared at her now, feeling alarmed by what he saw.

"What's wrong?" he asked.

"Let's just go to the hospital," she said.

His back stiffened and he shifted into drive. When she wanted to keep something to herself, nothing could get it out of her. She'd always been the same. He shook his head, angry at himself. Had he honestly hoped she'd walk out this morning and tell him she'd had it with the religious life, that this was the final straw, that she was all his? He glanced over, saw her sitting there in her black lightweight-wool habit, pictured her in jeans and a sweater, exhaled loudly.

"How did we go on, working with each other all these years?" he asked. "We never had any trouble—not like this."

"We kept it bottled up," she said. "And that's what we have to do again. As soon as this is over."

"What do you mean, 'over'?"

"I mean after we go to the hospital records office today," Bernie said. "Whatever we do or don't find, this is the end of the road. If we find out the information, good. If we don't, then it's meant to be. In either case, we fly home."

"Yeah?" Tom asked, glancing across the seat. "That's what we do?"

"Yes."

"Whatever you say, Sister," he said. "You're the boss."

He said the words, sounding more convincing than sarcastic. But he didn't believe her. He felt the energy pouring from her and knew that she was far from at peace with the plan she had just laid out. Worried by her pallor and the timbre of her voice, he looked over again, saw her hands shaking. He fought the urge to reach for them, lace fingers with her, tell her it would all be okay.

They drove across the river, through an industrial area, into a residential neighborhood, saw Gethsemani Hospital looming up from among the houses. Its brick facade turned rose red as clouds broke and the sun shined through. Tom parked the car, waited for Bernie to say something. She didn't, so they climbed out.

They entered through the front door, as they had done the day their son was born. Tom glanced at Bernie, wondering whether she was thinking the same thing. He remembered their first time in

Ireland. She had been right by his side when he'd needed to come over and research his family history.

Dublin had been their base. They'd loved it here instantly, falling in love with the city and the entire Irish way of life. The Kellys had, predictably, embraced them—maybe a little too much, because the longer they stayed together, the more Tom wanted Bernie all to himself. Just thirty days after arriving in Ireland, Tom had known he had to take her away.

At the beginning of May—Mary's month, Bernie had later pointed out—he'd convinced her they had to take a break from tracking his roots and spending time with the family, and they'd traveled west to County Clare. They found a B&B in Doolin, a tiny fishing village on the edge of the Atlantic. Famous for traditional music, the town felt magical, as if it had been created just for them.

The accommodations were cheap; they'd taken separate rooms on the same floor. Tom couldn't walk Bernie to her door without feeling ravaged inside, but he'd fought every urge. Instead of doing what he really wanted to do, they'd hung out, eating good food, listening to Irish music, walking the narrow streets and laughing.

They'd borrowed bicycles from the B&B and explored the rugged coastline, the spectacular and haunting limestone expanse of the Burren. They'd bicycled along the sea road toward the Cliffs of Moher. Young and in shape, they'd made the ride in time for sunset.

God, the sight was breathtaking. The cliffs rose six hundred and fifty feet straight up from the ocean, their sheer rock face glistening for five miles in the golden light. Bernie had leaned into his arms.

"I can't believe we're here," she'd whispered.

"I'm so glad I'm seeing it with you," he'd said.

"Tom, think of our ancestors standing here, looking across the ocean toward America," she'd said. "Imagine their dreams...."

"They dreamed of better lives," he'd said, wrapping her in a strong embrace. "Of having families, and loving each other forever."

"That's how I feel about you," she'd said.

"It's how I've always felt about you," he'd said.

They'd kissed with such tender passion. Her lips had tasted of the salt air, and he'd shivered because he'd never felt anything close to this before. Never letting go, they'd led each other off the well-trod path into a thatch of sea grass and wildflowers. The Irish spring weather was still chilly. A cool breeze blew off the water, keeping tourists away, making Bernie and Tom press closer together as they tore off clothes, their bare skin hot against each other.

They'd conceived their child alone together at the top of the Old World. There, on the very brink of the Cliffs of Moher, on the edge of Ireland, facing America. The entire earth had fallen away. Tom and Bernie were a new family.

Summer passed, and fall. And then, just after the new year began, after it all, after everything that unfolded, Bernie had been in labor, her contractions coming hard and fast. They were standing on a new edge, so much more treacherous than those western cliffs. Tom had supported her, his arms around her, afraid she'd have the baby before they got to the delivery room.

Even now, walking into the hospital beside Sister Bernadette Ignatius all these years later, he could still see Bernie's long red hair, her narrow shoulders, her belly protruding from her unbuttoned dark green coat. He could see her face, in pain, but so alert to what was happening.

"You okay?" he asked her now, standing in the entrance hall.

"I am," she said. "I want to do this."

"Then we'll do it," he said. Doctors, visitors, and nuns walked by. Tom waited for Bernie to recognize someone, but she didn't. Walking over to the front desk, he asked for the records department, was directed down one flight. "They're in the basement," he told Bernie.

She nodded. They went to the bank of elevators, but when all four were going up, she glanced at him; they were thinking the same thing, and ran to the stairs, hurrying down.

They walked along a long olive-green corridor with fluorescent lights overhead. When they got to the records office, Bernie put her hand on his arm. She looked at him with huge blue eyes, and he knew what she was about to ask.

"Forget it, Sister," he said.

"Tom, I really think I should go in alone," she said.

He shook his head. His heart was in his throat. He didn't want to have to tell her how huge this was for him. Couldn't she see? "I had to let you go in to Eleanor Marie alone, Bernie," he said. "But not here. He's my boy, too. I'm coming."

She looked up at him. Maybe she was thinking about saving face with the nuns working here, or maybe she thought she could be more persuasive without him—but Tom was past the point of backing off.

"Are we going in or not?" he asked.

"I'm doing the talking," she said.

Tom nodded as he held the heavy door for Bernie, and they walked inside. A tall counter separated a small waiting area from a work space with two desks. A nun about Bernie's age occupied one, bent to a task on the computer; Tom saw another, younger nun back in the stacks of records that ran like shelves in a library, one row after another.

"Excuse me, Sister," Tom said.

Bernie gave him a sharp, dark look; he let her take over when the older nun came over to the counter. She was small, pretty, with warm brown eyes and an open smile. Tom saw her glance at Bernie without recognition, but taking in the distinctive habit and cross that marked them as members of the same order.

"Good morning, Sister," she said, then, looking at Tom, "And you, too!"

"Good morning," Tom said.

"What can I do for you?" she asked in a gentle brogue.

"Sister, we're looking for some information," Bernie said. She sounded strong, like her administrative self. Only Tom could detect the shakiness deep down in her voice.

"Of course," the nun said. "From the sounds of you both, you've come a long way. America?"

"Yes," Bernie said, smiling. "Connecticut."

"Ah! I have cousins in Hartford and New Britain. And some in Springfield, Massachusetts. I hope to get there someday; on my sabbatical, maybe."

"Well, you'd be welcome at our convent in Black Hall," Bernie said. "Star of the Sea; I'm Superior there."

Good going, Bernie, Tom thought; *way to throw your weight around.*

"Maybe one day, God willing, if I don't die of old age in this basement first," the nun said, chuckling. "I'm Sister Dymphna, by the way. So now, what are you looking for?"

"A baby boy," Bernie said. "He was born on January 4, 1983."

"And what is his name?"

"I don't know," Bernie said.

Sister Dymphna gazed across the counter, confused. Tom felt a trickle of sweat run down his back, between his shoulder blades.

"His birth name was Thomas Sullivan. But he was put up for adoption," Bernie said.

A look passed between her and Sister Dymphna, a ripple of understanding. The nun glanced at Tom, then back to Bernie, her brown eyes more kind than curious.

"What are the parents' names?" she asked.

"Bernadette Sullivan and Thomas Kelly," Bernie said.

"We're not supposed to release information on adoptees," Sister Dymphna said quietly, "without going through a lot of paperwork."

"I understand," Bernie said, but her tone was beseeching, and her eyes . . . Tom had been watching her come apart for a day and a half now, and he was pretty sure Sister Dymphna had the compassion to see it, too.

"We just want to know where he is," Bernie said. "That he's had a good life."

Sister Dymphna cast a quick look over her shoulder, as if to make sure the younger nun wasn't close by. She was back in the stacks, crouching down, replacing an armload of manila files.

"We're slowly computerizing," Sister Dymphna said. "We're not through entering the eighties into our database yet, but I'll see if those names are in here." Her fingers flew over the keyboard, and she frowned at the screen. "Nope," she said. "Not yet." She glanced up. "Wait just a minute, and I'll check something else."

Tom watched her make her way back into the archives. He was aware of Bernie standing close beside him, leaning against the counter, as if she had lost faith in her legs to support her. He wanted to hold her up, but he held himself back. His own heart was pounding so hard, he felt it all through his chest.

A minute later, Sister Dymphna emerged from the stacks. She held a large brown envelope, but she was frowning.

"What's wrong, Sister?" Bernie asked.

"It's very strange," she said. "I have the birth records here. The boy was born at seven-thirty a.m., on January 4, as you said. He weighed 3.36 kilograms. Baby Boy Sullivan."

"He was called Thomas that first day. Thomas James Sullivan," Bernie said, and Tom couldn't let himself look at her. Thomas after him, James after her father, and Sullivan—her last name because she wouldn't marry him and take his.

"That's not in the file," Sister Dymphna said. "And neither is any information on where he went from here."

"What do you mean?" Bernie asked.

"It's customary for the pediatrician to make notes in the file, in terms of the child's placement with an agency."

"Agency?" Tom asked.

"Yes. The child normally goes from here to one of the agencies approved by the Irish Adoption Board. Our order has several facilities—St. Thomas Aquinas, St. Maurice, and St. Augustine's." She paused, scanning the documents. "I would expect to see that information here, stapled to the birth certificate. But it's been removed."

"Removed?" Bernie asked, reaching for the paper. There were the staple holes in the top left corner. "Who did this? Why?"

"I have no idea," replied Sister Dymphna. "There is no way of knowing who accessed the records, or when. I've worked here for many years, but I don't recall anyone ever asking for this information before."

"So there's nothing?" Bernie asked. "No way of knowing where he went?"

Sister Dymphna shook her head. "Not unless the mother stayed in one of our homes. Sometimes they move into the convent before or after birth. If that is the case, the convent would have information about the child."

"We tried that," Tom said.

"The information doesn't exist," Bernie said.

"Oh, it has to exist somewhere," Sister Dymphna said, growing agitated. "Perhaps it's this office's mistake. Transferring files onto the disk, sometimes things get misplaced. It doesn't happen often, but it does happen. We're only human, after all."

Tom stared down at his feet. He felt pressure building in his chest. He wanted to explode, to grab Bernie and tell her what they had to do. But he'd sworn to behave, to let her try this her way.

"Sister Brigid?" Sister Dymphna called, turning toward the young woman in back. Slowly, almost reluctantly, she approached the front desk. "Would you know anything about the placement certificate from this file? Perhaps it's on your desk, waiting to be entered into the database?"

"No," Sister Brigid said.

"No it isn't, or no you don't know?" Tom asked harshly.

"Tom!" Bernie said, her tone sharp.

"No, it's not on my desk," Sister Brigid said, reddening.

"That's all right, Sister," Sister Dymphna said. "I didn't really think it was. It was just a long shot. Thank you."

The younger nun hovered for an instant, eyes troubled, seeming to be unsure of what she should do next. Tom homed in on it right away, and he saw that Bernie did, too. Bernie was an angel with young nuns. Tom had watched her over the years, back home at Star of the Sea. She treated the young women as daughters—loving them, wanting the best for them, guiding them, and when they lied or evaded the truth, seeing through them. That was happening now.

"Sister Brigid," Bernie said. This was a tough one; Tom could see her walking the fine line between wanting to respect Sister Dymphna's authority and needing to get to the bottom of the story. "Please," Bernie said.

Sister Brigid's blush deepened. Her eyes flicked from Sister Dymphna to Bernie. She looked so uncomfortable, Tom felt sorry for her.

"One of our sisters called last night," Sister Brigid said. "She asked me about this very file. Sullivan-Kelly, she said. She asked me to look inside and check to make sure the placement information was gone."

"You removed it?" Sister Dymphna asked, frowning.

"No," Sister Brigid said, shaking her head vehemently. "No, Sister. She made it sound as if it had been removed long ago, and she just wanted confirmation of the fact. That's all! I only checked for her."

"What was her name?" Bernie asked.

"Sister Theodore," the young nun said.

Bernie thanked the two nuns. Her tone was flat, dull; Tom could tell she thought it was over. He held the door for her, and they walked into the stairwell, their footsteps echoing as they climbed. Emerging in the main lobby, Tom felt wild. So alive, on fire, ready to move.

"I'll get my things," Bernie said. "And then we'll leave."

"No, Bernie," he said.

"What are you talking about? It's finished, Tom."

He shook his head, grabbed her shoulders. Could she see in his eyes the way he felt? She stared up at him, not trying to break free, seeming not to care that crowds were swarming around them, seeing him look at her this way.

"This is the hospital where our baby was born," he said. "Can you feel him?"

"I could," she said. "But not now."

"Don't let her take him away from you."

"She got to the records here, too," Bernie said. "Eleanor Marie. She claims she did it to protect him."

"She did it because she has it in for you," Tom said. "And she always has."

"This is evil," Bernie whispered. "It's not about me—it's about *him.* . . ."

"Our baby."

Bernie nodded.

"You're going to get her back," Tom said. "And you're going to do it tonight. We are."

"Tom, we're going home...."

He held her, hands on her shoulders, gave her a soft shake. Staring into her blue eyes, he tingled. Here in this crowded hospital lobby, he felt the breeze coming across the Atlantic, across the Cliffs of Moher, across Ireland.

It belonged to Long Island Sound, and he knew it had come straight from the Star of the Sea vineyard, a breeze full of salt and grapes. It was the smell of home, their home. And he knew they weren't returning until they'd gotten what they'd come for.

"She didn't destroy the records," Tom said.

"Yes she did—she told me—"

"And you believe her? Think about it, Bernie. She's trying to hide something, and she's desperate enough to have her henchman call here yesterday to make sure."

"What could she be trying to hide?" Bernie asked. "About our son?"

"I don't know," Tom said. "But we're going to find out."

"How?" Bernie asked, and her eyes began to shine again.

"Listen. We tried it your way," Tom said. "Now we're going to try it mine. And we're going to do it tonight."

Six

The convent was dark. Everyone was asleep. The red sanctuary candle flickered, and Bernie blessed herself as she walked by. She had taken off her shoes, left them in her cell, so her footsteps couldn't be heard echoing through the house.

She hurried down the hall, not wanting to keep Tom waiting. A shadow crossed the wall, startling her, but it was just her reflection in the glass of a framed picture of Saint Marie-Joseph, the founder of their order. Street light came through the tall front windows, slanting onto the wood floors and threadbare Oriental rugs.

When she got to the parlor, she saw Sister Anne-Marie waiting. They nodded at each other, and Anne-Marie went to the alarm panel. Bernie had filled her in, enlisting her help—she knew she'd have to disarm the burglar alarms in order to carry out Tom's plan.

The convent contained several valuable paintings and pieces of furniture, gifts from wealthy patrons, as well as gold and silver chalices and other religious items. The records of the order in Ireland were stored here. Besides, it was a house full of women, and even back home, Bernie took precautions to protect her Sisters. So the alarm was expected, and Tom had reminded her it needed to be disarmed.

At Bernie's signal, Anne-Marie typed in the code on the keypad. A tiny chime sounded, and Bernie winced, watching the stairs. When no one appeared, she carefully pulled open the heavy door. Sticking her head out, she breathed in Dublin's night air. It smelled of the sea. She heard leaves rustling overhead, the breeze picking up and blowing through the trees up and down the block.

Tom was waiting across the street. At the sight of Bernie, he hurried up the steps. His wavy dark hair glinted in the lamplight, and his eyes looked young and bright. He wore jeans and a black sweater.

"You ready?" he asked.

She nodded, her mouth too dry to speak.

"Hello, Tom," Sister Anne-Marie whispered.

"Hi, Annie," he said. "Thank you for all this."

"You're welcome. I'm with you and Bernie."

Bernie's heart tightened. Annie's loyalty and friendship had not diminished one bit over the years.

"Let's go, then," Tom said.

They mounted the stairs, all three of them. Tom wore boots, and when he realized they were making noise, he took them off. It struck Anne-Marie funny, three people walking barefoot through the convent on a stealth mission, and she put her hand over her mouth to hold back laughter. Bernie loved her for it. They had plotted all afternoon, working out the best scenario, trying to imagine what Eleanor Marie would have done with the paperwork.

Annie had joked that Eleanor Marie probably slept with it under her pillow—they would have to brain her to get it, but first they would have to get past Theodore, who slept in the next cell.

"She's a regular watchdog," Annie had said.

"Why does she do it?" Bernie had asked.

"Eleanor Marie provides a safety net, in a way."

"Go on..."

"She is zealous about so many things," Annie had said. "She is a true believer, there's no doubting that. She has such a sense of morality, a black-and-white idea of right and wrong. Gray areas don't exist to her, and that can be a very appealing notion. It stops the questions, you know?"

"I know," Bernie had said grimly. Some women were drawn to

being nuns because of their contemplative natures, their desire to go deeply into the mysteries of life, love, eternity. But once there, the silence could prove too much. Questions led to other questions, and a person could get lost. Some nuns, like Eleanor Marie, became absolutists.

The Superior's own upbringing had been so painful. She'd been born to a single mother, had never even known her own father. An old nun who had known her growing up said that her mother had been a prostitute, leaving her daughter alone for nights on end. Even worse, one of the men once went after Eleanor, and her mother had failed to protect her. Bernie understood that great hurt had hardened in Eleanor Marie's heart, freezing it with hatred.

"Sister Theodore is devoted to her. Most of the rest of us just put up with her. She's very ambitious, and I think she wants to go to Rome. I'm just hoping the next Superior is less evil."

"'Evil' is a strong word," Bernie had said softly after a long moment, because she wasn't at all sure the word was wrong. She thought of the young Eleanor, of all she had endured.

"Rigid, then."

Bernie had nodded. The concept of evil was one for the theologians. "Eleanor Marie certainly takes things—and people—into her own hands, and shapes their destinies. She did it with me, back before I first joined."

"Are you saying she made you decide to give the baby up?"

"You were there, Annie," Bernie had said. "You know she influenced my decision."

Annie had nodded, taking her friend's hand. "You know what people were saying back then," she'd said. "We were all in awe of you. Some were so jealous—Eleanor Marie, for example. There was talk . . ."

Bernie had closed her eyes, transplanted back to the Blue Grotto.

"There was talk of a miracle. And then you showed up, pregnant. Some people were saying you'd been chosen, that the baby was blessed, the Second Coming. . . ."

"He *was* blessed."

"It enraged Eleanor Marie," Annie had said. Her gaze had flickered, not wanting to hurt her friend. But Bernie had given her the signal that she wanted to hear, for her to go on. "She said you had gotten pregnant out of wedlock. That the child was a bastard. She'd raved about fornication, sin, shame. You can imagine."

"Oh, yes," Bernie had said, thinking how that would have reverberated with Eleanor's own troubled history.

"She said that you'd had a vision—she wanted to call you a liar, but she couldn't dispute the Vatican's findings. That the Virgin Mary had appeared to you, alone among all of us, and you'd chosen to throw that gift right back in Mary's face. She'd called you to a life of purity and prayer, and you'd gone and gotten yourself pregnant."

"I was in love," Bernie had said.

"Sister Eleanor Marie was obsessed with the idea of sin. You remember. She still is. She says the Blessed Mother called you, and you turned your back."

"She did call me."

"I know. I believe you," Annie had said, taking her hand.

"I think I heard the wrong message," Bernie had whispered, shuddering with the doubt that had been growing for weeks now, since she had first seen Brendan McCarthy and his red hair, since she'd started thinking and dreaming about her son.

"What do you mean?"

"She's the Blessed Mother," Bernie had said. "And when I became a mother, I turned my back on my child to join this convent...."

"You mean, you think she called you to be a mother, not to be a nun?"

"That's what I sometimes think," Bernie had replied.

"Do you think Eleanor Marie knew that, back when you came to us? And steered you in the wrong direction?"

"I wonder," Bernie had said. "I think maybe she did."

"She was so jealous of you. Still is. You're just a few years younger than she is, but you're already as powerful within the church. I'm sure she never expected you to become a Superior. Look, we both know that when she looked at you, she saw her own mother."

A prostitute. Bernie had nodded slightly, imagining how Sister

Eleanor Marie would process that. Had she thought Bernie had given herself so freely out of desperation? How wrong that was, Bernie thought; how much she'd loved Tom...

"She thought you'd be hidden in the cloister, repenting for your terrible sin," Annie had said, making a face to let Bernie know what she thought of that.

"I did repent," Bernie had said. "But not for loving Tom. I repented for hurting him and our son. And I was forgiven."

"In the eyes of Eleanor Marie, two sins are unforgivable," Annie had said.

"What are those?"

"Having a vision without her, and being as highly or better regarded than she within the church. I almost feel sorry for her."

"Almost," Bernie had said. "She's gone over the line, hiding the evidence about my son. I can't imagine what motivated her to do that; I'm not sure I even care. All I want is to find him."

"I'll help you, Bernie," Annie had said.

Bernie had stared at her, long and hard. Annie's goodness was so deep, and her friendship was beyond question. But Bernie knew a little about Tom's plan, and she knew that Annie would be better off not getting involved.

"The only thing I'll ask," she said, "is whether you know the alarm code to the front door."

"To the convent?" Annie had asked, looking shocked.

"Yes. I want to let Tom in tonight. He's going to help me get behind the iron grate, to look for our son's records. I can't do it alone."

"You'll need my help, too," Annie had said. "I know the code; I'll let Tom in. And I'll help you tear the place apart till we find your boy. Bernie, I have an idea of where his file might be."

"Under Eleanor Marie's pillow, like you said?"

"Maybe," Annie had said, dimpling. "But if it's not there, I can think of another place. It's behind the grate, as you say. And I don't have the keys to it. Eleanor Marie keeps them close at all times. None of us gets in there without her."

"We will tonight," Bernie had said. "Tom will get us in."

"But it's locked tight!"

"We're always locking ourselves out at the convent back home," Bernie had said. "Locking keys in the car, or the truck…Tom can break into anything."

"Well, he can walk right through the front door here. I'll open it for him," Annie had vowed.

She had kept that promise, and now they were moving silently down the hall to the offices. Although the office door was alarmed, Annie had disarmed it with the master code. She didn't have a key to the heavy door, and looked up with helplessness in her eyes. Tom brushed her aside, removed a set of lock picks and a small pry bar from his back pocket. Bernie glanced up at him, saw the concentration on his face. Only Tom would come to Ireland and know how to lay his hands on burglars' tools.

He tried two picks before the lock opened; it took eight seconds to get inside. They hurried in, quietly closing and locking the door behind them. Bernie started to turn on the light, but Annie stopped her.

"Someone might see," she said. "Both Eleanor Marie and Theodore sleep right across the courtyard." She ran to the windows, pulled down the blinds. But even so, Bernie worried that light would be visible through the slats.

"Don't worry about it yet," Tom said. "Where's the iron grate you told me about?"

"Over here," Bernie said. She took his hand, led him through the dark room. She bumped into Eleanor Marie's desk, banging her hip, and she bit her tongue to keep from crying out.

The wrought-iron grate, heavy and tall, was locked tight. Bernie grasped it, holding on to the ornate curlicues with both hands, giving it a swift shake.

"Patience, Sister Bernadette Ignatius," Tom said, trying the picks on the lock. They didn't work; it was very old, and Bernie remembered the skeleton key it took to open it. She started to tell him, but he'd moved on to a cruder method. He held the pry bar between the wall and the grate, wedging it into the space, working it down. One hit, and the lock popped with a crashing sound. Bits of plaster rained down on the floor.

"We're in," he said.

"But we can't see anything," Bernie said, peering into the darkness.

"Hang on," Annie said. Knowing her way in the dark, she rushed into the outer office, returned with a handful of devotional candles and a box of matches. "Here," she said nervously.

Bernie grabbed her hand. "Annie, you've done enough. Let Tom and me take it from here."

"No," she said stubbornly. "I believe in this, and you. I want to help you find him."

"You've helped us already. Please, you have to live here. When Eleanor Marie finds out, there'll be hell to pay. It's for me and Tom to deal with. Please, Annie. Go upstairs. I'll come find you when we have it."

"Go, Annie," Tom said. He had lit his candle, and was giving her a look of deep gratitude. "I'll never forget you for this."

"Okay, then," she said reluctantly. "I don't want to leave you, but I know that this is your mission. Bless you both."

"Thank you," Bernie said, giving her friend a hug. Then Annie slipped out of the office, letting Bernie lock it behind her. Hurrying back to the vault, she took a candle from Tom.

"How much time do we have?" Tom asked.

"Two hours," she said. "It's just before one, and matins are at three-fifteen."

"Let's go, then," he said.

Bernie led him down the long row of old wooden filing cabinets. They passed the S's, where she had already looked. Annie's idea had been to look in the drawers containing folders for the adoption agency homes: St. Thomas Aquinas, St. Augustine, and St. Maurice. The very last cabinet in the aisle was labeled "Institutions."

Tom stared at the drawer, ran his hand over the fine wood. Bernie knew how much he admired the craftsmanship, hated the idea of damaging it. But in went the pry bar, and the lock popped open with one crack. He had done it with almost no damage to the wood, but the lock was ruined.

He held the candle, and Bernie started to rifle through. They pulled the folders out, spread them on the floor. She brushed aside anything before 1983, concentrating on the first months of their child's life. January, February, March, April. Name after name: Ardigeen, Bannon, Bower, Charles, Darigan, Geary, Howe, Killeen, Mahoney, O'Brien, O'Byrne, O'Malley, Reilly, Sullivan.

Bernie's heart pounded. She pulled open the file, read through the first lines, Tom looking over her shoulder.

"Rosaleen," he said. "Wrong Sullivan."

"It has to be in here," she whispered.

May, June, July...

More names, no more Sullivans. They looked through documents from each home. St. Thomas Aquinas in Blackrock, St. Augustine's in Phibsboro, and St. Maurice behind St. Stephen's Green.

"Phibsboro," Tom said, gazing into the drawer that held the information for St. Augustine's. "That's where we lived after the cliff..."

"I know," she whispered.

"I hope he went there," Tom said. "I hope he was in Phibsboro for a while. So he could feel us. Even though we'd already gone, our love was there, Bernie."

"Shhh, Tom," she said.

"There's nothing here," he said. "Not one paper with his name on it. Maybe she really does sleep with it under her pillow. Could it be in her desk out there? I'll jimmy every goddamn drawer."

"It's just a writing desk," she said. "There's no room to store a file. She was telling the truth. She destroyed it."

Silently they started cleaning up. Bernie felt overwhelmed. She hadn't known the whereabouts of their son all this time. But the desire to know was so powerful; once it took hold, it just kept growing. She felt it pouring through her body, a sense of desperation and helplessness, the feeling that he was right here—just an arm's length away, if only she knew where to look.

Tom replaced every file in its proper folder, stuck them back in the drawer, closed it as best he could. Splinters of wood around the broken lock glinted white in the candlelight. They started down the aisle, and Bernie knew Tom's heart had to be as heavy as hers. She put her hand on his arm. Her fingertips prickled, and she knew there was something she had to say to him.

"What is it?" he asked.

She felt dizzy. Emotions flooded through her, and she leaned back, hand behind her for support. Tom stood there, frowning, concern in his dark blue eyes. She saw them glinting in the candlelight. Years melted away, and for a second she imagined them back in time, together, in love.

"Tom…" she said.

"What's wrong, Bernie?"

And then she saw. She'd never know what made her stop right there, at that precise spot in Eleanor Marie's record room. Over Tom's shoulder she saw a drawer in the highest row, and she knew. Their baby's records were in there.

"Open it," she said, pointing.

"Bernie, what are you talking about? Why?"

"Look, Tom," she said, and he followed her gaze.

The drawer was marked with the letter *K*.

"Kelly," he said.

He wasn't careful this time. He jammed the iron bar in, hit it with the heel of his right hand, and the fine wood splintered loudly. Pulled the drawer open so hard, all the contents spilled onto the floor. Bernie's heart was racing so hard; she kept standing, while Tom crouched down to look.

Baby Boy Sullivan. That was the name used by the hospital. But Bernie had called him Thomas, after his father. Eleanor Marie had said he was a bastard child, but she couldn't deny his Kelly lineage, and she had found it a convenient place to hide the records.

"Here he is," Tom whispered, slowly paging through the file. Looking up, he met Bernie's eyes. "Our son is right here. Thomas James Sullivan. Filed under 'Kelly.'"

Bernie nodded. She had to look away to stop herself from shaking, and to keep from seeing the tears running down Tom's cheeks. He reached for her hand, pulled himself up. He blew out their candles and held her, their son's file pressed between them, and she let him.

Footsteps sounded in the hall outside. Heavy thumping, followed by a lighter pair. By the time the door to the outer office flew open and lights were turned on, Bernie and Tom had broken apart, stepped over the pile of shattered wood and mixed-up files, placed the smoking candles in a brass wastebasket, and started to leave.

"What do you think you are doing?" Sister Eleanor Marie asked, her voice booming.

"Taking what's ours," Tom said.

"How dare you!" she exclaimed, flying at him, trying to wrest the file from his hand. Bernie watched him hold her off, holding the documents out of her grasp.

"Those belong to the order," Sister Theodore said, sounding panicked but almost apologetic, both at the same time.

"They're about our son," Bernie said.

"I'm calling the garda," Sister Eleanor Marie said. "And then I'm calling Rome. You'll be sorry about this, Bernadette. You'll regret it until the day you die and beyond. Your days as a Superior are over. I hope you know that."

"We're leaving," Bernie said. Her voice was so choked, she could barely speak. Her thoughts were whirling, and she could barely register the determination on Tom's face, the triumph on Sister Eleanor Marie's.

"You'll hear about this," Sister Eleanor Marie said. "You're a fraud. I tried to help you back then, and I saw it in your eyes. Coming to this convent twenty-three years ago, you had hidden agendas. Didn't I tell you, Theodore?"

Sister Theodore nodded, but didn't speak. Bernie saw sadness in her eyes.

"You came in here to hide from something," Sister Eleanor Marie said. "To bury your shame. What better place to avoid facing yourself than a house without mirrors? You should have looked more deeply into your soul—I consider it a shortcoming of mine, that I didn't force you."

"Bernie, come on," Tom said, sliding his arm around her shoulders. She trembled, holding back a sob.

"I want that file," Sister Eleanor Marie said, blocking the door.

"You'd have to kill me for it," Tom said, staring her down.

"Dial the gardai," Sister Eleanor Marie ordered, and Sister Theodore fumbled the phone, rushing to obey. "You're not leaving with that file."

"We're not leaving without it," Tom said. He started to turn away, and Sister Eleanor Marie stepped between him and Bernie.

"You're a whore," Sister Eleanor Marie said, staring into Bernie's eyes.

Bernie felt a surge of rage and despair, but before she could say a word, she felt Tom stop, turn, and face Eleanor Marie. She sensed him lunging forward, just like a wave rearing up from the ocean's depths.

"How dare you?" he roared, grabbing Eleanor Marie by the throat. Bernie saw the satisfaction in her eyes, as if she'd provoked him just to see him reveal the baseness of man.

"No, Tom," Bernie shouted, hauling him away from Eleanor. "It's not worth it!"

His eyes flickered, and she knew that he heard. He stepped away, but still—as if he couldn't stop himself—he brushed Eleanor Marie aside, swatting her off like a fly. She tumbled down, crying out with a sort of masochistic triumph.

Tom held on to Bernie, led her right past the fallen nun. She felt him trembling as he bent down to pick up the boots he had kicked off.

Bernie looked around. This was her home—not this building, but the sisterhood. She had been a Sister of Notre Dame des Victoires for nearly her entire adult life. It was her sanctuary, her refuge, her life. She had believed herself called here by Mary, and she stood in front of the small alabaster statue now. Her heart raced, and she looked for a sign. Anything to tell her what to do.

She saw only white marble, a pretty expression, open arms carved by an artist in another century. Tom's arm tightened, and he said her name. Bernie glanced up the stairs, saw Sister Anne-Marie standing on the landing. Behind her, Sister Eleanor Marie shouted for Theodore to call the gardai.

"Annie," Bernie said.

"I love you, Bernie," Annie cried back.

"We have to go," Tom said.

Turning from her friend to look up into Tom's eyes, Bernie tore the veil from her head and dropped it on the floor. And she touched the folder he held in his hand, and she followed him out the front door, down the stone steps, through the iron gate, and she left the convent.

PART TWO

Seven

Oakhurst was tiny as Newport mansions went, but try telling the family that. To them, it might have been The Breakers, or Marble House. Granted, it had a fine address, right on Bellevue Avenue. But it was at the wrong end—closer to the shopping center, with the grocery store and Brooks Drugs, than to Ocean Drive and Bailey's Beach. And it was faced with white clapboard instead of limestone, the material favored by the Vanderbilts, Astors, and most other self-respecting robber barons.

The white house had eight bedrooms, formal living and dining rooms, parlor, library, and flower-arranging room. The kitchen was in back, with a huge stove and refrigerator, for all the entertaining the family did; it reminded Kathleen of an institutional kitchen, something she was quite familiar with. There was an enormous butcher-block counter for chopping, and a center island with six stools around it, although very few people ever sat there. The kitchen window overlooked a carriage house that held the family's silver Rolls-Royce, their Mercedes station wagon, and the two sons' matching Porsches.

The house sat on a small piece of property—about a quarter acre—nearly filling every inch, so that there were just two patches of grass, one in front, by the avenue, one in back, between the kitchen door and carriage house. The namesake oak tree rose from the back-yard, shading the peaked roof, keeping the downstairs rooms so cool the air-conditioning rarely needed to be turned on.

The help lived in the attic, under sharply sloping eaves. There was no air-conditioning up here. Even with all the windows open, it was oppressive. Kathleen had her own room, and she had bought a fan for it, which she kept going almost all the time. The heat bothered her terribly. She wasn't used to humidity like this; they didn't have anything like it in Dublin. She had noticed a boarded-up section of the attic, just across the hall. Sometimes she imagined breaking down the door, opening any windows inside, just to get a cross breeze.

As the family's cook and upstairs maid, she had somewhat exalted status among the other help. In the hierarchy of service, she was right up there. The other servants were Beth, a local girl, hired to be the maid who answered the front door; Miss Langley, the nanny for Wendy's children; Samantha, the babysitter for June's children; and Bobby, the chauffeur. The staff shared one bathroom, with a stall shower whose water never quite got hot.

The family relied on Kathleen for all their meals, as well as for the parties they gave. Kathleen lived for the nights they entertained, when she could cook lobster with black truffle porridge; cinnamon-braised short ribs; potato soufflé; ricotta bruschetta topped with marinated grapes. Cooking for the family was another story. "Plain" was too adventurous a word to describe their culinary tastes.

The first day Kathleen started working for them, Mrs. Wells had taken her aside to explain how she liked things prepared. "The employment agency said you are a very good cook, and that's why we hired you—for parties. We like to be known for our table."

"Then you shall be, madam," Kathleen said, with pride.

"When it's just us, however, we like things just so."

"Anything you like, I can prepare."

"Beef," Mrs. Wells said. "Roast beef, steak, and hamburgers. Mashed potatoes every night, with a side dish of mixed vegetables. We like Birds Eye."

"Excuse me?"

"Birds Eye vegetables."

"But they're frozen," Kathleen said, thinking she must have misunderstood.

"I know. We prefer the mild flavor. Get the kind with the sauce packet."

"I can make any sauce you would like," Kathleen said. "Béchamel, hollandaise, Mornay..."

"We like the sauce packet," Mrs. Wells said steadily. "Now, as for potatoes..."

Kathleen had listened politely, with growing alarm, as the woman told her how to make potatoes: "Use instant," she'd said. "But not powdered—the flakes. Use plenty of butter, and half-and-half. Not milk, understand?"

"I don't mind peeling real potatoes," Kathleen had offered, hiding how appalled she was by this suggestion.

"They don't taste any better," Mrs. Wells had said. Small, tan, with neatly turned-under blond hair and wearing her customary abundance of diamonds, she sounded perfectly confident.

Kathleen had nearly quit right then. Frozen vegetables with a sauce packet? Beef every night of the week? Those were strange enough, but insisting that instant potatoes tasted as good as *real* ones? That nearly did Kathleen in. The woman was delusional. What other insanities lurked in her mind?

"And peeling takes too much time. Just make sure you use the butter and half-and-half—delicious. Now, I'll need you to pitch in with the housework when you're not cooking. It will be your job to make the beds after breakfast. I need Beth downstairs, to answer the door in case people come to call."

Kathleen had nodded. The family was all about show. God forbid a visitor would arrive while Beth was upstairs, slapping clean sheets on a bed. She had to be somewhere in the front of the house, tidying up with her feather duster, dressed in her black uniform and white apron. Since Kathleen's domain was the back of the house, her uniform was white, simple, not so formal.

The boys noticed her. There were two of them, Andrew and Pierce, ages thirty-one and twenty-nine, respectively. They were playboys, two of the most eligible bachelors in Newport. When they got home from parties at night, they fought each other viciously for first crack at the Social Register, to look up the women they had met, to see if they were listed, worthy of being called.

Something was wrong with Andrew. He drank too much, for one thing. Beneath his dark tan was the greenish-yellow tint of liver. He sneaked bottles from the kitchen when he thought himself unobserved, then placed them, empty, in the trash at night. He was arrogant, yes, but there was a distant and tender quality about him. He was divorced; Patricia, his ex-wife, lived in New York with their son, whom Andy never saw. The reasons for the divorce were never mentioned, nor was the reason he didn't see his son.

He'd sit at the kitchen counter, smoking cigarettes and drinking gin and tonics while Kathleen worked. She didn't really mind—she felt sorry for him. He talked about "the Gulf," how he had been deployed in the first Desert Storm. When Kathleen did the math, however, she realized that he had to be lying. He would have been too young to go. Other obvious lies included talk about several patents he held on things he had invented that would make him millions—much more than Patricia's family. Her father held the patent on the hose clamp, and had three hundred and twenty.

Three hundred and twenty million dollars, that is. That was how the Wells family talked. This family had forty, that family had eleven. Some families had more than one hundred. That Andy had been married to a woman whose family had three hundred and twenty—and then lost her—was considered a great family tragedy and scandal.

So Kathleen indulged Andy, letting him keep her company while she prepared his family's meals. He was always very appropriate. He respected the boundary between them, never making a pass or a suggestive comment. As she had in other positions, working for other families, in these moments Kathleen felt a bit like a therapist, listening in silence as a person unburdened himself. In this case, Andy spoke mainly about how his three siblings got all his parents' favor—

and money. They all received higher allowances than he did; his father would never forgive him for getting divorced.

The closest Andy came to stepping over the line came one August afternoon. Kathleen had been taking her break outside, sitting under the oak tree, writing a letter she knew she'd never send. This was how she got by—writing to a boy she hadn't seen in ten years. She poured her heart out on paper, knowing that no one had ever understood her the way he had, telling him her deepest fears, sorrows, dreams, wishes. Tears began to flow as she thought of him, wondering where he was, and she'd buried her head in her hands.

Andy had seen. Just before dinner, he'd found her in the kitchen.

"Seeing you out there, sitting on the ground," he'd said, "cross-legged, bent over writing, concentrating so hard…sun coming through the leaves, tears on your cheeks…you looked so sad, and oh, Kathleen…"

"I'm fine," she'd said, frowning as she made hamburger patties.

"I feel connected to you," Andy had whispered.

"Connected?"

"You know what it is to feel lost," he'd said. "Lost and sad. I'll never forget that sight.…I'll remember it forever."

"What sight?"

"Of you, Kathleen," he'd said. "Sitting there in your white uniform, the sun in your hair. Crying. You looked so beautiful.…There's a mystery about you.…I just wish I could be the man you were writing to."

"Oh, Andy," she'd said. "I'm a cook, a maid. I'm not in the Social Register! I'm not a girl for you.…"

"Still," he'd said passionately, torment in his liquid brown eyes, "I wish you could be."

"Things like that don't happen," she said, smiling sadly. "Only in fairy tales, maybe…"

"That's what my sister said," Andy said, his mouth dropping open with shock, as if Kathleen had just suggested the Second Coming.

"Your sister? Which one, Wendy or June?" Kathleen asked, thinking that never had she met two less romantic, fairy-tale–like women than those two.

"Neither," he said. "Louise."

"Louise?" Kathleen asked. Why had she never heard of her?

"We don't talk about her," Andy said. "My sister who believed in fairy tales..."

"I used to, too," Kathleen said, thinking back to St. Augustine's, when she would look at James and see their future together. "But I don't anymore. Fairy tales don't come true, Andy."

She had smiled at him, her brow furrowed with pain and worry. He had seen something in her she always kept hidden, and she had to remind herself not to write outside again. He had sat there, silently drinking and smoking, lost in whatever thoughts were making his eyes so dark and anguished...possibly thoughts about this sister no one talked about, Louise.

Outside, Pierce pulled into the driveway, parked his Porsche behind Andy's, blocking him in. It was a metaphor for their relationship. Pierce always took the best parking spot. And everything else.

Pierce was tall, dark, and gorgeous. He had a deep Bailey's Beach tan, slicked-back brown hair, green eyes that lived up to his name—piercing, like a shark's. At night he wore clothes from Prada; he wore shoes from Bottega Veneta. By day he dressed in candy-colored garments, each shirt costing more than Kathleen made in a month. Pink-peach lisle softer than rose petals; yellow linen crisper than his mother's monogrammed stationery.

Walking past Kathleen in the kitchen, he'd give her a look beneath hooded eyes and say, "Behave yourself, baby." Then he'd leave. Returning, he'd toss his car keys in the basket by the door, stop to drink her in, his gaze lingering on the front of her white uniform, where the fabric pulled tightly across her breasts, and say, "One of these nights..."

Kathleen heard his sisters talking. She knew that Pierce had left a trail of broken hearts from Spouting Rock to the Clambake Club. He was a rising star at their father's small brokerage house. He had memberships in fancy New York clubs, an apartment on the Upper East Side, and a Porsche.

Pierce Wells had been engaged to Madison Weatherby of Palm Beach, but had broken it off when he'd met Paulette Lander of Greenwich. Then Paulette had caught him in bed with Lisa Davis of Locust Valley, and that was the end of that. Kathleen pictured the streets Pierce walked paved with discarded diamond rings.

His eyes were sharp but blank, as if he hardly saw the people he was staring right at. Sometimes he came into the kitchen while Kathleen was cooking, watched her without saying a word. His gaze made her skin crawl but somehow excited her at the same time. He'd stare at her while drinking juice out of the bottle in a way that let her know he wanted her. It gave her a feeling of power that she didn't really like or understand.

"You have an Irish accent. What made you come here from Ireland?" he asked one day.

"My parents brought me here when I was fourteen," she said.

"Are they American?" he asked.

She bent over the salad she was making, pretending not to hear him.

"Are *you* American?" he asked.

If I was, and I had half the advantages you did, do you think I'd be making fake potatoes and picking up after your family? she wanted to ask, but just stopped tearing up lettuce leaves and picked up a paring knife to cut tomatoes for the salad.

"Two kinds of girls turn me on," he said, moving closer. "Ones with dark skin, and ones with Irish accents."

"You don't find many of either in Newport," she said.

"You do if you know where to look," he said.

"Like in the kitchen?"

"You're fresh," he said, slapping and caressing her behind, making her jump.

She flashed the knife at him, still dripping with tomato juice. "Don't do that again," she said.

"Or what?" he asked. "You'll stab me? Should I be scared?" A burning look spread across his face, actually splashing some warmth into his cold green eyes. A slow smile tugged his mouth, and she put the knife down.

"Just don't touch me again," she said.

"The next time I touch you," he said, "you'll be begging for it." He tossed the words over his shoulder, not even bothering to look at her. "One of these nights," she heard him say.

Kathleen hated him for his arrogance—even more, she despised herself. His gravelly voice and nasty eyes did something to her insides, and she found herself wishing he'd come back.

His father drove her to Almac's, the grocery store, in the Rolls-Royce Silver Cloud every Monday morning. The car had red leather seats, and she sat up front next to Mr. Wells. Wearing her white uniform, she went into the grocery store. Sometimes Mr. Wells pushed the cart for her.

Occasionally Kathleen wanted to ask him about Louise: where was she? But she had grown up in a world where parents banished their children to places like St. Augustine's Children's Home; she just didn't think it could happen in families like the Wellses. Here, when parents wanted to abandon their children, they did so to the care of servants. In any case, Kathleen and Mr. Wells didn't say a word to each other on those grocery trips—not one word.

He was heavy and white-haired—much older than his wife, who was at the beach. Kathleen knew that Mrs. Wells thought Bobby, the chauffeur, drove her to market after dropping the family off on Ocean Drive. Kathleen had no idea what strange things went on between the Wellses, why Mr. Wells liked to push her grocery cart, and why Mrs. Wells never asked him to go to the beach with her.

At home, putting the groceries away, she would see Mr. Wells just standing there. Like Pierce, he would stare at her breasts. But Mr. Wells had the saddest, most hopeless expression in his eyes. It made Kathleen nervous, but she also felt compassion for him. She knew what it was like to long for something she could never have. She wished she had someone to tell about it, but she wasn't friendly with

Beth. Miss Langley was English, suspicious of Kathleen's Irishness. And Samantha was just young.

One day, Miss Langley punished little seven-year-old Jackie for being rude at Bailey's Beach—sticking his tongue out at the grand-daughter of Jean Trevor, the grande dame of Newport society.

Miss Langley stuck Jackie in the kitchen with Kathleen, telling him he had to stay there all day. Kathleen watched the small, frail blond boy fidget on the counter stools, coloring pictures and holding back tears. She tried to talk to him, get him to sing her a song, but he told her that Miss Langley had said he wasn't to have any fun.

"But you're a little boy," she said. "You're supposed to have fun!"

"She said I'm not allowed to."

"What you need is a friend," Kathleen said. "Someone who under-stands the oppressor."

"The what?"

"The person bossing you around, telling you that you can't have fun."

"What do you mean?"

"You can always have fun, Jackie," she said, thinking of the old days in St. Augustine's. "Any time you want to. No one can take that away from you."

"But I'm not at the beach with the other kids," he said. "Playing in the sand and the waves...having ice cream."

"Sometimes you can have more fun in a place no one else would ever want to go," she said, thinking of the old courtyard, surrounded by a tall chain-link fence, weeds growing out of cracked pavement. How much fun she and James had had there...And to think of all the years she had fantasized about her real parents, their wonderful life, their beautiful yard. She shivered, remembering her old dreams.

"Like here, you mean?" he asked. "Instead of the beach?"

"Yes," she said. "I'll be your friend."

"But you're just the cook," he said, staring at her coldly. "I'm not allowed to be friends with the cook."

That was a little knife in the heart—but just a little one. Kathleen had experienced much worse. She smiled at the little boy, gave him a scoop of ice cream. He pushed the dish away, saying Miss Langley had told him no treats. An hour before dinner, when Miss Langley finally returned from the beach with Jackie's sister Phillippa, Kathleen watched his face.

The kitchen door opened. Miss Langley waddled in—she wasn't as fat as Sister Theodore, the nun who used to show up unannounced to check on James, but she was very stout and dour, and reminded Kathleen of the rotund nun. Her face was humorless but not cruel. At the sight of her, Jackie jumped off his chair and flung himself sobbing into her arms.

"I'm so sorry, Nanny," he wept. "I'm sorry for being bad. Please take me back, love me again!"

"I do love you, Jackie," Miss Langley said, her English-accented voice breaking, and somehow Kathleen knew that she meant it, and was reminded of the nuns, women who took care of other people's children the best they could. Miss Langley was Jackie's nanny, just as she had been his father's.

The moment made Kathleen cry, but she turned her back so Miss Langley and Jackie wouldn't see. Her mind swirled with memories, of where she had grown up and where she had moved at thirteen, of people who said they loved her versus people who really did, of cobbled-together families compared to blood relations. Her heart split open—as it did so often—thinking of James. Where had he gone that summer day when she'd last seen him on the beach?

Oh no, she thought. It was going to be a James day. She tried to fight it, but it was too late. Once he entered her consciousness this way, the sorrows and regrets began to flow, and it was all over. She'd be overtaken with a grief so enormous and complex, it was as if every single person she'd ever known or loved had just died. Her heart ached, and her knees felt weak. The hurt rolled in, washed over her.

There were variations she used, methods for chasing the sorrow; she had used them over and over these last ten years, in differing ways. That night, sweating in her attic room, she lay on her back with the window open. Oak leaves rustled in the breeze, and crickets chirped in the garden three floors below.

When the downstairs clock struck midnight, she climbed out of bed. The Wellses were already in bed; the daughters and June's husband were at a party on someone's yacht, and the sons were at a party at Hammersmith Farm. Soon Andy and Pierce would be home, brawling over the Social Register.

Naked beneath a white robe, Kathleen padded barefoot down the hall and the back stairs. She walked silently along the second-floor hallway, past the parents' closed door. Mr. Wells's snoring was loud and constant.

When she reached Pierce's bathroom, she went in, closed the door behind her, and looked in the mirror. Her face was bright, flushed from the heat. Her eyes sparkled—only James would know that the light in them was from splinters of grief, little ice chips that had migrated from her heart into her gaze. Someone else might take the sparks as happiness, excitement, or lust. But James had them, too, and he would know what they were.

The bathroom was marble, and the stone felt cool under her bare feet. Sitting on the edge of the tub, she turned on the faucet. A stream of water flowed in, filling the tub slowly. She kept one ear cocked, listening for cars in the driveway. Only when she heard the low hum of the brothers' Porsches did she light a votive candle.

The flame illuminated her face in the mirror. She looked straight into her own eyes. Is this what a zombie looks like? she wondered. Behind the sparks, she saw death, as if her soul had already left her body. Her spirit was gone. All that remained was flesh, screaming to be touched. That's how she knew she was still human, because she still needed to have someone hold her now and then.

Footsteps and voices in the parlor downstairs—Pierce and Andy scuffling lightly for first look at the Social Register. Then Kathleen heard Andy go to the kitchen for a nightcap, and Pierce start upstairs.

She let her robe fall to the floor, set the candle on the tub's rim, slipped into the cool water. She poured a thin stream of bath oil, borrowed from Mrs. Wells's bathroom, into the tub. Lying back, she closed her eyes and pretended to be an actor. Her assignment was to play an exhausted young servant, stealing a moment in the master's bath, because there was only one broken shower on the third floor. The fact that it was true made the scene no less difficult to play.

The bathroom door opened. Pierce walked in—exclaimed and jumped a mile.

"Jesus!" he said.

"Oh, I'm so sorry," Kathleen said, feigning modesty as she pretended to cover up. She was desperate, and so lonely, and she'd seen him looking at her; she knew how to use her body, and she hated herself for it, but her skin hurt, just *ached,* every inch of it, craving to be touched, her body needing to be embraced. "I was just so hot upstairs, and I didn't think you'd be home so early. Please, forgive me...."

Pierce was already taking his clothes off. He dropped them to the floor, pulled her onto her feet. He kissed her so hard, his teeth drew blood on her lip. Stepping out of the tub, into his arms, Kathleen heard water slosh all over the floor. His hands were all over her body, touching her breasts, sliding between her legs. Towels thrown down on the floor, the bathmat, her robe...

In the hallway, she heard Andrew stumbling toward his own room. Kathleen's stomach clenched as the nice brother, the one who cared about his phantom sister Louise, who had seen something of Kathleen's true self outside under that tree—her white uniform in the sunlight, he'd said—passed by. Her eyes filled with tears. She couldn't go for the kind one, no, she couldn't. It had to be Pierce, the cold, shark-eyed brother—that's who it had to be for Kathleen.

Pierce entered her, right there on the hard, stone bathroom floor, not even wanting to take her into his bed, and she didn't care. She had arms around her, a man's lips on hers, and he was inside her, filling her up, whispering that he'd known she'd wanted it, had known all the time, she hadn't fooled him for a minute.

Eight

Before going to work, Seamus made tea. He sat at his kitchen table, reading the *Irish Times*. His flat was small, but it was all his. It was a stretch, affording it by himself. Before Kevin had asked Eileen to marry him, he'd been pestering Seamus to share a flat with him. "Seeing you at work is bad enough," Seamus had teased. "You think I want to see you on my days off? Think again!" Someone else might have wanted a roommate, but not Seamus. After living his first thirteen years in a group home, he liked his privacy, didn't want to share his space with another guy.

Outside his window, the city of Dublin was still asleep. He knew he had to get going, to catch the bus to work. Late August was a busy time at the hotel, with lots of people coming over from America on holiday, many of them wanting to see the countryside. Seamus hoped someone would feel like going to the sea today.

Dressed in his black suit and tie, he buffed his black wing-tip shoes. Glancing in the mirror, he combed his red hair. He wanted to look professional, as if he belonged behind the wheel of a fine car, driving wealthy people.

He headed out the door and locked it behind him, paper tucked under his arm. The subscription cost him, but it was worth it. He liked to be informed so he could sound intelligent to the people he drove. Besides, if he was going to become a barrister someday, he had to be up on law cases, both Irish and international.

He caught the bus, took a seat halfway back, and opened the paper. He always read the front page and looked at the football scores. But there was another reason he subscribed to the *Times,* as well. Even more since Kevin and Eileen had gotten engaged, he'd found himself scanning the news, running his eyes over every story in each section, whether it interested him or not, looking for her name.

Over the years, he'd seen "Kathleen" plenty of times, and "Murphy" as well. But he'd only seen the two names together three times; the Kathleen Murphys in question had once been a high school student from Meath, the winner of her school's science prize; once a banker at an international summit in Geneva; and once a grandmother of twenty, dead at ninety-two.

Seamus wasn't even sure his Kathleen Murphy still had the same name. Perhaps her parents had christened her something different after they took her home. Murphy might not have been their name after all, just something she was called at St. Augustine's. Names were a strange commodity in foster care. Seamus's birth certificate had him down as "Thomas James Sullivan," but he'd been called James at St. Augustine's—there were already two Toms there.

Now he was called Seamus, Irish for James. He wanted no part of his birth name, or of the people who had given it to him. Who would bother to take the time naming a baby, then shove him into the system? It made no sense to him.

Taking the bus to work, he scanned the paper—never giving up hope. She had to be out there somewhere. What would he do if he actually saw Kathleen's name? The idea of it gave him energy, kept him moving forward through his days.

Seeing Kevin and Eileen, so happy and about to make a life together, had gotten him thinking. Sometimes, when he felt discouraged about ever seeing Kathleen again, he told himself that looking for Kathleen's name was just a pastime. It was a game he played, the way other people did the crossword puzzle. But that was just a lie he told himself, biding time until he saw her again.

He needed to know that she was happy and well. He imagined that her parents had given her a pretty good life, after all. At least, she'd never returned to live at St. Augustine's. He knew, because he'd gone back to look for her.

When he was fourteen, one year after running away during that trip to the beach, he'd walked right back through the door. Sister Anastasia had nearly fallen on the floor with shock, weeping and hugging him.

"Oh, James, sweetheart, we thought you were gone forever."

"I'm here, Sister."

"Thanks be to God, James. Where have you been living? Tell me it's not on the street. . . ."

He couldn't lie to her, so he didn't answer. She hugged him again, fed him a hot meal, held his hand, and brushed his long, dirty red hair back from his eyes. He sensed her wanting to throw him into the shower. He was shaking with the reason he had come in the first place.

"Sister, I need Kathleen's address," he said.

"I can't, James," she'd said, looking shocked and pained by his question. "You know that it's a private matter."

"She might need me," James had said, not wanting to spill the truth about some bad dreams he'd been having lately, of Kathleen standing at a window crying, locked in a room and unable to get out.

"Well, she's with her family now," Sister had said kindly. "I know how close you both were, how you looked after each other here. I love Kathleen, too, and miss her very much—just as I miss you. But we have to let her go, James. Let her be with her parents, make a life with her family."

I'm her family, James had wanted to say, emotions boiling over.

"I can't stand it, Sister," he'd said. "Not for another day, not even for another minute. I promise I won't bother her, or get in the way of her new life. I just have to see her, make sure she's all right. Won't you give me her address? I swear I won't cause problems. . . ." He'd broken down, ashamed of himself for it. Trying to be tough, living on his own, he never cried. But here at his old home, with the nun who'd raised him, he couldn't hold it together.

Sister Anastasia held his hand. He didn't pull away. She was obviously affected by what he'd said. When he was calm again, he saw the disturbance in her eyes.

"Her parents were adamant," Sister said. "They wanted her to sever ties with this place."

"What do you mean? How do you know?"

"When she came back," Sister Anastasia said quietly, "they were very angry."

"Came back?" James asked, his heart skipping. "Why did she do that?"

"To look for you," Sister Anastasia said.

James's body could hardly contain his feelings. His blood was wild, pounding so hard in his veins he thought it would kill him. "What did she say?" he asked.

"She wanted to know what had happened to you, after that day when you left; if you'd returned here to live. Or if I'd heard from you."

James nodded, waiting.

"You hadn't come back, of course. Come home now, James. Please—I worry about you so terribly."

"Sister, what else did she say?"

"Nothing, James. She was very discouraged to know that you hadn't been back."

"Did she leave a note, or a message for me?"

"She did. But then her father came to see me and demanded it back."

James's heart tore in his chest. Tears burned his eyes again—to think that she had written words intended only for him, that he would never read.

"What did it say?" he whispered.

"I didn't read it."

"Then tell me where she is, Sister. I swear I won't make trouble. You know how much I care about her. I would never do anything to bother her. . . ."

James watched the nun as she closed her eyes, trying to make up her mind. He understood that in the eyes of the church and the institution and even the world, he had no right to know Kathleen's whereabouts. But he had appealed to Sister Anastasia in a different way: through her enormous heart. She knew about life here at St. Augustine's; she had seen James and Kathleen together over the years.

"I'll give it to you," she said. "If you'll come back here to live. Until you're eighteen."

James's hands had started to shake. He thought of the hardships he had faced, the bridges he had slept under, the bad people he had fought off. He thought of the sleepless nights, the pit in his empty stomach, the horrible loneliness. He knew that returning to St. Augustine's without Kathleen would make the loneliness ten times worse, but he was so tired of being cold and hungry, of trying to stay alive. He nodded.

"Okay," he said.

"Here it is," Sister Anastasia said, writing the address on a piece of paper, sliding it across the desk.

James had grabbed it, tucked the paper in his pocket. He vowed to Sister that he'd be back that night, after he found Kathleen.

Now, on the bus moving through Dublin, he looked up from the paper and stared out the window. Dawn was breaking in the east, just a thin line of gold at the bottom of the darkness over Dublin Bay.

He'd gone to the address Sister Anastasia had given him. It was just outside Blackrock, a place of bungalow blitz just south of Dublin, where the developers had come in and mowed down the countryside. One house after another, all looking alike. James had felt so excited, knowing he was about to see Kathleen, he didn't care what her neighborhood looked like.

He'd walked up the steps, rung the doorbell. A woman came to the door—tall, thin, no resemblance to Kathleen. James cleared his throat.

"I'm looking for Kathleen Murphy," he said.

"Who?"

"Um, Kathleen…" he said, in case they'd changed her last name.

"Oh, would she be about your age?" the woman asked.

"Yes," he said. "Fourteen."

"She must have been part of the family that lived here before—they had a teenaged girl. They moved out months ago," the woman said.

"But this is the address I have," James said, holding up the paper as if it were a stone tablet decreeing the house as Kathleen's residence.

"I see that, dear," the woman said. "But as I said, they've gone."

"Where?" James asked, his voice rising to a wail, his fists clenching. "Where is she?"

"They left no forwarding address," the woman said, drawing back in alarm. "Which is a shame, because we keep getting their catalogues and bills."

James had turned and run. He'd made a promise to Sister Anastasia, and he kept it, returning to St. Augustine's. When she asked him if he'd found Kathleen, he just shook his head. He didn't have to speak; she could read the despair in his eyes. She was kind to him, giving him a job helping out with the younger kids and working part-time in the office. He had to answer the phones some mornings, and he never stopped hoping that it would be Kathleen on the line, asking if she could come back.

She never did. And he only lasted there a few more months. Without Kathleen, it had felt like an institution—not a home.

Now, the bus dropped him off at the foot of Bannondale Road, and he strode up the street to the Greencastle. He went inside, checked his orders for the day, and went down to the garage to get the spanking-clean silver Mercedes.

When he drove into the courtyard, he met up with Kevin—standing by a different Mercedes, also just washed, wiping a few stray water spots with a chamois. The two friends grinned, shook hands.

"Where're you off to today?" Seamus asked.

"Driving two Belfast businesspeople around town," he said. "As directed. You?"

"I've got a couple on holiday," Seamus said, glancing at his dispatch form. "They want to see Powerscourt."

"Nice," Kevin said. "Eileen loves it there. The Japanese gardens, and the pet cemetery. She likes that old cow who died after giving one hundred thousand gallons of milk."

"Who wouldn't like such a grand cow?" Seamus asked, smiling. It was always fun to start the day joking around with Kevin. "So, what's the weather for today?"

"A bit iffy, I'd say," Kevin said, peering up at the gray sky. "We'll have to wait till noon to know for sure. My grandfather is a firm believer that if the weather is unsettled coming into midday, that's when it decides what it's going to do for the rest of the day."

Seamus nodded, wondering what it would be like to have such a wise grandfather. As it was, Seamus had to rely on weather reports and his own best guesses, and he filed away bits of borrowed wisdom—like the ones passed on from Kevin—to use with his own children someday. He shook his friend's hand and turned to greet Mr. and Mrs. Whelan, the couple he was to drive.

Even before they hit Dalkey, they'd told him that they were from Waterford, and this four-day trip to Dublin was a twenty-fifth wedding anniversary present from their children. Seamus looked at them in the rearview mirror. They looked to be in their early fifties and were sitting close to each other, holding hands. He saw tired affection in their faces. His heart constricted as he looked back at the road.

They must have a happy family, he thought. Kids giving them a present like this—a stay at the Greencastle didn't come cheap. His parents would be about their age, he thought. His and Kathleen's.

There were roads not taken in life, Seamus knew. So far, he had missed the turn that led to family life. Listening to the couple in back joking and laughing, deciding to call their kids on the cell phone, tell them about their trip so far, he felt that he was listening to people speaking a foreign language.

How did people do it? Get together and stay together? From his earliest days, he had thought that he and Kathleen would go through life with each other. Once they'd parted, he had lost his connection to love. In a way, he felt he'd lost his ties to the human race. He was alone in life, kept going by the dream that he would one day find Kathleen again. Listening to the long-married couple in the back seat, he felt like an alien, trying to make sense of something that everyone else had been born knowing about.

"Seamus," the man said from the back seat, "are you married?"

"No, sir," Seamus replied.

"Darling, he's much too young!" the woman said. "But I'll bet he has a girlfriend, don't you, Seamus?"

"Not at the moment, ma'am."

"Well, you will," she said. "And when you decide to get serious, I hope that you're as happy as Frank and I are. Twenty-five years together..."

"Congratulations," Seamus said, smiling politely into the rearview mirror.

"Where are your people from?" the man asked.

"Dublin," Seamus said, although he didn't know. But Dublin had been his only home.

"Ah, you're from the city," he said. "We're from a small town, but it doesn't matter. When you love someone, you hold on to them. That's what you do. That's what I did with Sheila here."

"Very good, sir."

"That's what I've passed on to my boys. Three of them, all married."

"We have four grandchildren," the woman said. "They're the light of our lives. I'm sure your parents hope that one day you'll marry a wonderful girl and have little ones of your own, bless them with grandchildren...."

Seamus nodded, but he didn't speak. Kevin and Eileen would be getting married, having children, making their parents happy grandparents. He turned his attention to the road. His thoughts flickered to his parents—had they ever really been together, as a couple? Or had his father just gotten a girl pregnant, abandoned her, like so many of the women who'd left their babies at St. Augustine's?

Or had they been too young to raise him, given him up, but stayed together? Maybe they had other children that they'd kept. Perhaps Seamus had brothers and sisters. He didn't know, and he didn't care.

Kathleen and the nuns had been his only family—and he'd never stop believing that Kathleen would be his family again.

Heading south, concentrating on driving, Seamus half listened to the couple in back. He wanted to hear how they talked, watch how they behaved with each other. When the day came for Seamus to find Kathleen again, he would get engaged, as Kevin and Eileen had done, and he needed to know how to act.

"You're a good driver, young man," the man said from the back seat.

"Thank you, sir," Seamus said, glowing with pride.

The couple in back wouldn't know—none of them ever did—that their words of praise meant so much to Seamus. He took them as he would a parent's encouragement, and in some ways, many ways, he felt that he had been raised by the Sisters of Notre Dame des Victoires and the parent-aged people he drove in his silver Mercedes for the Greencastle of Dublin. It meant everything to him, that he know how to act, how to *be*: for Kathleen.

When it was over with Pierce, once again Kathleen lay on her back, calming herself with a memory of James. They were almost thirteen. It was winter, nearly Christmas. Everyone had decorated the Home with boughs of pine, red ribbons, and boxes of ornaments donated by one of their benefactors. There was a feeling of cheeriness in the air.

James was an explorer, and he'd always had fun climbing into St. Augustine's attic, into the storerooms, even down into the spooky basement. When they were children, he and Kathleen had turned it into one big adventure—pretending to be spies or treasure hunters.

That year, James had found a way into the warmest part of St. Augustine's basement, near the furnace. He'd led Kathleen down the stairs, and her heart had felt clutched by the usual trepidation—whenever they explored, they worried that they'd walk into a spider's web or surprise a mouse or get caught by one of the nuns. But this time her heart beat fast in a different way.

"Where are we going?" she'd whispered.

"To a secret land," he'd whispered back.

That wasn't a new or surprising thing for James to say, but the look in his eyes and the melting feeling in Kathleen's chest and the way he'd taken her hand were brand new indeed. Her stomach flipped as they inched their way along the dark corridor, pipes clanging overhead from the heat pouring through them, James's body pressed up against hers as he led her deeper into the basement.

There was almost no light down there—they didn't have flashlights, and James didn't want to turn on the overhead fluorescent lamps. They'd held hands, each step making them move closer to each other. Kathleen had felt his warm breath on her neck, making her tingle all the way down her legs.

When they got to the last room, James pressed open the heavy door. The furnace roared in the corner; a small flame flickered within, throwing warm orange light into the room. James led Kathleen over to the other side, behind the furnace. The room smelled musty, of oil and dust. She barely noticed, gazing into James's eyes.

"Is this the secret land?" she asked.

"It is."

"I thought we were having an adventure," she said.

"We are," he said.

"Aren't we too old for adventures now?"

He shook his head, his blue eyes gleaming in the firelight. "Not at all."

She shivered, as if a cool draft were coming from somewhere. But there wasn't anything cool happening in that basement room. It was all so hot—the furnace blazing, and the emotions swirling inside her chest. James looked into her eyes, kissed her lips lightly. They had done this before, once or twice—enough so she'd felt the difference from the innocent little-kid kisses they'd once had.

James's kiss was gentle and tentative, but the way his lips felt, his tongue touching hers, made Kathleen feel she was going to explode. She held him tightly, her heart hammering so hard it almost hurt.

He gathered some old cloths and pads from a shelf—used for

wrapping and moving furniture, donations from wealthy patrons—and arranged them on the concrete floor. The maintenance staff stored brooms and mops here, and James pushed them aside. Holding Kathleen's hand, he eased her onto the makeshift bed.

Her heart was going so fast, she felt almost dizzy enough to pass out. Her body ached, and instinctively she knew it was from desire to be touched by James. It made her feel almost crazy.

"We're best friends," she whispered as he caressed the side of her face with his hand.

"Always."

"So how can this be happening?"

"It's what I feel for you," he whispered. "I can't explain it. It's just that I have to be with you, Kathleen...."

"Isn't it wrong, though?"

"No, Kathleen. It's right. Don't you feel it?"

She nodded, because she *did* feel it. Alone in her room at night, all she thought about was James. Standing by her window, waving at him before they went to sleep, she would imagine the day they were grown-up enough to get married.

He kissed her again, still a little uncertain. But she suddenly felt so sure, she lay on her back, pulling him closer. She wanted to feel his weight on her body, pressing against her, almost as if she could pull him into her very being.

They stayed dressed; they hugged and kissed, wanting to do more but not really sure how to get started. Their souls merged that night, in the stuffy warmth of the St. Augustine's furnace room. Kathleen held James, and he held her.

It was the night they started growing up. When she returned to her room later, to stand by her window and gaze across the courtyard at him, she knew that she was no longer a child in the same way.

Yet waving at James in the darkness, a part of her had felt so empty. Her body ached to be held by him, yet she felt a nagging feeling inside. What lay ahead for them? Would there be more adventures, exploring each other's body as well as new places to hide and kiss?

She wanted to be James's family, and for him to be hers. Other girls her age had mothers to show her how it was done. She'd see them sometimes, at church or in school, mothers and daughters together. Kathleen never felt envious of those family girls' nice clothes or good shoes, their pierced earrings and pretty necklaces—no, she felt jealous because they had mothers who could teach them about life and love.

Even at twelve, she thought of the future. She wanted to know how to be, how to act. She felt panicked, falling in love with James. They had lost their childhood, but she wasn't sure how to step into adulthood.

That night, standing at the window, she'd raised her eyes over the chimneys of St. Augustine's, wishing on a star that her mother would come and find her. It was a crazy wish, considering how deeply she felt for James. Maybe that was why—maybe the depth scared her.

In any case, her wish came true.

The next summer, her mother came out of the shadows of the past and took Kathleen out of St. Augustine's. Kathleen had wished on that star, and it had delivered.

And now, huddled in the attic of Oakhurst, thinking of everything her parents had taught her, how far they had taken her from James and that innocent love they had started to discover together, Kathleen held herself as tightly as she could, crying into her pillow, already soaked with too many tears.

Nine

The flat was a fourth-floor walk-up, in a building inhabited mainly by students. Its gray stone facade reflected in the River Liffey below, and its windows overlooked a row of brick buildings across the river, and the domes and spires of the city beyond.

The apartment house was owned by Loyola Manhattan, for students in Ireland for their junior year abroad. When she had moved out of the convent, Bernie had called an old friend, a Jesuit who sometimes made retreats at Star of the Sea and who taught philosophy at the New York campus. He had made a call, and she was given the use of a flat reserved for visiting lecturers.

Sister Anne-Marie took the bus from the convent to see her. Bernie buzzed her in, opened the door, and waited as her friend climbed the stairs, her sensible black shoes clicking on the linoleum. Bernie stood in the doorway, her heart pounding.

"Bernie," Anne-Marie said, standing in the hall, gazing into Bernie's eyes. She looked startled to see her without her habit. Bernie tried to hold her head high, show that she was strong and in command of her emotions, but the minute Anne-Marie opened her arms, she fell into them.

"Oh, Bernie," Anne-Marie said. "It's all right . . . bless you, Bernie."

"I couldn't go back to the convent," she said.

"No, I understand. Most of us want to wring Eleanor's neck," Anne-Marie said.

"Did she call the gardai?"

"Of course not!" Anne-Marie said. "She doesn't want to be found out for what she did."

"What did she do?" Bernie asked, wiping her eyes, holding the door open wide so Anne-Marie could enter. They walked into the small flat, and Bernie led her through the narrow kitchen into the sitting room. They sat opposite each other in shabby armchairs, light reflected in the river bouncing off the chipped ceiling.

"She cleaned up the mess," Anne-Marie said. "And told Theodore to do damage control. Which meant talking to all of us, asking if we knew where you'd gone."

"You didn't tell her?"

"Of course not."

"Why is she taking this so personally?" Bernie asked. "What does she care about whether Tom and I find our son or not?"

Anne-Marie tilted her head, eyes sparkling, waiting for Bernie to figure it out for herself. But Bernie felt so dull and exhausted, she couldn't make anything come together in her mind. The tall windows were splashed with raindrops, and they overlooked the river winding to the sea, and Bernie stared at the gray sky and felt cold.

"You know that the community is just a microcosm of life," Anne-Marie said. "Just because we're nuns doesn't mean we're perfect, or even close. You of all people know we don't have all the answers."

"I know I don't," Bernie said quietly.

"She's jealous. Of your holiness, of the fact you're well thought of. Also, believe it or not, she thinks she's doing the right thing. Hiding him from you…"

"But why?" Bernie asked.

"Well, because she hates unwed mothers."

"I'm a nun," Bernie said dryly.

"Maybe she thinks that she's protecting your son from you; if someone had taken her away from her mother, maybe her life would have gone better…."

"The situation is so different," Bernie murmured, shaking her head, then looking back at her friend. "Did you know where he was, Annie?"

Anne-Marie shook her head. "I hadn't any idea. I've never worked in any of the Children's Homes; I've always taught in our schools. Nobody ever talked about him, after you left Ireland to go to the convent in Connecticut—I took that as protection of both of you. So few people knew that you'd had a baby...."

"Sister Eleanor Marie, Sister Theodore, you," Bernie said. "I showed up on the convent steps, four weeks before I had him."

"Yes, but so did many girls. Most of them don't then join the order. Those of us who were there back then were so young ourselves, focused on our own vocations. Hardly anyone put it together, after you returned as a novice, that you were the same young woman who had shown up pregnant a month earlier. Besides..."

"What, Annie?"

"Well," she said, raising her eyes to meet Bernie's, "you were much better known as the Sister who'd seen Mary."

"Same girl, two lives," Bernie said.

"What do you mean?"

Bernie closed her eyes. Back when she was young, there had always been Tom. They had grown up together, playing on the beach and green fields of Star of the Sea. He had been one of her closest friends and first love, but she had felt pulled in another direction as well.

The convent there in Black Hall, Connecticut, right on the beautiful coastline, had always seemed such a sanctuary. She'd felt drawn to the nuns, wondered what their lives were like. Some days she felt called to join them—give up worldly pursuits and enter the order.

She'd dream of becoming a Sister, kneeling in prayer and devotion, opening her heart to the Holy Spirit and all of God's love. She'd imagine wearing a habit; she'd put on her mother's black dress, high-collared and lined with silk, and pin a black mantilla to her hair.

Then she'd tear the veil off, go running outside to meet her friend Tom. They'd have so much fun—laughing, swimming, sneaking grapes in the vineyard. When she was young, the two desires had seemed to go together: a love of God and a love of Tom. But when she got older, when she'd finished college and begun to realize how serious religious vows were, she came to understand the gravity of the decision she was facing.

To choose one life, she would have to give up the other.

Tom had started talking about a trip to Ireland, and wanting her to go with him. His Irish heritage was so important to him—it always had been, and no one knew that better than Bernie.

The summer before he was scheduled to take his trip, Bernie had walked the grounds of Star of the Sea. She'd entered the Blue Grotto and knelt on the hard ground. Praying for guidance before the statue of Mary, she had watched as the stone became flesh and Mary came down to wipe her brow.

Visions, apparitions, were controversial in the church. Many people believed they were figments of a person's imagination—a psychological solution to a deep, personal problem. The church always tried to keep such things quiet—and so had Bernie. She'd told her priest, and an investigation had taken place. Rumors about the Blue Grotto had begun almost immediately. People whispered that Bernie had the calling. But then she'd come to Ireland with Tom, gone to the Cliffs of Moher, and everything had changed.

"I told Eleanor Marie because she was the Novice Mistress," Bernie said.

"That was the right thing to do," Anne-Marie said.

"And she told me my vision meant I was being called to be a nun. She was so adamant about it," Bernie said, her hand drifting to her belly now, remembering how it had felt to carry her son. "The thing was, I wasn't sure. I didn't know what to do."

"You made a good choice," Anne-Marie said. "You've run a school and a convent, shaped so many young minds, given great numbers of girls a wonderful education."

"But what about that one boy?" Bernie asked.

Sister Anne-Marie leaned forward, reached for her hand. "You have to trust that he's had a good life. That he's been loved and cared for."

Bernie nodded. She wanted to believe that so badly.

"Bernie," Anne-Marie said, gazing at her street clothes, "I have to ask. What does this mean?"

Bernie glanced down at the jeans and thick white sweater. Her closet door was ajar, her black wool habit hanging on a hanger inside. Their order was permissive about wearing lay clothing during retreat time. Bernie had often gone incognito on short prayer weekends. And when she'd go to the Abbey of Gethsemani in Kentucky, the monastery where she made her annual retreat, she would walk the hills of bluegrass in jeans and sneakers and an old Aran sweater Tom had bought for her that week in Doolin.

"Bernie?" Anne-Marie pressed.

Tears filled Bernie's eyes. This felt different. Her heart was gripped with such doubt and anger. She felt as if she'd come to a dead end. Her chest ached with hurt and panic. This morning her prayers had fallen like stones into the Liffey. They'd felt hard and inanimate, without life or hope, sinking to the bottom, into the river mud.

"Tell me you're not leaving the order," Anne-Marie said.

Gazing at the pale gray sky, Bernie didn't reply.

"Take some time off. Give yourself a chance to think. But don't make any rash decisions," Anne-Marie said.

Bernie sat still, aware of her friend's concerned gaze. But she couldn't move or respond.

"Tell me one thing. Are these old doubts? Dating back to the vision? Or do they spring from what Eleanor Marie did?"

"Both," Bernie managed to say.

"You did get the file, though," Anne-Marie said. "Right?"

"Yes," Bernie said. "Tom's coming in a few minutes, and we'll start looking."

"Well, please let me know what you find," Anne-Marie said, standing. She reached into her black knapsack, pulled out a small package neatly wrapped with brown paper.

"What's this?" Bernie asked, accepting it, opening the paper. She saw the folded black square and knew immediately.

"Your veil," Anne Marie said. "You left it the other night. I thought you should have it, for when you decide to put it on again."

"Thank you," Bernie said, hugging her friend. Then she put the veil on the top shelf of the glass-front oak bookcase and walked Sister Anne-Marie to the door. Hearing her footsteps going down, she walked back into the sitting room.

Tall windows overlooked the river, and Bernie rested her forehead against the cool glass. Rivers made her think of home, Star of the Sea, located where the Connecticut River flowed into Long Island Sound. She had always found peace in the water's flow. But right now, gazing down at the Liffey, she felt unsettled, unsure of where she was being taken.

Turning from the window, she closed her eyes and prayed she would find out soon.

Tom had parked on the quay, and sitting in his car, he stared up at Bernie's window. He felt tired and sore, as if he'd run a marathon. His heart was going so fast, a thought flashed that maybe he should get checked out. The thing was, all he'd been doing was sitting still. After the scene at the convent, Bernie had retrenched so deeply into herself, he'd been powerless to get through to her. His bones and muscles ached from having to restrain himself. He held the file in his hand, and all he wanted to do was run with it.

Now, climbing out of the car, he saw the front door to her building open. Expecting a student to come out, he was shocked to see Sister Anne-Marie. Hurrying across the cobblestone quay, he felt the wind picking up and bowed his head to walk into it. There was a storm out at sea, and the atmosphere felt charged.

"Tom!" she called, spotting him.

"Hey, Sister," he said. "How is she?"

Sister Anne-Marie shrugged, cocking her head to look up toward Bernie's windows. "She's troubled, that's for sure."

"She hasn't talked to me at all. I've got the file right here— we practically got arrested, taking it—and she hasn't even looked through it."

"Be patient with her, Tom," Anne-Marie said, looking worried.

"She's going through something profound. Doubts about herself—the decisions and choices she's made, even her life as a nun."

"What are you talking about?"

"You'll see, when you get upstairs," Anne-Marie said. "The standard term for what she's going through is 'discernment.' But I'd say it's much deeper than that. It's a classic 'dark night of the soul.'"

"Don't let Bernie hear you say that," Tom said. "Back at Star of the Sea, she said that's the most overused phrase in the church—everyone from kids mooning over each other to rich people having a bad stretch in the market uses it to describe feeling bad."

"She's right, of course," Anne-Marie said in her gentle Kerry accent. "Bernie's not one to coddle someone for a little angst. But I know Bernie, and I see it in her eyes. She's tormented over something. And remember..."

A truck rumbled past, windows open and radio playing, struts and axles bouncing over the cobblestones.

"Remember what?"

"The original 'dark night of the soul' was described by St. John of the Cross...a mystic."

"You're saying Bernie is a mystic?" he asked.

"Bernie would never call herself that," Anne-Marie said. "But she sees things, and feels things more intensely than many of us. St. John wrote about a night of dark contemplation, of grief and purgation, of the terrible pain that afflicts a person in that state."

"I can't stand to think of her feeling pain like that," Tom said.

Anne-Marie squeezed his hand. "Remember, St. John also said that the night brings darkness to the spirit in order to illuminate it and fill it with light. Bernie will get through to the other side, and she'll have new understanding."

"I hope I do, too," Tom said.

Sister Anne-Marie smiled. "Of course you will," she said. "In many ways, you *are* the light for Bernie right now. You'd better go up to her now...."

"I will," Tom said. "Thank you, Annie. If you wait a minute, I'll give you a ride."

She shook her head, already crossing the quay. "I love the bus," she said. "It's like going to the movies, watching the story of life unfold right in the seat in front of me!"

Tom watched her go, then rang the buzzer to 4B. Bernie had refused the idea of staying in one of his cousins' homes on Merrion Square. Tom had tried telling her she wouldn't have to stay at Billy's, under the same roof as him—she could go to Sixtus's or Niall's. But she wouldn't even listen, didn't want him to tell his cousins anything. She was so private, and so used to running the show at Star of the Sea. He'd tried to get her to sit down at O'Malley's with him, maybe order a pint of Guinness and talk things over, but she'd refused.

Standing on the front step, leaning back to look up at her window, he started feeling worried. Why wasn't she answering the door? Sister Anne-Marie talking about a "dark night of the soul" made his skin crawl. It smacked of both hokey pop-psychology and crazy mysticism, and Tom didn't like either.

He stared at the front door, assessing the lock. He'd left the lock picks he'd bought for the convent back in his room, figuring he'd never need them again. Running his fingers over the hardware, he knew that with one good hit with his shoulder, he'd break the doorframe.

Just then the door flew open and a beautiful red-haired woman stood there. She was tall and lean, with a thick cream Aran Isles sweater over jeans. Even in the gray light, her red hair glinted with strands of gold. They framed her delicate pale face, highlighted the sadness and purpose in her clear blue eyes.

"Bernie!" he said.

"Hi, Tom."

"I was just coming to pick you up."

"I know," she said. "I was watching for you out the window, saw you talking to Anne-Marie."

"She's worried about you. And so am I."

"There's no need for that," Bernie said sharply, sounding like the Star of the Sea Mother Superior he knew and loved. "Do you have the address?"

"For the Children's Home?" Tom asked. "Yes, I do."

"Then let's get started," she said. "I'm ready now."

"If you say so, Sister Bernadette Ignatius," he said. He stared at her, wanting to hear her say that was no longer her name. His spine tingled, and he knew he was still aching to hear those words he'd always dreamed of—Bernie telling him that she'd made a mistake, that after all these years she'd figured it out, realized that they were meant to be together.

But she remained silent. She just stared back, her blue eyes grave, reflecting the stone-colored sky and river. Then, after the line of traffic passed by, she ran ahead of him across the street and stood by the BMW, waiting for him.

"Have you eaten?" he asked as they settled themselves in the car.

She shook her head.

"Then we have a stop to make before we go."

Bernie was too upset to fight him. He drove her to a familiar spot: O'Malley's Pub. They had come here so often when she was pregnant; it seemed fitting to be here again now. They took a scarred wooden booth in the back, at the end of the long bar, and Tom ordered for both of them: shepherd's pie. He had a Guinness as well, but Bernie passed.

The front door and windows faced the street. They were open, and from inside the dark room, Tom could see the window boxes planted with fuchsia. Brilliant explosions of color. He tapped Bernie's arm so she would look and see.

She nodded, gazing out, appreciating the pretty flowers. They barely spoke, but Tom didn't care. He just wanted her to have some sustenance, gain her strength back. Did this feel as familiar to her as it did to him? All those months twenty-three years ago, when they'd sat here together and he'd tried to get her to eat....

"Our own personal Tir na Nog," he said. "Remember?"

She nodded. "This was our sanctuary," she said.

"It hasn't changed at all," he said.

"The shepherd's pie is as good as ever."

"The Promised Land of the Saints," he said, translating *Tir na Nog*, "should have really good shepherd's pie."

That made her smile. She raised her fork to her mouth, smiling at him as she ate a little more. He felt that he was egging her on, enticing her to eat a few more bites, just as he would have done with a child who was a difficult eater.

"Thank you, Tom," she said when she was done. "That was good."

"It was," he said, finishing his Guinness. He left her sitting at the table for a minute while he went up to the bar to pay the bill. His heart was racing as he thought of what they had to do next. But when he returned to the table and held out his hand to Bernie, he caught the eye of a man at the next table, sitting there with his wife.

Tom saw a sort of recognition in the man's eyes—as if the man thought Tom was just another guy out to lunch with his wife—that gave Tom a pang in his chest. It brought back so clearly how he and Bernie had come here to forget that they weren't like other couples.

They still weren't.

Giving a friendly nod to the guy at the next table, Tom put his arm softly around Bernie's shoulders, and led her out the door to the car. It was time to find their son.

Ten

The Dublin neighborhood was filled with nice houses and tall trees, small gardens and station wagons and minivans. Families lived here. Bernie took it all in, wondered what the children living in St. Augustine's thought of that. Walking home from school or the park, did they look at these houses and wonder why they didn't have places like this to live?

Tom drove down the street, not saying a word. Bernie held the documents in her hand; it felt sticky with sweat. Her throat was closed tight; if she saw her son right now, she wouldn't be able to speak.

They pulled past the sign, the name in cold black wrought iron: *St. Augustine's Children's Home.* A circular drive brought them to the front of a large brick building, unadorned by shutters or columns. Even with the car window down and Bernie straining to listen, she couldn't hear the sounds of any children playing.

She held her hands in her lap to keep them from shaking. The papers said that this was the right place; Baby Boy Sullivan had been sent here directly from Gethsemani Hospital, the same day that Bernie had signed the papers.

Gazing up at the front door, she wondered who had carried him through. Had it been Sister Eleanor Marie? Sister Theodore? Had he clutched at her with tiny baby hands, not wanting to be left behind? Bernie remembered the way he'd flailed his arms, wailed to be fed.

"Let's go," she said to Tom, opening her door, forcing the words out, partly to keep from remembering their son's cry.

"Sister Eleanor Marie has had plenty of time to warn them we're coming," Tom said quietly, as if she had to be reminded.

"It doesn't matter," Bernie said. "Our son came here first. She can't erase the truth of that. And he's surely not here now.... Come on. Let's go in."

Tom climbed out, but Bernie was already halfway up the wide granite steps. She glanced over her shoulder, waiting. The look in his eyes pierced her; the years fell away, and he was the young man she'd fallen in love with. She shivered, overwhelmed. He saw, and put his arm around her shoulder.

Walking up the steps, she felt herself trembling, and she knew it wasn't just because of where they were going, but also because of where they had been. When she and Tom had had their child, she'd been on the verge of becoming a nun. They'd never given themselves a chance to be a family, never given their boy a chance at being their son. It felt bizarre to be here in street clothes, yet that morning, getting dressed, she had felt unable to put on her habit. Going to O'Malley's, she had seen that couple looking at her and Tom as if they belonged together.

Inside the main hall, all was quiet. An office lay straight ahead. Through glass doors, Bernie saw nuns at desks, on the phone, bustling around. She stood still, listening hard. From the left she heard distant laughing and calling, almost as if it were happening in an echo chamber. It frightened her, thinking of their son in such a quiet, sterile environment.

"Do you hear that?" she asked Tom.

"No," he said. "What?"

"Just ... where are the children? I don't see any, and the only laughing I hear is coming from way down the hall. Do they keep them locked up?"

"Calm down, Bernie," he said. "We'll find out."

And then he took over. He held the glass door, and she walked into the office. He stood at a waist-high Formica counter, strangely like the one at the hospital's records office, as if the order had gotten a bulk rate on office equipment, and cleared his throat. "Excuse me," he said loudly.

"Hello there," a nun said from across the room, making one last note on a yellow legal pad before walking over. "Welcome to St. Augustine's."

"Thank you," Bernie said.

"Thank you," Tom said. "We're—"

"Why aren't there any children around right now?" Bernie asked shakily.

"They're on a day trip to the beach," the nun said, smiling. "We try to take them at least twice a summer. It rained so much in August, here we are, into September."

"But what are those voices, coming from over there?" Bernie asked, pointing down the hall.

"That's the infirmary," the nun said. "A couple of our kids are just getting over bad colds. The doctor thought it best they stay behind this time. Don't worry, we'll make it up to them...."

Tom raised his eyebrows at Bernie, as if to say "See?" She ignored him, but felt reassured. Ever since walking through the front door, she'd felt on edge, assessing every inch of the place.

"We've come to find out about a boy who lived here. Our son," Tom said.

"Ah," the nun said, standing very still. She was in her early thirties, thin and wiry, with a kind, steady gaze and unflappable smile. Opening a drawer, she pulled out some papers. "These are the forms for you to fill out. It's a slow process, but you can get started today. Start with his birth date, and any—"

"He was born January 4, 1983," Tom said.

The young nun nodded. "Well, as I'm sure you must know, we have to be very careful about giving out information about our residents. As a matter of fact—"

"Sister Felicity," an elderly nun said from the back of the office.

Hearing her name, the young nun turned around. "Yes, Sister Anastasia?" she asked.

"I know who these people are," the old nun said, coming forward. She was tall, gently stooped, with a lined face and bright gray eyes. Crossing the office, she looked past Sister Felicity, past Tom, straight at Bernie. Feeling the nun's gaze upon her, Bernie's skin tingled. She touched the counter to steady herself.

"Did Sister Eleanor Marie warn you about us?" Tom asked, putting himself between Bernie and Sister Anastasia. "It doesn't matter if she did. I swear, we've come all the way from America, and..." Bernie read the old nun's expression, saw the love and warmth in her gaze, and put her hand on Tom's arm to stop him.

"No one had to warn me about you, Thomas," Sister Anastasia said kindly. "And dear Bernadette...I've been waiting for you. Please, come with me."

She came around the counter, reached for Bernie's hand. Bernie took it blindly, and crying as if she were a lost child who'd finally, after longer than she'd ever thought she could bear, found her way home, let Sister Anastasia lead her down the long yellow hallway, with Tom walking close behind.

The office was large, with one half devoted to a desk, chair, and sofa, and the other half given over to a dollhouse, toys, and a child-sized table and chairs painted in primary colors. Pictures covered every inch of wall space: finger paintings, drawings, pictures colored by children of all ages. And photographs—school portraits, group pictures, candid shots of kids at the beach.

Tom watched Bernie wipe her eyes, blink blurrily at the wall. Was she wondering, like Tom, whether their son was up there? Tom waited for her to sit on the sofa, then lowered himself beside her. Sister Anastasia handed her a box of tissues and took her own seat behind the desk.

"What did you mean," Tom began with a protective glance at Bernie, "when you said you've been waiting for us? We've heard that a lot since we got to Ireland."

"Several things," Sister Anastasia said. "First of all, you were right—Sister Eleanor Marie did call, to tell me that you had James's file."

"James?" Bernie asked, her voice breaking.

"Yes," Sister Anastasia said. "Your son."

"We named him Thomas," Bernie whispered.

"I know," Sister Anastasia said. "But we already had several boys named Tom and Tommy. So we used his middle name, to help him have his own identity."

Tom watched Bernie take that in, register the information. It moved him to think his name meant so much to Bernie, even now.

"What did it matter," Bernie asked, "how many Toms there were? Once he got to his adoptive family's home, he'd be the only one. . . ."

"Yes," Sister Anastasia said slowly. "Theoretically."

"'Theoretically'?"

"You're assuming he was adopted, dear."

"He . . ." Bernie stopped, stunned. "He wasn't adopted?"

Sister Anastasia shook her head, and Bernie cried out. The truth washed over Tom in waves, and he saw Bernie sitting there frozen, and Sister Anastasia just gazed across her desk with unwavering love and compassion.

"Why else were you waiting for us?" Tom finally managed to ask. "You said there were other reasons."

"Because over time I came to know about Bernadette. Her identity was protected for most of James's stay here, but after many visits by Sister Theodore, I asked questions. And learned about who Sister Bernadette is, and how she came to the convent. I've believed for some time that the force that led her into our order would eventually lead her here, to search for James."

Tom was silent, watching Bernie. She was pure white, eyes wild blue, filled with pain and terror.

"Was something wrong?" Tom asked. "Is something wrong? Is that why you thought she'd be pulled to look for him?"

Sister Anastasia stood up. Her hands clasped behind her, she walked around the desk, gazed out the window at the courtyard. It was blacktop, with weeds growing through the cracks, basketball hoops at either end, two large plastic tricycles left on the side, several balls strewn around. Realizing that that was where the children played hit Tom like a punch in the stomach.

"This is hard to say to any parent," Sister Anastasia said without turning around. "You made the best decision you could, and no one here will ever question that. But this is a difficult place to grow up. As much as we love each child, there aren't enough of us to go around. Even if it were one-on-one, and the reality is far from that, St. Augustine children are needy. They've lost so much, before they even get started."

"It was hard for James?" Tom said.

Sister Anastasia nodded. "It was," she said.

"Oh no," Bernie said, breaking down. She sat on the sofa, face in her hands, and sobbed. Tom wanted to soothe her, touch her, but he couldn't move. He stared out at that tarred-over playground and felt tears scalding the back of his throat.

"What was it like for him?" Tom asked harshly. He could see that Bernie's heart was already broken—he didn't believe that any answer could be worse than what she must be imagining.

"He was, and is, very loved," Sister Anastasia said. "And very bright. He made friends easily. His personality is great, exuberant, wonderfully mischievous."

"He had good friends?" Tom asked.

Sister Anastasia nodded. "Oh yes. He certainly did."

Something about her tone made Tom start, give her a searching look. Bernie was sitting on the edge of the sofa, staring at Sister Anastasia, hanging on every word.

"He had one friend in particular," Sister Anastasia said. "Almost from the first day he came here."

"What was his name?"

"Her name, actually," Sister Anastasia said. "Kathleen Murphy. They were inseparable. Their cribs were next to each other in the nursery, and they bonded instantly. They were the same age, in the same classes, had the same interests...."

"Did they remain friendly?" Tom asked.

"They did," Sister Anastasia said. "For a long time." She fell silent, turning back to the window.

"He lived here his whole childhood?" Bernie managed to ask after a few moments.

"Until he was thirteen," Sister said, her back to Bernie and Tom.

"What happened then?" Tom asked.

"It had to do with Kathleen," Sister Anastasia said. "She was taken home by her birth parents. James ... well, he couldn't bear to be here without her. He left."

"Ran away?" Bernie asked, her voice hollow.

"Yes, dear."

"Where did he go?"

Sister Anastasia shook her head. "He never told me. He returned for a short time—hoping he could learn where Kathleen was living. I gave him her address, but by then the family had moved away. James came back to St. Augustine's—keeping a promise he'd made to me. But it didn't last." She paused, looking over at Bernie.

"Why didn't you contact me?" Bernie asked, standing up.

"I thought about it, believe me," Sister Anastasia said.

"But you didn't?"

"I was ordered not to, by the powers that be. As I said, at first your identities were kept completely secret. But the more Sister Theodore came to check on James, the more I realized that his family was somehow connected to the church, or our order. She let it slip one day ... and of course I knew who you were."

"You did?"

Sister Anastasia nodded. "We're proud of you, Sister Bernadette. You run a wonderful school in the United States, and many of us have dreamed of making trips to see the Blue Grotto, where you saw the Blessed Mother."

"It's still there," Tom said, thinking of how much work he'd done over the years, keeping the grotto in good shape, touching up the masonry, scrubbing the moss off the shaded stone walls. He thought of the words Bernie had carved into the stone this summer, how they'd been one signpost leading them to this moment.

"So, why didn't you contact me?" Bernie asked. "Once you figured out who I was?"

"Sister Eleanor Marie, through Sister Theodore, was very persuasive. Theodore argued that it would be harmful for all concerned. You were in no position to claim your son—you had left him in our care, and we were doing the best we could. It's just that no one could have predicted that an adoption would fail to materialize."

"Do you think Eleanor Marie sabotaged it?" Bernie asked.

Sister Anastasia shook her head. "No, dear. I don't. I think James did."

"James? But he was just a child! How—"

"His love for Kathleen," Sister Anastasia said. She looked old and frail, but her voice was strong, filled with warmth.

"He didn't want to leave her," Tom said, knowing immediately, and to the depths of his own heart, what that felt like. All these years, working at the Academy beside Bernie. Passing up the chance to marry, to have other children, to make a life with a family of his own. All that had ever mattered to him was being near Bernie, as close as possible, no matter that he'd never have a chance at anything more.

Bernie turned to look at him, and Sister Anastasia gazed at him, too, her eyes bright and shining, as if she could see straight into his soul.

"That's right," Sister Anastasia whispered. "That's exactly right, Thomas."

"He loved her so much," Tom said.

"And still does, I suspect," Sister Anastasia said.

"Where is he, Sister?" Bernie asked. "We have to find him."

To Tom's shock, Sister Anastasia reached into the folds of her habit, withdrew a folded paper. "That's where you'll find him," she said. "He works as a chauffeur, every day of the week."

"The Greencastle Hotel?" Bernie asked, her hands trembling as she read from the paper.

"Yes, dear."

"How will we recognize him?" Tom asked.

Sister Anastasia walked over to her wall of pictures. She scanned it, looking for the photograph. Removing its pushpin, she took it down. Then, reaching up again, she took down the photo beside it.

She handed one picture to Bernie, who held it toward Tom so they could look together. There was their son, Thomas James Sullivan. The photograph must have been taken when he was about twelve. He had his mother's red hair, and he had Tom's dark blue eyes. His face was thin, with cheekbones chiseled like Bernie's, freckles across his nose and cheeks, warmth in his eyes, and an easy, playful smile on his lips. Tom couldn't look away, and Bernie couldn't stop crying.

"Here's another," Sister Anastasia said, handing Tom a photo of a pretty young girl with long brown hair in a braid over her left shoulder, with clear blue eyes that made Tom think of a deer surprised by headlights.

"Kathleen?" he asked.

"Yes," she said.

Tom stared at the picture of the girl his son had always loved, and he felt a great connection with him. To love someone forever, to not be able to have her, to give your whole life for her and not know whether she knew it or not—Tom had that in common with his son.

"I received a postcard from her," Sister Anastasia said, opening a desk drawer, removing a card from it. "Her family moved to the States. She lives there now, in a grand house in Newport, Rhode Island. She asked for him."

"When did it come?" Tom asked, taking the postcard Sister Anastasia held out to him.

"Just two weeks ago," Sister Anastasia said. "The anniversary of the day James ran away from St. Augustine's. I've been meaning to get to the Greencastle myself—to let him know. But something made me wait...."

"You knew we were coming," Tom said, holding the card, gazing at the kind old nun. Bernie seemed not to hear; she sat perfectly still, staring at their son's picture, as if she was memorizing every feature.

"There's more than one way to have a vision," Sister Anastasia whispered.

Tom nodded. Bernie didn't reply. Tom tried to hand the postcard back to Sister Anastasia, but she just shook her head. After a moment, he understood, and put it in his pocket.

Bernie's eyes remained on the picture of their son. Sister Anastasia's lips began to move, and Tom knew that she was silently blessing them—Tom, Bernie, and the boy who had called St. Augustine's home.

Eleven

Seamus pulled into the Greencastle, enlivened after his long day of driving. He had taken his passengers, a Nashville singer-songwriter and her manager, in Dublin for a sold-out concert at Temple Bar Music Center, on a coastal tour of Newgrange and Bru na Boinne—"the Palace of the Boyne," the river valley considered to be the cradle of Irish civilization.

Not only was he a driver, Seamus was also—if he did say so himself—a first-rate tour guide. All the time he had spent on the road, after leaving St. Augustine's the second and last time, had taken him many places in Ireland. Wherever he went, he imagined returning with Kathleen—showing her the most beautiful sites, places they'd never dreamed existed beyond the walls of St. Augustine's. So over the years, he had committed to memory many historical facts and bits of Irish legend and lore.

These were things he'd learned on his own, he was proud to say. If he'd had parents, taking him out on weekend excursions, they would have been the ones to teach him about Newgrange—a passage grave from the New Stone Age, five hundred years before the pyramids in Egypt. They would have shown him the Roof Box—an incredible detail, an opening cut just above the door, precisely placed to catch the rays of the rising sun on December 21—the winter solstice—and hold the sun's light for twenty minutes.

Seamus had decided long ago that his somewhat limited background wasn't going to hold him back. He had learned all he could about the ring forts and sacred enclosures, things he could tell his passengers. Sometimes he dreamed of teaching his own children about these things, but for now his study had paid off by making him one of the most requested drivers at the Greencastle.

The singer was in her late twenties, a pretty blond American woman from Nashville, wearing jeans and cowboy boots, here in Ireland for her show, and to look into her Irish roots. Her manager was her aunt, in her forties. She'd booked Seamus on the recommendation of another Nashville star—Mark Riley, who'd visited last spring, come to Ireland to perform and research family origins. "Lot of hillbillies came from Ireland," Mark Riley had said. "That's why you hear so much fiddle music in bluegrass music. It's our Celtic roots."

"That's song material!" the songwriter, Randi-Lu O'Byrne, had exclaimed as she'd walked around, hearing Seamus talk about the Neolithic passage graves. "I'm going to call it 'Roof Box' and dedicate it to you, Seamus."

"Don't think she won't," her aunt said. "She's got her guitar up in the room; you can bet she'll be playing the song at her show this weekend."

"That's amazing," Seamus said.

"You know, I want you to come to the show," Randi-Lu said. "There'll be two tickets with your name on them, waiting at the box office."

"Thank you, ma'am," he said.

"'Ma'am'? Jesus, how old do you think I am?" she said, laughing.

"Randi-Lu, I'm going back to the parking lot, make a few calls," her aunt said, leaving them alone.

"Got a girlfriend, Seamus?" Randi-Lu asked as they strolled through the shade of the prehistoric tombs.

He thought of Kathleen, hesitating just long enough for Randi-Lu to grin and chuck him in the shoulder.

"You do, don't you?"

"Well, there's someone I used to know...."

"Yeah? Where is she now?"

"I don't know. I lost track of her on a beach long ago."

"Why, that's another song right there. You're inspiring me left and right! 'Roof Box,' and now 'Lost on a Beach.' Key of E. What's her name?"

"Kathleen," he said.

"Well, if you come to my show," Randi-Lu said, "I'll dedicate a song to Seamus and Kathleen. We'll put it out to the universe, your names, the two of you together. That's what my music's all about... love and connection. *Big Love*, Seamus. Capital 'B,' capital 'L.' Not just romance—that passes, dies, and fades. I'm talkin' love that's meant to be. In fact, that's what my latest single is about."

"Big love," he said, echoing her words.

"Love you hold in your soul," she said, gazing at him with sharp green eyes.

"Yeah," he said, and a shiver ran down his spine as Kathleen's face filled his mind.

"Not many men know what I'm talking about when I say that," she said, taking a step closer. They stood in the shadow of a Stone Age megalith, toes nearly touching. She looked about twenty-eight, not much older than he was.

"You said you lost her," Randi-Lu said.

"That's right."

"I lost someone, too," Randi-Lu said. "He's another singer, down in Nashville. We used to tour together; we planned on coming to Ireland together."

"But it didn't happen?"

Randi-Lu shook her head. "He left me for someone else. A girl he met on the road. They're living together now, have a baby and everything. Is that what happened with you and Kathleen?"

"No," Seamus said. "We never got that far, never had the chance. It's a long story."

"I'm a country singer," Randi-Lu said, moving even closer. "I love long stories."

Seamus felt a blast of attraction, felt her coming on to him. It had happened before with women he drove, here in Ireland for business or family, far from home. He'd never acted on it, and never would.

"This story's too long," he said gently, not wanting to hurt her feelings.

"Oh, big love," she said, smiling, backing away. "You got it bad."

"Yeah, I guess I do."

"Well, wherever Kathleen's lost, I hope she knows you're waiting to find her."

"Thanks," Seamus said. And then Randi-Lu's aunt came back from making her calls, saying it was time to get back to Dublin. Seamus held the doors for them as they climbed into the back seat of the Mercedes 600. Randi-Lu gave him a copy of her latest CD, and he put it on.

The very first cut was called "Big Love," and he heard her singing about the man she'd just told him about.

It's bigger than life, it's bigger than the sky,
It's bigger than always, it's bigger than why....

They listened, no one talking, all the way back to the hotel. The music tugged Seamus's heart, the place where Kathleen had always lived. When Seamus pulled into the driveway of the Greencastle, he saw Kevin standing in the shade, talking on his cell phone.

As he opened the back door, Randi-Lu stopped to look him in the eye.

"Thanks for the ride," she said. "And the talk."

"You're welcome," he said. "About your show..."

"Front and center," she said. "That's where your seats'll be."

"I can't come without Kathleen," he said.

"No?" she asked, not really seeming surprised.

He shook his head, gestured over at Kevin. "There's another couple who'd really like to hear you, though."

"No problem," she said. "We'll save a seat for Kathleen at another show, somewhere down the road. Okay?"

"Thank you," he said. "We'll be there. It's a promise. That fellow..." he began.

Randi-Lu looked up at him, waiting.

"The one you were supposed to come to Ireland with? It's his loss, not to be here with you," Seamus said. "He was a lucky man, and he just didn't know it. He missed the whole thing; it just passed him by."

"Another song." Randi-Lu grinned. " 'Don't Know You're Lucky Till It Bites You in the Ass.' I may get a whole new CD's worth of music out of this trip. Thanks again, Seamus. Say hi to Kathleen for me, when you find her."

"I will," Seamus said, shaking her hand.

He was walking over to tell Kevin about the tickets when he caught sight of a couple standing across the courtyard. They were watching him, and at first he thought maybe they were his next fares—perhaps the Greencastle had booked him for one more ride that afternoon. The woman had red hair, as bright as Seamus's, and a warm, excited look in her blue eyes. And he recognized the man—he was wearing the same shabby tweed jacket he'd worn when he'd come here for breakfast with the Kellys a few days ago.

Seamus nearly started toward them—there was something in their gaze, the way they were watching him so eagerly, that made him think they really wanted to hire him. But then Kevin called out his name, and Seamus couldn't wait to tell him about the tickets. And when he turned back to look at the couple again, they were gone.

They had gotten in the car, and Tom had pulled it away from the hotel, around the corner. They were both so overwhelmed—it had bowled them over, seeing their son. No matter how often Tom had imagined this moment, the reality was a thousand times more intense. He leaned across the front seat to hold Bernie. His eyes were scalding with tears. They'd seen their son, and he looked just like his mother.

Holding Bernie now, Tom couldn't get over how grown-up their boy was. Counting the years was one thing; seeing the evidence of them was another. The last Tom and Bernie had seen him, he'd been a baby; now he was a grown man. Tom had watched him drive the car under the portico, open the back door for his passengers—and do it with such skill and grace. Tom was a good judge of people, and he could see with one glance what a fine person their son was.

Little things. The way he'd signaled, going slowly up the drive, giving a departing driver the right-of-way, along with a friendly, playful salute. Tom had watched him open the door, help the passengers out of the back seat with a bright smile—a genuine, authentic smile, not just something pasted on his face to get a big tip.

Tom had watched the smile light up his face. Something his passenger—an attractive young woman—was saying made him bend closer, nod his head. Then he'd pointed over at one of his colleagues, another driver, a kid about the same age, standing across the courtyard, talking on a cell phone.

The whole time, Tom stood close to Bernie. She was trembling against him, and he felt her wanting to run right over to their son, take him into her arms. He had never seen or felt her this way—there was a wildness to her that almost scared him. For the last twenty-three years, she had been Sister Bernadette Ignatius—the rock-steady Mother Superior of Star of the Sea. Over here, in Dublin, she was Bernie Sullivan again—the tender, vulnerable, sweet girl he'd fallen in love with, and who had given birth to their baby, and who'd let him go.

"Bernie," he said now, his mouth against her hair, her head pressed into his chest.

"Did you see him?" she cried. "It was really him...."

"Yes," Tom said. "There's no doubt."

"His friend called him Seamus."

"Irish for James."

"We have to go back to him now—why did you hold me back?"

"What are we going to say to him?" Tom asked.

"You know..." Bernie said.

"No, I don't. I don't have any idea."

She looked up at him, almost as if she felt sorry for him. He saw the life in her face. There was always something going on behind her eyes—worlds of thought racing there. She looked so different without her black veil, without the stiff white framing her face. She hadn't explained to him why she'd taken off her habit, and Tom didn't care. He wanted to touch her cheek, her beautiful hair, and take her in his arms and kiss her.

"He's our son," Bernie said. "We'll know what to say. We can't plan it."

"But we don't want to upset him, scare him...."

Bernie blinked, her eyes red-rimmed. The color was returning to her face, her freckles standing out in not-so-stark contrast to the pallor. She wiped tears from her eyes and took Tom's hand.

"Let's go," she said.

"Right now? Shouldn't we—"

"Don't be scared, Tom. This is what we've come thousands of miles to do. He's waiting for us."

"Are you sure you're ready, Bernie?"

"I'm ready," she whispered. And by the way she was looking behind him, beyond him, at the courtyard of the Greencastle Hotel, just over his shoulder, Tom knew that she was.

Bernie tugged the white wool sweater down over her hips, stood by the car catching her breath. Wearing regular clothes—jeans, a sweater, her head uncovered—made her feel exposed. And she knew that that had been her intention all along. With what she had to say to her son, she didn't want to hide behind a habit and veil.

Walking beside Tom, she felt him wanting to take her hand. As tempting as it was for her, she didn't let him. She didn't want to give any wrong signals—to either him or their son.

During the hours since Sister Anastasia had given them his information, Bernie had run many scenarios through her mind. She and Tom could have hired him to drive them, told him what they had to say somewhere away from this place, out on the road. But she had discarded that idea—it seemed too dishonest. She didn't want to manipulate anything.

As they watched, he finished speaking to his friend, then started across the courtyard toward the road. He was finished with work for the day, probably heading home. Bernie felt Tom tense up beside her, lurch forward as if to catch him.

"James!" Bernie heard herself say.

The young man stopped dead in the middle of the sidewalk, looked straight at her.

"Are you speaking to me?" he asked.

"Yes," she said.

"My name is Seamus."

"Thomas James Sullivan," she said.

"What are you talking about?" he asked, looking shocked.

"That's your name," Bernie said.

"I'm Seamus Sullivan," he said, eyes darting between her and Tom.

"But you used to be called James, right?" Tom asked.

"How do you know that?"

"We just . . . we were speaking to Sister Anastasia," Bernie said.

"At St. Augustine's?" he asked, his eyes lighting up a little. "Are you friends of Sister's, then?"

"We just met her today," Tom said.

"What was she doing, telling you about me?" he asked, laughing. Then his eyes clouded over with worry. "Is she all right? Did something happen to her?"

"No," Bernie said quickly, touched by the concern in his eyes and voice. "She's fine. She . . . told us where we could find you."

"I'm sorry we called you James," Tom said. "We didn't know that you preferred Seamus."

"I do," he said. "I haven't gotten around to telling Sister, though. She, well, she gave me the name James. It's not the one I was born with, but the one she called me. So it might seem ungrateful to tell her I've changed it. I don't see her often enough . . . you've reminded me I should stop by to see her more often." He stood still, and for a few moments, no one spoke. Bernie's heart was pounding in her chest. He laughed nervously. "I don't know why I just told you that."

"I think I know why you did," Bernie said softly.

Seamus looked puzzled, raising upturned palms, shaking his head. "What are you talking about?"

"Look at us," she said. "Can't you tell by looking at us? I knew the instant I saw you...."

"I'm not following you."

"When you were born," Bernie said quietly, "I named you Thomas, after your father."

Tall, mature trees arched overhead, and the leaves fluttered in the wind. They sounded terribly loud against the silence. She saw panic rising in his eyes, suddenly sensed him wanting to bolt.

"There were too many Toms at St. Augustine's," she said. "That's why Sister called you by your middle name. James."

"How do you know this?" he asked.

"You know the answer to that," Bernie whispered. "It took us so long to get here, James...Seamus...But we've thought of you every day."

"Thought of me? You don't know me! Who are you?"

The words caught in Bernie's throat. She looked to Tom, who seemed frozen, standing this close to their son, struck by the passion in the young man's eyes and voice. But suddenly Tom stepped forward.

"We're your parents," he said.

"No," Seamus said. Then, wildly, "I saw you here with the Kellys the other day. They're important people, barristers, from Merrion Square."

"They're my cousins," Tom said. "My name is Tom Kelly. I'm your father, Seamus."

Bernie's eyes filled with tears, hearing those words come from Tom's mouth. Seamus's expression was shocked, and he shook his head hard.

"No," he said. "I don't believe you."

"And this is your mother," Tom said. "Bernadette Sullivan. Look at her, Seamus...you can see it, can't you?"

The young man raised his eyes to her, and she felt herself melting, turning liquid, every inch of armor draining away. His hair was her hair, his skin was her skin, his eyes were Tom's eyes; and she could see that Seamus saw it, too. He took her in, every detail and feature, then turned to look at Tom.

"You're my parents?" he asked, the words tearing out from somewhere so deep they almost didn't sound like words at all. "You really are?"

"Yes, Seamus," she said. "We are."

"You're together? Twenty-three years, you're still together?"

"It's not like that," Bernie said. "It's complicated. . . . We want to tell you."

"It's not complicated for me," Seamus said, his eyes burning and the words slashing out. "It's damned easy. I don't want to hear, don't want any part of you."

"Seamus," Tom said, reaching for his arm. But Seamus wheeled, smashing his hand down on Tom's wrist.

"Get away from me," Seamus said. "I swear to Christ, get away. Other kids at St. Augustine's? They dreamed of this happening—counted on the moment their parents would come into their lives. Not me. I don't want it, don't want you—"

"Please," Bernie said, standing still and quivering, every inch of her, staring into his blue eyes as tears flooded in her own. "I understand, Seamus. I do, I do . . . But please, just talk to us for a few minutes. We just want to talk to you. . . ."

"You don't understand," he said. "You can't! See, you don't exist to me. You never did."

"Seamus, please listen," Tom said. Bernie was in shock, and Tom's voice was breaking.

"You think I need you? I'm living just fine on my own. I've got plans that have nothing to do with you. I'll be a barrister, just like the Kellys. Better! I've got my own life!"

"We know that," Bernie said. "Oh, Seamus . . ."

But Seamus just turned and ran, the hard soles of his black shoes ringing on the sidewalk as he tore down the street, around the corner, out of their sight, leaving Bernie and Tom to stand there with their hearts breaking and so much left to say.

Twelve

Walking to St. Malachy's for six o'clock mass the next morning, Bernie saw everything differently. The weather was gray and rainy, but Dublin had become luminous. Every stone, every brick, each building, every spire was different—glistening, glowing, infused with hope—because Bernie had met her son. Rain fell steadily, splashing off her black umbrella.

When she knelt in church, she knew that she had never felt anything like this before. Joy at having met Seamus, but pain beyond words, to feel his anger and rejection, and to remember back to the beginning. She bowed her head, eyes closed, feeling shock waves pass through her body. Even now, twelve hours since meeting him, she could see him as clearly as if he were standing right here.

Looking into his eyes, she could see the man he was today—tall, strong, honorable—and the baby he had been two decades and the blink of an eye ago. It overwhelmed her, to think that the last time she'd gazed into those bright blue eyes, he'd weighed just over seven pounds.

She had held him after he was born. He'd come early but he was healthy. The nurses were astonished by his size. He had cried and cried, and Bernie had fed him and whispered to him that she loved him. The nurses had left her alone with him. There in her hospital bed, holding him to her chest, she had cradled his head, touched each of his fingers and toes, rocked him back and forth.

She remembered how loudly he had cried. She'd hardly believed that such a tiny baby could make that kind of noise, and it had pierced her straight through—because she'd believed that he must have somehow known.

"For him to cry this way, he must know something's wrong," she'd said to the charge nurse. "He must know that I'm giving him up...."

"No, he's just hungry," the nurse had said, handing Bernie a bottle filled with formula. "Give him this, and he'll quiet down."

Bernie had waited for her to leave the room. And then she'd pulled down her nightgown, given her son her breast. The feeling was beyond description, the most intense love she'd ever felt. This baby had come from her body, hers and Tom's, and now she was feeding him. It felt as if every ounce of love she had were flowing into him, and in that moment she'd decided she couldn't give him up.

Now, kneeling in mass for the consecration, Bernie remembered how he'd fit in the crook of her arm, his tiny hands patting her breast, eyes squeezed so blissfully shut as he'd drunk his fill. She'd felt as one with her baby—she, Tom, and their son could be a family. They could stay here in Ireland, or they could move back to Connecticut. She didn't care where they lived, as long as they were together.

In that instant, her mind had been completely made up—she admitted that to herself now. It didn't matter that she'd signed the paperwork, agreeing to give him up for adoption. Tom loved her, wanted to marry her, and he'd been begging her to change her mind.

Now, in the middle of mass, everyone stood. They prayed the Lord's Prayer. Bernie's voice joined the congregation. Her gaze fell on the statue of Mary. Her heart kicked over. She remembered how Sister Eleanor Marie had visited her in the hospital; she'd held the baby, promised that he would go to a good home.

"I've changed my mind," Bernie said, staring at the tall, austere nun, holding her infant.

"What do you mean?"

"Sister, I've made a mistake. I can't join the order...."

"But everything is in motion," Sister Eleanor Marie said. "You've been accepted into the novitiate. There's a place waiting for you....

And as for this baby—there's a good Catholic family waiting to adopt him. Surely you don't want to spoil that, do you? Ruin his chances to be raised by a real family—a married couple who can give him everything he needs?"

"I know," Bernie said. "I feel terrible about getting their hopes up. But I didn't know I'd feel this way! I love him so much, Sister. I had no idea I had that kind of love in me—for Tom, yes, but this is different."

"Your hormones are out of control, having just given birth," Sister Eleanor Marie said. "And is it true, what the nurses have told me, that you've been breast-feeding him?"

Bernie nodded, not understanding why the nun's question made her feel such shame. She felt the blood rise into her face, and she could barely stand seeing the look in Sister Eleanor Marie's eyes.

"That was very foolish, Bernadette. There are rules against it, for the benefit of both the mother and child. It bonds you to each other in a damaging way."

"How can it be damaging?" Bernie whispered. "I'm his mother."

"Stop thinking in those terms. You gave birth to him, but now it is time for you to do what is right—what you've already *promised*."

"Sister," Bernie said, holding out her arms, "please give him to me."

But Sister Eleanor Marie had held him closer, wrapping him in her black-sleeved arms, peering over his head with cold, angry eyes. "Don't you know," she asked, "what a slap in the face this is to the Blessed Mother?"

"What?" Bernie asked, shocked. She had been thinking of Mary and Jesus—for the first time ever, she had a real sense of what their lives had been, the depth of love and connection possible between a mother and son.

"She appeared to you—*you* of all people on this earth. Before you even came to Ireland, before you sullied your body. Our Lady stepped down from her pedestal to wipe your tears. She gave you the sign you'd been praying for—to join the convent and become a Sister of Notre Dame des Victoires."

"Notre Dame," Bernie murmured. Our Lady...

"You didn't listen to her—you came to Ireland with that man, and you gave yourself to him instead of God. This is your last chance to make things right."

"What do you mean?"

"Mary appeared to you for a reason."

"But Sister," Bernie said, reaching for her son, aching to hold him, "I hadn't had my baby yet. I couldn't imagine how this would feel, what it would be like. She wouldn't want me to give him up—she couldn't!"

"But she does," Sister Eleanor Marie said coolly. "Didn't she tell you?"

"I don't know what she meant," Bernie said, so confused and muddled by emotion, by the pain of labor and birth, and by the ticking clock—she was scheduled for discharge tomorrow, and that's when she was supposed to say goodbye to her son.

"You don't know because you no longer want to know," Sister Eleanor Marie said. "Bernadette, you're a devout enough Catholic to know that you are choosing to move away from the visitation you received in Connecticut. This is your choice—to give in to these doubts or to proceed with your vocation."

"Give me my baby," Bernie said, no longer able to process one word she was saying.

"A vocation is a sacred thing," Sister Eleanor Marie said.

"Having a *baby* is a sacred thing," Bernie screamed, jumping out of bed, grabbing her son from Sister Eleanor Marie's arms, accidentally raking her nails across the nun's hand.

"Nurse!" Sister Eleanor Marie called, rushing to the door. "Nurse!"

Bernie crouched down, sheltering her baby with her entire body. She rocked him, feeling his tiny hot breath on her neck. He had started to cry, and so had she. She wept, burying her face against his. Hearing footsteps, she recoiled, holding him closer.

"She's hysterical," Sister Eleanor Marie said. "Look what she did to me!"

"Oh, you're bleeding," the nurse said.

"She scratched him, too."

At that, Bernie pulled back enough to see her baby's face. Oh God—it was true. Grabbing him from Sister Eleanor Marie, she had nicked his cheek. It wasn't deep, but there were tiny drops of blood. He cried so loudly, and suddenly she realized that she had hurt him.

"I'm so sorry," she whispered. "Sweetheart, Thomas...I didn't mean to."

"Of course you didn't," the nurse said, bending down beside them.

"I love you, Thomas," Bernie whispered, as if the nurse and Sister Eleanor Marie weren't there. "More than I've ever loved anyone...."

"Let me take him," the nurse said gently. "I'll see to the scratch, and then give him back to you."

"I need to feed him," Bernie wept.

"Of course. I'll bring him to you in a few minutes...."

The nurse had taken Thomas away. Bernie had climbed back into bed, crying as if they'd ripped her heart out of her chest. Sister Eleanor Marie left the room. Bernie hoped she'd never see her again.

When they brought Thomas back to her, they had already fed him. Given him a bottle full of formula. He was docile, sleepy. The scratch on his cheek was small, but red and puffy. Bernie held him, trying to quell her rage at the nurses for feeding him. She felt herself boiling over—at the nurses, at Sister Eleanor Marie, even at the Virgin Mary.

How could she be in this position? Why had she ever gone into the Blue Grotto in the first place? If she hadn't done that, she never would have had the vision. Mary had been so loving—wiping the tears she'd been crying because she felt so torn, over loving Tom, and a desire to join the convent.

Mary had seemed illuminated from within. Her blue robe had seemed almost like gossamer silver. It had shimmered in the grotto's shadowy light. When the Blessed Mother touched her face, Bernie's tears had dried instantly. Mary had whispered words in Bernie's ear that made her heart leap.

"Love my son," she had said.

Of course she had meant Jesus....

Even in the hospital, holding her sleeping baby, Bernie had known in her heart that that was true. Mary had been telling her to love

Jesus, serve Him. She had been told by her parish priest and the Vatican's detective that she was being called directly—no vocation had ever been clearer. Bernie was to become a nun.

But first, she had promised Tom she would take that trip with him—before she joined the order, went behind the wall, she had told her old, dear friend that she would accompany him to Ireland, to search out where the Sullivans and Kellys had come from. And they had traveled here, to Dublin. . . .

And they had tumbled into love. Bernie knew that love had been brewing their whole lives—but the minute they'd landed in Ireland, she'd felt something new. It was as if they were suddenly all grown-up, far from home, together in a different way.

His Kelly relatives had besieged them in Dublin, so they'd taken a week away. They'd gone west, to County Clare. Bernie had always wanted to see the Cliffs of Moher. She had seen pictures, known that they were spectacular, and she'd thought that standing there, facing back toward America, would help her say goodbye to an old dream; she'd tell Tom that she'd really made up her mind.

But when the time came, she couldn't. Tom had held her, standing so high over the sea. It was the first of May, and the air felt so fresh. She'd shivered in his arms, knowing that she'd never wanted anything more. Her eyes weren't closed, not at all. She'd held his hand, walking together away from the path, into a field of flowers.

They'd lain down in the tall grass, undressed each other so tenderly, and made love for the first time. She'd arched toward him as he entered her, and he'd looked into her eyes so directly, she'd felt he was seeing straight into her heart.

He'd never left. Bernie's heart had never stopped belonging to Tom, and from that moment on, it had also belonged to their son. They'd returned to Dublin. She'd given up the room she'd rented, moved into the small Phibsboro apartment with Tom. With all the local shopkeepers and the waitresses at O'Malley's—the only people they saw—they'd pretended they were married. Tom even avoided his Kelly cousins, and it wasn't easy, considering how prominent they were in Dublin. Bernie had avoided the nuns until the end, in her eighth month, when she'd known she needed help—finding a hospital, and deciding what to do about her baby.

Lying in her bed, the lights dim and Thomas breathing softly against her breast, Bernie had let both experiences wash over her: the divine gift of meeting Mary, and the human miracle of her son's birth. Tears had welled up in her eyes. Why was she being tested this way? How could she be expected to make the right choice, when each option was both so beautiful and terrible?

She closed her eyes and prayed to be given a sign. She'd started to cry silently. If only Mary would appear to her right then, tell her exactly what she was supposed to do. She remembered Sister Eleanor Marie's words, about giving her son the right kind of home—with parents who were already married, with a mother who wasn't ripped apart by a burning desire to become a nun. She'd mentioned her own mother, a fallen woman who'd sacrificed her child's well-being; did Bernie want to be like that?

"Please, God," she'd prayed, "through the intercession of the Blessed Virgin Mary, help me do what's right...show me what I'm supposed to do."

She'd fallen asleep and dreamed of being with Tom. They were in a rowboat in the Connecticut River, just off the grounds of Star of the Sea. The sky was dull gray, and Tom was rowing them toward shore. Bernie looked down—she was holding their child. Suddenly thunder cracked and lightning split the sky. Silver light poured through, as if the dark sky had been a curtain, torn in half. Scalding light spilled into an inlet, behind a row of rushes, drizzling silver over the water's surface.

Tom rowed them closer. Bernie began to cry—both in her dream and in reality. Tears fell from her eyes, onto the baby she held in her arms. Tom's oars sliced the water, gently splashing. As they got closer to the marsh grass, the river water merged with the spilled silver light. It was blinding—too bright to see.

When they reached the shore, Tom jumped out and tied up the boat. He reached for their son, and Bernie kissed him, knowing that she was saying goodbye. Her tears spilled onto his cheeks; he smiled.

Tom placed him in a tiny boat, hidden in the bulrushes. He pushed him, and the boat drifted away.

Bernie woke up. The hospital room was filled with gray light slanting through the windows. She was still crying, but when she touched her face, she felt grainy crystals. Her tears had turned to salt. They'd fallen from her cheeks, onto her son's face.

Looking down, she saw that they'd healed the scratch.

It was gone, completely. Not a trace of blood or swelling remained. Thomas's cheek was completely smooth. Bernie gasped, and stared, thinking she had to be mistaken. She'd prayed for a sign, but this wasn't what she wanted. . . .

Married couple, parents together, the Blue Grotto, *Love my son*, crystal tears, ice tears, the healed scratch . . . Bernie's mind raced with messages. Her heart knew one thing only: that she loved her baby more than her own life. If she was supposed to give him up, if that's what was best for him, that was what she'd do.

"Nurse!" she cried. "Help me!"

Within seconds she was surrounded by nurses—asking what was wrong, comforting her, taking Thomas from her arms. She trembled, kissing him, reaching for him. She would see him again; she and Tom would have the chance to kiss him and hold him, to say goodbye to him for good. But when she looked back on the entire sequence, Bernie knew that that was the moment she had really said goodbye to her son: when she'd wakened from her dream of silver water.

"The mass is over, go in peace," the priest said now, a lifetime later. "To love and serve God and each other."

"Amen," the congregation said.

"Amen," Bernie said, blessing herself, rising to her feet.

She filed out the back of the church along with everyone else. The priest stood on the sidewalk outside, shaking hands. Bernie nodded, thanked him for mass. She walked several blocks through the neighborhood, then turned to walk the rest of the way along the river.

Wondering where Seamus lived, whether he saw the Liffey every day, she gazed east, toward the river's seaward end. Morning sun had broken through the clouds. Silver light poured through, bright rays slanting down from the sky onto the river's surface.

The river gleamed, as if molten silver. Bernie stared at it, the hair on the back of her neck standing up. She wondered whether there were rushes in the Liffey's marshes, a place for a tiny boat to drift and find safe harbor. She thought of Moses, and she thought of her son.

Faith was a true mystery, she thought. On good days, it all came together. She would wake up in the morning, and she could see everything lined up before her. She would know that if she took a certain action, she could count on a predicted outcome. Any fears and doubts would be assuaged by her knowledge of God's love.

On bad days, she felt as if she were standing in thick fog. She couldn't see where she'd come from, and she definitely couldn't see where she was going. Whatever lay around the bend might hurt her or the people she loved most. Demons could be lying in wait—they almost certainly were.

On bad days, she needed her favorite line in the Creed, to get her through: faith in that which is seen and unseen. Usually it was the *unseen* part that scared her. Today it was the *seen*.

She saw that silver light, and she couldn't stop seeing the look in Seamus's eyes. Only she knew what it meant—she doubted that Seamus himself was aware. All that anger, hurt, fury in those beautiful, clear blue eyes had been caused by Bernie herself.

Her son had loved her. She knew that down to every bone in her body. She had felt it while he was growing inside her, but she had *seen* it when he'd lain in her arms, looked into her eyes. They had loved each other, mother and child. They'd only had two days together, but that was enough. Sister Eleanor Marie had been right: they had bonded.

And she had betrayed him.

She hadn't meant to, but that's what had happened when she gave him away. Strangers had taken him from his mother's arms. She had known that she wouldn't see him again, but he hadn't understood that he wouldn't see her.

Bernie had counted on something, and believed in it all these years she'd been a nun—until this trip to Dublin: the myth of her son's happy family. If he'd had a real family, would the pain in his eyes have been so vivid? She would never know.

"Thomas James Sullivan," she said out loud, staring at the silver ribbon of light, spread across the mouth of the River Liffey.

When Tom got to Bernie's apartment that morning, he climbed the stairs with his heart pounding and thoughts racing. He had lots of ideas, plans, ways to make everything better. Until midnight, he'd lain awake in his room overlooking Merrion Square. When it was obvious he couldn't sleep, he'd climbed out of bed and slipped outside.

He'd walked the streets of Dublin, haunting the places he and Bernie had gone, hoping for clarity. Past Trinity College, the Custom House, O'Connell Street, then back across the Liffey, up Grafton Street to O'Malley's Pub. It was closed of course, but he could have used a pint.

Walking through St. Stephen's Green, past homeless people sleeping on benches, he stopped and stared. Young people, some of them. Tom stared down at one redheaded kid, praying that that hadn't ever been Seamus. Their son had made something of himself—and Tom was overcome with pride, just thinking of it.

Bernie was wracked with guilt for what Seamus had gone through, and Tom could understand. He sometimes felt the same way, for not talking her out of the decision she'd made. But instead of feeling worse for having Seamus reject them, Tom actually felt better than he'd felt in years.

The young man had tremendous heart and strength, belief in himself, in his own convictions. He had a good job, driving for the Greencastle, and he had big dreams, to start a law degree. Tom had worked hard nearly every day of his life, and he knew that a strong work ethic had gotten him through. Bernie, too. Seamus had inherited that quality from his parents, and Tom hoped that work brought him the same rewards it did them.

Seamus had every reason to resent, even hate, his parents. Tom had seen Bernie scanning his cheek for evidence of that goddamn scratch. Back when it had happened, Tom had tried telling her that it had probably been just a nick from her fingernail—nothing serious at all. If it had "healed" during the time it took for her to dream that dream, it probably hadn't been one bit serious in the first place.

But that damned scratch, coupled with Bernie's dream of their son in that tiny boat. Moses all over again, Tom had said at the time. Jesus Christ—it didn't mean they should set him adrift on the sea.

Now, finally, twenty-three years after the fact, Bernie was seeing the light. The real light—of love, not of religion. Sister Eleanor Marie had shown her true colors, hiding the documents related to Seamus's birth and transfer to St. Augustine's. Whatever had gone on there to keep him from being adopted, Tom could only imagine.

Bernie had to be wondering herself. Tom thought of what Sister Anastasia had said, about Kathleen, how their son had been so loyal to her, he'd wanted to stay. Tom understood the power of love, and he believed that his son was capable of something like that.

But Tom just hoped that Bernie's heart was finally open enough to allow for new possibilities. Maybe she would feel so betrayed by Sister Eleanor Marie, and so inspired with love for Seamus, that she would rethink her vows.

Climbing the stairs to her flat, he heard her open the door. She stood there waiting as he reached her landing. Seeing her dressed in jeans, a soft sea-green shirt setting off her hair and pale skin, he felt a shiver go through his whole body.

"How'd you sleep?" he asked, standing beside her.

"I didn't, really," she said. "How about you?"

"The same," he said.

They seemed frozen in place. She was gazing up at him, and he was doing everything he could to hold himself back, not touch her. He wanted to hold her; he'd wanted that all night. After what had happened, he felt closer to her than ever.

"What should we do?" she asked after a few minutes.

"Try to see him again," Tom said.

"Should we go back to the hotel? I don't want to upset him in front of his coworkers."

"Where else, though? We don't know where he lives."

"I know," Bernie said. "You're right."

They gazed at each other, and it was harder for Tom to restrain himself. She looked so beautiful, standing there. Seeing her in normal clothes unlocked something in him—he'd been so well behaved for so many years, seeing her day after day in her long black habit and veil, rosary beads hanging from her belt, reminding him she wasn't his and never could be.

"We could call the hotel, ask for his home number," she said.

"They wouldn't give it out," he said. "I could ask Sixtus or Niall to have one of their investigators look him up."

"Investigators?"

Tom nodded. "Lawyers use them all the time."

"We don't want to involve your cousins, do we?" she asked.

"I want them to know, Bernie. I always have."

"Know what?" she asked, frowning.

"That we have a son. That we loved each other . . . That I still love you."

"Tom," she said, stepping away.

He couldn't help himself. Reaching for her hand, he held it with both of his. He was staring into her blue eyes with such intensity, he thought he could see straight into her soul. Her emotions were so raw, pouring out, impossible for him to read.

Even though Tom had known Bernie most of his life, she was still a mystery to him. She kept so much of herself hidden; even the parts that she showed seemed too complicated for him to understand. He often felt he needed her to translate, explain the look in her eyes or the expression on her mouth. But she never would—that was the point. Bernie was a puzzle—even to herself, he strongly suspected.

"Bernadette," he said, cupping the back of her head.

She closed her eyes, leaned into the pressure of his hand. He saw her fighting with herself; her forehead was furrowed with worry, eyes moving behind her eyelids like someone having a troubling dream.

He bent down, brushed her lips with his. She didn't pull away, and he felt electricity all through his body.

"I love you, Tom," she said, her voice barely a whisper.

"Bernie—"

She stiffened slightly, stepped away. Her tangled red hair looked so beautiful and disheveled; he wondered how she had ever fit it all under her veil. His heart was pounding, and he held on to her hand a few more seconds, until she pulled it back.

"I love you," she said again. "I always have."

Suddenly his heart fell. She'd told him she loved him before, many times. Nuns had no shortage of love, and Bernie was no exception. The thing was, she wasn't using her "nun's love" voice, the one he'd heard her use with her students, the novices, the other Sisters back at Star of the Sea, even Tom's helpers on the grounds crew. This was different, deeper, troubled.

"What are you trying to say to me, Bernie?" he asked.

"We're in the midst of something enormous," she said. "We've just met our son, Tom. You and I are both stirred up, and we can only imagine what it's like for him."

"It makes me want to be with you," he said. "That's never changed, but now I know it more than ever."

"Don't talk like that!" she said. "This is confusing enough, Tom."

"Then let's make it less confusing!" he said. "Let's make it really simple. I love you, Bernie. I want us to be together."

"I'm a nun," she said.

"You don't look like one," he exploded, gesturing at her jeans, her lovely green shirt, red hair tumbling over her slim shoulders.

"I'm trying to figure things out," she said. "And I didn't want to be wearing my habit when I first met him. I didn't want anything to be between us—any excuses or symbols, anything that would distract him from seeing me as his mother."

"He's not here now," Tom said, his pulse racing. "And you're still not in your habit. You're questioning your vows, Bernie. It's so obvious. I've known it since that night at the convent, when you threw your veil on the floor."

He saw her shaking, backing away. She turned her back to him, staring out the window. The river flowed past the quay below, dark and austere. Out by Dublin Harbor, it took on a silver cast, reflecting the argent dawn.

"We're not going to talk about this now," she said, and he could hear in her voice the effort it was taking to stay calm. "We need to find Seamus, talk to him. He must be very upset, Tom. It was a tremendous shock for him, meeting us."

Tom knew that she was talking about herself, too; it had been a great shock for her, reuniting with her son. As great a mystery as Bernie was, Tom believed he knew her better than she knew herself. He knew how she'd suffered all these years, the penance she had done day after day, night after night, for giving birth to a little boy and then giving him away.

Tom had seen the pain in his friend's eyes, and he had witnessed the message she had carved into the Blue Grotto back in Connecticut: *I was sleeping, but my heart kept vigil.* It came from the Bible, from Song of Songs, the canticle that Bernie had always said was a love song.

"Bernie," he said, standing behind her, hand on her shoulder.

"Don't, Tom," she whispered.

"I won't push you until you're ready," he said.

"You don't understand," she said, her voice falling so low he could barely hear.

"I think I do understand," he said. "Better than anyone. 'I was sleeping, but my heart kept vigil.'"

"Oh God," she said.

"Come on, Bernie," he said, giving her shoulder a gentle shake. "Let's go find Seamus."

And after a moment she turned around and, without meeting his eyes, got her jacket. His hands tingled, holding it for her as she put it on. Then she locked the door behind her, preceded him down the stairs. And they climbed into his cousin's car, and headed back to the hotel.

Thirteen

H e's not here," said the doorman at the front door of the Greencastle, when Bernie and Tom showed up asking for Seamus. "He's out sick from work today."

"Is he all right?" Bernie asked.

But then a cab drove under the portico, and the doorman shot Bernie and Tom an apologetic glance, and he opened the door and started to help unload the passengers and their luggage.

Bernie stood off to the side, feeling unsure of what to do next. She had pushed Tom away pretty hard, and he was being uncharacteristically silent, waiting for her to speak.

"What do you think?" she asked after a moment.

He shrugged. "I don't know. Maybe he really is sick, and he'll be back tomorrow."

"He doesn't want to see us," Bernie said. "That's the reason, don't you think?"

Tom didn't reply. He was gazing across the courtyard, to a row of silver Mercedes parked along the wall. The young man they'd seen polishing his car yesterday, talking to Seamus, wasn't there. Bernie wished he was, so they could speak to him, find out if Seamus was okay.

Just then a horn blared, and Bernie jumped. Tom's arm came protectively around her, and he pulled her out of the way. She figured it was just an aggressive driver, arriving at the hotel in a hurry, but when she peered through the car's windshield, she saw two familiar faces grinning at her.

"Hold on tight," Tom muttered. "The Kellys have arrived."

"Well, look who we have here!" Sixtus exclaimed, bounding out of the driver's seat, throwing the keys to the valet. "Cousin Thomas and Sister Bernadette. How are you, Bernie?" he asked, coming around the car and giving her a huge hug.

"I'm fine, Sixtus. It's so good to see you. . . . And Billy, too. Hello there!"

"Sister, wonderful to see you!" Billy said. "Tom told us you'd come to Ireland on business, but he's been very recalcitrant, not bringing you to the house for dinner. Liza is most displeased with him."

"I'm so sorry," Bernie said, smiling. There was nothing like the boisterous Kellys to cheer her up, make her forget her darker thoughts of a few minutes ago. "I've just been very preoccupied."

"Traveling incognito?" Sixtus asked, raising his eyebrows at her street clothes.

"Don't give Sister Bernadette a hard time," Tom said.

"Ah, that's right. You're her designated protector. Well, whatever you're wearing, Sister, it's great to see you," Sixtus said.

"Thank you for what you did for my niece," Bernie said, changing the subject quickly, referring to the legal situation that had brought her brother's family to Ireland just a few weeks earlier.

"Yes, Regis Sullivan—quite a lovely girl. Her father didn't deserve the trouble he got over that business at Ballincastle, and neither did she. I was glad to represent her at Children's Court. The judge was quite happy to let her go."

"Still, we're so grateful," Bernie said. She shivered, knowing that her brother John's return home to Connecticut after six years in Irish prison for a crime he hadn't committed, his reunion with his children, had sparked her and Tom's deep longing to see their own son. Families were amazing, with all their secrets and connections, the way present events always seemed to echo what had happened in the past. A great deal of her family's history had taken place on the west coast of Ireland.

"It's very rewarding," Sixtus said, "to be able to help a young person. Seeing your niece, helping her to let go of all that pain, to move on from the events at Ballincastle and be able to live a good life—that's worth everything."

Bernie listened to his words, unable to look at Tom. Was he thinking of Seamus, as she was? A silver Mercedes, part of the hotel's fleet, pulled slowly into the circle. Bernie's heart leapt—could it be him? But a different driver, much older, with dark hair, stepped out to greet some passengers waiting under the hotel's awning. Her heart fell again.

"Come in, join us for breakfast," Sixtus said.

"Absolutely," Billy agreed. "As Tom knows, we're regulars here—and frankly, bored with our own company. Come talk to us, Bernie. Tell us what you're doing in Ireland, and how things are going at Star of the Sea."

"How I love visiting the Academy," Sixtus said. "To think of Great-Grandfather Kelly building such a splendid place. With all the retreats we've spent with you there, and your tremendous generosity to all us Kellys, it's time you let us reciprocate. Come to breakfast now, and dinner tonight."

"Oh, I can't," Bernie began. "We were actually just leaving now... we have an errand, something important..."

"What are you doing here at the hotel in the first place?" Billy asked. He chuckled. "Don't tell me the Vatican has started putting nuns up at the Greencastle? I knew I've been giving too much at the Sunday collection...."

"We were just looking for an old friend," Tom said quickly. "Someone who works here. That's all." The lie slipped out effortlessly, and Bernie gave him a glance of pure gratitude. "But now we really have to get going, on to the next stop."

"That is most unsatisfactory," Sixtus said, frowning with mock displeasure. "Only one thing will set it right. Sister Bernadette Ignatius, you must agree to come for dinner tonight. Emer would feel very slighted to think you'd come to Dublin and not accepted our hospitality. So. What will it be?"

"Yes," Tom said, before Bernie could open her mouth. "We'll be there."

"Excellent," Sixtus and Billy said at once. They hugged Bernie, shook Tom's hand, and told them they'd see them at dinner at eight.

"Why did you do that?" Bernie asked as Tom's cousins walked into the hotel.

"Because they love you," he said, gazing down at her with clear blue eyes. "Don't you get it, Bernie?"

She stood there, her heart pounding hard at his question.

"You of all people should understand," he said. "You've spent your life being a nun. Isn't that supposed to be all about God's love? Well, there's human love, too. And it's just as powerful. The Kellys love you, care about you. You're here in Dublin, and they want to reciprocate for all the great times you've given them at Star of the Sea."

"They don't have to reciprocate," she said. "I welcomed them because I wanted to...."

Tom stared at her long and hard. His eyes twinkled, and his mouth twitched in a half-smile. She saw him trying to hold back laughter, and something else.

"What's so funny?" she asked.

"I always think you're so smart," he said. "The smartest person I know. You're a scholar of so many things: philosophy, theology, literature...But when it comes to the human heart, Bernie..." He shook his head, grinning. "Stick with me, kid. I'll show you the way."

His happiness was infectious. Bernie smiled, wanting to give in to it. Tom came from a big, wonderful family, and she could see how proud he was to be a part of it. Bernie felt that way, back in Connecticut, about her brother, sister-in-law, and nieces. For so long, she had felt that the community of Sisters of Notre Dame des Victoires were her larger family.

But a new feeling was starting to grow. She looked into Tom's laughing blue eyes, saw reflections of Seamus. These wonderful men, the Kellys, were her son's relatives. Bernie shivered, thinking of what it could be like to introduce him to them. To bring him back to the States, have him meet everyone there.

"Tom," she said, reaching for his hand. She felt waves of love and hope washing over her—no matter what Seamus had said last night, once he got past the shock, realized that they loved him without any reserve or expectations, he would open up. It might be a slow process, might take a very long time.

"We're going to have dinner on Merrion Square tonight," Tom said. "And tomorrow we'll come back, right here, and keep coming back until we see Seamus again."

"Yes," she whispered, feeling such warmth. She was so over-whelmed, she barely noticed the car pulling up the drive. It was one of the hotel's vehicles, and its driver parked it with the other cars by the wall, climbed out, started across the circle.

"And you know what else?" he asked.

"What?"

"I'm taking you to Doolin," he said, grabbing her hand. "That's right, Bernie—we're going to the Cliffs of Moher again. Will you come with me?"

She was about to say yes—her heart was overflowing and she was caught up in the moment—when Tom looked over her shoulder, dropping her hand.

"Look," Tom said suddenly. "There's his friend."

Bernie turned in time to see the young man dressed in a black suit and shoes, the same one Seamus had been speaking to yesterday, striding toward the hotel's service entrance.

"Hey!" Tom called. "Hold on!"

The young man stopped, surprise all over his narrow face.

"Yes?" he asked. "Is there something I can do for you?"

"It's about your friend," Tom said. "Seamus Sullivan."

"Oh," the young man said, starting to grin. "He told me you might be looking for him."

"He did?" Bernie asked. Now it was their turn to be surprised. "What did he say?"

"Just that if anyone showed up asking for him, I was to give them something. Hold on a minute," he said, dashing back to the car.

"What does he have?" Bernie asked, looking up at Tom.

"Hang on, Bernie. Don't get worried," Tom said, placing his hand on her arm, making her shiver. She felt nervous and excited, as if she were standing at the threshold of a whole new life. Her mind raced, and her heart had never felt so full. Her faith had never wavered, and it didn't now, it was just that it had become, sometime during the last several days, all about love. A deeper love than she had ever felt before—suddenly she wanted nothing more than to stand on the cliffs with Tom and tell him how she felt.

"I'm Tom Kelly," Tom said, shaking the young man's hand as he ran back.

"I'm Kevin Daly."

"And this is Bernadette Sullivan," Tom said, his hand on her shoulder.

"Hello, Kevin," Bernie said.

"Sullivan?" Kevin asked, shaking her hand. "Like Seamus?"

"Yes," Bernie said. She held herself back from saying more, focused on the white envelope Kevin held in his hand.

"I'd ask if you were his long-lost relatives," Kevin said, chuckling. "But I know he doesn't have any."

"How do you know?" Tom asked.

"Well, because he came from St. Augustine's," Kevin said. "He's the greatest guy in the world, and he had the rottenest childhood, stuck in that institution. You'd never know; he's so up and positive. Eileen and I are having him as best man at our wedding. We wouldn't have anyone else."

"He's a wonderful person," Bernie murmured, stung by Kevin's words.

"Anyway," Kevin said, "what a coincidence, you both being named Sullivan. He didn't tell me that part, but you must be the people he meant. No one else has come asking for him!" He held out the envelope; Bernie's hands were shaking, so she let Tom take it.

"When will he be back at work?" Tom asked.

Kevin shrugged. "Don't know. He's never sick—this is a first. Yesterday he gave me and Eileen his tickets to a show Friday night— tonight, that is. Maybe he came down with something."

"Did he look sick when he gave you this?" Tom asked, tapping the envelope.

"Kind of pale, tired, but nothing too serious," Kevin said. "He had me stop by his flat to pick it up, said it was important I give it to a couple who'd be stopping by the hotel, asking for him. Don't worry about him, now. He never gets sick. It's probably just a cold, some- thing like that. Are you friends of his?"

"Yes," Bernie said. "We're his friends."

Kevin nodded, smiling. "Glad to hear that. He needs 'em. Friends, that is. Sometimes I think I'm the only one. He keeps to himself...."

"He does?" Tom asked.

"Yes," Kevin said. "He works all the time, saving money for his future."

"His future?" Bernie asked. She was aching to read what was in the envelope, but also hungry for any detail his friend could spare.

"He said he wants to be a barrister," Tom said.

Kevin laughed. "Yes, that's Seamus. Very aspirational. You know why, of course..."

"Why?"

"Well, for Kathleen," Kevin said. "She's all he ever talks about. When he finds Kathleen, what he'll do, the life he wants to give her. He has great dreams for himself and Kathleen—just like me and Eily."

"He's in love...." Bernie said.

"Well, he hasn't seen her in a long time. But he will! Don't doubt it!" Kevin said in a warm, good-natured brogue. "Seamus is the kind of person who sets his mind to something and never lets go. He'll search for Kathleen to the ends of the earth. And he's inspiring me to think about another career, too."

"Another career?" Tom asked.

"Other than driving, I mean," Kevin said. "It's good work, very honorable. But Seamus has got me dreaming, just like him. I'm not so much cut out to become a barrister, but there are other things. We meet a lot of influential people here. Maybe one of them will hire me."

"We wish you all the best," Bernie said, shaking his hand. She had educated so many young women, never tired of their dreams, of the shining look in their eyes as they imagined their futures. It pierced her heart to think of Seamus spurring his friend to think big, dream large.

"Yes, we do," Tom said. "Thank you for this," he said, gesturing with the envelope. The sight of it made Bernie's blood leap—maybe Seamus had given thought to seeing them, talking to them. Their presence in Dublin was a shock, yes, but such an open young man would surely want to hear what they had to say.

"You're welcome," Kevin Daly said, waving and heading in through the service door.

"Come on, Tom," Bernie said, tugging his hand, pulling him toward their car. Her mind raced with so many ideas: Seamus would give them his address, they would drive straight there, spend the day together. She and Tom would have to postpone dinner with the Kellys—or maybe Seamus would want to join them. Would that be too much? It was *all* too much, and not enough, both at the same time.

Tom held the door, and she climbed in. She watched him come around the car, wondering why his expression looked so dark and guarded. Usually he was so optimistic; why wouldn't he be imagining that Seamus had slept on it, come to the conclusion that he should meet with them today? Or even tomorrow...

"Let me read it," Bernie said as soon as Tom got into the car.

"Are you sure, Bernie?" he asked, holding on to the envelope.

"Why don't you want me to?" she asked.

"I...I just don't want you to be hurt," he said.

"He can't hurt me," she whispered. "He's my son. Nothing he says..."

Tom gave her a long, almost pitying look, as if he knew how very wrong she was. How had he been able to intuit such a thing? She'd been so strong and guarded for so many years, worn her habit like a shield. Right now, she felt as if her armor, even her skin, were stripped away. She sat across the front seat from Tom, holding out her hand, asking for the letter.

"Bernie," he said. "Please let me."

Reluctantly, she nodded. Tom's hands were trembling as he slipped his thumb under the flap, tore the envelope open. He read the words through silently once. Bernie felt nearly crazed with impatience— why wasn't he reading the letter out loud?

"I can't," he said, staring at the page, after a long minute.

"What are you talking about?" she asked.

He turned toward her, looked at her with such love and despair, she felt her heart crack in two.

"I can't read this to you. I thought I could, but I can't," he said, but he let her take the paper from his hands. She held it in her lap, read what Seamus had written:

Dear Mr. Kelly and Ms. Sullivan,

Your visit yesterday surprised me, to say the least. I can't say that I didn't know who you were, the minute I saw you standing there. As you pointed out, there is quite a strong resemblance— the red hair, the blue eyes. But that is all—just the superficial similarity of physical features. You can't tell me that red hair and freckles make people into family. Because I know they don't.

I know many things that you don't know. I have lived my entire life without you. You say that you have "thought of me every day." I can't tell you how little comfort that brings me. I could probably describe to you the time I had chicken pox, along with every other kid at St. Augustine's, how I scratched my skin raw and the nuns were too busy with the other kids to stop me. Or about the times I dreamed of monsters, coming through the light fixtures overhead, coming to kill all the children at the Home. Or about holiday dinners—you get the idea.

The point being, I didn't have you then, and I don't want you now. You're after something that doesn't exist. I can't even imagine why you thought finding me would be a good thing. Maybe you thought I'd be grateful for giving me life. From that standpoint, I guess I can say "Thank you." Thank you for giving me life.

As for the rest of it, I don't think you want to know what I think. Or what I have to say. It's not one bit complicated, it's dead simple: Stay away.

By now, if you are reading this letter, you know that I skipped work today. I guarantee you, I'll skip work for the rest of my life if it assures me I won't have to see you again. Go back home to America, to your nice house and other kids if you have them, to the life you've been living for the last twenty-three years without me.

You obviously didn't need me, and I don't need you. If you look for me again, I'll disappear. I've done it before.

Goodbye,
Seamus Sullivan

Bernie read the letter, then folded it, placed it back in the envelope. She felt Tom's eyes on her, but she knew he wasn't expecting her to speak. She couldn't if her life depended on it. She felt as if they had driven to the West, as if she'd fallen off the cliff's edge. Sitting there, holding the letter, she felt so grateful to Tom for one thing: for not telling her that she'd been wrong about her son being unable to hurt her.

Her eyes stung as tears spilled out, and she knew she wasn't hurt now. Not for herself, anyway. But for the tall, thin young man, with her red hair and Tom's blue eyes, she began to cry as if her heart was broken. And it was, for him.

Fourteen

Tom had no idea what to expect, what he'd find. He'd dropped Bernie off at her flat after they'd read Seamus's letter—not because he'd wanted to, but because she'd refused to talk, seemed unable to unlock the thoughts and feelings that had to be pouring around in her mind, as they were in his.

All she had said, very quietly, in a voice nearly too low to hear, was, "Please take me home."

"Home?" he said, not wanting to drive her back to her flat, that small, sterile academic walk-up across the Liffey. He imagined all the kids gathering. It was the start of fall term, and the air was charged. Hearing young adults' voices wasn't what Bernie needed right now.

She nodded, though, staring out the windshield, not looking left or right, as if she was unable to take one more thing in.

"If you're sure, Bernie," he said. "But why don't we stop at O'Malley's instead? We can talk... Or not talk, whatever you want. We need a little Tir na Nog, don't we? We can kill time until we go to Sixtus's for dinner."

"I can't," she said.

He glanced across the seat. "Come on, Bernie," he said. "It'll be good for you. For both of us. We can get some perspective and then start fresh tomorrow. Look, if you want to go home now, and rest, or think, that's fine. I'll take you back to your apartment...."

"Not my apartment," she said.

"Doolin?" he asked, his heart jumping. "That's what we'll do! We'll drive west, go to the cliff. Bernie, I'll hold you. I swear, I'll make it better. We'll find that same B&B, and..."

"No, Tom," she whispered. "Home."

"The convent?" he asked, his heart skipping. Jesus, no. He wanted to take her to the Cliffs of Moher, prove to her how much he loved her. Not the convent. He'd never stopped dreaming, praying, that she'd want to be with him. "Please, Bernie—don't ask me to take you there."

"No," she said. "Home...Star of the Sea."

"Bernie," he said, "what are you talking about?"

"You read his letter, Tom," she said. "He doesn't want us here. He's right, in every single thing he says...."

"No," Tom said. "He's wrong in every single thing he says."

Bernie turned away, gazed out the window. Tom wanted to grab her shoulder, throttle her, make her pay attention to what he was saying. But he saw her shrinking into herself, knew that she was going through something even he couldn't understand.

All he could do was drive her back to her flat, drop her off. He watched her climb out of the car, taking Seamus's letter with her. Before she closed the door, she leaned into the front seat again.

"You know I can't go to Doolin with you," she said.

His heart fell, and he couldn't speak.

"Or even to dinner tonight," she said softly.

He nodded. His voice wouldn't work.

"I'm sorry," she said.

"So am I," he managed to say.

"Thank Sixtus for me," she said.

"Yeah. I will," Tom said. Did she think he was going without her? He'd drive around for an hour, come back, see how she was doing then. Maybe she'd be feeling better. Perhaps she just needed to lie down, clear her head. Or pray. Bernie had always gained clarity through prayer. Tom couldn't count the times he had come upon her at Star of the Sea, kneeling in chapel, or at the Blue Grotto, or at the outside altar where the bishop always said Easter mass at dawn.

So here he was—he'd given her not one, but two hours. He buzzed the downstairs bell, got no response. Standing on the doorstep, he gazed over the river, watched the water flowing seaward, clouds reflected in the dark surface. After a few seconds, he rang again.

Although Bernie didn't answer, two students came hurrying out. Tom caught the door behind them before it closed. He started walking up the stairs—but before he reached the first landing, he began to run, taking the steps two at a time.

When he got to the fourth floor, his heart was crashing in his chest. He knocked softly on the door, just in case she was sleeping and hadn't heard the buzzer. She didn't answer, so he banged loudly.

"Bernie?" he called. "Hey, it's me."

But there was no reply. Tom stood in the hallway, sweat pouring down his back. He took three steps downstairs, then turned and stood outside her door again. Knocked once, twice more. His mind raced, thinking of options. Maybe she'd gone out for a walk. To church, or St. Stephen's Green, or Trinity College, or O'Malley's, or maybe back to the Greencastle.

Maybe she'd headed back to St. Augustine's. But why wouldn't she have called him? And besides, what could she hope to accomplish? By the time his thoughts quit cycling, his heart felt like lead, and his mouth was dry as cotton. Fumbling in his pocket, he knew what he had to do.

He'd never intruded on her like this, had always respected her privacy. No matter how much silence or space she needed, Tom had always given it to her. They worked alongside each other at the Academy—she in the school and convent, he on the grounds. Not a day in twenty-three years had gone by with Tom not wanting to get into Bernie's life, into her heart, into her mind. But he'd always respected the way she removed herself, locked herself behind closed doors.

Right now, he reached into his pocket, pulled out his wallet. Took out a credit card, worked it in between the door and the frame, slid it down toward the lock. He felt the spring hesitate, then give, and he was inside.

"Bernie," he called, blood charging through his veins. She wasn't in the living room or the kitchen. What was he expecting? He didn't know, but he'd never felt so afraid in his life as he opened her bedroom door.

The room was empty.

The clothes she had been wearing were on the chair beside the bed, neatly folded. Her jeans, the sea-green shirt, the big white sweater. Tom walked over, picked them up. He held her clothes to his chest, as if he were holding Bernie. Opening the door to her closet, he already knew what he'd find.

Her habit was gone. He saw an empty hanger, knew with absolute certainty that it had been hanging there. Placing her clothes back on the chair, he walked back into the living room.

The nondescript furniture was just as he'd seen it that first day: a muddy-green tweed sofa, plaid armchair, table with two chairs. Her Bible and prayer book were on the table, along with Seamus's letter.

What was missing was the folded square of black fabric. Tom had seen it on the table when he'd come to pick Bernie up yesterday. She hadn't mentioned it, and he hadn't wanted to ask. He'd just been so glad to see her veil there, lying on the table, instead of on her head.

Bernie had put her habit back on.

All the hope, and all the plans Tom had felt flowing through him since they'd left the convent with their son's information, died inside him. They swirled and fell, just like sand in a last gust of wind.

Bernie had said she wanted to go home, to Star of the Sea. Tom couldn't begin to stop her, even if he knew how to try. Wherever she was right now, he had no doubt that it had nothing to do with him. He was starting to realize that, ultimately, very little in her life did.

But he had one thing left to do before he returned to Connecticut with Sister Bernadette Ignatius. He tucked Seamus's letter inside his jacket pocket, took one last look around, and then locked Bernie's door behind him. His footsteps echoed on the stairs as he walked down to the street. He had the letter, the picture, and the postcard from Kathleen, and he knew what he had to do. He had never been surer of anything in his entire life, and he was positive that two people's lives depended on it.

After Tom had dropped Bernie off at the apartment, she'd gone upstairs, every step taking its toll, her legs so heavy, as if they were made of iron. But once she reached the third landing and heard her phone ringing, she started to run. It was crazy, she knew, but she thought maybe Seamus had found her—he had tracked her down, had a change of heart, decided he had to see her and Tom after all.

Fumbling with her key, throwing open the door, she'd flown to the telephone and nearly dropped it, grabbing the receiver to her ear.

"Hello?" she asked

"Bernie?" came the female voice.

"Honor?" she asked, her heart splitting—she loved her sister-in-law, but it wasn't Seamus.

"Yes, it's me. How are you, Bernie? Have you found him?"

"Oh, Honor," Bernie said, her voice breaking. "We did find him. It's been incredible. But he doesn't want anything to do with me—with us."

"Bernie, I'm so sorry," Honor said, falling silent as Bernie sobbed quietly for a few seconds. Then, "How is Tom taking it?"

"You know Tom. He's trying to be so strong for me, but that only makes it worse. I look at him and see him holding it together, trying to," Bernie said, sniffling, wiping her eyes.

"This trip has been a dream for Tom," Honor said. "You know that. The culmination of a whole lifetime of them..."

"Yes," Bernie said. "Just looking at him, I can see those dreams swirling around his head."

"He can't hide them from you, of all people," Honor said. "You probably wouldn't even want him to."

"At this point, I'm not too sure about that," Bernie said softly, picturing his eyes, filled with passion and hope. "How is John? And the girls?"

"We're all fine. Just thinking of you so much—you, Tom, and your son."

"His name is Seamus," Bernie said. "That's what he wants to be called."

"Well, he has three cousins who'd love to meet him. You know that you'd only have to say the word, and Regis, Agnes, and Cece would fly over there and tell him what's what."

"I can imagine," Bernie said, thinking of her three headstrong nieces. "We saw Sixtus Kelly today."

"Give him our best, okay? He was amazing with Regis. He counseled her through everything and when they went before the judge, he helped her to have the courage to tell what happened. She's doing so well now, Bernie. Tom has such wonderful cousins."

"He and I were supposed to have dinner with them tonight, but I can't. I can only think of Seamus. . . ."

"I know, Bernie. I'd be the same way. Do what feels right to you, okay?"

"Thank you, Honor."

"Listen, I'll let you go. I only called to say I love you—we all do. We're rooting for you, Bernie. Don't give up hope. . . ."

"We'll be home soon," Bernie said. "Tom and I."

"Give Tom our love," Honor said.

"I will," Bernie said. She hung up the phone, and almost instantly it rang again. Once again she grabbed the receiver, said hello.

"Bernie," came another woman's voice—Irish this time.

"Annie?"

"Yes, it's me. How are you?"

"Oh, Annie," Bernie said, her voice catching. "Don't ask."

"Listen," Sister Anne-Marie said. "I have a surprise for you. A shock, in fact."

"What's that?"

"Someone asked me to set up a meeting with you. Face to face. And it has to be a secret."

"Who?" Bernie asked, skeptical.

"Sister Theodore. She made me promise not to tell Eleanor Marie. She wants to see you on her own, and not here at the convent."

"What does she have to say to me?" Bernie asked, feeling empty.

"You should hear her out," Sister Anne Marie said. "But I think it's important, something you really should hear."

Bernie hesitated, clutching the receiver. Thin gray light came through the big window, breaking through rain clouds over Dublin, rippling across the river's surface. Bernie looked for silver, but right now there was nothing but flat, pewter gray.

"All right," Bernie said. "Where?"

"She said she'd meet you anywhere you want."

"At St. Augustine's, then," Bernie said, her voice breaking. "At the Children's Home, where my son spent his childhood. Tell her I'll see her there."

And an hour later, after Bernie had changed from her street clothes into the garment she had worn all these years—that defined her inside and out, that reminded her of the choice she had made—she knelt by the window, praying for guidance. Taking her habit off had been a very mindful decision, having to do with meeting her son. Even more than that—and she could barely admit it to herself—it had had to do with Tom. Putting it back on was no small act, and she prayed she was doing the right thing. Blessing herself, she left the apartment and she walked north through the city streets in her black habit and veil.

Nuns were not an uncommon sight in Dublin, but perhaps seeing one practically run along the sidewalk, her face twisted with grief, looking as if she was about to do battle, was enough to give people pause. Because Bernie got a wide berth, people parting like the Red Sea as she hurried along.

When she got to St. Augustine's, she felt her heart constrict, her blood freeze, as if she had just entered the Arctic Circle. The children who had been absent on her visit here with Tom—off on a trip to the beach—were now back. She saw them in the courtyard, playing basketball, drawing on the pavement with chalk, two kids pushing each other while a nun tried to break them up.

She glanced around for Sister Anastasia, didn't see her. An office worker—a layperson, not much older than Seamus—gave her a form to sign. Because she was a member of the Sisters of Notre Dame des Victoires, she wasn't asked many questions; it was assumed she had a reason for being there. Bernie cast an eye over the playground, wondering what Seamus had liked to play, what his favorite games had been.

"Sister Bernadette."

Bernie was so distracted by the children playing, she didn't hear her name being called. She watched the kids, heard them talking, couldn't stop thinking of Seamus.

"Sister Bernadette!"

This time she heard. She turned around, saw Sister Theodore walking heavily up the sidewalk. She was extremely overweight, but here at the Children's Home, away from the home turf of her convent, she looked almost fragile. Her brown eyes were watery, worried, darting around. Bernie saw the spirit draining right out of her, heard her wheezing breath, as if she was having a hard time walking.

"Sister Theodore," Bernie said, alarmed by how she looked. She gestured toward a bench in the shade at the edge of the play area. Bernie helped her sit down, felt concerned by her pallor, the sheen of sweat on her face and neck.

Bernie took a deep breath, gathering herself together. She felt like stone. She asserted herself, as Superior of this nun, giving her the coldest look she could summon. Back at Star of the Sea, when she had to deal with problems, she had a certain way of sitting: erect, hands folded, waiting for the other Sister to start talking, so she knew what she was dealing with. At the same time, she felt worried about Theodore's health.

"Are you all right?" she asked.

"Please, don't be concerned," Sister Theodore said.

Bernie was, however, and offered her a handkerchief. Sister Theodore took it gratefully, wiping her face, balling it up in her hand, trying to catch her breath.

"Why did you want to see me?" Bernie asked after Sister Theodore had composed herself.

"To tell you something," Sister Theodore said. "You were wise to suggest meeting here. This is exactly the right place for us to have this conversation."

"What do you mean?"

"Here at St. Augustine's. Where Thomas grew up..."

"He calls himself Seamus now," Bernie said. "He obviously wants no reminders of the name his father and I gave him."

"Sister, I have to confess something to you."

"I'm not a priest," Bernie said. "I can't absolve you of anything; you should go to confession."

"You're the only person who *can* absolve me," Sister Theodore said, grasping Bernie's hand. Bernie recoiled at her touch, but forced herself to sit still.

"Look around here," Bernie said quietly. "Please, Sister Theodore. The broken tar, the weeds growing up, the children...they have such wild looks in their eyes, don't they? I was just watching them, thinking how alone they must feel. How abandoned by the universe."

"I see that, Sister."

"I never wanted to abandon my son," Bernie said. "It was a terrible decision I had to make. I'd felt called to the convent. It tormented me, as dramatic as that sounds. I'd been yearning for a life of prayer and contemplation. And then I made what I thought was an awful mistake. I got pregnant."

"Many girls do," Sister Theodore whispered. "And many babies come here, to St. Augustine's. And they are placed in wonderful homes."

"But my baby wasn't."

"No," Sister Theodore said, shaking her head. Her breath came heavily, sounding labored. She'd started wheezing again, and her eyes flooded, overcome with emotion.

"Is that why you needed to see me? To tell me about that?"

Sister Theodore nodded.

"Please, Sister. What is it?"

"Thomas, your son," Sister Theodore said. "He was the sweetest, most gentle boy I've ever seen. I used to come here, to see him. Sister Eleanor Marie wanted me to, to make sure he was getting along well. I thought it was because you were one of us, a Sister . . . and not just in an ordinary way. The most blessed of us, the one who had received a visit from the Virgin Mary. I thought that we were giving special treatment to your son for that reason."

"But that wasn't it?"

Sister Theodore shook her head. "No."

"Tell me, Sister. . . ."

"There was a young girl," Sister Theodore said. "Your son and she were inseparable. Truly, it was a sight to see. I would come here, sit on this very bench . . ." She gazed out across the playground, and Bernie shivered, knowing that her son and Kathleen had played here.

"Kathleen?" Bernie asked.

"Yes. Kathleen Murphy," Sister Theodore said, sounding confused that Bernie would know.

"Sister Anastasia told us about her," Bernie said. "She said that she and Seamus had done everything they could to stay together, even sabotaging adoption attempts."

"Not every attempt," Sister Theodore said, her voice throaty and low.

"What are you talking about?"

"Because someone wanted to adopt them both—keep them together."

"What?" Bernie asked, her stomach lurching.

"A couple came to Dublin from Connemara. He was a poet, and she was a playwright. They were very kind, they saw right away the bond between Thomas—Seamus, I mean—and Kathleen. They had such heart, and the kind of creative spirit that allowed them to see the children's connection. They wanted to adopt them both, keep them together."

"Why didn't they?"

"Because Sister Eleanor Marie interfered," Sister Theodore said.

"Why? For what reason?" Bernie asked, her eyes wild. "I thought the only reason Seamus was never adopted was that he'd refused to leave Kathleen!"

"He never even found out about this couple. They never got as far as the interview. When Sister Catherine Laboure, Sister Anastasia's Superior, first heard about them, she was so happy, she called Sister Eleanor Marie directly. And Eleanor Marie…"

"What did she do?"

"She instructed me to investigate. I called the couple's parish in Westport. The priest told me that he had had a problem with drink several years back, but seemed to be doing better. The woman had been a widow, with an older child from her first marriage. And that child had had some behavior problems at school."

"And Sister Eleanor Marie used that against them?"

"All of it, taken together. The alcohol problem, the older child… she'd made a case to Sister Catherine about how precarious the situation could be, trying to take not one, but two children into a home. She said she believed that adopting two children at the same time would cause a great deal of stress on all concerned in this particular family…."

"Do you think she really believed that?"

Sister Theodore hesitated, her lips pursed. Then she shook her head. "No," she said. "I wish I did, but in all honesty, I do not."

"Why are you telling me this now?" Bernie asked.

"Because you have come to Ireland for answers," Sister Theodore said, her voice spiraling away into nothing.

"You helped Sister Eleanor Marie hide the truth all this time," Bernie said, rising from the bench, pacing around it, eyes never leaving Sister Theodore. "Tom Kelly and I had to break into her office just to get our son's records. She's gone to a great deal of trouble to keep this buried, and you have been with her every step of the way."

"I know," Sister Theodore. "I've protected her."

"She's evil, if she really did what you say," Bernie said. "I've never wanted to believe that before; I know she suffered when she was young, but to do this…"

"She's ill," Sister Theodore said. "That's what I believe, Sister. Not evil. Do you know about her mother? She used to bring men home to their house; little Eleanor used to hear them night after night. She'd pass her mother's room on her way to the bathroom and see what was going on. Once, when she was thirteen, one of the men went to her bed; it was a miracle Eleanor didn't get pregnant."

"Sister," Bernie said, shaking, "I grieve for everything Eleanor went through as a child. But right now you're telling me she destroyed my son's chance for happiness, for a good family life for both of them, him and Kathleen!"

The older nun bowed her head, tears rolling down heavy cheeks.

"She's so envious," she said. "You seemed to have everything. A calling… not just within your own heart, but from Mary. You had that, and a child, too. Eleanor Marie feels abandoned by the world, by Mary, by God. You forgave yourself for your sins—she can't do that for herself."

"But she didn't sin!" Bernie said. "She was an innocent child!"

"As I said, she's ill. Her mind is warped with all that's happened. A downfall of being a Catholic woman," Sister Theodore said. "Where sex comes in, guilt is sure to follow. We have a long way to go in that area."

Amen to that, Bernie wanted to say, surprised by Theodore's point of view.

"When you went to America and were made Superior of the order over there, it was too much for Eleanor Marie. Don't you see how troubled she is? Please, you're good. You're such a good person, Sister Bernadette Ignatius."

"What do you want me to do?"

"Forgive her. I plan to tell our Provincial Superior. I'll do it today. Sister Bernadette—it will destroy Sister Eleanor Marie, although I'm doing it out of love. I can't live with what I've done, and I don't believe she can either."

"It bothers her?"

Sister Theodore nodded, tears spilling from her eyes. "She's haunted by it. I'm sure that's why she didn't want you to find Seamus. She's wracked by all that guilt, and it's eating her up. She hid the files because she couldn't bear for you to know what we'd done to him. Or to Kathleen..."

"Where is Kathleen now?" Bernie asked. She remembered the postcard from America Sister Anastasia had given Tom. How specific had it been, in terms of her address?

Sister Theodore shook her head. "Keeping track of Kathleen Murphy never had the same priority as Thomas James Sullivan. I'm so sorry, Sister Bernadette. Please forgive both of us."

"It's not for me to forgive," Bernie whispered, staring out at the playground, at the lonely children playing in the shadow of St. Augustine's. She pictured Seamus and Kathleen, sticking together through everything. She imagined their separation, what it must have done to each of them. And she saw the look in Seamus's eyes, and the words in his letter, the same fury tearing through both. "It's for them," she said.

"Them?" Sister Theodore asked.

"My son and Kathleen," Bernie said. "It's for them to forgive us all."

Fifteen

The day after the couple came looking for him, Seamus called in sick to work—something he'd never done. He had such a good reputation at the Greencastle, no one would suspect that he was shirking. Everyone thought him such a good worker, such an honorable man. He knew they'd all be shocked to see him up and about, completely healthy, just hiding out. Kevin, his best friend, had given him such a sympathetic look, when he'd come by to pick up the letter.

It was seeing the couple—Seamus wouldn't call them his parents. What had they said their names were? Thomas Kelly and Bernadette Sullivan. So, that's where his last name came from—they weren't married. He was a bastard. Who cared, and what did it matter? Whether they were married or not, they hadn't wanted him.

He was grown-up now, with a good life of his own. Why was this bothering him so much? They came to see him—big deal. He had moved far beyond the trials and hurts of St. Augustine's. Most of the time, in fact, he thought he'd had it pretty good there, as institutions went.

No, his reaction to the couple was shocking him. It was like being stung by a bee, and not knowing you were allergic. You think it's just an insect, you assume the sting might hurt a little. But suddenly you're all swollen, finding it hard to breathe, seeing the world go black before your very eyes. You can't catch a breath because your throat has shut tight, and next thing you know, you're dead.

That's how Seamus, sitting in his armchair, felt about meeting the couple. Over the years—not as often as some St. Augustine's kids, but more than he'd like to admit—he had imagined what he'd do if someone came looking for him. A woman saying she was his mother, a man saying he was his father, or both together.

Oh, Seamus had had quite the speech imagined. At one point, he'd dreamed of spitting on their shoes. That was a nice touch. He'd thought of showing them his class pictures—all the way through eighth grade. To him, staring at the group shots, he'd always thought he looked ridiculous, like a bird. Too skinny, too tall, with his sleeves not fitting right, and his red hair sticking out in tufts.

He'd gone to a school that took students from St. Augustine's as well as kids from regular homes, and he remembered looking around the class, always being able to tell which kids had mothers and which didn't.

Mothers combed their kids' hair. They made them wash their faces, so they wouldn't have sleep in their eyes. They straightened their ties and collars on picture day. They checked out their sleeves, and if they'd outgrown their shirts, they'd set them aside for the younger kids and pull a new shirt from the closet.

For motherless girls, it was even more extreme. Girls without mothers either tried too hard or not hard enough; as they got older, they sometimes wore extra makeup, as if it could mask the fact they didn't know what to do, how to act.

Kathleen had been the opposite. She had had such natural beauty, she hadn't needed makeup at all. Her skin glowed, and her dark hair was as shiny as silk. But Seamus had always had to remind her to brush her hair, to wear the sweater without the hole in the cuff, to put on socks with elastic that hadn't given out, that didn't droop over her shoes.

Yes, Seamus had often imagined showing his "parents" these old school pictures, pointing out what a ragamuffin he'd looked like compared to his classmates. He pulled them out now, from the box under his bed where he stored important things. Getting them hadn't been an easy task. Because he'd run away from St. Augustine's when he was thirteen, he obviously hadn't taken his pictures along.

But when he'd returned the next year, looking for Kathleen, and Sister Anastasia had convinced him to stay, she had helped him. They'd gone through all the yearbooks of his school, finding the class pictures of him, and those of Kathleen, and then Sister had helped him write letters to the yearbook company, asking for copies of the pictures. Although the pictures had originally been free—one to each student, included in their school fees—getting copies had cost money. Sister Anastasia had paid for them, letting Seamus work off his debt by washing windows in the school and convent, on top of his normal chores.

Seamus gazed at the pictures now. He wondered what the couple would think, to see him as a child. Spreading the class pictures out on his bed, he stared at himself, wondered what he'd been thinking. His eyes always looked too wide and wild—as if startled by the flash. Deep down, Seamus remembered always being scared. He'd always felt unsure, off balance, worried about what was going to happen next.

He looked at Kathleen. They had attended grammar school together, but once they'd reached sixth grade, they'd gone to single-sex academies. That was just how St. Augustine's did it; but staring at the pictures, Seamus remembered how wrenching it had been, to be separated from each other for entire days at a time. Even at night, after school, he was living in the boys' wing and she in the girls'. Her job was cooking, his was cleanup. Some days their only conversation had been before school, walking to the bus, or in the kitchen, after meals, dead tired on their feet.

Some days, on their way to the bus, he'd tuck her hair behind her ears. Or she'd hand him a tissue, to shine his shoes. His favorite mornings had been times she'd ask him to braid her hair, and they'd hang back, him fumbling with sections of her long, smooth hair, smelling her shampoo and never wanting to stop.

He stared at a picture of her now, one with her thick braid coming forward over her shoulder, so long it nearly obliterated the school insignia on her green blazer. Running his finger over her face, he stared into her big eyes and saw that same startled expression that he always saw in his own. He wondered what she looked like now, where she lived. Did she still have long dark hair? Was someone else braiding it for her?

A knock sounded at the door, and Seamus looked up. Who could that be? Not Kevin, he was sure—it was late in the day, and his shift was over. He should be home by now, showering and getting changed, on his way to pick up Eily for Randi-Lu O'Byrne's concert.

Leaving the pictures on the bed, Seamus crossed the room. His flat was small, so it only took him a few steps. What if it was his boss from the Greencastle, coming to check and make sure he was really sick? Taking his chances, Seamus opened the door.

Tom Kelly stood there.

Seamus leaned back, shocked to see him.

"How'd you find me?" he asked.

"I needed to see you. It's important."

"Yeah, who told you where I live?" Seamus asked belligerently.

"Look, I'm a Kelly," Tom said. "I pulled some strings."

Seamus peered at him through narrowed eyes. He knew the Kellys were powerful; it was a world beyond imagining. Seamus drove people like Sixtus Kelly all the time. He'd pretend to be deaf, listening all the while to what went on in the back seat. He'd hear state secrets, dark plots, the details of romantic assignations. He knew that people like that had access to anything they wanted: detectives, operatives, everything short of magicians.

"What, you paid someone to find me?"

"Never mind how I did it," Tom said. "Look, can I come in?"

Seamus wanted to slam the door in his face, and he started to— but Tom's hand shot out fast and hard, caught the door's force with a sharp crack. Tom's expression didn't change, even though the impact must have killed his palm and wrist.

Without asking again, Tom stepped inside. He gently closed the door behind him. Seamus glared at him, his heart racing. He wanted to attack the man—thinking he could just invade his home this way! But something in Tom's eyes took Seamus aback; it was beyond words, a sadness and resignation that Seamus hadn't seen yesterday. As if overnight, Tom Kelly had gotten old.

"Rich people like the Kellys do things differently," Seamus said. "They do what they want. They get things done."

"Yeah," Tom said. "You're right."

Seamus gestured at Tom's tweed jacket—the same one he'd been wearing both other times Seamus had seen him. It was old, kind of beat up, as if Tom had worn it outside in the rain plenty. The cuffs and pockets were frayed, the shoulders sagging; there were patches on the elbows. Oddly, it looked like something Seamus would have worn in one of his school pictures.

"If you're so rich," Seamus asked, "what're you wearing that for?"

"Who said I'm rich?"

"You're a Kelly. You just said—"

"Do me a favor, Seamus. Don't assume you know anything about me, and I'll do the same for you. My cousins are rich. I'm not."

Seamus felt stunned, as if he'd been slapped. Tom's eyes were hard, injured—they reminded Seamus of the toughest kids at St. Augustine's. Like himself, the kids who had been there the longest, gone through the most. Had Tom grown up in an institution?

"Did you live in a Home?" Seamus asked suddenly, surprising himself.

Tom shook his head. "Nope. I grew up in a big house. A mansion, actually. Lots of land, servants, big cars. I went to the fanciest schools in Connecticut. Could have gone to Yale if I'd studied harder; my family donated a science building and a gym. But I blew it."

"You didn't work hard?"

"I worked hard," Tom said. "But not at school. I like the land. Dirt, rocks, trees, gardens. Things like that. I like the weather, too. Doesn't matter if the sun's shining, I just like being outside. Snow, hail, all of it."

"So, you keep the gardens nice on your property?" Seamus asked, not bothering to hide the sarcasm.

Tom shook his head. "I don't have any property."

"But you just said—"

"I walked away from Kelly family money," he said. "It didn't mean anything to me. Big houses, fancy cars, those Mercedes you drive—I couldn't care less about them. I have plenty of relatives who are happy to get my share. When I visit Dublin, you know where I like to go?"

"The Greencastle?" Another dig.

Tom shook his head. "Nope. Rutland Fountain."

"In Merrion Square? That's where the Kellys live—in all those Georgian houses along the north side. I know, I've dropped people off for dinner parties, business meetings...."

"Yeah," Tom said. "That's where they live. They make fun of me for visiting the fountain. Do you know about it, Seamus?"

"Of course," he said. "I give tours of Dublin to the people I drive around."

"Why don't you tell me what you'd tell a passenger," Tom said, and his voice sounded dangerous, as if he wouldn't take no for an answer. Seamus remembered the crack of the door as Tom had forced his way in, his mind in turmoil. He didn't like being boxed into a corner, forced to perform like a trained monkey. On the other hand, he didn't want to cross someone who was this angry.

"I'd tell them that Merrion Square, for all its fanciness, once served a terrible function—it held a soup kitchen in the Great Famine. People starving, dying, all through Ireland. Tremendous suffering. That's what Merrion Square used to be—not just a place for the Kellys to live their rich lives."

"And Rutland Fountain?"

Again, Seamus felt confused. Tom was testing him for some reason, and Seamus didn't like it. He felt fury boiling inside, under his skin. "It predated the Famine. Installed in 1791, for Dublin's poor."

Tom nodded. "That's why I visit it," he said. "It reminds me of something."

"What can it remind you of? You just told me you went to fancy schools, lived in a mansion."

"It reminds me of water," Tom said quietly, as if the fight had just gone out of him.

"Yeah? Water?"

"Water is what people need to survive," he said. "It quenches the deepest thirst, and you don't have to be rich to drink it. There's nothing better than cold water...."

Seamus stared at him. That's what Kathleen used to say to him. He'd be doing the dishes after dinner—piles of crusty pans and dirty plates and grimy glasses. And he'd be thirsty, his hands elbow-deep in sudsy water, and she'd fill a glass and hold it to his lips. He could still feel the pressure of her hand cupping the back of his head as she'd tilt the glass up, letting him drink.

"It's nice to romanticize the poor," Seamus said now, "when you're not poor yourself. You use a lot of water on your gardens, don't you? Oh, that's right—you say you don't own property."

"You're right, though. I do use a lot of water—irrigating gardens, lawns, and vineyards. At a very large estate in Connecticut, where the river meets the Sound. It belonged to your great-great-grandfather, Seamus. Francis X. Kelly."

"Shut up!" Seamus said, backing away. "He's not my great-great anything. Why are you telling me this? I don't want to know."

"It's called Star of the Sea Academy," he said. "Francis X. donated the land and buildings to the Sisters of Notre Dame des Victoires...."

That got Seamus's attention. The Sisters who had raised him. Still, he peered at Tom with all the hostility he could muster; it wasn't hard. Tom didn't react to the dirty look, though. He just kept talking.

"There's a nun who runs the place," he said. "She's the reason I walked away from the Kelly money. Don't tell her that, though."

"How would I tell her?" Seamus snapped. "I don't know her, and I sure as hell have no plans to visit."

"She's one of those pure types, you know?" Tom asked. "You meet them, and you think they're too good to be real? They're kind, and humble, they don't give a shit about the clothes you wear or the car you drive. They only want to help others. You know what I mean?"

Seamus didn't reply, but he did know what Tom meant. He

thought of Sister Anastasia, some of the other nuns at St. Augustine's. He wouldn't give Tom the satisfaction of identifying, though. So he just stared.

"This woman. Back when she was young, before she became a nun—she got under my skin. Even with all my family money, I'd never seen anyone as happy as her. It was as if she'd tapped into her own private spring, Seamus. Cool, clear water all day long. And you know—it had nothing to do with money."

"So you decided to forsake your family fortune for a girl?" Seamus asked meanly.

"Yep," Tom said, Seamus's sarcasm passing right over his head. "I surely did. A sweet, pure girl. You could even call her holy."

"Not many people on this earth are holy. The nuns are, the ones at St. Augustine's. They're saints right here on earth," Seamus countered.

"So was she . . . she had a vision."

"A what? You mean, like Lourdes?"

"Exactly like Lourdes. The Virgin Mary appeared to her in the Blue Grotto at Star of the Sea."

Seamus tingled, hearing the words. Something was coming back to him now—stories trickled down, from the convent to the Children's Home. A story about a nun, one of the Sisters of Notre Dame des Victoires, who had had a vision in America before she joined the order—something mysterious about it, the reason she entered the convent. Kathleen had loved the story. She'd always been praying for a visitation from Mary.

"Why are you telling me this?" Seamus asked.

"Because I want to put things in perspective. So you'll understand."

"Understand what? Why you didn't want me? I don't care about that. My life is fine now, it always has been. I don't give a crap about Star of the Sea, or the money you gave up, or why you like going to Rutland Fountain. Okay?"

"Yeah," Tom said. He stood there nodding. Seamus saw that hard look in his eyes again—as if he really wanted no part of Seamus, as if he wasn't here to act all fatherly, to bond with the son he'd thrown away. No, it was something else.

"So, why don't you leave now?" Seamus asked.

Tom exhaled. He reached inside his old tweed jacket, fumbled his hand in the inside pocket. "I am going to leave now," he said. "But I want to give you this first."

Seamus didn't want to take anything from him, not one thing. He half expected the guy to pull out a wad of cash—in spite of all his words about renouncing family money, about water and thirst, maybe he thought leaving Seamus with some blood money would kill his guilt.

But it wasn't cash. Tom held out a picture of Kathleen.

Seamus grabbed it; it was a school picture, not the group kind, but an individual portrait taken the year he and Kathleen had parted. She was smiling at the camera—that wildness in her blue eyes, that insecurity Seamus knew so well. Her cheeks were pink, her skin flawless. And she wore a braid—long, thick, and dark, swung over her left shoulder. Seamus had braided her hair that morning...he saw the little bump where he hadn't pulled one of the strands tight enough.

"Where did you get this?"

"Sister Anastasia," Tom said. "When we went to St. Augustine's, looking for you."

Seamus saw the tiny hole in the top white border, where Sister had pushed the thumbtack, holding it to her office wall. He ran his thumb over the small hole.

"Why did she give it to you?"

"I wanted to see Kathleen," Tom said. "Because she's so important to you."

"Well, she's gone," Seamus said harshly. "I lost track of her. So it doesn't matter anymore."

"Sister gave me this as well," Tom said, reaching into his pocket again, slowly pulling out a postcard. He handed it to Seamus, and even before Seamus took it, he knew. He felt electricity shooting through his body, from the postcard that Kathleen had touched, written, and sent.

The picture on the front was an aerial shot of coastline—wild waves crashing on jagged rocks, with a row of tremendous mansions looking over a rugged path along the top of a seawall. *The Cliff Walk, Newport, Rhode Island,* was written in white script over blue sky at the top.

Seamus tried to keep his hands from shaking. He turned the card over, and there was her handwriting. Kathleen's tiny script, trying to fit as many words on the card as possible...He ran his thumb over her name, felt his eyes blur, making it hard to read.

> *Dear Sister Anastasia,*
>
> *This is where I live now, with a family in a house like one of these. I'm a cook! Who would have thought that all my years in the kitchen at St. A's would have paid off like this? I love my work, and have never been happier. As you might have heard, my parents brought me to America, and I've never left. I think of you, and all the Sisters, so often. I think of James, too. Do you ever hear from him? If you do, will you tell him I send my best regards?*
>
> *Blessings and love,*
> *Kathleen Murphy*

Seamus read and reread the words. He hadn't been this close to Kathleen in nearly ten years. There was so much information encoded in the postcard's photo, in her words, in her mention of her parents. Seamus wanted to be alone with the card so badly, his body was screaming for it—he wanted to push Tom Kelly out the door, just fall into his chair and be alone with Kathleen's postcard.

"She asks for you," Tom said.

Seamus just stared at her writing. He didn't care that Tom had given him the card, that he had done that kindness. He just wanted to shut the man up, get him the hell out, let Kathleen's presence fill him up.

"She doesn't know you as Seamus," Tom said. "She doesn't know where you live, where you work."

"No," Seamus said sharply. "And I don't know where she lives, where she works either. Except that it's someplace called Newport, Rhode Island, and it's far, far away."

"It's a plane ride away," Tom said.

Seamus glared at him. He wouldn't give the man the satisfaction of knowing he'd never been on a plane, didn't even have a passport.

"She calls you James," Tom pressed. "Doesn't it bother you, that she doesn't know you're known as Seamus now?"

"Jesus Christ! She knows me," Seamus said, shooting him a look of fury. "Names don't matter with us. You don't know what we've been through. We have a connection that goes beyond names, words, post-cards, pictures."

"Connections die," Tom said harshly. "Get that through your head. No matter how strong you think they are. If you don't take care of them, they're gone."

"What do you know about it? *You're* the one who kills your con-nections with people. Where's that girl who had the vision? You for-sake your fortune for her, and then what? And what about your family? The Kellys? You just walk away from what matters to them? And what about me?"

"Seamus," Tom said, his voice shaking. "That's why I'm here. Because of you. Because I don't want you to make the mistakes I've made. Fight for what you love, Seamus. Fight for Kathleen."

"I don't have to fight for her! I have her, in my heart. We have each other. You talk about holy? That girl who had the vision? You say you gave up so much for her? Kathleen's more than that to me. You could never understand!"

"The hell I couldn't," Tom said. "I love someone like that, too."

"Not like me and Kathleen," Seamus said stubbornly.

"More," Tom said.

And that was all Seamus needed. Rage filled him like hot lava, flowing over, making him shove Tom Kelly against the wall. How dare he say he loved someone more than Seamus loved Kathleen?

"You don't know what love is!" Seamus shouted, punching Tom in the face. Blood poured out, all over the tweed jacket. Tom tried not to fight back, but Seamus didn't want to give him any choice. His fists flew again and again. "She's everything to me! You can't know love like what we have." Seamus landed another punch, bone cracking against bone. Tom tried to hold him off, arms stiff, face twisted in a grimace.

"I do know it, and I have it for your mother," Tom said, ducking as Seamus pounded him.

"You're lying, you're delusional," Seamus said, slamming Tom against the wall. "If you loved her, you'd have married her. You'd have kept me! Goddamn you, don't say you love her like I love Kathleen!"

"Seamus," Tom said, dodging a blow, Seamus's fist crashing through the plaster of the wall behind.

"Don't say you know what love is," Seamus yelled. His hand was broken, but he didn't care. He swung again, trying to claw Tom's face. "First you say you loved that girl who had the vision, now you say you love my mother—you fucking bastard!" He wound up, ready to give it to Tom once and for all, and Tom clocked him. Reeling from the blow, Seamus retched.

"They're the same person," Tom said, catching Seamus in his arms, holding him in a bear hug. Blood was streaming from his nose, and from Seamus's knuckles. Seamus weaved, dizzy and sick.

"What?" Seamus asked, his head spinning.

"Your mother," Tom said, holding him, tears mixing with the blood on his face. "I've loved her my whole life. She's the girl who had the vision. She's a nun, Seamus."

"No, I saw her . . . Bernadette Sullivan . . ."

"Sister Bernadette," Tom said with a sob. "Sister Bernadette Ignatius."

"I don't get it," Seamus said, shaking.

"She joined the convent," Tom said. "That's what her vision was about—making that choice. I let her, Seamus. That's what I'm saying—I didn't fight hard enough. We had you, but she had already made up her mind."

"She became a nun? My mother?" Seamus asked.

Tom nodded. He went to the sink, soaked a dishtowel with cold water. Then he went to the freezer, filled it with ice cubes. Pressing it to the side of Seamus's head, he looked into his eyes. The blueness there shocked Seamus; he saw that exact color and intensity every morning, shaving in front of the mirror.

"I never wanted to hit you," Tom said. "You have a hell of a punch. I thought you were going to kill me."

"I got carried away," Seamus muttered.

"God," Tom said, looking down at Kathleen's postcard. Blood had spattered all over it. Seamus grabbed it, began to wipe it off. Of everything that had just happened—the fight, the news that his mother was a nun, learning that Kathleen lived in the United States—none of it affected him like seeing Kathleen's words obliterated by blood. Seeing that was too much for Seamus, and he bent his head so Tom wouldn't see him crying.

"Seamus," Tom said, his hand on his shoulder, "I'm so sorry."

"It's all I have of her," Seamus said through hot tears.

"No," Tom said. "That's not true. You just said yourself, you love her. You have the deepest connection I've ever heard of."

Seamus held on to her card, eyes closed shut, trying to feel her with him now. It didn't matter whether she was across the Atlantic or right here in Dublin—the fact was, he hadn't seen her in nearly ten years. She still called him James. Their bond had been broken, probably the moment he'd walked away from her on that beach outing, just before her parents came to take her away.

"It's not real," Seamus said. "I've been lying to myself."

"No," Tom said. "It *is* real. That's what I came here to tell you. Don't let her slip away, Seamus. Don't make the mistake I did. If you love her as much as you say you do, go find her."

Seamus didn't look up, just kept staring at the bloodstained postcard he held in his hand.

"Whether you want to hear it or not," Tom said, still holding the ice pack to Seamus's head, "that's why your mother and I came looking for you. Because we love you. We've messed it up as badly as two people can do, but we had to find you, and tell you."

"It's not the same," Seamus whispered. "You weren't in my life.

Kathleen was. She's everything to me. We were everything to each other. . . ."

"You're right," Tom said. "It's not the same at all."

Seamus nodded, shaking, wanting him to go now. As if Tom sensed it, he reached for Seamus's hand so he could hold the ice pack himself.

"You should go to a clinic," Tom said. "Have your hand seen to. I could take you—"

"No," Seamus said. "I'll go myself."

"I'm going to leave now," Tom said. "We're going to fly back to Connecticut on the late flight tonight. Your mother and I." He stopped himself, and Seamus couldn't look at him. He heard Tom trying to pull himself together, hold in whatever it was he wanted to say. "I'm just so glad to have met you," Tom said.

Seamus didn't reply.

"Nothing has ever mattered to me more," Tom said. "Nothing."

"Yeah," Seamus said. "Well . . ."

Tom walked to the door. When he was safely across the room, Seamus looked up. He met his father's eyes. Their gazes locked and held, and Seamus felt his heart pounding hard in his chest. Tom's eyes were blue, clear, gleaming with an emotion Seamus had never seen before. He didn't even know what it was called.

"You go find her," Tom said, his expression changing, hardening.

"I'll think about it."

"I'm leaving this right here," Tom said, reaching into his pocket again, placing a small square of paper on the counter by the door. "It's my cousin's card. Sixtus Kelly. He'll get you a passport overnight. Like you said earlier, the rich get things done."

"I'm not rich. I couldn't pay him."

"He wouldn't take your money. By the time I fly out tonight, Sixtus will have heard all about you. He'll be expecting your call. Do it, Seamus. Get yourself to Newport and find Kathleen."

Seamus found himself staring. "What's that?" he asked, seeing Tom lay something else on the counter.

"The address of Star of the Sea. The phone number is for my cell phone. It doesn't work from Ireland, but it will once you get to the States. You'll get me if you call. And I'll help you find Kathleen."

That was it. Tom took three strides across the floor, shook Seamus's hand. Seamus looked up at him, thinking of a thousand things he suddenly wanted to say. He hated the man who had abandoned him at birth, but he understood the man who stood before him now—he looked like a ghost of someone who had once been in love, who had once loved a woman enough to forsake everything.

"Goodbye, Seamus," Tom said. "Make sure you get that hand looked at." And then he walked through the door and was gone.

Seamus heard his footsteps descending the stairs, fading away. The strangest thing was, he found himself thinking it would have been nice to have Tom drive him to the clinic. It was just a fleeting thought, and Seamus pushed it away. He always took care of himself. But still, it would have been nice to have someone drive him, someone who cared.

Now, holding Kathleen's postcard, Seamus sat back and closed his eyes, his broken hand throbbing. His body quivered from the fight, but it had all gone out of him now. Across the room, on the bookshelf beside his bed, he had an atlas. He knew he could look at it, find Newport, Rhode Island. Find Kathleen...But for now, he just held the Cliff Walk postcard; knowing that she had written it was almost enough.

Sixteen

Tom made an excuse, and the Kellys were understanding about the sudden change of plans. At least that's what Tom told Bernie, before he fell silent and stopped talking. They sat together at the airport, by the gate, waiting for their flight to be called. Bernie wore her black habit and veil, her white wimple, rosary beads hanging from her belt. Tom had arrived at her door to pick her up, given her a disgusted look, helped her with her bags.

"Tom! What happened to you?" she asked, reaching out to touch his face. He had a black eye and bruised cheek, and an obviously broken nose.

"Nothing," he said. "Are you ready?"

"No, I'm not ready! We can't get on a plane like this—you have to go to the hospital!"

"All they'll do there is ice it," he said. "Come on. Let's get out of here."

"Your nose is broken!" And it was, obviously: long and aquiline, it had always had an appealing bump from where he'd broken it once before, when he and John were horsing around as kids. Now the bump was even more prominent, bruised and red. Dry blood streaked his jacket.

"Who cares?" he said. "Look, I got us the last two seats on the last flight. If we're leaving, let's make that plane."

"I'm surprised you're in such a hurry," she said, gazing up at him.

"You said you wanted to go home, Bernie," he said. "When you say you want something, I take you seriously. You don't want to go back to Doolin, we won't go."

"Tom..." she said, touching his arm. But he flinched, pulling away, grabbing her bags.

She had left the key with the Loyola resident advisor, climbed into the waiting car. She'd been afraid it would be one of the Kellys, insisting on driving them to the airport, but she needn't have worried; Tom didn't want to explain things any more than she did, and he'd arranged for a cab to drive them. Nice and anonymous.

Now, at the airport, her mind spun with questions. Mainly, what had happened to Tom? She had to know, but was afraid to ask. He'd gone into the men's room, taken his jacket and shirt off, changed into a blue T-shirt and black windbreaker. When he came back, she saw that the swelling around his eye and cheek had gone up; his eye was nearly swollen shut.

"Who did you fight with?" she pressed.

"What's the difference?" he asked.

"Was it Seamus? You went to see him, didn't you?"

"Yes, I went to see him."

"Why didn't you take me with you?"

Tom gave her a long, cool look that made her squirm with discomfort. He was staring straight through her, regarding her in a whole new way. "Because I had to speak to him privately," he said quietly. "Father to son."

"How did he take it?" Bernie asked.

Tom didn't reply, but raised his eyebrows. His bruised face said it all, and Bernie felt herself blush.

"He did that?"

"We got into it," Tom said.

"Why?"

She watched him attempting to contain himself. She'd known Tom so well for so long, she could read every mood, often know his thoughts before he spoke them out loud. Right now, seeing him try to control his emotions, viewing the cuts and bruises their son had given him, she bowed her head, trembling, afraid of what he was about to say.

"Because he's angry," Tom said. "He hates what we did to him. Who wouldn't? Put him up for adoption, left him in an institution his whole childhood?"

"But we didn't know that would happen," Bernie whispered. "We never intended it. We wanted love for him, Tom. A life with a wonderful family..."

"He didn't get that," Tom said harshly.

"I know." Bernie thought of her meeting with Sister Theodore. She'd told Tom the bare bones of what had happened with Sister Eleanor Marie. "By now, Sister Theodore has probably called the Provincial Superior, told her what Eleanor Marie did to him and Kathleen."

"Bernie," Tom said, "are you that bureaucratic to think it makes one bit of difference? So what if the Provincial Superior finds out? What'll she do? Strip Eleanor Marie of her 'command'? Send her for therapy, to heal her rotten childhood? Who cares, Bernie?"

"Tom," she said, shaking and shocked by his tone.

"Lives were ruined," he said quietly. "Our son's and Kathleen's."

"I know," she whispered.

"I gave him her postcard. A postcard, Bernie! That's all. Nothing can bring their childhoods back, give them the chance to be part of a family." Tom paused, staring into space. Was he seeing their son as a little boy, imagining games of catch, fishing trips, walks along the beach? Bernie blinked, seeing the same things.

"I know," she said, her throat catching. Her head was spinning. Tom had hustled her into the cab so fast, but she'd made him take her past the hotel where Seamus worked. She'd climbed out, walked over to the desk, asked for him.

He wasn't there, of course, so she'd left him a note. She didn't know that he'd want even that, from her. And Tom hadn't told her this until now. What had he been thinking, watching Bernie stand by the bell desk, staring emptily at the row of cars lined up? Her heart had been thumping, she'd thought of all the trips he'd driven, all the people he'd taken around Ireland—her son, and she was leaving, and she couldn't even say goodbye.

She stared over at Tom now, wondering how they could be doing this to each other—it seemed like the latest in a strand of hurts, unintentional maybe, but still, straight to the bone. She had stood at the hotel weeping, and now he sat in the airport silent and empty.

Just then the loudspeaker crackled, and their flight was called. Their seats were all the way at the back of the plane, in the tail section. They lined up with the other passengers, and Bernie felt numb as they inched forward along the jetway. She showed her passport and boarding pass, saw Tom do the same.

"Sir, are you all right?" one of the flight attendants asked with alarm. Tom's face was a mess, and he weaved slightly—as if still dizzy from the punch—keeping his eyes down to keep from looking into curious faces as they made their way to the back of the plane.

Bernie watched as people reacted to her. They always did whenever she flew. Complete strangers would approach her, ask her to bless them, or their babies, or just the flight in general. Others would gaze at her with alarm; she knew that some people considered nuns to be bad luck. As she walked down the narrow aisle, she tried to keep her expression serene.

To disguise the turmoil she felt inside. It was so great, so extreme, she almost thought she should get off the plane. Her heart was beating so hard, twisting with such anguish, she felt sure she'd send the flight off course. If only people could know how human nuns were; how they didn't have any extra answers or powers, even any extra holiness. By the time she got to her seat in the last row, she felt so broken, so wrecked, she could only turn to Tom with wide, beseeching eyes.

"Why are we leaving?" she asked.

"The better question," he said, shoving their luggage into the overhead bins, "is why did we come?"

They sat beside each other. Bernie had the window, and Tom the middle. A stranger had the aisle. He nodded at them once, then pulled eye shades down and went instantly to sleep. Bernie glanced at Tom—tall, rangy, stuck in the cramped middle seat.

"Want to switch?" she asked.

"You like to look out the window," he said.

She nodded her thanks. It was true; she did. Right now, waiting for the plane to push back from the gate, she watched fuel trucks and luggage carts, food service vans and cleaning crews. People buzzed around the tarmac, doing their jobs. She pressed her forehead against the cool glass; in a few moments they would take off. She'd be gazing down at Dublin, as she had just a week earlier, when they'd first arrived.

Everything is different now, she thought. It's both better and worse.

"What you said before," she said, turning to Tom, "when you asked why we came?"

"Yes?" he said.

"We came to find him," she said. "And we did."

"That part's true," Tom said.

"Leaving is so hard," she said. "I didn't think it would be this hard."

He listened, his lips pursed, gazing out with his good eye. The other was swollen shut, angry red.

"That's because you don't live in this world," he said.

"What are you talking about?"

"You don't want to know," he said darkly, evenly.

"I do, Tom," she said. "Tell me."

"You wanted a life of prayer and meditation all those years ago? Well, that's what you've got. You and the Holy Spirit. The rest of us, living here on earth, have to fight it out, Bernie. You didn't think leaving would be this hard, because you've always been able to consign the people you love into the care of God."

She listened, knowing that he was right.

"The rest of us don't have that luxury. For us, it's flesh and blood, dog eat dog. To me, loving someone means carrying them, and feeding them, and holding them when they're scared. God might be up there"—he nodded his head back, tilting up toward the ceiling—"but I'm down here."

"We're all down here," she said. The plane jostled, then began to push back. It pivoted, then bumped slowly into traffic waiting to take off. "We're all human, all the same, Tom."

"Nah," he said, shaking his head. He sounded so bitter, looked so tired.

"Yes," she said stubbornly.

"Bernie, you know what I said before? About Eleanor Marie ruining lives?"

"You said she ruined our son's and Kathleen's."

Tom fixed her with his dark gaze. "She ruined ours, too."

"No," Bernie whispered. "We've had good lives...."

"Tell yourself that if you want to," he said. "And maybe you'll even believe it."

"Tom!"

"We were meant to be together, Bernadette. From the day we first met. You had a vision? Well, so did I. My vision was of a little cottage with a pretty garden. You and me raising our kids. Me working the Academy land, you teaching—you always wanted to be a teacher."

Bernie closed her eyes. The flight attendant had come to the back of the plane. She handed Tom an ice pack, and then began walking up the aisle, looking left and right, making sure everyone had buckled their seatbelts. Tom was right, that she had always wanted to be a teacher. She had started with her younger brother, John, right around the time they'd met Tom Kelly at a summer picnic at Star of the Sea.

The flight attendants took their seats, the captain came on the loudspeaker, told them they were next in line for takeoff. Bernie blessed herself. She sat with her eyes closed. The plane began to taxi down the runway. It picked up speed; she felt the thrust in her lower back. Bernie had always loved to fly. But right now, taking off filled her with sorrow.

Lifting into the air, the plane slowly climbed over Dublin Bay. The sun was setting, but there was a soft golden gleam over the city and surrounding fields. Bernie scanned the ground for the Liffey. There it was, running right past the brick apartment house where she had lived this last week. She blinked, searching southeast Dublin for Merrion Square, and for the convent. She caught sight of a rooftop that might have been O'Malley's: Tir na Nog...

"Where is he?" she whispered.

"What do you mean?"

"Show me now," she said, turning to Tom. "Before we fly out of sight. Where does he live? I want to be able to picture it, find it on a map."

"I can't right now," Tom said. He might have meant because his eye was too swollen, or it might have been something else.

Regardless, Bernie welled up. She stared down at Dublin as the plane banked west, heading across Ireland on its way to the United States. She was leaving her son behind, as she had done once before.

The realization made her shiver, feel so cold. What had Tom and he talked about?

"Do you think he'll ever come to America?" she whispered. "To look for Kathleen?"

"Of course he will," Tom said.

"Did he say so?"

"He didn't have to. It's just the way it is. That's how much he loves her."

Bernie pressed her face to the window again. Dublin was slipping away, its flickering lights left behind, as the plane climbed into the next layer of clouds. Bernie glanced down at her habit. She had taken it off, and she had put it back on. She harbored no illusions about the effect either of those things would have on Tom. She wanted to tell him, but couldn't quite, that putting it back on had been one of the hardest things she'd ever done.

"Tom," she said, turning to look at him. He had pushed his seat back a little, was sitting there with the ice pack on his eye. The way he was sitting, he couldn't see her, and she was glad. She reached toward his face, wanting to touch it. She held her palm open, trembling slightly. Just then he lowered the ice, and she pulled back.

"I have to tell you something," he said.

"Okay," she said.

"I've been thinking about it for a while," he said.

"Sometimes it takes time for thoughts to gain clarity," she said.

"Spoken like a true nun," he said, flashing her a quick, bright smile.

She smiled back, relieved to hear Tom Kelly joking again. But his grin quickly faded, and the seriousness was back on his face.

"I'm leaving the Academy," he said.

For a moment she was confused, thinking she'd heard wrong. "Leaving?"

"Yes," he said. "I'm leaving Star of the Sea."

"But Tom," she said, panicking, "it's your home. It's where you live...we need you."

"I'm just a groundskeeper. There are plenty more like me."

"But you know everything! You know us." She swallowed. "Tom," she said, "you know *me*."

He shook his head, and one stray tear slipped from his bruised, swollen eye. It took him a long time to speak, and when he did, she could barely hear him.

"I thought I did," he whispered without looking at her. "And I wanted to, more than ever. But I don't, Sister Bernadette Ignatius. And I know I never will."

"Tom," she begged, "don't say that. I know you're upset, but you'll change your mind."

He shook his head. "I'm tired," he said. "Let me sleep, okay?"

She couldn't take her eyes off him. She reached for the small pillow wedged beside her hip, tucked it against his head. He left it there for a few moments. But either it was uncomfortable, or he didn't want to touch anything that reminded him of her. He gently lowered the pillow down, slipped it into the seat back in front of him.

The plane flew west, just ahead of the darkness, bringing the night with it, trailing blackness and clouds and millions of stars, including the ones Bernie had named for Tom and their son, over Ireland, over the Cliffs of Moher rising over the open sea. She, who always loved to look out the windows on planes, tonight slid down the plastic shade, blocking all the stars, and that beautiful cliff where it had all begun.

She closed her eyes, praying for Seamus and Kathleen, for Tom and herself: the four lives Tom said had been ruined. She hadn't believed him when he'd first said it, but she did now as the plane flew home across the Atlantic from Ireland, through a night without stars.

PART THREE

Seventeen

"W hat's Seamus like, Aunt Bernie?" Agnes asked.

"Tell us," Cece said. "Is he coming to Connecticut?"

"Do you have any pictures of him?" Regis asked. And then, "What happened to your eye, Uncle Tom?"

"I walked into a door," Tom had said. The whole family oohed, except for John, who just looked across the table with withering pity that Tom couldn't come up with something better than that.

The family had gathered at the Sullivans' house, on the beach side of the Star of the Sea campus, to welcome Bernie and Tom home from Ireland. They had flown into Boston's Logan Airport, driven down to Black Hall in Tom's truck, retrieved from long-term parking. The swelling in Tom's eye had gone down, but it was still black and blue.

Honor had cooked dinner, John had opened a bottle of good wine. Regis had taken the train home from Boston College, even though she'd only been back there for a week and a half. Cece was wide-eyed, wanting to hear every detail about Seamus. Agnes sat beside Brendan McCarthy, her boyfriend. And Sister Bernadette Ignatius sat between Honor and Tom, as frail as a new leaf, trembling in her seat. Tom was pretty sure no one but he and Honor noticed.

"Tell us about him," Regis said.

"We've been dying to hear!" Cece exclaimed.

"Girls," Honor said gently, "give your aunt and Tom a chance to relax. They must be so tired from traveling." She glanced at Bernie with such sensitivity, Tom realized she must have heard some of the story. But her daughters wouldn't let up—they were constitutionally incapable of anything less than total love and enthusiasm when it came to their family members. They practically bounced on their chairs, wanting to hear.

"He's tall," Bernie said, shakily. "And so beautifully handsome."

"Beautifully!" Regis said, grinning.

"He has bright red hair, just like Bernie," Tom said.

"And lovely blue eyes," Bernie said. "Just like Tom."

Her words sliced through him. He felt her watching him, but he couldn't look her way. A dam had broken somewhere inside, and he was a rushing torrent. If he even glanced at her, he'd wash her away—onto the beach, out to sea.

"What does he do?" Agnes asked.

"He's a driver," Bernie said. "For the Greencastle Hotel. He wants to go to law school, though."

"Being a lawyer sounds very Kellyesque," Regis said, laughing. "All except for Tom, that is."

"Working the land like Tom does," Brendan said, "is just as good as being a lawyer."

Tom smiled his thanks. Brendan's red hair and freckles were so like Seamus's. The way the kid moved and laughed, his inflections, the wounded look just behind his blue eyes were all reminiscent of Seamus—but while Seamus had grown up at St. Augustine's, Brendan had been adopted by a couple here in Connecticut.

Meeting Brendan in August had been the catalyst that had sent Tom and Bernie over to Dublin to look for their own son. Seeing him now made Tom's stomach clench. He had promised Brendan a job on the grounds crew, to supplement his work at the hospital, saving money for medical school. But Tom knew that he had another promise to keep as well: the one he'd made on the plane, the one that would take him away from here.

"Does Seamus have a girlfriend?" Agnes asked, holding hands with Brendan.

That question, Tom felt ready to answer. "He loves a girl named Kathleen Murphy."

"Ohh, Kathleen!" Regis said.

"Does she live in Dublin?" Agnes asked.

"Newport, Rhode Island."

"She's American?" Regis exclaimed. "That's great! He'll come over from Ireland to see her, and we'll invite them both here, and we'll all get to know them."

"Tom, is something wrong?" Brendan asked.

Tom shook his head reassuringly, as he would to his own son. Brendan was so eager, but also a little insecure. He'd been so disappointed to find out he wasn't Bernie and Tom's son—that their child, although the same age, had been born in Ireland. What he didn't fully realize yet was that Bernie would hold on tight—she'd love him no matter what, help him in his search to find his real birth parents. That had been Tom's plan, too....

"All is well," Tom said.

"I started working on the grounds when you were gone," Brendan said. "The other guys are nice."

"That's great," Tom said.

"Tom trained them well," Bernie said, fixing Tom with a tentative, hopeful gaze. "He has such a particular way of doing things around here."

"It's a long tradition," John said, giving Tom a light punch on the shoulders. "Kellys and Sullivans rampaging around the grounds of Star of the Sea."

"Yeah, it was a long tradition," Tom said.

Everyone looked at him, hearing something in his voice, taking note of the past tense. He felt the blood rising in his face. Bernie's smile faltered and dissolved. John clued in to the fact Tom needed help fast. He was Bernie's brother, but he was also Tom's best friend.

"Hey, Tom," John said, standing up, "can you step outside for a second? I noticed some pipes are leaking. Let me show you before I forget."

They went out the kitchen door, leaving everyone else to stare after them and wonder what was wrong. It was getting dark. Twilight silhouetted the hills, and a few stars had started coming out. Tom breathed in the salt air, trying to calm himself. John walked him away from the house, up the first hill, toward the old stone wall.

"There aren't any leaking pipes up here," Tom said.

"Nope," John said, stopping at the hilltop so they could lean against the wall and look down at the beach, where long waves rolled in, lacy white spume blowing off in the cool breeze. "Like Brendan asked: is something wrong?"

"I don't know," Tom said, staring out to sea. Looking east, he could see lights blinking seven miles across the Sound, in Orient Point on the North Fork of Long Island. Beyond that was the South Fork, and after that the Atlantic Ocean. Beyond that lay Ireland and Seamus. "I met my son."

"I know," John said. "Man, that's great."

"He didn't want anything to do with us."

"I'm sorry."

Tom shrugged. "I can't really blame him. The fantasy we've been living with all these years, that he grew up in a great Irish family? Didn't come true."

"What do you mean?"

"He spent his childhood in an institution."

At that, John turned to look, incredulous. Tom felt anguish just saying the words—he saw it reflected in his friend's eyes. "How could that have happened?"

"I don't know. It's a combination of a really misguided nun and a stubborn boy, if you can believe that. The nun was Bernie's Novice Mistress, when she first joined up with the order. The stubborn boy..."

"Let me guess," John said. "Your progeny?"

"I don't feel I deserve to call him that," Tom said.

The summer air had turned chilly, and fall was sweeping in.

August's constellations had given way to September's, and the stars hung low in the dark blue sky. Bats flew over the vineyard, catching the last bugs. Soon everything would change. The temperature would continue to fall. Ducks and stripers would migrate south, by air and sea. The grapes would be picked, and the vines would die.

"What did your stubborn boy do?" John asked.

"He fell in love," Tom said in a low voice.

"We both know how that feels."

"Yep."

"Kathleen Murphy?"

"Of Newport, Rhode Island. I gave him a postcard she sent to Sister Anastasia at the Children's Home, and you would have thought I was handing him the Holy Grail. Then I bled all over it, so he couldn't read her writing."

"Damn those doors."

"I didn't walk into a door, as you surmised earlier."

"What did you do—open a vein right then and there?"

Tom shook his head. "We scuffled a little," he said. "Something to do with his not being too thrilled about his mother and me showing up, him making the point he'd be happier if we left him alone."

"I thought your nose looked more crooked than the last time you broke it," John said, peering through the darkness. "Plus, your eye is a mess. The kid landed some good ones."

Tom nodded. "He's done some street fighting, that's obvious."

"Takes one to know one," John said.

"Yeah, there's some of that," Tom said. "He hasn't done things the easy way."

"Like father like son, there again," John said.

"He's slept on the streets," Tom said.

"I know it's not the same thing," John said, "but so have you."

Tom nodded, knowing that John had watched him rebel against the Kelly stronghold—the boarding-school life, and debutante manners, and cotillion nights, and country club ways. He'd hitchhiked away from that, and it hadn't always been pretty. There'd been more than one bar fight along the way.

"What does Bernie think of it all?" John asked.

The question was a punch in the stomach. Just hearing her name—after that flight home, and just now seeing her sit at the family table, looking for all the world like a woman about to fall apart—but knowing she never would—made Tom feel like he might go crazy.

"You wouldn't have recognized Bernie," Tom said. "For one thing, she helped me break into a secret drawer in a locked room in the convent over there. Then she threw her veil on the floor."

"Really? My sister did that?"

"Which part surprises you more? The fact she'd commit B and E, or the thought of her removing her veil?"

"Both, honestly," John said. "Although, in a way, I don't know...all these years I've half expected her to walk away from the convent. I know about her vision, how she chose the religious life. But I also see how she is with my kids. And with the students. She was a great older sister. I'd have said she'd be a great mother. And then there's you."

"What about me?"

John shrugged. Tom looked out over the long stretch of black water, shimmering under the bright autumn stars. It was slow moving and mysterious, and something about it made Tom shiver, and know that whatever his friend was about to say would just make everything harder, just cement the decision he'd made on the plane.

"I've never understood it," John said quietly, staring in the same direction. "Why God did that to her."

"What do you mean?"

"She's such a good person," John said. "So full of love. She would have been great at either thing—being a nun, or having a family. Why the hell did God test her this way?" He turned toward Tom, tried to smile. "You, too. Why'd He test you with all this?"

"You'd better ask a theologian," Tom said. "I can't figure it out. I have to stop trying."

He took a few steps away—not toward the Sullivans' house, where dinner was still going on, but in the opposite direction, toward the river, where his own cottage was located.

"Do me a favor?" he asked. "Tell everyone I had to fix those broken pipes. I'm heading home."

"Come on," John said. "The girls are so glad to see you. Brendan, too. He's so happy you've asked him to work with you here. Watch it, or he'll change his mind about going to medical school and go into landscaping instead."

"I think maybe Brendan would be better off finding another role model," Tom said. "I'm leaving."

"Skipping dinner? Fine, then. But—"

"Nope," Tom said. "I'm leaving Star of the Sea."

"Tom!"

"Brendan will be fine—you know Bernie will do everything she can for him."

"I'm not talking about Brendan—I'm talking about you."

Tom just shook his head and started walking away. He knew John wouldn't follow—there'd be time for a better explanation later, along with a request for help. Tom had a few plans about what he wanted to do next, but he couldn't really depart without knowing Brendan and the Academy were in good hands.

And Bernie. He couldn't leave without knowing her brother would look after her. She'd say she was in the care of God, and that was fine and true. But Tom was a man, and he thought in human terms, and he knew he had to make sure Bernie had John to turn to once he left this place. Not for her peace of mind; for his.

The Greencastle concierge desk was bustling with people wanting restaurant reservations and tickets to the Abbey and Gate theaters, but Seamus wedged his way to the back counter and quickly logged on to one of the computers. The hotel never minded him checking his e-mail or doing a quick Internet search, and he'd been burning to do this ever since Tom Kelly had left his apartment.

"Seamus, what happened to your hand?" Matthew Killian, the head concierge, asked, during a short lull between customers.

"I slammed it in a door," he said. He'd been ready with the story ever since he'd been to the clinic.

"Not getting into any fights, I hope," Matthew said kiddingly.

"No, not at all! Just a close call with the Mercedes."

"Well, take care of it," Matthew said. "You're my best driver. I don't want to lose you to carelessness or those heavy German doors."

Seamus flushed. He never wanted to seem ungrateful or disloyal, for the Greencastle had been so generous with him. But staring at the computer screen, typing slowly with his good hand, Seamus knew that lose him they would. And soon.

Tom Kelly couldn't give him much, but he'd passed on that postcard. Seamus Googled "Newport," "the Cliff Walk," and "Kathleen Murphy," and got hundreds of hits. When he looked at Google Earth, an image of Newport came up. He homed into it on the computer screen, the picture zooming into focus.

It was as if he were a spaceman, circling the globe. He watched the earth get closer, moving from Ireland, across the Atlantic Ocean. There was Rhode Island, the smallest state in the union, way up in the Northeast between New York and Boston.

Lots of Irish lived in those two cities; plenty of older friends had gone over, taking jobs as gardeners or domestics. Now, with the Irish economy what it was, there was more money to spare, and they were applying to college or graduate school. The cities were filled with Hibernian transplants.

Maybe Newport was, too. As Google Earth got clearer and closer, he saw the ocean spreading out before him, the points of land as rocky and craggy as those in Kerry, as if the two places had been torn apart by the Ice Age. The picture got smaller, and Newport slid into sharp focus: there, right on the computer screen, was nearly an identical view of the town as on Kathleen's postcard.

"What's that you're looking at?" Matthew asked, leaning to see.

"Newport, Rhode Island," Seamus said.

"Ah," Matthew said. "Lots of money there."

"Do you think they have a Greencastle?"

"No. But there are other fine hotels, I'm sure. Why, Seamus? Are you thinking of moving to America?"

"There's a girl I know there," Seamus said, not wanting to lie or say more.

"Ah. A girl," Matthew said.

Just then Kevin came in, to tell Seamus his car was clean and ready to go pick up his passenger at the airport. Seamus quickly logged off, thanked Matthew for letting him use the computer. Kevin had heard the exchange, and he grinned as they walked through the hotel's front doors toward the line of cars.

"What are you smiling about?" Seamus asked, scowling.

"Eily's bet me you'll meet back up with Kathleen before the wedding," Kevin said.

"It would be a long shot," Seamus said.

"Well, that couple gave you her postcard," Kevin said. "Even if you did have to go and bleed on it."

"He bled, not me."

"He seemed nice," Kevin said. "They both did. When I told them you'd left them a note, they looked so happy. Overjoyed. You'd have thought you offered them the seats to Randi-Lu O'Byrne instead of me."

"Yeah, well," Seamus said. His hand was throbbing. It bothered him to think of Tom Kelly and Bernadette Sullivan looking so happy, *overjoyed*, before reading his letter. They hadn't had any idea what was inside. They'd been filled with hope. He had dashed that, all right. And he didn't even feel bad about it.

Or not *very* bad, anyway. They had brought it on themselves, coming to see him. What had they expected, after all? Jesus, how could they have thought he'd be happy? It was difficult, at best. That's what it was. The nun—he couldn't call her his mother—Sister Bernadette—had left him a note on her way out of town. It had been in Seamus's cubbyhole here, and he'd read it quickly. "Dear Seamus," it said. "Be well. Know that you are loved. Always, Bernadette." *Loved.* He'd stuck the note in his wallet, although he should have thrown it out.

He reached into his pocket with his good hand, felt the edge of Kathleen's postcard. This was something worth reading. Tom Kelly had given it to him. He was grateful for that, at least. It made him feel he owed them something. Not a lot—not anything like affection, or wanting to get to know each other, or get together at that place in Connecticut he'd mentioned—Star of the Sea? That was it, the name of the Academy where his mother—Jaysus!—where his mother was a nun.

"You okay to drive with that hand?" Kevin asked.

"Sure. It's not a problem at all."

"Thanks again for those tickets," Kevin said. "Eily loved the show. Now she wants to go to Nashville for our honeymoon, see Randi-Lu again. She can't believe she was staying here at the hotel, and you got to drive her."

"She was pretty nice," Seamus said, thinking of that song on her CD. "Big Love" . . .

"Well, see you later," Kevin said. "End of shift, maybe we can grab a pint."

"Maybe," Seamus said, heading for his car.

He climbed into the Mercedes, stuck Randi-Lu's CD into the player. He skipped the first two tracks, went straight to "Big Love." As he started out of the parking lot, he noticed Sixtus and Billy Kelly driving in.

His father's cousins. Seeing them nearly made Seamus drive off the road. His heart was beating so fast, he had to pull himself together. What was it Tom had said? That if Seamus wanted to get a passport, Sixtus would be willing to help him, that he'd be waiting for Seamus's call.

Newport, Rhode Island, Seamus thought, driving away, watching the Kellys in his rearview mirror. That's where Kathleen lived.

It might be half a world away, but as Tom had said, all he had to do was get on a plane. "Big Love" played on the stereo, and Seamus's heart began to pound.

Eighteen

The granite buildings, Gothic in architectural style and stature, were clustered at one end of a long gravel road running straight in from Route 156, through two imposing stone posts, one bearing the sign *Star of the Sea Academy.*

Francis X. Kelly had donated his estate to the Sisters of Notre Dame des Victoires, so what had once been his family dining room was now the nuns' refectory; the children's bedrooms were used for boarding students; the wing that had once been the site of so many family parties and gatherings was now the cloister, where the contemplatives lived. Devoutly Catholic, Francis X. Kelly had had a chapel built for his family. It was small and intimate, filled with rows of oak benches, and very dark. The only light came through blue stained-glass windows, created by a master of the craft in Rouen, France. A cross topped the austere spire; the chapel was now used for daily mass and prayers, by the nuns and all the girls who attended the school.

The campus was nestled at the very foot of the Connecticut River Valley, where the great river opened into Long Island Sound. On the river side, there were golden marshes, a haven for waterfowl. Along the Sound was a pristine white sand beach, lapped by gentle waves and scoured by the sea wind.

The land was covered with grapevines. Twenty acres were devoted to chardonnay, five to merlot, and three to pinot noir. The nuns taught school, but they also worked the vineyard. During the spring, they would train the vines onto trellis wires. Buds would form, tiny clusters emerge. Summer was devoted to repositioning the vines along the wire, cutting and pruning to optimize growth, and making sure they got enough water. By late September, the scent of ripe grapes spiced the air, and the nuns prepared for the harvest.

The Academy's gentle hills were crisscrossed by beautiful, intricate stone walls built by workers the Kellys had brought over from Ireland in the late eighteen hundreds. Among them was Cormac Sullivan, great-grandfather of Sister Bernadette Ignatius—head of the school for years.

Today, an afternoon in late September, the hills of Star of the Sea were washed in butterscotch sunlight. It spread over the hayfields and vineyard, the marsh and tributaries; it made the stone walls glisten. The air was crisp, with a sharp breeze off the Sound. Girls in their navy blue blazers and plaid skirts ran back and forth between buildings, on their way to class or sports.

Sister Bernadette Ignatius stepped out of her office, into the bright light. She blinked, looking around. Two fourth-grade girls flew past, waving. "Hi, Sister!" they called. One of her nieces, Cecilia Sullivan, hurried to catch up with them.

Bernie waved to all three girls, heading across the courtyard toward the beach. Running this place took all her attention; in fact, she needed twice as many hours in the day just to keep from going backwards. With students in grades K through 12 to oversee, novices to observe, teachers to supervise, grades to review, seniors to advise, and the entire physical plant that was Star of the Sea Academy, she had her hands full. Even now, something had come up, and she needed an answer right away.

If she were the art teacher, where would she be? Honor Sullivan, her best friend and sister-in-law, was also in charge of the school's art department. Bernie knew Honor's favorite painting spot, so she made for it now. On the way, she saw hedges that needed trimming, stones that had tumbled from walls, weeds that had sprung up along the edge of the path. She swallowed hard, trying not to get upset.

Cresting one low hill, she saw Honor and her students halfway up the next. Bernie followed the stone wall down. She hurried along, her veil blowing out behind her. Honor hadn't yet seen her; she was walking slowly among her students, bending over to admire their watercolors, offer suggestions. Bernie watched how the girls focused on their work, dipping their brushes in small bottles of water, trying to capture the scene.

"Excellent work, girls," Honor called. "Now's a good time to notice the quality of light we have here at Star of the Sea . . . isn't it amazing? Well, if you think so, you're in good company. Back around the turn of the last century, when the Black Hall art colony came into being, many artists were attracted to these hills for the light."

"The American Impressionists?" Megan Bailey asked, sitting cross-legged, leaning against the wall.

"And the Tonalists?" Heather McDonough called from up the hill.

"Yes," Honor replied. "Both groups. Very good . . . the Tonalists, the Barbizon School, believed the light we have in Black Hall was very like the light they'd found near Fontainebleau and Barbizon in France. It's very special and elusive . . . wonderful for artists. Can you tell me why?"

"It makes the landscape come alive," Agnes Sullivan said. Bernie hung back, waiting to hear her niece say more. Honor and John's middle daughter was shy and spiritual, as talented an artist as both her parents. A student in her mother's class, Agnes liked to stick close to home, Bernie knew, embracing her deeply felt kinship to the shoreline community.

"Alive? What do you mean?" Jenny Kilcoman asked. "I see rocks and grass and grapevines."

Agnes hesitated, always shy about speaking. But because her love for art was so great, and because she was a teenaged mystic who saw the Spirit everywhere, she couldn't hold it back. "The light moves," she said. "It changes every second—depending on the time of day, and whether there are clouds or not. It's different at every time of year. So what it touches changes right along with it. Like that stone wall." She pointed. "It glimmers like silver when the sun is bright, but it's black and grave when the sun goes behind a cloud."

Turning toward her own easel, Honor spotted Bernie standing on the path. Honor wore camel hair pants and sweater, with one of John's old shirts thrown on as a painting smock. The sleeves were rolled up, the front streaked with paint. Her light brown hair was tied back in a ponytail, and she wore a ball cap.

"Hello," Honor said, smiling and walking over.

"Painting *en plein air* today?" Bernie asked.

"Yes," Honor said, looking happily around. "This day is too beautiful to stay in the studio. I'm so glad you found the chance to get outside, too. I know how busy you've been."

Bernie nodded. "Yes . . . start of term, harvest ready to start, and the whole place falling apart."

"Falling apart?" Honor asked, keeping her expression neutral.

"Yes," Bernie said. "The high winds during that storm over the weekend knocked two limbs down from the sugar maple behind the cloister. One branch came right over the wall, nearly hitting a novice."

"Is she okay?"

Bernie shrugged. "She's taking it as a *sign*. To rethink her vows. Last I heard, she was on the phone with her mother in Norwalk."

"Signs can be very powerful," Honor said mildly.

Bernie gave her a sharp glance, looking for hidden meaning. But Honor didn't react. "Anyway," Bernie said, "the reason I came looking for you was to ask if you and John will help out with the grape harvest. It's this weekend, and there's so much to do, and with Tom gone . . ." She trailed off.

"Of course we'll help," Honor said. "Have you heard from him?"

Bernie shook her head. "No, and I don't expect to. The whole point of his leaving was to sever ties. I thought maybe you had heard from him."

"I haven't," Honor said. "Maybe John has, but if so, he hasn't mentioned it."

"I know it's for the best," Bernie said, staring at the hillside dotted with young artists. They were all far enough away that they couldn't hear what she was saying.

"Why is it for the best?" Honor asked softly. "This was Tom's home. He loved it here. He's been caretaker forever.... I know he felt he was carrying on his great-grandfather's love for the land."

"He just felt it was time for him to move on. To go somewhere new," Bernie said. "I'm just surprised he left Brendan . . . they'd gotten very close."

"Maybe he's still in touch with Brendan. I doubt he'd just abandon him, Bernie."

"No," Bernie said. "He wouldn't do that."

"You're devastated, aren't you?" Honor said. "That he left?"

Bernie tried to shake her head.

Honor raised her eyebrow. She gave Bernie a long, questioning stare, letting her know that she wasn't buying it. Ever since their return from Ireland, Bernie and Tom had had to face the reality of their relationship. It was a friendship—no, wait, it was a thwarted love affair. It was pure—they'd kept it so, all these years, since Bernie had taken her vows. Or had they?

"You can't answer my question," Honor said.

"I don't know how to feel," Bernie said. "In some ways, it's a relief to not see him every day. Not to see him doing his hard work, and know how disappointed he was that . . ."

"That he couldn't be with you the way he wanted."

Bernie nodded. That was hard to admit, to say, even to her closest friend.

"And it got even more intense after Ireland," Honor said. "After Seamus."

The mention of his name did something to Bernie. She felt all that soft golden light—flowing over the land, the vineyard, and walls—trickle across her skin, her hands and face, making her melt, start to cry.

"Yes, it did," Bernie said, holding back tears so the girls wouldn't see. "I'm not sure what I expected. I prayed for a healing—for all three of us. Myself, Tom, and Seamus. I've held such anger at myself for so long for making such a mistake, creating a life that I then abandoned. I think I wanted to be let off the hook. To see that he was healthy and happy."

"You said Seamus was healthy," Honor said. "And relatively happy."

"He's incredible," Bernie said. "To think of what he's overcome."

"He sounds it," Honor said.

"It just undid Tom, though," Bernie said. "He's so compartmentalized—I've always known it. The way he was able to live here, on campus, going about his duties as caretaker and groundskeeper, pretending there'd never been anything between us."

"Do you *really* think he pretended that?" Honor asked softly, with great patience, as if Bernie were a naive, somewhat misguided student.

"I think he had to," Bernie said stubbornly.

"Bernie," Honor said, "you can't honestly believe that was possible for him?"

"Then how," Bernie asked, feeling as if she were falling, "could he *stand* it?"

"How could *you* stand it?" Honor asked.

"Prayer," Bernie said. "That we could both come to love and accept the divine within ourselves. To quote Martin Buber, 'All real living is meeting.' Isn't that so true?"

"Bernie," Honor said. "Could we please leave Martin Buber out of it?"

Bernie glanced over, shocked by the vehemence in Honor's tone. She saw her dear, oldest friend shaking her head with great exasperation.

"You're being a nun," Honor said.

"That's what Tom always used to say," Bernie said, gazing into the middle distance. The golden light seemed to hover in the air, holding particles of dust and pollen and salt spray. She heard waves breaking on the beach, just over the rise.

"Well, he had a point," Honor said. "Sometimes you see everything through the prisms of the spirit and the intellect...it distances you from life down here in the trenches."

"Believe me," Bernie said in a low voice, "I feel very much in the trenches right now."

"Which part, Bern? You've barely talked about it at all, since you've gotten home. The part about meeting your son? Or the part about taking off your habit for two days?"

"How do you know about that?" Bernie asked, her head jerking back to look at Honor.

"Tom told John."

"I thought you said you didn't know where he was!"

"I don't. This was before he left. Your first day or so back, while he was packing up his things."

"What did he say?"

"John went over to try to find out what was going on. Tom told him about Seamus, and St. Augustine's, about that nun, he called her your nemesis...."

"Eleanor Marie," Bernie said.

"Right. And then he told John how you'd stopped wearing your habit after you finally got Seamus's file. He said that he'd looked into your eyes, known that you were questioning your vows. No, more than that. He said that you knew."

"Knew what?" Bernie whispered.

"That you wanted to be with him. With them," Honor said. "Tom and Seamus."

Bernie shook her head, closing her eyes. "He was wrong."

"About which part?"

"There's no being 'with' Seamus," she said. "He's a grown man now. He doesn't need his mother and father to raise him—he's already raised."

"That's not what Tom said," Honor said gently. "He wasn't talking about the reality of what should happen...he was talking about what you *wanted* to happen. They're different, Bernie. Don't you get that?"

Of course Bernie got it. She understood the difference between a deep desire and life's reality extremely well. Over the years, when her students, the nuns, or her spiritual directees would come to her with a dilemma, hashing over in their minds the terrible and wonderful choices of life, she would always tell them to listen deeply.

That was really it, her message as a nun and a child of God: listen deeply to your heart. That was how and where God communicated with people. Not so much in burning bushes or on mountaintops, in blue grottos or apparitions of the Virgin Mary, but more often in the depths of their own hearts.

Bernie's throat closed, remembering how she'd passed by Tom's cottage that night just before he left. Located on the far end of the property, it overlooked the salt marsh and the banks of the river. He had the windows open, and she'd stood just outside, watching him fold his clothes, take books down from his shelves, box up his papers. She had held herself back, not knowing what to say, wanting to find a way to tell him to stay.

Her own heart had been so broken. Twenty-three years ago, when she'd made her choice to come here as a novice, Tom had stayed quietly beside her, supporting her and helping her believe that her reasons— whether he agreed with them or not—had merit.

Now he had reached his limits. Whatever strength it had taken for him to stay close, let her find her way, was depleted. Or maybe he'd found new strength—the inner conviction he needed to pack up and move on.

"Bernie, Tom saw you put your habit away and thought that meant that you finally knew you wanted to be with him."

"He said that to John?"

"Of course he did. And Bernie, I love you—you're my best friend. I know you pretty well. So don't tell me, please don't try to tell me, that you weren't thinking that. Or, at least, that you didn't realize he'd *think* you were thinking that."

"Honor! I took the habit off because I didn't want it to shade my meeting with my son! I didn't want him to see me as a nun before I had the chance to tell him I was his mother!"

Honor nodded. She reached for Bernie's hand with her own paint-streaked ones, clasped it tight. "I'm sure you did. I can understand your thinking about that. But aside from Seamus, can't you see what it must have been like for Tom? And Bernie—I swear I'm not trying to give you a hard time here. But didn't you maybe want something yourself?"

It was a testament to how much Bernie loved and trusted Honor, that she didn't just turn and walk away. "Want what?" she asked.

"Well, a life with Tom," Honor said. "That's what."

"I gave that up a long time ago," Bernie said. She looked long and hard into Honor's eyes, saw skepticism brewing. Then, checking her watch, she backed away. "I'd better get back—I have a call in to Admissions at Princeton. Monique Blaschka wants to apply early decision, and I want to check out the lay of the land. Anyway, thanks for saying that you and John will help with the harvest."

"Anything for our Bernie," Honor said, giving her a big hug.

Bernie held on a few seconds before letting go. When she looked out at the hillside, she saw several of the students watching. She knew that there were school administrators who would never show their feelings in front of students, keep up a front of imperviousness to human emotion. Not Bernie. She knew to the depths of her being that the greatest lesson she could teach her students was that of love: the ability to open their hearts to the world and each other.

Perhaps that had been Tom Kelly's legacy, she thought. Having him so close by all these years had reminded her that God's love came through people: the quiet eloquence of his backbreaking work, the way he'd respected her choices and decisions, the times he'd served as her sounding board on everything from trouble with the new irrigation system to a student injured in a soccer game.

"You okay?" Honor asked now.

"I'm fine," Bernie said. "I'm glad we talked. Wherever Tom is, I'm sure he made the right choice. I wish him nothing but the best."

"Uh-huh," Honor said, raising that eyebrow again as she turned back to her painting class.

Bernie caught Agnes's eye just before she walked away. Her middle niece was, in some ways, her closest. There had been times Bernie had wondered if Agnes had a vocation. But then Brendan McCarthy had come along and, at least temporarily, thrown that off track.

Although Tom was gone, Brendan remained on the grounds crew. Bernie saw him now, on the next hill, working in the vineyard. His bright red hair gleamed in the sunlight. Her stomach fell, as if she had just started on the downhill side of a roller coaster.

Agnes and Brendan were signaling each other. Bernie watched as she walked slowly away. She saw Agnes flash a silver paint tin and Brendan signal back with the blade of his pocketknife. She thought of young love, how it thrived on these hills: Honor and John, Bernie and Tom, now Agnes and Brendan.

Then she thought of another red-haired young man, all the way across the sea. Hurrying back to her office, she tried to listen deeply to her own heart, but all she could think about was how empty it felt.

Nineteen

That night, after Cece went to bed and Agnes settled at the kitchen table, writing an English paper, Honor made some coffee and brought it to John in the studio. He hunched over a drafting table, sketching out plans for his next project. Sisela, their old white cat, lay sprawled across the surface; he worked around her.

Honor stood back, watching him. He wore black jeans and a blue chambray work shirt, his dark hair was short and shot with gray, and even in the dim light, she could see the lines in his face. He had aged during his time in prison.

So had she, during his time away. Missing someone that badly for that long did something terrible inside. It encased the heart in stone, made it almost impossibly too heavy to carry. But when she looked at him now, so grateful to have him back home, she felt as if the opposite was happening: they were both growing younger. Their hearts were free again.

"Coffee?" she asked, stepping out of the shadows.

"Thanks," he said, looking up. "Did I hear the phone ring before?"

"Yes—it was Regis. She's thinking about coming down for the weekend."

"Get her to bring her roommates and friends," he said. "They can help with the harvest."

"Good idea," Honor said. "But don't you think it's a little odd, that she wants to come home again so soon? She just went back to college, and she was already here for Bernie and Tom's homecoming...."

"I think she wants to check up on everyone," John said, absently petting Sisela. "Make sure we're all still together."

John was a sculptor and photographer, known for working on a grand scale. He worked with ice floes and fallen trees, canyon walls and cliff edges. His last work had been a labyrinth, built right here on the beach, from the remnants of an Ice Age boulder he'd destroyed in one night of passion and rage; the sculpture before that had been a soaring chapel built of driftwood, granite rubble, and an iron cross, installed on the cliffs of Ballincastle, in West Cork. With their daughter Regis standing right there, a man had attacked it and them, and John had gone to jail for killing him.

For six years, Regis had kept the secret of that day locked inside. She hadn't told a soul what had happened, because she hadn't been able to remember. Trauma had taken a toll on their family, and it wasn't really until their last trip to Ireland, at summer's end, when Regis had been able to face the judge and tell the truth.

She'd broken up with her fiancé Peter, and headed off to her sophomore year at Boston College. Honor knew that her nightmares, of what had really happened at Ballincastle, had helped her break through, somehow guided her toward a new stage of healing. But the experience had left Regis, the daughter most likely to follow in her daredevil father's footsteps, more tentative and insecure than Honor had ever seen her.

"You're worried about her?" John asked now.

"Not really," Honor said. "She seems to be doing really well. But I think you're right about why she wants to come home."

"To check on us?"

Honor nodded, sipping her coffee. "All of us," she said. "Because we're not *really* all together."

"Ah. Are you referring to the elusive Thomas Kelly?"

"Yep," Honor said.

"Guess he finally got tired of hanging around my sister, hoping she'd break her vows."

"John, you make it sound so..."

"So futile? So crazy? So like a pipe dream?" he asked, holding the coffee mug between his two hands. The nights were chilly, with a steady breeze coming off the water. The crickets were silent, replaced by the low, throaty call of geese flying overhead; the fall migration was under way. "Think about it. My sister took religious vows, but Tom's been just as celibate. He might as well have become a priest."

"Where is he now?" Honor asked.

"I'm not really sure," John said. It wasn't so much the tone of his voice as the way he wouldn't meet her eyes that made Honor think he was being evasive.

"Come on," she said. "I know you're in touch with him."

"Maybe," John said.

"Then tell me!"

"I swear, I don't know," he said, smiling, pulling her close. "He didn't give me the details. All I know is, it has to do with Seamus."

"Seamus, their *son*?" Honor asked. "But he's in Ireland; Bernie told me he said he never wanted to hear from them again."

"That's what he said," John said. "But since when did something as blatant as a nun's vows or a kid's demand to be left alone ever keep Tom from hoping?"

"He didn't go back to Dublin, did he?"

John shook his head. "No, I can tell you that much. He said something about 'paving the way' for Seamus. Not sure exactly what he meant beyond that."

"Maybe Seamus is coming over," Honor said, her eyes shining. "Oh, I'd love so much to meet him. Can you imagine Bernie, if that happened?"

"I'm almost afraid to," John said.

"What do you mean?" Honor asked.

John stared down at his drafting table, line drawings he'd done of one huge boulder and what looked like a ring of Christmas trees. Sisela stretched, jumped down, ran away. John took a long drink of coffee, then raised his eyes to Honor's. Sometimes she felt so glad to have him home, she almost couldn't bear it.

"My sister can seem so strong," he said. "Act so tough. She's got that sense of justice, of doing battle for the cause, for God. It's what makes her get up in the morning, run this place like a Navy ship, never let anything get to her. But *this* is killing her."

"I know," Honor said. "Of course."

"Not just meeting Seamus. I know she's been moving toward that this whole time, and even now, I'm sure she's trying to figure out a way to have a relationship with him. I think between her prayers and persistence, she's working that out. But Tom's another story."

"He always has been, when it comes to Bernie."

"Too much so," John said. "It wasn't honest, when you get right down to it."

"How can you say that?" Honor asked, leaning back, stepping slightly away.

The studio was spacious and dark, except for the circle of light over John's drafting table. Tall windows along the north wall reflected the lamplight, and outside the wind blew, making leaves rustle overhead.

"Bernie can't admit certain things to herself," John said.

"She's extremely self-aware and totally honest," Honor said, loyal to her best friend.

John shook his head, using his pencil to shade some areas on his sketch, frowning as he worked, as if he were thinking thoughts he didn't want to say.

"What, John?"

"I'm not sure."

"Try. I know she's your sister, and you love her. But so do I…"

"I know," he said. He looked over, met Honor's eyes. She saw in his face the young man she had fallen in love with, right here at Star of the Sea. They were a couple, and so were Bernie and Tom. Honor had been touched that John and his older sister had been so close.

"She was just an ordinary girl," he said. "I mean, to me, she made the sun rise. She was the greatest sister. But she seemed—I don't know, just like everyone else. Normal, I guess. She prayed more than

I did, went to mass more regularly. But art was my church, so it didn't take much…"

Honor nodded. It was true that John met God through his work. Loving nature, being out in the wild, vulnerable to the elements, many miles from other human beings. In some ways, his spirituality had always seemed more extreme and austere than his sister the nun's.

"We were just run-of-the-mill Catholics. Who doesn't imagine becoming a nun or a priest? When we were little, we used to play at it."

"Communion made from little circles of Wonder Bread," Honor said, remembering how her friends had played, too.

John nodded. "Bernie would never play with us. She'd just shake her head, as if she didn't want to take the sacraments lightly. And her eyes would get that glow…."

Honor knew what he was talking about. A clarity in her eyes, as if she was seeing so much more than the rest of them. Even during times of stress, like when John had gone to prison, she had exuded a sense of peace. Honor had spent a lot of time with Bernie during those years, because she'd made her feel everything would be all right.

"When she started going out with Tom," John said, "I just thought that was it. They'd be together forever. I figured he'd be my brother-in-law."

"I thought that, too," Honor said. It was all so mysterious. For her, whose greatest dream had always been to marry John, raise their kids, be an artist, Bernie's choice to join the convent had at first seemed shocking.

"That's the part I'm not sure she's ever really been honest about," John said. "She joined the convent, but she never really let go of Tom. And he never really let go of her."

"Well, he's letting go of her now," Honor said sadly, gazing toward the tall windows.

John reached for her now, pulled her to him. They kissed in the big dark studio, holding each other and feeling how close they'd come to losing each other. Love was so deep and powerful, a couple could think it would last forever. But life was a series of surprises, each one catching them off guard. It wasn't so much what happened, but the way people reacted, that determined the future.

John turned off the light and came back to slip his arms around Honor again. His kiss was so hot, and the wind blowing against the north windows was so chilly. They held hands, walking each other through the dark of their studio, down the hall, and into their bedroom.

When they closed the door behind them, they were alone together. Honor knew that she had never wanted anyone, or anything, more than this. Her husband undressed her on the bed they had bought the year they got married. Her body arched with desire, his hand caressed her. She knew his touch by heart, yet it surprised her every time.

The fact that they had almost lost each other made every second more precious. She reminded herself of that every day. But right now, time blurred, and her thoughts drifted away. Making love, she and John were together forever. They always had been, and they always would be, and she knew it, because her skin was his and his skin was hers, and they melted together under the covers of their old bed.

Kathleen Murphy couldn't sleep. The attic of Oakhurst had been so hot during the summer, but now autumn's chill seeped through the uninsulated roof and walls, through windows badly in need of caulking. A stiff wind rattled the panes, making her jump, sit straight up in bed.

She was alone on the top floor. Except for Beth, her fellow help had all left Newport, and Beth lived "out," with her boyfriend, in an apartment on Spring Street. Miss Langley had gone with Wendy and her family back to Manhattan, for the start of school. Samantha had returned with June and her children to Rhinebeck, where India was in her first month of kindergarten. And Bobby the chauffeur was now living in the carriage house—which suited Kathleen just fine, after that night last month when he'd stumbled upstairs so drunk he could barely walk, came into her room, and pretended he thought it was his own. She'd fought him off just fine—a lamp to the side of his lecherous head. Taught him a lesson...

Hearing the wind whistle under her door, she almost thought someone was calling her name. The sound came from behind the boarded-up door across the hall. Kathleen knew the family ghosts lived in there; she had haunted the place herself on one or two occasions. That's how she'd learned the truth about Louise. Asking Pierce about her had gotten her a cold stare, and then he'd ignored her for three days. But Kathleen had found out herself, one afternoon off, when she'd pried off one of the boards, squeezed underneath, and let herself into the secret attic....

But the voice she heard tonight didn't belong to Louise or anyone else from the Wells family. This was a ghost of Kathleen's past. She heard the faintly whistling wind, coming through cracks in the wall, and could swear it was calling her name. Oh, she felt him coming for her—he'd never stopped needing her, any more than she had him. The hair on the back of her neck stood on end; but instead of pulling the covers more tightly around her, she jumped out of bed, flung open the door.

"James!" she whispered. Peering up and down the dark hall, she could swear she heard his voice.

But he wasn't there. She stood still in her white nightgown, looking left and right. Her senses were finely tuned. They always had been, ever since St. Augustine's. Sister Anastasia used to pick her up, rock her sometimes. She'd whisper in her ear, "Why are you still awake, little one? Who are you watching for?"

Sister Anastasia had said she was "vigilant." Kathleen knew that was right. She was always on guard. Nothing got past her. If something happened, it was because she wanted it to.

Well, most things, anyway.

Standing in the drafty hall, she wondered whether Pierce would come up to see her tonight. The family was still in Newport, and would be for a few more days, before they went to Palm Beach for the winter. Trust funds were vile curses or wonderful things, depending on one's perspective. They allowed grown men to stay boys forever. Shivering, Kathleen knew that it was warmer downstairs—every bedroom had a heating duct, and forced hot air made them warm and cozy.

Sometimes she wished Pierce would take her to his warm feather bed, let her stay with him there, in the toasty heat, instead of freezing up here. She could easily slip out before dawn, get back upstairs before his parents woke up. But except for that first time, they had never been together in his quarters. He liked to sneak up here when he felt like it—without any real rhyme or reason, or planning, or courting. He'd just come up in the dark, lie down on top of Kathleen, kiss her with his eyes closed, get busy with what he'd come for.

Standing in the darkened hall, Kathleen hated herself for harboring any romantic notions about such an obvious cad. As she'd once told Andrew, she used to believe in fairy tales. Not that the poor servant girl could make the prince fall in love with her if she was pretty, smart, and sexy enough; if she let him do anything he wanted, things his Social Register debutantes would never dream of. That was no fairy tale.

No, Kathleen's fairy tale had always been about James; that he'd find her somehow. Never stop looking for her, no matter how long it took... Her spirit was stretched so thin, though. Her heart was turning to stone, a little bit at a time. These cold nights in the attic, wishing for Pierce's loveless visits, were destroying her. She loathed herself for desiring—not him, but the feeling of his arms around her shoulders. So that even if James did find her, it might be too late.

Kathleen might already be lost....

Hearing voices downstairs now, she crept closer to the staircase to listen. It was dear Andy, saying good night to his mother.

"Darling, if only you wouldn't drink quite so much," Mrs. Wells said. "I'm not saying you should stop entirely, even though Dr. Malahyde seems to think it would be a good idea."

"Mother, I'll get a liver transplant."

"That's not funny, Andrew! Prevention, that's what you should be thinking. You've seen your brother at parties, dear. The way he has *one* cocktail and makes it *last*. That's what you should do."

"He doesn't care as much as I do," Andrew said sadly.

"Care? What does caring have to do about anything?" his mother asked, as the impatience she'd been suppressing came pouring forth. "I don't like oversensitivity, and you know it. Yes, the world is a cold, cruel place. But wallowing in it will just ruin you. Do you see me sniveling over your father's situation? No."

"Doesn't it hurt you, that he goes to her every weekend?"

"I don't even think about it, Andrew. And you shouldn't either. It's just what men do. You might feel better if you..."

"I'm not like that," Andrew said. "And I wouldn't want to be. The way Dad and Pierce are with women?"

"No. You just get drunk every night, watching reruns of *Law & Order* while life goes on without you. Other people your age are wearing gowns and tuxedos, having delightful times, while you lie on the sofa in *sweatpants*."

Listening upstairs, Kathleen could practically see Mrs. Wells cringe as she said the words. Everything in the Wells world was supposed to be beautiful, elegant, without mess or fuss or rough edges. Women were to be wives, or hidden off to the side. Parties went on all night, on torchlit paths leading to white tents, or under crystal chandeliers in Belle Époque ballrooms, or on curved stone terraces overlooking the shining sea. People had titles—Princess this, Countess that.

And the help lived in the attic, without heat, waiting for their lovers to sneak up the back stairs, use them, and leave them alone again. Kathleen crouched down, gripping the banister, aching for a life she wasn't sure existed.

"You have only yourself to blame," Mrs. Wells said harshly to Andrew, her voice receding as she walked down the hall to her room. "You let Patricia get away. She was more than you could handle, and now she's gone."

"We never loved each other," Andrew said, his voice wavering. "You knew that, Mother. You wanted me to marry her because it looked good in the society pages. You wanted me to make up for Louise."

"That is a vile thing to say, Andrew," Mrs. Wells gasped.

"Don't you ever miss her, Mother?"

"How dare you ask me that? She's dead to me—to all of us. Don't ever let me hear you say her name again. You're drunk, and you know I don't like to talk to you when you're drunk!" With that, Mrs. Wells walked into her bedroom and slammed the door.

Kathleen closed her eyes. She could feel Andy's pain seeping upstairs, just like a cold draft. When she thought back to her childhood and the motherless girl she was, she remembered dreaming of having a mother love and nurture her. She had imagined someone brushing her hair, speaking softly to her about life and dreams, reading to her and tucking her in at night. Her own mother hadn't, even after she'd reclaimed Kathleen.

Had Mrs. Wells ever done that for Louise? And if so, how could she have stopped loving her? Or was Kathleen's vision of motherhood a complete fantasy? She had to know, and she had to know soon.

Andy sighed audibly, then headed down the back stairs to the kitchen. Even from up here, Kathleen could hear the bottles and ice clinking. She wrapped her arms around herself, shivering on the top step. Closing her eyes, she sent good thoughts down to Andy, and hoped he could feel them.

That's what she and James had done for each other. Not in their earliest years, when their cribs were right next to each other, and they could reach through the bars to touch hands. But later, when they were moved into the boys' and girls' wings. At first, the separation had been so terrible, Kathleen felt as if her arms had been cut off.

But over time, they'd learned how to deal with it. They'd stand in the windows of their respective wings, looking across the central courtyard, waving at each other. Kathleen would have stood there all night if Sister Anastasia hadn't gently spun her around, walked her back to bed, tucked her in.

"I know you love James," Sister had said, stroking her hair.

"I do," Kathleen had said. "I miss him so much it hurts...."

"Oh, it doesn't have to hurt," Sister had said. "You have him with you always."

"But he's over there, and I'm over here!"

"Yes, but you're together always, in a very special way."

Kathleen had swallowed hard, wanting to believe that. Sister Anastasia would never lie to her. Peering up, she'd watched the nun for any sign she was telling Kathleen a story. But Sister had always had such light and goodness in her face, it was impossible to imagine anything but pure truth coming from her.

"How?" Kathleen had asked.

"Close your eyes," Sister had said, "and think of him. Picture his eyes, his freckles, and that carrot top. Got it now?"

"Yes," Kathleen had said, her eyes squeezed tight, an image of James so vivid, smiling, reaching for her, that she felt she could hold his hand right then.

"All right, then," Sister had said. "When you fall asleep, take James with you into your dreams. Have wonderful adventures, Kathleen! Run on the beach, go swimming in the sea...climb Croagh Patrick!"

"We will," Kathleen had promised. The year before, the St. Augustine's patrons had treated the children to an excursion to Croagh Patrick, Ireland's holy mountain. She knew just what it was like, rising into the clouds over Clew Bay, and she and James could climb it again tonight....

"Don't let him go," Sister had said, leaning over to kiss Kathleen's forehead. "You just keep him with you...if you let go of his hand, close your eyes and think of him. You can always get him back."

Sitting on the top step, eyes closed now, Kathleen wondered whether Sister had ever told James the same thing. Whether she had ever told him to hold tight to Kathleen, never let her go.

If only her parents hadn't come for her that summer day, she thought now. If only she and James had stayed together... Everything would be different.

She was so distracted, she barely heard footsteps on the stairs.

Pierce started up, his face in shadow. Kathleen's heart beat faster; not from desire, though—from the opposite.

"Waiting for me?" he asked, his voice low and dangerous.

She didn't even answer. There were no words. Shivering in the late September chill, she rose and preceded him to her room. She was so cold, and even more, so lonely. Her narrow bed creaked as they climbed in. His hands were soft, as if they'd never done a bit of work in his life, but they touched her so roughly, as if she were wooden, as if he had no idea that there were bones and muscles inside her smooth skin.

He grunted, kissing her, and he jammed himself inside her. She cried out a little; she wasn't the least bit wet. That just made him push harder, more insistently. His legs felt hairy, like an animal's, and they scraped her calves. Kathleen bit her lip, not caring if she drew blood. She squeezed her eyes as tight as she could.

There had been times in life when she'd called on James, from the depths of loneliness and despair, connecting with him wherever he was. At these times, she did the opposite. She blocked him out; shut the iron door of her mind on James, Sister Anastasia, all the angels and saints.

Kathleen somehow unlatched herself from the pain of Pierce's rhythmic thrusting, the smell of his cologne, the click of his teeth against hers. She let herself feel the crush of human connection and the warmth of another body. She felt the wet explosion inside her, and wrapped her legs around his waist and cried.

He took it as pleasure, and that made him tender for a moment: he hugged and kissed her, smoothed her hair back from her forehead, whispered that she was great. Then he kissed the tip of her nose and pulled his pants on. They weren't sweatpants, but Armani. Kathleen would be hanging them up in his closet after she made his bed tomorrow morning.

"Night, baby," he said then, closing her door behind him, sneaking down the hall so his mother wouldn't hear him, going somewhere warmer: his own room.

He didn't notice that Kathleen's little cry had kept going, gaining velocity, that she was silently sobbing now, holding her pillow, thinking crazy thoughts about a baby doll she had once had, a doll with red hair that her foster parents had thrown into the trash.

She hung onto her pillow, thinking of that doll instead of James, because although they both had red hair, only the doll wouldn't see Kathleen's life as something she probably should have left in the garbage.

Twenty

The law firm of Kelly, Walsh, and Fitzpatrick was instrumental in the regeneration of Dublin's Docklands, and therefore had one of the finest offices in the brand-new Global Financial Center. Given the choice of locating the firm here or in the equally desirable nineteenth-century Custom House Quay, Sixtus Kelly had really thought there was no contest—for a Kelly.

For as charming and historical as the old brick buildings were, Sixtus enjoyed having an office on the top floor of this glass structure. There was a time no self-respecting person would come down to the Docklands. The port had fallen into decline, and it was an area of crime and skulduggery. There had been shipbuilding at Ringsend, a glassworks making bottles for Guinness stout, and flour mills opened after the Famine for non-Irish-grown wheat.

Other, more sordid trades thrived. Dereliction was rife, and jobs disappeared. Buildings crumbled or burned. Then came regeneration. Sixtus was proud of his part in bringing the waterfront back to life. His office overlooked Dublin Bay, and what a body of water it was! A great wild expanse of water, embraced by Howth and Dun Laoghaire. Back in the seventeenth century, it had been treacherous for shipping, storms blowing in, causing frequent shipwrecks. Weathering storms in Clontarf to the north, ships could be held up for weeks, waiting for the wind to die and make it possible to reach the city. It wasn't until 1716 that a bank was constructed on the south side of the channel, making the bay safer for ships.

So much history in Dublin Bay. So much *Kelly* history. From the day he'd moved into this office, Sixtus had made sure his desk was positioned so he had a good view over the bay's northernmost reaches. Yes, from his desk he was looking toward Clontarf...where those ships had gone for safe harbor, and where his brave ancestor had died.

His intercom buzzed, letting him know the young man had arrived. Sixtus glanced down at his notes. Tom had explained the situation weeks ago, just before he and Sister Bernadette had left Dublin—the day they'd canceled dinner at the last minute, most inconsiderately, especially considering the trouble to which Emer had gone, cooking a roast and generally trying to be as hospitable as possible to the nun who had so often welcomed them for retreats in Connecticut.

That day, Tom had been very clear. Sixtus gave him credit, considering the turmoil Tom must have found himself in. He had called the office, said he was coming by, and for Sixtus to cancel all appointments. Well, the fact Sixtus had a meeting with the Prime Minister's sister's solicitor was of no matter. Family came first: meeting canceled.

Tom Kelly had sat directly across Sixtus's desk, laying out the whole story. He and Bernie had a child. A son, twenty-three years old, named Seamus Sullivan. The young man had grown up at St. Augustine's Children's Home, was now employed as a driver by the Greencastle on Bannondale Road.

Sixtus had been rendered speechless. His cousin had a son who had grown up at St. Augustine's? Emer sat on the board of directors of St. Augustine's! Her cousin Father Tim Donnelly had just been named the pastor! Sixtus had wanted to vault across the desk, throttle Tom, ask what in the name of God he and Bernie had been thinking.

But it was quite clear that Tom had been throttling himself. He'd looked like death—face beaten, black and blue, nose as crooked as a prizefighter's. And Tom's physical condition had been the least of it: the spirit had gone out of him. In the short time since Sixtus and Billy had run into him and Bernie, Tom's heart had been broken.

Sixtus Kelly might have been a shrewd, tough hired gun, but he was also Irish. He knew that poetry ran through the veins of all Kellys. They lived for love, loyalty, and victory; above all, for love.

"What the hell were you thinking?" Sixtus had asked. "Once you found out she was pregnant, how could the convent have even been an option for Bernie?"

"Don't question her," Tom had said.

"But my God! Bernie should have known better. Did she honestly think she could just forget she'd had a child? When she told you, did—"

"I told you," Tom had said, his voice a threatening growl, "I don't want you questioning Bernie! She did what she had to do!"

"Fine, Tom," Sixtus had said, backing down.

"What's done is done."

"All right. What can I do, to help you move forward?"

"Here's what I want," Tom had said. He'd written out all the information, told Sixtus to sit tight and wait for the young man to call. Sixtus was not to look for him, not to approach him, not to stand in the courtyard of the Greencastle trying to guess which driver was Tom's son.

"Fine," Sixtus had agreed.

Of course he had kept his word. The shame was, he couldn't even talk to Emer about it. Nor Niall, nor Billy. Tom had told him in confidence, and Sixtus would never breach such a thing. But he'd been unable to help himself from trying to figure out which livery driver was Seamus.

Therefore when the young man walked into Sixtus's office, he wasn't one bit surprised. It was the tall, blue-eyed redhead with the quick smile and warm wave. At the Greencastle, he always looked friendly, even solicitous. Here, however, he walked in with his shoulders hunched slightly, looking tentative and intimidated.

"Hello, Seamus," Sixtus said, crossing the big office to meet him.

"Hello, Mr. Kelly."

They shook hands, and Sixtus led him to the chair Tom had sat in several weeks earlier.

"Did you find the office all right?"

"Oh yes, sir," Seamus said. "I've dropped many people off here, and picked them up as well." He looked out the enormous windows to his left, at Dublin Bay sparkling in the sun.

"I've seen you at the Greencastle," Sixtus said, peering at him.

Seamus nodded, turning red. He kept staring out the window, as if too embarrassed to meet Sixtus's eyes.

"You like the view?" Sixtus asked.

"Incredible. You'd never know from down on the street."

"Yes," Sixtus agreed. "It's nice. It's also inspiring. Do you know why?"

Seamus shook his head. "No," he said.

"Do you know about the Battle of Clontarf?"

"I'm Irish," Seamus said, smiling.

Ah, the ice had been broken. Sixtus nodded. "Then you know our ancestors were warriors. Back in the Middle Ages, we were in an almost constant state of war. The tribes were fierce, Seamus. Dubliners used to prove themselves by going to the Connaught and killing a man. We'd go to battle, cut the heads off our enemies. Or we'd stick our spear point between our enemy's teeth while accepting his surrender. So we were ready, when the time came."

"When the Danes invaded?"

"That's right. In the year 1014. Brian Boru might have been High King, but Tadhg Mor O'Kelly fought his heart out for our tribe and Ireland. We in the family are proud to say 'he died fighting like a wolf dog.' See that crest?" Sixtus asked, pointing at the framed heraldry hanging behind his desk.

"It's a sea monster," Seamus said.

"That's right—rising from the waves, just as in the legend; during and after the battle, as O'Kelly fought and lay dying, the monster came from the sea to protect his body from the marauders."

Seamus listened intently, staring at the family crest as Sixtus gazed at him, taking in the similarities—his clear, intelligent eyes, ferocious concentration, straight nose, wide mouth, slightly—the only blight on the family beauty—protruding ears. The freckles and red hair came from Bernie.

"The monster was supposed to protect him?" Seamus asked.

"*Did* protect him," Sixtus corrected.

"But the Vikings killed him."

"Seamus," Sixtus said patiently, "people die in battle. The sea monster did his best, and he kept the body safe from being stolen. That's what the Vikings *would* have done. Who knows what desecrations would have been perpetrated?" At the sight of the young man frowning at the Kelly sea monster, Sixtus began to squirm in his seat. "What's wrong?" he asked.

"It's nothing," Seamus said.

"That's good," Sixtus said. "Because that's your family crest."

Seamus looked up, turning redder.

"You're a Kelly, son."

"My name is Sullivan."

"Look. My cousin Tom told me everything. I know that you were born Thomas James Sullivan, and that's the name we'll be using to get your passport—that's why you're here now, isn't it?"

Seamus nodded.

"Fine. You had your pictures taken?"

"Yes. They're right here." Seamus tapped his breast pocket.

"Excellent. Sign this paper, and take it to the government office on Molesworth Street, Dublin 2. Ask for Clodagh. She'll be expecting you, and will issue the passport on the spot."

"Thank you, sir," Seamus said, pushing back as if about to rise and leave. Sixtus motioned him back down.

"You said you want to leave Ireland as soon as possible," he said.

"Yes, that's true."

"Well, once you have the passport, you can leave tomorrow night—if that's what you want."

"I do," Seamus said, his eyes shining. "I have a reservation on Aer Lingus."

Sixtus breathed steadily. Just like a Kelly, he was: moving fast, eyes on the ball, getting it done. Staring across the desk, he was struck again by those Kelly blue eyes—it was almost like looking into the mirror, or Tom's face.

"Well, since time is of the essence, that's why we're doing it in the Sullivan name."

"Sir?" he asked, frowning.

"Seamus. You're a Kelly." Sixtus got choked up just saying the words, welcoming this bright-eyed young man into the family fold.

"I wasn't born with that name."

"You're Tom's son. That's good enough for me."

"I don't even know him, though," Seamus said.

Sixtus shook his head impatiently. He wanted this young man to understand so badly. "Do you really think that matters? Seamus, why do you think I have my desk facing out the window? I'm a busy, important barrister, more cases than I can shake a stick at—I don't have time for pretty views. *That's* not why I look out."

"Then why?"

"*Clontarf*," Sixtus said, narrowing his eyes in the hopes of holding the tears inside. He peered hard across the desk, out the window, gazing toward the north end of the city, for which the battle was named. Seamus swiveled in his seat so he could look as well. "That's where our brave ancestor died defending Ireland."

"Tadhg Mor O'Kelly," Seamus said.

"That's right." Sixtus's heart constricted, thinking of what the young man had said about the sea monster a moment ago, hoping he wouldn't say the same thing again. "I'm looking out for him now," he said.

"Who?"

"The sea monster," Sixtus said, his voice falling.

"Because you need him to protect you?"

"No, son," Sixtus said. "To thank him. For looking after one of our own. You see, that's what we Kellys do." He raised his eyes to Seamus, who really looked like not much more than a boy. Thin, wide-eyed, stunned by the twist life had sprung on him. "We look after our own."

"That's good," Seamus said quietly.

"And you're one of us now," Sixtus said. His voice broke—he had to face it, it had to happen. "You're Seamus Kelly to me, son. I'll have that passport for you tomorrow, and you'll go wherever it is you have to go."

"America," Seamus whispered.

Sixtus nodded once, hard. "Fine. So be it. You have Tom's number over there, and I know he expects you to use it."

"I don't need his help," Seamus said.

"Perhaps not," Sixtus said, seeing the flint and pride in his eyes. "That's up to you. The point is, when you get back to Dublin, you call me again. Come here, and I'll file the paperwork necessary for you to be called Seamus Kelly."

"But—"

Sixtus raised his hand. He wasn't used to being interrupted by colleagues, enemies, or even family members. "Tom told me you want to become a barrister."

"Someday."

"When you are ready, there will be an office for you here. That's all I'm saying for now. You will have to prove your capabilities, but I have no doubt that you will. You're a Kelly, after all."

"Thank you, sir," Seamus said, suddenly looking ready to jump out the window. If there were a sea monster passing by in the bay, Sixtus had no doubt that Seamus would hop on board and hightail it as far from the Docklands as he could get.

But perhaps Sixtus was wrong. For Seamus picked up the passport documents, lingered for a moment gazing at the family crest. He seemed to examine the beast's writhing body, fiery eyes, sharp fangs, green scales. Blinking like a young boy, he glanced at Sixtus, as if afraid to ask a question.

"What is it?" Sixtus asked. "Go ahead."

"Before," Seamus said. "When you told me that Kellys look after their own..."

Sixtus nodded. Was he thinking of how Tom and Bernie had abandoned him to an institutional existence? How Tom Kelly had left him there, on the shores of the battle of life, to fight without any family support?

"I screwed up with that," Seamus said.

"You mean someone screwed up with you?"

"No." He shook his head. "I mean, there's someone I consider family. I swore I'd always be there for her, that I'd always look after her. But I didn't."

Sixtus held his tongue, not wanting to reveal what Tom had told him about Seamus and the girl from St. Augustine's.

"How do you know you didn't?" Sixtus asked.

"I walked away," Seamus said.

Sixtus took a deep breath. That didn't sound very Kelly-like. He had to give this some thought. Gazing out the window at the gleaming bay, right where he'd expect to see the sea monster if it was ever to surface, it came to him. He cleared his throat.

"Did you walk away because you wanted to, or because you felt you had no choice?"

"She was going back to her real parents. I didn't want to go back to the Home without her."

Sixtus smiled. He'd known there was a loophole. "Then you didn't walk away. You were both children. You thought she was about to be cared for by the people who could love her most—her parents. And that's probably what happened...."

"Probably," Seamus agreed, but he sounded uncertain.

"You're going to find her," Sixtus said, and he wasn't betraying any confidences from Tom; it was written all over Seamus's freckled face.

"I am," Seamus said, the words sounding like an oath.

"Then you'll need this," Sixtus said. Sliding his gold crest ring off his finger, he handed it to Seamus. The young man reddened and frowned as he looked at the well-worn oval, engraved with the same sea monster roaring and rising from the waves behind his desk.

"I can't take it," Seamus said.

"I insist," Sixtus said. He smiled magnanimously even as he held back emotion. He walked the young man to the office door. "Don't forget. Call Tom if you need him."

"But I won't," Seamus said, still trying to hand back the ring.

Sixtus had to practically push him out the door. When he got to his desk, he made a note for himself. He'd call Columba Jewelers tomorrow, have another ring struck. They had the die on hand—Sixtus had had many rings made over the years, for his brothers and their wives, his two sons, both living in America, and all his nieces and nephews, everyone's spouses, even close friends. He liked to think of Kellys pro-liferating, all of them wearing the crest ring of Tadhg Mor O'Kelly, all of them ready at a moment's notice to go to battle for each other.

He sat back, gazing at the bay, thinking of what Seamus had said when Sixtus had told him to call Tom for help. "I don't need his help," he'd said. No, perhaps not, Sixtus thought now. But Tom needed to give it.

Taking a deep breath, he punched the international calling code into his phone, rang Tom's number. It rang a few times, and then Tom answered.

"Hello?"

"Tom. It's Sixtus. He just left."

"He's getting his passport?"

"Yes. Picking it up tomorrow."

"Did he say anything about flying out?"

"He has an Aer Lingus flight tomorrow night. Into Boston, I would presume—Logan being closer to Newport than JFK. But I'll find out the details from my source at the passport office."

"Sixtus—I don't know how to thank you."

"Don't you dare, Tom. Not after all you and Bernie have done for us over the years. Have you found anything on your end?"

"I know where she works," Tom said. The connection was bad; he was on his cell phone, and perhaps he was driving. It sounded that way anyway, from all the noise rushing through the receiver.

"Tom, are you there?" Sixtus asked. "Tom? Give my love to Bernie!"

But the line had gone dead. Sixtus Kelly replaced the phone in its cradle, sat back in his chair. He had several clients backed up, including the solicitor for the Prime Minister's sister. But first he needed to compose himself, gazing out at Dublin Bay—once so dangerous to ships and fighting Kellys—thinking of his cousin and his son, of love, loyalty, and victory.

Right now, they needed all three.

Twenty-One

Regis Sullivan, a sophomore at Boston College, was having what she knew her aunt would call "adjustment problems." Getting back to college after the summer she'd had was like walking off the deck of a burning ship onto safe, dry land—and trying to enter into normal life again. She was a philosophy major. Going to class each day, hearing Jesuits teach about truth, mysteries, and preambles of faith, actually helped her get her bearings.

Her roommates were great. Monica, Juliana, and Mirande really shored her up, made sure she didn't spend too much time dwelling on her part in Gregory White's death in Ireland. When BC kids heard Regis had been to Ireland, they all chimed in with their own experiences: going to Dublin Castle, drinking in Temple Bar, trying to get tickets for U2, visiting the Guinness Brewery, kissing the Blarney Stone, wanting to buy their mom some Waterford crystal but realizing it was too expensive and getting her a scarf instead.

Regis's roommates knew that her trips to Ireland had been different. On the first one, six years ago, she had stood on the cliffs of Ballincastle with her world-famous father and his sculpture, fighting for their lives with a deranged man. For six whole years, Regis's memory had gone blank. Completely erased, when it came to that fight. Last year, when they were freshmen, her roommates had put up with her nightmares, crying in the night, sometimes screaming, as little bits of that terrible day had come up from the depths.

And then, when her father was released from prison and finally came home, it all came flooding back in one tidal wave of memory: the rain, the blood, the shouting, and that final thudding impact. Regis's family had flown over to Dublin with her so she could tell her side of the story. Tom Kelly's cousin Sixtus had represented her, and the Irish authorities had said there would be no charges filed.

All that, and now it was supposed to be back to school as usual. At least the nightmares were gone. Instead, Regis would just lie in bed, staring at the ceiling, exploring the strange new world of insomnia.

Sometimes she'd glance over, and there would be Mirande, wide-awake, drawing in her sketchpad. With two artists for parents, Regis had felt comforted by the sound of charcoal whisking across paper. Of all her roommates, she felt the strongest kinship with Mirande. Her name, for one thing. It was so cool—she was named for the beach on which she'd been conceived, a hidden cove with a crescent of sand, on a visit to her father's family on the Côte d'Azur.

Mirande wore a beret at all times, even when she went to bed. She had long chestnut hair, pale skin, and a Mona Lisa smile. She wore many bracelets: several woven by her mother of brilliant, jewel-colored embroidery thread, and two made of green glass beads from her American aunt, who had had them blessed by the Dalai Lama before she died. Her favorite purse was amber wool stitched with turquoise yarn, from her other aunt, who lived in Aix-en-Provence. She always wore a small gold cross around her neck, from her grand-mother in St. Paul de Vence.

Regis loved Mirande for her artistic nature, her eccentricities, and her closeness to her family. It made her feel she had a true friend, someone who would understand. Irish on her mother's side of the family, Mirande was proud that her middle name was Grace, after the fearless Irish pirate Grace O'Malley. Regis—a little shell-shocked since the summer—needed to find her fearlessness again, so she stuck close to Mirande.

"We need a road trip," Mirande announced on Friday afternoon, when they were all in the room studying.

"You could all come home with me," Regis said. "It's the grape harvest at Star of the Sea, and I said I'd help."

"Honey, you're going home an awful lot," Monica said, leaning down from her upper bunk bed.

"She needs her family right now," Mirande said, sliding her arm around Regis's shoulder.

"I know, I know," Monica said. "I just miss her when she's gone."

"Then come to the harvest," Regis urged.

"I'd like to," Juliana said.

"Sounds good," Monica agreed. "I went to Catholic boarding school, and the one thing we lacked was a vineyard. It would be cool to see."

"All right," Mirande said, her beret dangerously low over one eye. "But I say we take a little excursion on the way."

"Where to?" Monica asked.

"The land of sailors, pirates, robber barons, domestics, Rolls-Royces, and debauchery—my hometown, Newport, Rhode Island!"

"Color me there," Juliana said.

"What are we waiting for?" Regis asked.

Traveling light, they packed overnight bags and jumped into Mirande's car. It was her mother's old Volvo station wagon and had Buddha beads, crosses, and a lei of blue, pink, and yellow flowers hanging from the rearview mirror. They left Chestnut Hill driving south on I-95, then got off the highway in Providence to meander down Narragansett Bay through Barrington, Bristol, and Portsmouth. The foliage was turning, so Regis just sat back and let the fall colors—oranges, yellows, reds, and nut browns—soothe her soul. When they reached Newport, they went straight to Mirande's house, located in the Fifth Ward, two streets back from the bay.

"The bus tours don't come through this section," Mirande explained. "It's for the working class, and it's mainly Irish."

"I like it," Regis said, looking up and down the street. The houses were tidy and well kept, with pumpkins on the steps and chrysanthemums blooming in the yards. She thought of how Tom Kelly always said that Irish people were natural gardeners. She'd been devastated to hear that he'd left Star of the Sea, and she couldn't quite imagine the harvest without him.

"How long are you staying?" Mrs. St. Florent asked, surprised and happy to see the girls. She'd been at her loom, making a tapestry for a monastery in Vermont, but she put her work aside to serve them cider and doughnuts.

"Till tomorrow morning. Then we're going to Regis's place to pick grapes."

"Oh yes," Mrs. St. Florent said. "The Sisters do make some delicious wines...."

"I'm sorry to subject your daughter to backbreaking work," Regis said. "But I promise we'll send you a few bottles of chardonnay to make up for it."

"Her father and I thank you in advance!" Mrs. St. Florent said. "I just hope you'll be able to see Elizabeth before you leave. She'll be beside herself if she misses you again, Mirande."

"Is she still working at Oakhurst?"

"Yes," Mrs. St. Florent said. "Although she's living with Jeff now, instead of up in that cold attic with the other girls, and counting the days until the family leaves for Palm Beach."

"We'll go see her," Mirande promised.

So the girls all got back into the Volvo and drove up to Spring Street on their way to see Mirande's older sister. Graceful Victorians with gingerbread, peaked roofs, and wraparound porches were crammed side by side in a sort of summer-resort urban madness. From there, they headed up to Bellevue Avenue, where every house was a mansion. Driving along Bellevue, Regis was awed by one limestone palace after another. Many had iron gates, spectacular stone walls, perfect hedges.

"A lot of us work up here at least once in our lives," Mirande explained. "My sister dropped out of Villanova last year, and came back to Newport to be closer to her boyfriend."

"What does she do?" Regis asked.

"She's the downstairs maid for a really snobby family. Answers their door in a black uniform..."

Suddenly they reached a relatively normal-looking house. Although still quite large, it was white clapboard instead of limestone, and had black shutters, a screened-in porch, and a tall oak tree towering in the backyard. A silver Porsche was parked in the driveway behind a silver Rolls-Royce.

"Welcome to Oakhurst," Mirande said. "Looks like the family is home, so we shouldn't all go to the door. I'll just run up and say hi to my sister, okay?"

Regis watched as her friend jumped out of the Volvo, hurried up the bluestone walk to the front door. Mirande rang the bell and stood there waiting. Monica and Juliana sat in the station wagon's back seat, watching. Craning her neck, Regis looked up at the house. There were tall floor-to-ceiling windows on the first floor, normal-sized eight-paned windows on the second, and small little squares up in the attic. As she stared up, she saw a face peek out.

There, in one of the tiny attic windows, Regis saw a young woman staring at the sky. She looked so forlorn and desperate, so full of yearning, the sight of her almost brought tears to Regis's eyes. Regis had known that feeling. During the last six years, when she was struggling with her dark secrets, she had felt that way all the time.

Downstairs, the front door opened, and another young woman answered the door. It was Mirande's sister Elizabeth, wearing a black dress with a white apron. She grinned, waving out the door at the girls. They waved back, but Regis's attention was drawn again to the woman in the window upstairs.

Two minutes later, Mirande was back, her black beret raking her green eyes.

"She gets off at six," she said. "She and Jeff are going to meet us at the Black Pearl for dinner."

"Mirande, who's that?" Regis asked, pointing up at the attic window. In that instant, the girl standing there locked eyes with Regis, then backed slightly away, into the room, leaving just a shadow.

"Must be one of the other help," Mirande said. "The English nanny, maybe, although I think Beth said she's gone back to New York City. Could be the Irish girl."

"The Irish girl?"

"Yes," Mirande said. "The cook and upstairs maid. She's leaving with the family on Sunday. They head south for the winter, to Palm Beach. Not my sister, though. She's staying in Newport, and she'll start up at Salve Regina next semester."

"That's good," Juliana said.

"Better than answering a door all day long!" Monica said.

The other girls started talking about the worst jobs they'd ever had, but even as Mirande backed out of the driveway, Regis couldn't stop staring up at the attic window. As the Volvo pulled into Bellevue Avenue, Mirande slammed on the brakes to avoid hitting a green pickup truck that was moving slowly along.

"Whoa, watch it," Mirande said.

Regis glanced at the truck. It was old and a little battered, as if it had been used for heavy work. Landscaping, maybe, to judge from the dents along the sides of the truck bed, and from the rack used to store rakes, shovels, and hoes. There were bits of concrete stuck to the mud flaps, and a few dead leaves wedged in the gate.

The truck's driver seemed oblivious to the fact he'd nearly gotten hit by the Volvo. He was too intent, staring upward, his gaze directed not at the sky but at a window at the top of the white house with black shutters. The man was staring up at the girl in the attic window. He looked completely absorbed and—in the two seconds Regis had to register his eyes, his mouth—heartbroken. Regis knew heartbreak when she saw it.

Especially when it was on the face of Tom Kelly.

Kathleen stood at the window, trying to hold herself together. She'd never been so sick in her life, and the idea of having to finish packing tonight, so they could drive to New York tomorrow night, get on a plane on Sunday, and fly to Palm Beach, made her feel like jumping off the roof right this instant. She was ill at the very idea of transplanting herself from one grand house to another, knowing it would be just the same wherever she went.

Although she'd only been with the Welleses since last spring, she had done the circuit with other families before. East Hampton in the summer, Boca Raton in the winter. Or Edgartown and Man-O-War Key. Or Northeast Harbor and Naples. The houses were all enormous, the estates pristine. Have Rolls-Royce, Will Travel.

Staring out the window, Kathleen saw a carload of girls pull into the driveway. The glass blocked their voices, but she could see them all laughing and talking. Oh, what she wouldn't give to go running downstairs, jump into the back seat, and drive away with them. What would the Welleses have to say about that? Considering everything, they might be happiest if she were to disappear right now. In fact, she was working on a plan to accomplish just that.

One of the girls, a young beauty with a jaunty black beret cocked over one eye, came running across the yard, tripping up the front steps. The sight of her made Kathleen smile. Not a usual visitor to Oakhurst, that was for sure... She recognized her as Beth's sister... what was her name? Something odd, something that had reminded Kathleen of the beach.

Beth had kept her picture on her bureau, before she'd left for the greener pastures of moving in with her boyfriend. Kathleen had loved the story of how her little sister never took off her beret; it had been her aunt's last gift to her, the Christmas before she died. Although the aunt was American and lived right here in Newport, she had given her niece a beret, knowing her love of all things Gallic. The aunt had understood her niece, and Kathleen knew that understanding was a gift beyond measure.

The story of Beth's sister and the beret had pierced Kathleen to the soul. Oh, she understood the power of talismans, the need to hold someone close at all costs. When they were right there, by your side and holding your hand, it wasn't so dire. But once they were gone—through death, or separation, or running away on the hard-packed sand of an Irish beach—then you needed all the talismans you could find.

Kathleen wished she'd had something of James to hold on to. The most she had had was that red-haired doll. She'd kept it with her all the years at St. Augustine's, and even her first few months with her real parents. She didn't care that she was almost fourteen, too big to need a doll. Her father had teased her about it, hidden it on her a few times.

He'd laughed when she'd panicked. She had tried to pretend she wasn't really falling apart just because she couldn't find her ragged, soiled, hugged-to-death redheaded baby doll. She'd thought that if she pretended she didn't really care, then he'd stop hiding it on her.

Then one day, after they'd moved from Blackrock to Cork City, the day before they would make the score necessary to finance their flight to Boston, she had torn the apartment up, looking for the doll.

"Where is he?" she'd asked, thinking maybe she was losing her mind.

" 'He'?" her father had asked, in that leering way of his. "It's a doll. A *girl* doll."

"Leave her alone," her mother had said, seemingly weary of it all.

"She, then," Kathleen had said, not wanting to argue or try to convince them. She had already learned that to survive, she was better off going along, not fighting back or trying to assert herself.

"Leave her alone?" her father had bellowed, going after her mother. "Who the eff are you to tell me to leave her alone? This was your idea, getting her out of the Home. Another mouth to feed, to drag along, and what does she do to pull her weight? Whines about a goddamn doll—knowing the pressure I'm under!"

"You're right, Clement," her mother had said swiftly, trying to head him off before it got too bad. "We both know the stress you're dealing with, trying to get the money for the trip, and making arrangements on the other side ... we do know, don't we, Kathleen?"

"Yes," she'd said, trying to keep her chin from wobbling, trying to contain her anxiety. Not over the trip to America, or even the fact she knew her parents were planning to go to the hotel bar later, get some rich man drunk so they could steal his wallet—his cash and credit cards. But just the simple fact that her father had her doll, and she needed it. Needed it to remind her of James, know that he was always with her. Always, always.

"This goddamned stinking, lice-infested, ugly doll," her father had raged, pulling it down from the closet shelf, too high for Kathleen to have reached on her own. She'd held herself back, knowing that if she reached for it or looked too eager, her father would just hide it again, maybe not give it back until they'd flown to Boston. And she needed him, her doll. . . .

She didn't like knowing her parents were thieves; they sometimes took her to the bars, to laugh and dance, distract people from paying attention to their wallets or briefcases or handbags. Sometimes she'd wondered if that's why they had gotten her out of St. Augustine's: so she could help them steal. She got by, thinking of James. That's what she'd tell herself: *Just think of James.* He was there with her, telling her she'd be fine. They'd be back together as soon as they could. Her red-haired doll was the reminder she needed, every day, that James was by her side, with her always.

That's why Kathleen loved Beth's little sister, in her black beret. She leaned against the windowpane, looking up into the sky, as if she could see all the way to Ireland. She knew that one day Beth's sister would learn that objects didn't matter. They couldn't save you, no matter how much you wished they could. Her father had burned her doll that day. Told her that it was filthy, and distracting her from doing a good job. Oh, that fire had never stopped burning. It had raged all around her all these years.

But Kathleen had survived, learned to live without the doll. She pictured the day she finally got it, finally had had enough of her parents. The sky was blue. The breeze was blowing. Kathleen packed the few things that mattered and started walking. She remembered wondering when they would notice she was gone. She knew they would be upset, but for all the wrong reasons: reasons that had nothing to do with love.

Kathleen knew that Beth's little sister could get by without her beret; she just hoped it wouldn't be before she was ready. Glancing down at the car, she noticed one of the other girls staring up. Their eyes locked—and Kathleen jumped back.

She felt ashamed to be seen. Up here in the attic, too sick to work, needing to finish packing. Tomorrow night, they would all drive to New York, to drop things off at the Fifth Avenue apartment, before flying out on Sunday to sunny Palm Beach—unless Kathleen could get the energy to come up with a plan.

Nice college girls, she thought. Nothing like this would ever happen to them. She prayed it wouldn't, at least. As she watched the Volvo backing onto Bellevue Avenue, she saw it nearly collide with a green truck. She banged on the window, opening her mouth to yell for them to watch out.

But her voice caught in her throat. Only the tiniest sound came out. . . .

"James," she whispered.

God help her, she saw him. Her beloved, the boy who had promised to be with her always. There he was, at the wheel of a green pickup truck. Blue eyes blazing as he stared up at her, that gaze as strong as a lifeline, promising without words to save her, rescue her from the fire.

"James," she said again, hand on the cold window glass.

The man saw her, thought she was waving at him. He raised his hand, as if to steady her, tell her to wait, that he'd come back and get her. She watched his green truck pull out of sight, and oh, she thought her heart would break to see it go.

She knew she was losing her mind, had finally gone mad. That had to be it. That man was a stranger—and old, besides. He had to be twice James's age, forty-five if he was a day. His hair was dark brown, going gray, not a bit of red to be seen. But those blue eyes . . . those clear blue eyes. Perhaps he was a spirit. Kathleen was having visions now, losing her mind in the attic, carrying the child of a fool.

Leaning her forehead against the window, she stared down the street, praying, as she always did, to see those blue eyes again. But the prayer caught in her throat. It was too late.

Twenty-Two

The girls parked at Bannister's Wharf, and Tom pulled in just a few cars behind them. His head was spinning—he needed to find Regis and find out what she'd been doing in that car coming out of Oakhurst. He pulled into the lot, had to run to catch up with Bernie's niece and her friends on their way to the Black Pearl.

"Regis!" he called.

"Uncle Tom," she said, spinning around. "I thought that was you. What are *you* doing here?"

"I'm here on . . . family business," he said.

She gave him a funny look. How much did she know about why he had left the Academy? He remembered back to that dinner, his and Bernie's first night back at Star of the Sea. All three girls had been so enthusiastic, so eager to hear about Seamus.

"Aunt Bernie?" she asked.

"Yes, indirectly," he said.

Regis introduced him to Mirande, Juliana, and Monica.

"Nice to meet you," he said. "I was driving along Bellevue Avenue, and I noticed you pulling out of Oakhurst. Does one of you live there?"

Juliana laughed. "We wish! What a fancy house . . ."

"My sister works there," Mirande said. "She's the downstairs maid, and so much more! Little do the Wellses know, they have a world-class artisan in their midst. Beth is hell on wheels with our mother's loom."

"That's why I love her so much," Regis said, putting her arm around Mirande's shoulders, pulling her beret down over her green eyes. "She's from a crazy artistic family like ours." Tom smiled with affection for Regis, whom he'd always loved like his own niece.

"Thank God Beth isn't going with that family to Florida," Mirande said.

"Florida?"

"Yes. They summer here, and winter in Palm Beach."

"La-di-da!" Monica said.

Tom's stomach fell. "When are they leaving?"

"They fly south on Sunday," Mirande said. "Beth has been count-ing the days until she's free...."

"Does Beth know Kathleen Murphy?" Tom asked. "The family's cook?"

"Oh, is she the Irish girl?" Mirande asked. "Beth said she's really quiet. Very nice, but shy. She pretty much keeps to herself. Except..." Mirande paused. "Well, Beth said she thought maybe something was going on between her and one of the Wells boys."

"Maybe she'll marry him and live happily ever after, like a prin-cess," Juliana said. "Someone will cook for her, instead of the other way around."

"I don't think she's in love with him," Regis said.

"How do you know?" Tom asked intently.

Regis hesitated. She stared out into space for a few seconds. "I think I saw her, up in the attic window. She was looking at the sky, and I thought..."

Tom held his breath; he had seen the same thing, and had thoughts of his own. In Kathleen's far-off gaze he'd seen himself, longing for Bernie. He'd watched the young woman staring with sorrow at noth-ing, and felt a kinship with her. She was longing for his son, and he was longing for his son's mother.

"I thought she looked like me," Regis said. "Last summer, when I was trying to fit into something that wasn't real. I was engaged to Peter, wishing that could make me whole again, so I wouldn't have to think about Ballincastle."

"You saw all that, looking up at an attic window?" Monica asked skeptically.

Regis nodded. Tom didn't speak, but he knew Regis. He believed her, that she *had* seen all that; she had her aunt's gift for compassion and insight. Tom's stomach jumped, and he suddenly knew there wasn't time.

"When did you say they're leaving?" he asked. "For Palm Beach?"

"They fly on Sunday morning," Mirande said. "But they leave Newport tomorrow."

"Tomorrow?" Tom asked, shocked. "What time?"

"I don't know. Beth said something about a brunch. I guess they're going to that first, then Beth and Kathleen will finish packing for them, and then they'll drive down to New York. Spend the night there, and fly out on Sunday. At least, that's what my sister said...."

"Uncle Tom, will you come back to Star of the Sea with us?" Regis asked, her eyes wide and pleading. "For the grape harvest? I know how much Aunt Bernie would love for you to be there.... It would mean so much to her."

In spite of Tom's anxiety over this new information, he fixed Regis with a gentle gaze. She was Bernie's godchild, and that made her almost a daughter. He was so glad she'd made it through this last rocky time; he knew that John and Honor were still worried about her, knew that she'd been emotionally fragile.

Tom hoped that she'd be able to handle what he was about to ask of her. His chest ached, as if he had an anvil sitting on it. His head was spinning, figuring out schedules and trying to factor this new information in. It could still work....

"Come on, Uncle Tom. The harvest?"

"No, Regis," he said. "There's something I have to do in Newport. And I wonder if I can get you to help me...."

"Help you, of course. What is it?"

"I'll explain everything. We'll have to work fast, though; we only have one day. It all has to happen tomorrow...."

As Regis and her friends gathered around to listen, Tom began to talk.

Saturday—the next morning—dawned clear and bright, with golden October light spreading over the hills and fields. Sunrise was Sister Bernadette's most peaceful time of the day, and she always tried to greet it with prayer and gratitude while walking the Academy grounds.

The sun rose straight out of Long Island Sound, illuminating its rippling waves, the beach, and the stone wall climbing into the vineyard. Bernie stood on the hill's crest, gazing out at the water. She had so much to pray for today and always. She called for the strong white light of the Spirit, all she could summon, straight from her heart, wishing the Savior's light and peace for everyone she loved, for the whole world. And, especially, for Tom and Seamus.

As she stared out at the water, she watched the surface change from orange to bright blue. Fall weather was here, and she felt a sharpness to the air. A chill by the sea put her in mind of that walk on the cliffs in May, when she and Tom had conceived their son.

As she held Tom and Seamus close to her heart in prayer, she thought of the love she and Tom had always shared. She knew that their trip to Dublin had opened old wounds, and that he was suffering now. She prayed that his decision to leave Star of the Sea was a movement toward healing, that wherever he was, he was moving ever deeper in that direction.

She sighed, made the sign of the cross, started back toward the convent to get ready for the harvest. This land was so blessed. Knowing that she had once met Mary here, realizing what a miracle that was, how could she ever doubt or complain? Star of the Sea was a sanctuary for the weary, a haven for the lonely, a home for the lost. God's love and presence were always present, and today's harvest was a perfect symbol for the abundance in all of their lives.

So walking along this beautiful morning, Bernie felt guilty for the feelings she had swirling around inside. These last few days had been hard. Knowing that Tom was gone, that there wasn't any chance of seeing him with his wheelbarrow, on the hillside or in one of the valleys, filled her with sorrow. As much as she understood his need to leave, she felt herself screaming against it. He belonged here—this was his home as much as hers.

The very un-nun-like truth was, she didn't know how she could go on here without him. She had been a nun for twenty-three years; she had gone straight to the convent the day after giving her son up for adoption. She had been a novice in Dublin and then right here, at Star of the Sea. She'd spent her first year cloistered, and in the course of the next year, as a postulant, decided that she wanted to emerge from behind the enclosure and join the larger community.

Sister Bernadette Ignatius had professed her solemn vows six years later, right here in the Star of the Sea Chapel. Blue stained-glass windows, dark oiled woods, and marble altar were a solemn backdrop to the ceremony. The archbishop had presided as seven women became Sisters of Notre Dame des Victoires. Each woman received a silver blessed-profession ring, symbolizing chastity, the seal of the Holy Spirit. And through the ring, each Sister was espoused to Jesus Christ.

Bernie's entire family had been present, and so had Tom. He had long since given up trying to convince her she was making a mistake. Giving birth to their son, leaving him in Ireland, had been the hardest thing Bernie had ever done. The second hardest, she admitted to herself now, was walking down the aisle after professing her vows, seeing Honor and John with Regis and Agnes, Cece having not yet been born, all smiling; and Tom sitting in the row behind them, his cheeks wet.

The finality of what she'd just done had hit him in that moment. So that after Communion, when the organ finished playing and the chapel doors were thrown open, she knew that Tom's heart had felt torn. Her own joy, at finally professing her vows, was so great; but in that moment, seeing the tears on Tom's face, she'd nearly stumbled.

She didn't see him for days after that. Although he had been working on the Academy grounds for many years, since long before she'd decided to join the order, he made himself scarce. Then one day, when she went to the Blue Grotto to pray, she found him there. Not working—just sitting still, before the statue of Mary.

"Excuse me," she'd said, backing up, not wanting to interrupt if he was praying. "I'll leave you alone."

"That's okay," he'd said. "Sister."

She'd heard the delay, followed by soft sarcasm.

"How've you been, Tom?" she'd asked. "I haven't seen you around at all."

"There's a lot of land here," he said. "Tunnels, aqueducts, marshlands... it's not that hard to get lost."

"Where have you been getting lost?"

He'd stood up at that question. She remembered seeing him unfold himself from the bench slowly, stretching to his full height. His shoulders were so broad, and he nearly filled the small space. Although he was still young, his face was craggy and weathered, and a shock of wavy brown hair fell across his blue eyes. Even in the grotto's dim light, she'd seen the burning in his eyes, and she'd remembered their time on the Cliffs of Moher.

How they'd lain on the grass behind the path, high above the Atlantic. How she'd looked across at him, reaching over to push the hair from his eyes, and how he'd grabbed her wrist, kissed her hard, told her he loved her.

"Where've you been getting lost?" she'd whispered again.

"What do you care?"

"I'll never stop caring," she'd said.

"I'm staying out of your way," he'd said, his voice low and dangerous even as he'd taken a step closer to her. "Isn't that what you want?"

"I don't know," she'd whispered.

He'd been standing so close, she could smell the scent of sweat and newly cut grass. Leaning over, he'd brushed the veil back from her face, caressing her cheek with his knuckles. Bernie's eyes had closed; she'd felt him bending close, brushing her lips with his. A cool breeze had swept through, just like the one that had touched them that early May day on Ireland's west coast. And then he'd left.

Bernie had stood there, her knees weak. There they were, in the Blue Grotto, where the Virgin Mary had consoled her eight years earlier. The walls were dark and damp with moss. Bernie had lowered herself onto the bench where Tom had been sitting. Her lips tingled with his kiss.

Now, the morning of the harvest, Bernie turned off one path, onto the one that led into the hollow behind the vineyard, hurrying toward the Blue Grotto. She started off walking, but began to run. Tom had been gone for days now, but part of her couldn't believe he'd really left. She'd go to the spot where it had all begun and ended, and he'd be there.

But he wasn't. She was alone in the cool sanctuary. The words she had written seemed stark in the stonework: *I was sleeping, but my heart kept vigil,* and *Set me as a seal on your heart, as a seal on your arm; for as stern as death is love.* But the lettering was softened by moss, the constant growth that covered every surface of rock in the grotto's damp shadows. Tom hadn't scrubbed it down before they'd left for Ireland, and no one else had since. Bernie looked around, felt his absence here as much as anywhere else, in that sinister, relentless moss.

As she brushed off the stone bench and started to sit down, she raised her eyes to the Madonna. And she gasped.

The statue of Mary was perfectly clean, gleaming in a shaft of sunlight. The sun slanted in from a crack in the eastern wall—facing dawn, the sea, and Ireland. Bernie walked closer, noticing that not an inch of moss grew anywhere on the statue. Had it always been this way? Had Tom treated the surface with some chemical? Or had Brendan or one of the other groundskeepers scrubbed the statue but not the rest of the grotto?

The rays of sunlight grew brighter, blindingly so. The rays seemed alive, darting around the small, enclosed space like tiny white hummingbirds. Bernie shielded her eyes, blinking into the sunbeams.

Suddenly the sun's position must have moved ever so slightly, because the light seemed normal again. Bernie caught her breath, looking at the statue.

It gleamed so brightly, alabaster in morning light. Bernie had always loved all images of Mary, but this one was her favorite. Francis X. Kelly had acquired it from a monastery near Clontarf. She knew that it had linked him to his family in Ireland; Bernie felt it connected her to hers as well: Tom and Seamus.

She stared at the delicate statue, the folds in the draped robe, the serpent beneath her bare feet, the outstretched arms—as if Mary wanted to embrace Bernie, Star of the Sea, the whole world. As Bernie raised her eyes even higher, to Mary's face, the sunlight came back, stronger than ever. It flooded the grotto with scalding white light, and Bernie heard herself cry out.

"Blessed Mother..."

Even though the light burned her eyes, she couldn't look away from Mary's face. As she stared, Bernie saw Mary's lips begin to move, and she heard the words, more kind, gentle, and loving than anything she had ever heard in her life:

"My child..."

Bernie fell to her knees, hands clasped at her breast, and began to pray.

Bees drawn to the ripe grapes, literally drunk on nectar, wove in and out of the vines, but no one got stung. The vineyard buzzed with other activity as well: every nun from the convent, each girl from the Academy, John, Honor, Agnes, and Cece, all the groundskeepers, including Brendan, some of his friends from his other job at the hospital, volunteers from Black Hall, and the winemaker—a man highly recommended by the Benedictines, for his knowledge and ability to coax the best out of the grapes—worked steadily.

They spread out, marking off their turf, dividing each row of vines into three or four sections, seeing who could fill their baskets fastest.

Honor stuck close to John, thrilled to be so near him. This was his first harvest in six years, and he seemed to be having the best time—picking grapes by hand, snapping off their dry stems, holding huge, lush bunches over Honor's mouth as she ate one after another.

"Regis doesn't know what she's missing," he said, moving along the trellis to the next vine.

"I know," Honor said. "She sounded so excited to be bringing her friends, but I guess they got sidetracked in Newport."

"It's nice of Mirande's mother to let them stay the weekend."

"Yes, it is," Honor said. She'd felt uneasy last night, when Regis had called to say they'd had a change of plans. For although Regis had sounded happy, even excited, Honor thought she'd heard something furtive in her voice. Six months ago, she'd have been worried that Regis was planning to do something daring and dangerous—climbing Tuckerman's Ravine, or trying to kayak out to Martha's Vineyard, or something equally intense—to forget about Ballincastle and the breakup with Peter.

But now, she didn't know what to think. Regis had seemed much more timid since the summer. As if her memories about Ballincastle had given her a new awareness of life and death, of her own mortality. But that morning there had been hints of the old Regis, of her capacity for secrets and surprises. Honor had asked if everything was okay. Regis had said yes. But Honor just wasn't sure....

"Where's Bernie, anyway?" John asked, looking around.

"I don't know," Honor said. "I wonder if maybe it's too hard for her."

"Because Tom's not here?"

"Yes," Honor said.

"I know that she's the Mother Superior and he's the caretaker, but they're like an old married couple. I honestly can't imagine them without each other," John said.

"Maybe he'll come back," Honor said. But something in her husband's eyes made her think that Tom had told him otherwise. "Do you know where he is?"

"He told me he had some business in Rhode Island. Newport, as a matter of fact. He called Chris Kelly, to help him track down some Irish girl."

"Do you think it has to do with his and Bernie's trip to Dublin? With Seamus?"

"He wouldn't say," John said, clipping off more bunches of grapes, dropping them in the wicker basket. "But I think so. He told me she was an Irish national, and he wanted someone from Chris's law office to look up her green card, find out where she was working."

"Kathleen," Honor whispered, dropping the basket.

"Who?"

"Don't you remember, their first night back? They said Seamus was in love with a girl who'd moved to the States. Didn't he even say it was Newport?"

"He did," John said, holding her shoulders, looking into her eyes. Honor blinked into the sun; she knew how tender Tom Kelly's heart was. If he couldn't have Bernie, he would help his son find Kathleen.

"Oh God," Honor said. "Regis..."

"What are you talking about?"

"That's why she stayed in Newport," Honor whispered. "Don't ask me how I know, or what she's doing, but it has to do with Kathleen and Seamus. Tom must have bumped into her there...."

John's eyes gleamed and he kissed her exuberantly at the thought that such a thing could be true. But suddenly they heard a commotion— a truck driving through the field, tearing up turf under the wheels, and John craned his neck to see over the vines.

"We might be wrong about that," John said. "Here's Thomas Kelly right now."

And it was true. Hurrying around the end of a thickly overgrown row of grapevines, Honor and John were just in time to see Tom barreling across the meadow. He threw the truck into park, opened the door, and stood tall on the door panel to look across the vine-covered trellises. The vineyard was filled with people, but not the one he was looking for.

"John, Honor," he yelled, "where's Bernie?"

"We haven't seen her," John said, striding over.

Honor started after him, but just then she saw a black figure standing on the top of the hill, appearing almost disoriented, gazing down at the vineyard, at everyone harvesting the grapes. Honor's throat caught at the sight, and she started up the hill toward her best friend.

Tom saw her at the same time. He jumped down from his truck, bounding past Honor and John, up the grassy hill. Honor followed close behind him. Something had happened; she knew the instant she saw her. Catching up with Tom, she saw Bernie's eyes, stunned but bright. She looked almost as if she had just woken up from sleep, from a deep dream.

"Bernie," Honor heard Tom say. "We have to hurry."

"No," Bernie said quietly. "We should slow down. Please, Tom…"

"You don't understand. Everything is happening very fast. We could miss our chance if we don't leave now."

"Why, what are you saying?" she asked.

"Bernie," Tom said, grabbing her hands, "come with me. It's important, more than I can say right now. I'll tell you everything on the way. Hurry, we don't have much time."

And Honor watched as her best friend and sister-in-law, holding hands with Tom Kelly, ran down the hill, her black gown and veil flying out behind her, and climbed into the old green truck. The sun gleamed on the tawny fields, green and golden grape leaves, and pale green fruit. Wheels spun as Tom shifted into reverse, turned around and roared through the meadow, dust kicking up behind. As the truck disappeared through the Academy gates, John looked down at Honor.

"What was that about?" he asked.

"I honestly don't know," Honor said, but she thought maybe she did. Her heart tumbling over, she had the feeling that although Tom had come with news about Seamus, Bernie had just had a revelation of her own.

Twenty-Three

Traffic was heavy the minute they hit I-95. Tom gripped the steering wheel, trying to concentrate on the road, but it wasn't easy, with Bernie sitting beside him. He hadn't seen her in over three weeks. In all their lives, he couldn't remember a time when they'd been apart for that long.

Sometimes she went on retreat—once a year, she'd go to Gethsemani, the Trappist monastery in Kentucky, to spend seven days in silence and prayer. Thomas Merton had lived and written there, and she would go to the monks' library and choose one of his books to read during her visit.

She'd come home and tell Tom about the bluegrass, and the monks, and the beautiful music played by Brother Luke at Sunday mass, on their Letourneau Opus 93 organ. The monastery had the same name as the Dublin hospital where she'd given birth, so she'd listen to the music and feel love for her son come welling up.

Or she'd go to Montreal or Washington, D.C., for conferences or her order's planning sessions. Business trips.

Occasionally it was Tom who went away, never for more than a few days. Skiing with his cousins at Mad River, or on a trek with John, scouting locations in Newfoundland or Manitoba for one of his installations. One year Chris Kelly had tried to talk him into going on

a two-week diving vacation in the Bahamas, but Chris had quit pitch-
ing about three minutes into it.

"You don't like being away from Star of the Sea," Chris had said
with a chuckle. "You think the place will stop running, fall apart if
you leave."

"Yeah, that's it," Tom had agreed, laughing, letting his cousin
believe that because it was easier than the truth: that Tom couldn't
stand being away from Bernie.

So these three weeks had felt unreal, a little like living in a wind
tunnel: nothing to hold on to, and the most profound sense of emptiness Tom had ever had. He drove north toward Boston now, trying
to concentrate on the road, steadily passing cars as he tried to make
time, instead of staring across the seat at Bernie, to make sure she was
really there.

"Are you going to tell me where we're going?" she asked after a
while.

"I'm surprised you didn't ask the minute you got in the truck," he
said.

She didn't reply. In fact, as he glanced over now, he could see that
she didn't look well. Her face was pale, her expression drained and
worried. He felt a rush of panic—was she sick?

"Are you okay, Bernie?" he asked.

She started to nod, then shook her head, raising her hand to her
forehead. "I'm not sure," she said, and Tom could see that her fingers
were trembling.

"Should I pull over?" he asked, his eyes darting between her and
the road.

"No," she said. "It's not like that." She paused, closed her eyes. Her
lips looked dry. Tom reached into the door pocket, pulled out a bottle of water.

"Here," he said.

Bernie nodded gratefully, opened it up, drank a few sips. As Tom
watched, a little color returned to her cheeks. She drank a little more,
screwed the top back on, and handed it back to him.

"Thank you," she said.

"Was that it?" he asked. "You were thirsty?"

She gave her head a quick shake, letting him know she didn't want to talk about it right now. Over the years, Tom had learned how to read her signals like no one else. They had worked so closely together. Leaving their personal history aside, they'd kept Star of the Sea running perfectly—and it wasn't easy.

Bernie basically oversaw the human aspect: the convent, with all the nuns, and the school, with all the students. Tom kept the rest going: he hired plumbers and electricians, roofers and carpenters, to maintain the old buildings; he kept a full-time grounds crew to stay ahead of the mowing, trimming, weed-whacking, pruning, and stonework. And he had hired a winemaker, a scientist and artisan with an agricultural degree from the University of Connecticut and eleven years of experience at vineyards on Long Island and in the Napa Valley.

With all that responsibility, Tom had no illusions about being the boss. Sister Bernadette Ignatius signed his paycheck; she was his employer, and she ran the place. She was a busy woman. More than that, she was his mysterious and complicated Bernie. So Tom had gotten very adept at listening to what she didn't say, as much as what she did. Right now, with her wide eyes staring out the windshield, he could see that she was in the grip of something big, and he knew she wouldn't tell him until she was ready.

They rode along in silence for twenty miles, heading north. Traffic seemed worse on 395, for a change—probably people in search of fall foliage, cider mills, pumpkin patches. So Tom stayed on I-95, finally breaking free of the flow and starting to make time.

"You asked me where we were going," Tom said after a while.

"I know. And you didn't tell me."

"Don't you want to know?"

"I asked," she said, giving him the first smile of the day. It did something to his heart, unexpected and forceful. Tom felt rattled by the softness in her eyes and her sudden warmth. "I trust you, Tom," she said. "I know if you tell me to come with you, it's important."

"I wasn't sure you still did," he said.

"You're the one who left," she said, reminding him gently.

"I did it for you, Bernie," he said.

"Shhh," she said, holding a finger to her lips, as if she were too tired for more recriminations. "Just tell me: where are we going?"

"Boston," he said. "Logan Airport."

"Tom," she said, instantly rattled, "the airport? But I can't leave now ... you don't mean we should go to Ireland again? Not now ..."

"No, Bernie," he said, reaching over to touch her hand, just to reassure her. Her skin felt hot, and he left his fingers there, touching her, unable to pull away. "We're not going anywhere."

"Then what?" she asked.

"He's coming here," Tom said.

"Who? What are you talking about?"

"Seamus. He's on Aer Lingus 124, arriving at two-thirty."

Bernie gasped, and when she turned to look, he saw tears in her eyes. His hand was already touching hers, so now he clasped her hand in his, holding it tight, trying to give her all the reassurance he could.

"Did he call you?" she whispered. "Did he say he wants to see us?"

"No, Bernie," Tom said. "Sixtus has been keeping me informed. He helped Seamus get his passport, and to rush it, the passport office required that he fill in his dates and times of travel. Sixtus found out that way, through his contacts in the government."

"Oh, Tom," she said, closing his eyes. "What do you think you're doing?"

"Picking him up at the airport."

"But don't you see? He doesn't want you to pick him up! If he did, he'd have called you. He's trying to work everything out on his own, and I think he'll resent us terribly if we interfere in his life right now, any more than we already have."

"Bernie, you don't understand," Tom said quietly.

"I do," she said. "Turn around. Take us back to Star of the Sea, right now."

"No," he said.

Her head snapped to look at him. She wasn't used to being defied that way. Tom had spent so long trying to work with Bernie's rules, but right now he knew he didn't have time for that.

"Yes," she said. "There's something you don't know, that I haven't told you yet...."

"Same here, Bernie. I haven't told you why we're doing this. And we *are* doing it," he said, not wanting to hear her reasons, her rationale, her philosophical construction for why they shouldn't pick their son up at the airport.

"Why, then?" she asked. "What haven't you told me?"

"I've found Kathleen."

Once more Bernie gasped. Her eyes were wide, disbelieving.

"Where is she? Is she all right?"

"Bernie, she's in Newport," Tom said. "And I don't know if she's all right or not. I only saw her for a minute, looking out the window." He pictured her now; as fleeting as his sight of her had been, he'd had the impression of despair, of someone at the very limit of herself. And Tom had experience, seeing a woman like that: that quick look at Kathleen had brought him back to Dublin, when Bernie was in the fight of her life, with her demons.

"Tom, you really found her?" Bernie asked, a tone of joy sounding in her voice.

"I did," he said proudly. "I did it for Seamus. And I wanted you to be with me, so we can tell him together."

"It can be our gift to him," Bernie whispered.

Tom nodded. His chest felt full, as if his heart was expanding. He held back the words he wanted to say: that it was really his gift to Bernie. Something they could give their son, that would make him know how much they loved him. They had missed so much of his life, but they could be completely present right now, for this. Tom had looked in Seamus's eyes and known that his love for Kathleen was the most important thing in his world. It ruled him, owned him, and gave him a reason to get up in the morning.

Tom knew how that felt. Right now, sitting beside Bernie, he knew that he had everything he had ever wanted in the world. Her presence, the sound of her breathing, the ever-changing expression on her face. They hadn't been together from birth, but they'd known each other as children. Tom had fallen in love the first day he ever saw her; he could see her now, in her yellow dress at a Star of the Sea picnic, as they chased each other over the rocks and through the fields.

"Tom," Bernie said, "I can't wait to see him."

"I know," Tom said. "Neither can I."

"Will we drive him straight to see Kathleen?"

"We have to," Tom said, thinking of Regis, hoping that she was able to work things out on her end. "She's leaving tonight."

Oakhurst was stuffy and pretentious in just about every way—and that was just the house. The people were even more so. When Mirande brought Regis to the front door on Saturday afternoon, both of them dressed in Beth's spare uniforms—lightweight black wool dresses with starched white aprons—you might have thought aliens had landed, judging from Mrs. Wells's reaction.

"Madam," said Beth, who had been filled in on most of the plan, "may I present my sister Mirande and her colleague Regis?"

Mrs. Wells, passing through the front hall on her way upstairs, stared in shock. Her blond hair, as always, was perfectly done. She wore a navy blue pantsuit with huge brass buttons, gold tapestry slippers on her feet, and her hands were laden down with diamonds on her fingers and wrists. "But what are they *doing* here?" she asked.

"We've come to help you pack," Regis said. Considering how this was going, she was glad she had told Monica and Juliana to wait in the car—getaway drivers ready at a moment's notice.

"But . . ." Mrs. Wells began. She would have frowned if her face hadn't been surgically immobilized. "I don't recall hiring extra help. . . ."

Beth had told Mirande that the Wellses often employed freelance workers—extra maids, butlers, servers; even manicurists, hairdressers, and masseurs—for parties, balls, and other special occasions. They used an employment agency on Spring Street, and occasionally the agent sent too many or too few people for any given event.

Mrs. Wells would always explode at Beth or Kathleen, somehow blaming them for something that couldn't possibly be their fault. Beth said Mrs. Wells tended to forget details, like how many waitresses she had asked for, or exactly which day she had told them to come.

"It's a bonus," Regis said, smiling. "For all the many times you have cheerfully used our services this summer!"

"You mean," Mrs. Wells said suspiciously, "it's free?"

"Yes," Regis said. Beth had said that although they were filthy rich, they were also shockingly cheap. "For being such a valued customer… we certainly want to keep your business for next year."

"So they've come to help me finish packing for you, ma'am," Beth explained with a slight laugh. Although Regis didn't know her, she could see that Beth felt nervous about lying. Her neck and cheeks were bright red, and she was about to start giggling. But she shouldn't have worried; Mrs. Wells was too self-centered to question the idea of a gift of free service landing on her doorstep.

"Hmm," Mrs. Wells said. "Very well, then. I need a pedicure."

"We're here to help with *packing*," Regis said, glancing up the stairs. She couldn't wait to tear up to the attic, find Kathleen.

"Yes, well, let the other two handle that. Come with me. My feet need tending to before that tedious drive to New York. We leave in two hours." Leading Regis up the wide, curving front staircase, she had an air of resignation, as if this young woman was quite an annoyance, but at least she'd be able to get her toenails painted before enduring the rigors of travel.

As they walked along, Regis scoped out the lay of the land. The second-floor hallway was enormous—quite long, and wide enough to drive a Rolls-Royce right down the middle. Glancing into the open doors, Regis saw several spacious bedrooms with four-poster mahogany beds, walls covered with pale silk moiré, chair rails and ceiling moldings, marble fireplaces with intricately carved mantelpieces, and portraits of dour ancestors.

Passing one room, she saw a man sprawled on his back, tangled in the sheets, arm flung off to the side, snoring. The winds of liquor blew from his bed into the hall, like a sirocco of hangover, depression, and regret. Regis could smell it from the hallway.

"Wake *up*, Andrew," Mrs. Wells said sharply as they passed. "You missed a lovely brunch at Eloise Craven's. You had better be ready to leave in two hours flat. Up, *now!*"

"Is that your son?" Regis asked, thinking of what Beth had said, about Kathleen being involved with one of the Wells boys, thinking that that poor, sodden lump couldn't possibly provide much competition for any son of Tom and Aunt Bernie.

Mrs. Wells threw her a dark glance, as if she couldn't believe what a disastrous faux pas she'd just made. Speaking without being spoken to? *Quelle horreur!* Regis ducked her head like a supplicant, reminding herself to behave so she could get this job done.

But she raised her eyes just as Mrs. Wells swept into her bedroom, in time to spot a narrow doorway at the shadowed, far end of the hallway. Regis had grown up at Star of the Sea, the main building of which had originally been a very grand house for the most successful Irish family in Connecticut. She knew how these places worked— that the aristocrats had wide doors and huge windows for their own bedrooms, and stuck narrow doors and tiny windows in the servants' quarters.

That door at the end of the hall went up to the attic, where the help slept—Regis's skin tingled, and she knew instinctively that that was where she would find Kathleen. But for now she followed Mrs. Wells into her bedroom. It was decorated in pale blue and gold, with crystal lamps and gilt-framed oval mirrors. Mrs. Wells reclined on a tufted chaise longue, pointing at her dressing table.

"My beauty tray is there," she directed Regis. "I'd like you to use the Elegante Rose polish."

"You got it," Regis said, pawing through the seemingly hundreds of bottles of makeup and nail polish.

"Excuse me?"

"I said, '*Certainly*, madam.'"

Making her way over to the chaise, Regis wasn't sure where to sit. Mrs. Wells directed her to pull the dressing table's dainty antique bench closer. Regis sat down, heard it creak, hoped it wouldn't shatter under her weight. She knew exactly how to do a pedicure—she and her sisters had given each other many. After she removed the old polish, she literally had to hold her hand steady to keep from dabbing butterflies, hearts, and smiley faces onto the woman's toenails. Meanwhile, she stayed attentive for any sounds coming from the attic.

"I would like to give you a gift," Mrs. Wells said suddenly.

"Oh, you don't have to," Regis said, although as a college student she knew how happy she'd be to be slipped a ten-spot, especially since holding this woman's bare feet had not been part of the plan.

"Please. Here is my gift to you. Have pedicures."

"Excuse me?"

"When you are older. It is a gift you give yourself, but I'm giving it to you first."

"Uh, thank you," Regis said, confused.

"And use good skin products. The face is one's most precious possession."

Regis nearly choked. She started painting faster, knowing that she was in the presence of madness. Besides, as she dipped the brush in the bottle, she swiveled her wrist and saw twenty minutes had passed since she'd started. Her stomach knotted up as she thought of what she had to do.

"You have good bone structure," Mrs. Wells said appraisingly, through narrowed eyes.

"Thank you, ma'am."

"Stay out of the sun. That's my last gift to you. I tell all the girls... do they listen? So rarely. I hope you'll do yourself a favor and take care of your face."

"Hmm," Regis said, thinking she'd like to take care of Mrs. Wells's face; unclip all the stitches and let her smile again. But instead, she just fanned her hand over the woman's newly lacquered toenails and said, "Voilà! Beautiful tootsies!"

"You certainly have a lot of personality," Mrs. Wells said distastefully. "Why don't you run along and help the other girl, the one you

came with? Send Beth up here, and tell her I need Kathleen. That girl
has been shirking all day, and I won't have it! She is leaving in the first
car, with Bobby and Mr. Wells, and she had better be finished packing for Mr. Pierce and Mr. Andrew!"

"Very good, madam," Regis said, starting to back out of the room.

She backed straight into someone, who caught her around the
waist with his hands. Jumping, turning to look, she came face-to-face
with the tannest, slickest man she'd ever seen: the new generation of
George Hamilton. He wore sleek chinos and a black lisle shirt, his
eyes were dark, his nose aquiline, and he was devastatingly handsome
in a vaguely reptilian way.

"Well, well," he said. "Who might you be?"

"Get your hands off the help," Mrs. Wells snapped. She didn't use
Regis's name, because she didn't know it.

"Why have I never met you before?" he asked, staring hungrily into
her eyes.

"Because I'm new," Regis said. "And here just for today."

"Are you coming to Palm Beach with us?"

Regis shook her head.

"Pierce," Mrs. Wells said, "let her do her work. Now, you go and
wake up your brother before I go stark, raving mad. We have an
eight-thirty dinner reservation at the Union Club, and Sophia
Stillwater will be there, and if Andrew makes us late, I'll be very
unhappy."

"You wanted me to get Beth for you?" Regis reminded Mrs. Wells
as she inched away.

"Yes. Please, right away," Mrs. Wells said, her voice clipped.

Pierce was watching Regis with hawk eyes; she wanted to slam the
door on him, make a break for the attic. But just then his mother
summoned him to help her walk to the bathroom without smearing
her nail lacquer—and Regis knew that was the best gift of all: distracting her son.

Out in the hall, she knew she didn't have time to run downstairs,
so she pulled her cell phone out of her uniform pocket and texted
Mirande: *hr mjsty nds beth!*

Then Regis looked both ways, up and down the hall, as if about to cross an extremely dangerous thoroughfare. The coast was clear; she hurried to the narrow door at the very end, turned the crystal knob as silently as possible, and began climbing the dark, steep stairs.

When she got to the top, she felt the chill: there was no heat up here. Tearing along the cold corridor, she looked into each bedroom. They were all small and spare, with skinny twin beds and bare light-bulbs. After the opulence downstairs, it seemed like something out of Dickens, and it made Regis's blood boil to think of people being treated so carelessly.

All the rooms were empty; Kathleen wasn't up here. Had Regis been wrong or misunderstood? Was Kathleen somewhere else, had she already left for New York? But no—Mrs. Wells had just said that Kathleen was to leave soon, with Mr. Wells and Bobby, whoever that was.

Regis glanced into one room, instantly knowing that it had been Kathleen's: there was a postcard of Ireland stuck in the mirror, the romantic sandy strand of North Beach in Courtown, County Wexford. Regis stared at the picture, feeling Kathleen's homesickness as she did so. She turned and looked around the room; the bed-clothes had been stripped off the bed, and a thin blue blanket neatly folded at the foot of the stained mattress.

There was a white bureau and straight-backed chair, but no night table or bookshelf. The only lamp was the bare bulb overhead. Regis glanced around, feeling choked up. To think of Kathleen living in this room, probably heading for another just like it in Florida, made her heart hurt.

But where was Kathleen now? Had she run away—made her escape from this job and these people? Regis felt a moment of panic, knowing that Bernie and Tom had to be on the way here with Seamus.

Just then, Regis heard a scraping sound, coming from across the hall. Standing perfectly still, she held her breath and listened. The sound was so subtle, barely audible, almost as if it were coming from mice nesting in the walls.

Regis's gaze fixed on an old door. It had been painted green, but the paint had peeled. It had been boarded up to prevent access, with splintery old wood that gave a feeling of menace and a warning to keep out.

Regis's mouth was dry, her palms sweaty, as she stepped closer. Someone had pulled one of the boards off, making a space just big enough to slide underneath. The peeling green door was cracked open behind the boards.

Regis ran her hand over the rough boards. She listened, her ear to the door, hearing nothing; whoever had been moving around in there must have frozen, waiting for her to leave. Her pulse racing, she gave the door a good push. It squeaked on its rusty hinges. And then she ducked her head, and stepped inside.

Twenty-Four

The flight had been nothing short of amazing, from start to finish. Seamus had had no idea what to expect. To be twenty-three and have never been on a plane—well, it seemed almost shameful. Especially when he'd spent so much time at the airport, picking up and dropping off hotel guests on their way to and from so many exotic places. So he'd been more than ready to climb aboard.

Once on the plane, he'd looked around. It was like being in a long, plastic room, with tiny little TVs dropping down from the ceiling every few feet. The seats were comfortable, slightly crowded, but not too bad, if you didn't mind having your knees folded up to your chest. It was close quarters, all right, but having lived at St. Augustine's, Seamus was very good at sharing space with others.

The woman in the seat beside him needed help in stowing her bag overhead. Seamus offered to help, and she seemed very grateful as he wedged her suitcase in between his and another. He liked the sense that he was a traveler amongst travelers. It didn't matter whether they were chauffeurs or judges—they were all on the same plane. He settled back, glad he had chosen a window seat.

Takeoff was spectacular. Seamus appreciated fine machinery, and he couldn't get over the throttle the pilot must have had to give the plane to get it airborne. Hurtling down the runway, Seamus stared out the small window, not wanting to miss a thing. Then—wow!

That thrust, right in the small of his back, as the plane rose up, veering right, then left, straightening out over Dublin Bay. Before one wide, banking turn west, Seamus peered out at Clontarf.

His throat actually felt tight. It was strange, unexpected, something he hadn't felt before. A surge of emotion every bit as powerful as the acceleration of the plane's engines. It rocked him, honestly. Because when he gave it a little thought, watching Clontarf disappear into the vapor trail, he realized that the feeling had something to do with Sixtus Kelly. Tom Kelly's cousin.

It was good of the man to have helped him, to have put Seamus on the right track for his passport. That's what this crazy feeling was about—Seamus's gratitude to a person, a stranger, really, the fact he was Tom Kelly's cousin notwithstanding, for helping Seamus get something he needed. And not making him feel like an idiot for not having a passport already. Sophisticated men of the world like the Kellys—they would have had passports and flown many places by the time they were Seamus's age.

But that thought made Seamus think of Tom's tattered tweed jacket, his old boots, the trousers that could have stood a pressing. He didn't have such a worldly air. Neither did Sixtus, really, when you considered how powerful a man he was; entertaining Seamus the way he had, taking all the time in the world to talk to him, show him Clontarf and tell him about the Kelly sea monster. He'd been very easygoing. No airs about him to speak of.

Now, as the plane flew west, Seamus slipped his hand into his pants pocket. Yes, the ring was right there. He still couldn't believe Sixtus had given it to him, and he didn't really feel right about wearing it. But having it close by made him feel good somehow. His throat tightened again, and he closed his eyes. New waves of emotion came over him, thinking of the ring. And suddenly, out of nowhere, came the image of a woman with red hair. Not dark, raven hair like Kathleen's, but golden-red hair: like Seamus's mother's.

He had a mother. The very thought of it made him hold tighter to the ring. To have thought himself parentless for so long, and then to have met Bernadette and Tom, face-to-face in the hotel courtyard—

it was all a great deal too much to handle all at once. That was the best that could be said.

That letter he had written . . . not that he regretted it, exactly, the letter was full of things that needed to be expressed, but perhaps he could have softened the tone. Maybe he could have said that someday—not right then, while he was reeling from shock—but another time, in the future, and possibly not even the distant future, perhaps then they could meet. Meet and—what? Talk, maybe. Something like that.

The truth was, and he had to face it, he probably wouldn't be making this trip if Bernadette and Tom hadn't come to Ireland. Not that Seamus wouldn't have found out Kathleen was living in Newport—Sister Anastasia would have gotten the postcard to him somehow. But he might not have considered such a trip doable, or even possible, if Tom hadn't told him to go see Sixtus.

The flight attendant was coming around, offering drinks. Seamus ordered a beer; he drank it, looking out the window. Ireland was so green from the air. He had so often heard the tourists say it, fresh off their flights from the States, and he'd thought they had to be exaggerating. But they weren't, he could see now: there were squares of emerald green everywhere he looked, some bisected by roads or stone walls.

There, those rocky promontories: that had to be Kerry. Great long fingers of stone, scraping into the sea. And there—just north—that had to be Clare: the Cliffs of Moher! Amazing to be seeing them from the air; the light was hitting them straight on, and they looked majestic and fantastic.

He watched, and then they were over the open ocean. Really under way now, crossing the Atlantic, on his way to Kathleen. How would he find her? He had downloaded maps and information from tourist websites on the hotel computer; it was all packed away in his suitcase, along with a Rhode Island travel guide and a New England road atlas.

He had saved a lot of money, working over the years. Although he had planned to use it for his continuing education, he'd taken most of it out of the bank, converted it to traveler's checks. Whatever it took, he was going to find Kathleen Murphy. He knew that Newport was a wealthy town, with mansions, yachts, and fine hotels. The prices would probably be sky-high, but if he found himself a good boardinghouse, for the minimum price, he could make his funds last long enough to find her—and then bring her home.

That was, assuming she'd want to go with him. Some nights, lying awake, Seamus would stare at the postcard, through the fine brown film of Tom's blood, looking at those enormous seaside palaces, imagining that Kathleen lived there. Maybe her parents were very affluent, and they had transformed her into a princess. The men she'd meet were probably all well-off, very successful; perhaps their houses were even bigger than Kathleen's parents'.

Seamus told himself that it was possible that she was married. He couldn't bear to think it, but he knew how beautiful she was, how smart, and wonderful, and funny, and how the men of America would all have to be idiots to have not caught her by now.

But deep down in his heart, the place where he knew the truth about everything that mattered, Seamus knew that she couldn't be married. Kathleen couldn't be in love, couldn't be engaged, couldn't be with anyone but him. As the plane flew west, and he got closer to her, it was almost as if he could feel her pull—she was the full moon, he was the high tide, and they were coming together....

Other people slept or watched the movie on those little ceiling TVs, but not Seamus. He just held on to the ring, staring out the window, through high, thin clouds, at the slate-colored ocean far below. Tiny whitecaps, freighters, tankers, then an island...another island...a land mass.

"America," he said.

He watched the great northern expanse of North America come into view. It seemed massive and solid, spreading out before him in shades of brown and green, throwing out its arms to welcome him. He wanted to get his bag down from the overhead bin, to be ready to jump off the plane the second it landed, but the flight attendant told him it would be another hour yet.

My God, was the country that big? he thought. Staying in his seat was no small challenge. Especially once the captain announced that they were starting their descent. Seamus's ears popped. He watched people heading to and from the bathrooms, freshening up. The woman beside him told him her husband would be picking her up. The couple in front of him were talking, and he overheard them say their son would be at the gate.

Suddenly, Seamus felt a chill. Out the window, the land was looking closer. It wasn't green here; the trees were a blaze of color—scarlet, orange, yellow. Everything seemed strange—what had he been thinking, taking this trip? Seamus Sullivan, who'd never been on a plane in his life? He had no idea about transportation in America; he'd ask about a bus or train to Newport, or maybe he'd hitchhike.

What if he found Kathleen and she rejected him? Or didn't remember him? God, it had been ten years. Why had he ever thought she'd even know who he was? No—he reminded himself of the postcard. She had asked for him by name...James...A new thought arose: what if he couldn't find her? What if he went to every door in Newport and she wasn't there?

And at that moment, a jolt of electricity passed through him, and he knew—Kathleen needed him. He felt it in his skin and bones, in every one of his five senses. He shivered, knowing that she was calling him, as surely as if she'd cried his name. It was as if he'd entered a different force field; here on the shores of America, he could feel her like never before—or at least not since their years at St. Augustine's.

His thoughts were so vivid, he barely noticed that they had landed. The plane roared, bouncing down the runway. They taxied to the gate, and people all jumped up at once, turning on cell phones, calling their families.

If Seamus had her number, he'd be calling her now. She didn't know how close he was, that he was moving inexorably closer to her, that nothing would get in his way. Something tore at his heart, as if she was in distress, or even danger. A sense of her despair filled him like a cold black fog, making him feel afraid.

With everyone thronging the aisles, struggling to get their bags down, Seamus sat still, gathering himself together. He was in a new country—where Kathleen lived. Slipping his hand into his pocket, he closed it around the ring. He remembered what Sixtus had said, that if he was going to find Kathleen, he would need it. Although he'd not worn it before, he slipped it on now.

Instantly, as if the ring had strong powers, he felt a little more sure of himself. He stood up and hauled down his suitcase and that of the woman beside him. She thanked him, told him to look after himself, and he said the same to her. The ring felt heavy on his finger; he wasn't used to wearing one. The gold was solid, the crest deeply scored. Seamus felt a pang—here he was, identifying himself as a Kelly. After the way he'd treated Tom, he wasn't sure he had any such right.

Once he hit the concourse, he began to run ahead of the people from his flight. Some had more luggage to pick up, but Seamus was traveling light, with just the one suitcase. He hurried along, the feeling of panic growing. How would he find her? He felt her needing him, but he had no idea of how to get to her.

The airport seemed to go along forever. He hit Immigration, and the line was long. It inched its way forward, and he wanted to shout. His blood was really racing, and he looked wildly around, wondering if there was someone he could tell—but what would he say? That he had a feeling that something was wrong with someone he hadn't seen in ten years?

But he held it all in, making it through Immigration with no problem—especially because the inspector was an Irishman named T. C. Devlin.

"Reason for visiting?" he asked.

"Love," Seamus said.

"You really just had to say 'business' or 'vacation,'" the man said with a smile. But he stamped Seamus's passport, gave him a nod, and that was that.

Through U.S. Customs—nothing to declare—and then Seamus ran for the exit. Others from his flight were with him, pushing forward, some coming home, others on a visit. The double doors swung open, and families shouted their hellos to each other. Seamus scanned the crowd, almost by habit, but this time he was on the other side, instead of standing with the uniformed livery drivers, holding up signs with their passengers' names written in big black letters.

Families everywhere—reunions, greetings, people overjoyed to see each other. Seamus swallowed hard; he'd never had anyone happy to see him since Kathleen, and this arrival in America just brought it home for him. He heard the woman who'd sat next to him on the plane cry "Frank!" and throw herself into her husband's arms. They kissed, and they seemed so happy. Seamus paused, looking for the exit.

Sliding his gaze away from the couple, he glimpsed a nun. Ah, that was nice—a Sister of Notre Dame des Victoires. He'd know their habit anywhere—the long black dress, the white underpart of her veil framing her face, and the black outer part of the veil falling over her shoulders. Seamus's throat caught to see her—it was like a homecoming, in a way, and he took it as a good sign for him and Kathleen. He raised his eyes to hers, to greet her, and what he saw there was the warmest, most loving expression he'd ever seen in his life.

The nun's blue eyes were glowing, smiling, making Seamus feel as if they knew each other. He stumbled, and started walking toward her. Had she been one of his teachers? Or at St. Augustine's? Just then, she said his name:

"Seamus."

But they had known him as James there....

"Sister," he said politely.

And then he saw: a few strands of red hair emerging from beneath her veil, and her clear, bright eyes. Standing beside her was the tall man, his blue eyes shining, his nose a little crooked but otherwise healed.

"Tom," Seamus said, reaching out to shake his hand. Tom did the same, and their rings clicked—two Kelly rings, emblazoned with the great sea monster.

"Welcome to America," Tom said.

"Yes, Seamus. Welcome," Sister Bernadette said. As if she couldn't hold herself back, she opened her arms. Maybe it was because he was exhausted from the flight, or maybe it was because she was wearing the habit he had so long associated with love, and care, and everything maternal, but he opened his arms also, and let her hug him.

And then it was over. He pulled back, she stepped away, and they all stood there looking at each other. Seamus felt awkward, for a thousand reasons he couldn't even name.

"Are you traveling somewhere?" he asked. "I'll let you get on your way now, because I'm in a hurry myself."

"Seamus," she said, "we came to get you."

"I don't understand," he said, his brow wrinkled with confusion. "How did you know I'd be here?"

"Tom found out," she said. "From Sixtus..."

"Oh," Seamus said. Had he mentioned to Sixtus what time his flight was leaving, or that he'd be flying to Boston? His head spun; was this what jet lag felt like? He didn't want to hurt their feelings; although he wasn't half as angry as he'd been when he first met them in Dublin, he didn't quite know what they wanted from him. Besides, he had to get to Newport, to Kathleen. "I'm sorry, but I have somewhere to go," he said.

"We'll take you to her," Tom said.

"But you don't know what I'm doing, where I'm going....I'm sorry for being rude the last time we met, and again now, but this is urgent...."

"He *does* know where you're going," Sister Bernadette said, putting her hand on Seamus's arm, looking into his eyes. "He found Kathleen for you."

"Kathleen?" Seamus asked in disbelief, his voice breaking.

"Yes," Tom said, hoisting Seamus's bag, slinging it over his back. "But we have to hurry—we don't have much time."

"I know," Seamus said. "Kathleen needs me."

"I think you're right; she does," Tom said, hurrying along, as if he understood Seamus with everything he had.

Bernie sat between Tom and Seamus in the pickup's cab. Her left arm touched Tom, her right Seamus, and she felt so close to each of them. Not just physically close, either. There'd been such energy in Seamus's gaze when he saw her—instant recognition. Perhaps not as his mother, not even specifically as Sister Bernadette Ignatius—but merely as a

Sister of Notre Dame des Victoires. She had loved seeing his reaction to her habit, knowing that he had good feelings about the Sisters who had raised him.

That made everything go a little easier. This was a day of miracles, but not in the usual sense. Bernie knew that most people used that word to describe moments of great joy—a healing, a cure, a resurrection. And in many ways, "joy" would be the right word to describe the day. Seeing her son again, sitting between him and Tom, his father. She felt energy pouring off both of them, through her body, back to each other.

And Bernie's time in the Blue Grotto; it had been over two decades since she had knelt at the feet of the statue of the Virgin Mary and Mary had come down from her pediment to wipe Bernie's brow, soothe her with words of love and grace. In the language of the faithful, that event was called a "Marian apparition."

But to Bernie, there'd been no apparition about it. Mary had been real, and Bernie had felt her touch, heard her words, shared time with her, and felt her presence. This morning, it had happened again.

Bernie's skin still tingled now, from that single touch that morning. Sitting in the middle of the truck's bench seat, Bernie caught sight of her face in the rearview mirror. There was a small mark on her right cheek, bright red, like a sting or a burn, where Mary's hand had been. Bernie felt it now, tender to the touch, but without any pain. Instead, she only felt the loving presence of God.

Mary had said, "Be ready." What did that mean, and why did Bernie's stomach jump to think of it? Just hours ago, Bernie had gazed into the Blessed Mother's kind, loving eyes. She had asked what the words meant, but Mary had just said them again: *Be ready.*

Tom sped, passing cars, driving as fast as he could. The truck weaved in and out of traffic. Seamus was very alert, watching out the window, probably thinking of Kathleen; Tom was intent only on making good time, getting to Newport as quickly as possible. Neither one of them talked.

Bernie was glad. She needed this time to think and pray. When the truck jostled her and Tom together, she sensed him wondering whether she was uncomfortable. At the same time, she knew what this meant to him—not just the overwhelming fact of having their son in the truck with them, but the simple, ordinary fact that he and Bernie were touching. She had only to look up at his face to know how happy it made him; his blue eyes crinkled at the corners, and his mouth lifted in a smile.

Bernie had to close her eyes; she was so grateful for this time. She prayed that Tom could know the depths of her love, her appreciation of the gift he had always been in her life. She asked for the words to tell him, when the time was right. And she thanked God for everything He had given her, given all three of them, especially this time together now, today.

Gifts came in small and large ways. Several years ago, when Sister Felicity developed multiple sclerosis, Bernie had read everything she could find on breakthroughs in research on the disease. Reading one article, she had been shocked to learn that mothers carry cells from their children years after they are born. The cells live on in the mother's body. Although the article said that this discovery brought medical hope, that the cells of babies born even decades earlier retain the power to regenerate, and help the mother fight disease, Bernie was struck with a much simpler truth.

She had lowered the scientific journal and wept. The knowledge had made her feel closer to her beloved child. She had always felt his spirit and presence; she had held him close in prayer each day since his birth. But to learn that his cells existed in her, that they were still united, mother and child, had felt like the most wonderful gift.

They hadn't been together, not really—not walking and talking and interacting. But now she knew that a part of her son was with her always. That night, reading in bed, she'd cried because Tom didn't have that. He hadn't carried the baby as she had. And she knew that Tom's grief was double, in many ways more severe than Bernie's.

Because Tom had had no choice. Not really. When Bernie decided to give up the baby and join the convent, Tom had had to stand back and let it happen. That was what Mary spoke to her about that morning. That and other things…

Now, speeding south, Bernie prayed for strength. She felt Tom's and Seamus's tension and knew that they worried they wouldn't be on time to intercept Kathleen. Bernie wanted to reassure them, tell them what she knew. But she didn't quite trust her own voice.

So she said the rosary, lips moving in silence. When they reached the Newport Bridge, soaring over Narragansett Bay, they saw the whole town spreading out below. Seamus pressed his face against the truck window. Bernie knew that he could *feel* how close they were to Kathleen; she believed that her son's intense love for his long-lost friend was guiding them like a beacon.

"We're almost there," she said now, catching Seamus's eye.

He nodded, and she saw his eyes gleam with a smile.

"That's right," Tom said. "Just a few more minutes…"

His words seemed prescient, and they pierced Bernie's heart. This time with their son, all sitting so close together, nearly overwhelmed her. She was a nun, but she didn't care. Reaching for his hand, she held it in hers. He looked over with shock and almost more happiness than she could bear. Bernie held her rosary beads in her right hand, and she kept silently praying; but she held Tom's hand in her left, and she wouldn't let it go.

Twenty-Five

Kathleen crouched on the floor in this secret, boarded-up part of the attic, across the hall from her bedroom, huddled in a blanket. Unseasonably cold October drafts blew through cracks in the walls and bare floorboards. In this mansion, where downstairs nearly every inch was gilded or silvered or intricately carved or marbleized, this spare and rustic attic made her feel as if she were home again.

Not only that, it gave her a place to hide. No one would find her here; the family would think she had run away. Her suitcase was stowed behind an ancient, cracked cheval glass, over in the corner. If she stayed very quiet, she would fool them into imagining she'd slipped out the back door. If she had one regret, it was that she wouldn't be able to say goodbye to Andrew...she hoped that he would understand, or at least drown his sorrows in his next drink.

She could stay here at Oakhurst, living in the dark so the neighbors wouldn't know she was here, until she figured out what to do next—not so much for her, but for her baby. Every move she made now had to be for him or her. Nothing else really mattered. She couldn't abandon her baby, not even for a second, not even in these early months. But no matter what hardships she faced, she knew she couldn't stay with the Wellses one more day.

Pierce wouldn't care; he wouldn't spare her a thought. Kathleen had kept her secret well. Her swelling breasts had turned him on, but he hadn't asked her what was happening. She didn't feel one bit guilty about not telling him. He didn't deserve to know.

The attic was filled with old trunks, wardrobes, and stacks of ornately framed portraits leaning against the rustic walls. Ever since Kathleen had forced her way past the boards, jimmying the nails with a screwdriver, she had spent her afternoons off exploring these rooms.

It was a museum of Wells family history. Old gowns of velvet, silk, and satin hung in dusty armoires. Ancient lace petticoats, turning brown, disintegrated to the touch. Hatboxes contained bowlers, homburgs, top hats, fancy flowered Easter bonnets, some over a hundred years old.

Wedding gowns were stored in special cases. They ranged from the opulent to the very spare, came from Worth of Paris, Balenciaga, Bonwit Teller, some with seed pearls and others of simple white silk. But there was only one veil, and it had been worn by every bride in the family for three centuries—from Mrs. John Quincy Adams III all the way down to June and Wendy. The oldest daughter hadn't worn the veil, however. Not Louise...

Scrapbooks of each Wells family wedding were stored downstairs, in the library. Kathleen had seen Beth dusting each embossed, red leather-bound volume carefully, knowing the scrapbooks were as priceless as the silver tea sets, Canton china, and Limoges figurines. But newspaper clippings describing Louise's wedding were here in the hidden attic—stuffed into a cardboard box with old grocery receipts and New York Yacht Club chits—to yellow and crumble into dust. From the way they were tossed aside with what amounted to trash, Kathleen almost wondered why Mrs. Wells had kept them at all.

Louise Wells had married a black man. They had met at Harvard. He was a doctor, a visiting lecturer from Mississippi. Louise had been a sociology student. The clipping didn't say much—torn from the society pages, it showed pictures of a lovely dark-eyed girl, her spirit radiating even now, fifteen years later. Kathleen noticed that she wasn't wearing the family veil.

So this attic seemed the perfect place for Kathleen to hide. She thought of Louise, who had defied her terrible family for love, and gathered her close—as an angel or a protector. She pulled the blanket around her shoulders, shivering and trying to sit still. Having to pee and throw up was her curse these days. But she had to hold herself back from doing either until the family left.

It wouldn't be long. She knew they had plans to meet friends for dinner at the Union Club in New York. They would do a quick search through the house for Kathleen, and when they didn't find her, they'd assume that she had run off, abandoned the family, like so many other thankless servants before her. She had heard the story of how the last cook, Vivian, had whipped off her apron and walked out in the middle of a dinner party for thirty—all because the chocolate soufflés had fallen. Or so Mrs. Wells thought...

Although Kathleen had never met Vivian, she felt she knew her. Pierce had told Kathleen about Vivian, lips against her ear, moving inside her, saying that Kathleen was hotter, wetter, sweeter than Vivian had ever been, that she was more willing, eager, sexier; that he liked Kathleen's Irish accent better than Vivian's French one; that Kathleen's tits were bigger, her nipples nicer.

Kathleen had tuned him out. She'd thought of Vivian with Pierce inside her, wondered whether Vivian had loved him, made him part of her fairy tale, or whether, like Kathleen, she had *known*. For Kathleen did know...she had to give herself that. She'd never bothered kidding herself, not even for a minute. Not once had she told herself that Pierce loved her—and she sure as hell knew that she didn't love him.

Oh God, she had to pee. That was part of the first three months, she'd learned from the baby book she'd bought. Not that she wouldn't know anyway—considering her bladder was screaming out right now, refusing to be denied. She looked around the attic for something, anything, to relieve herself in.

There—a cachepot. Herend porcelain, just like the priceless pieces downstairs, only this one chipped—just a tiny crack along the gold rim—and thus relegated to the dark attic. Kathleen lunged for it. Her body was betraying her, she had no choice. The need to go was so great, she felt her eyes overflowing.

But they were tears; of course they were. She had finally reached her limit. If only James had come for her this summer...she really had never given up hope. But now all was lost. Her last shred of hope was gone. She was a madwoman in the secret attic of a family who had millions of dollars and not an ounce of sense or love. Kathleen was shivering, her teeth chattering. Pulling down her pants, her bottom bare, she squatted over the chipped Hungarian cachepot. She thought of James, and began weeping in earnest.

Just then, mid-pee, the boards creaked.

Jaysus, she thought, who's this? The intrusion—with her stuck on the pot, unable to move—made her unable to stifle any sound, and she sobbed out loud. The jig was up. It was Pierce, here for one last visit before they hit the road for New York. He hadn't found her in her room, so he'd followed the sound of urination. Kathleen bit her lip, tears flying from her eyes and the stream down below continuing forever.

"Kathleen?" she heard the female voice whisper.

Oh God. Relief flooded through her. It wasn't Pierce....But Kathleen was so crazy now, she thought it had to be Louise. Or Vivian...Or Sister Anastasia, or the Virgin Mary herself, a kindred spirit come to find her, save her, take her to James.

"Help me," she wept. "Mother of God, help me...."

Holy crap, if help didn't come. The young woman poked her head through the cracked green door, wedging her way under the rough boards Kathleen had left in place to fool the family. Kathleen had the impression of brown hair, bright, compassionate eyes, and the black-and-white clothing of a maid or a nun.

"Kathleen Murphy?" she asked, eyes locking with Kathleen's.

Kathleen nodded dumbly, and at that moment saw everything register on the girl's kind face.

"Oh, I'm sorry," she said quickly, turning her back to give Kathleen her privacy.

"Close the door behind you," Kathleen whispered.

The brown-haired girl did so, stepping quietly into the attic, standing there until Kathleen was done. After pulling up her pants and stowing the cachepot off to the side, Kathleen cleared her throat.

"Who are you?" she asked as the girl turned around, coming toward her.

"I'm Regis Sullivan," she said. "And we have to leave now."

"What do you mean, 'leave'? What are you doing here?" Kathleen asked.

"I came to get you—"

"Get me? Jaysus! You have to leave me alone!" Kathleen felt the panic rising in her chest. Who was this girl? She was wearing a uniform like Beth's; she obviously worked in service, had come to join the staff. "And you have to save yourself, too. Get out now, Regis. Run, and don't look back...."

"I can't. I'm not going anywhere without you."

"My God, girl. You don't understand what's going on. They can't find us in here, or they'll take us with them. I'd rather die than go with them to Palm Beach."

"You don't have to," Regis said, taking her hand. "Just come with me...."

Kathleen shut her eyes, swooning. She knew that she was half crazy, and this was just making it worse. In a minute, she'd have to be sick. She'd had the morning sickness at bay, but Regis, whoever she was, had upset her so much, it was all over. "Look," she said, in as calm a voice as she could, "I don't know who you are. Or why you're here. I'm desperate, can't you see? I'm begging you...."

"Kathleen, I'll explain everything, as soon as we get outside," Regis said. Her eyes were so lively, almost jumping with joy. Kathleen could see she was trying to restrain herself, that she was holding on to a secret.

"Tell me now."

"I can't," Regis said. "If I do, it will spoil the surprise."

Kathleen's eyes flooded again. Surprise? What world did this girl live in? Kathleen was beyond the ability to be surprised by anything. Shocked, maybe. Stunned, horrified. But surprises were for children, adults young at heart, or people in love.

"There's no such thing as a surprise," Kathleen said.

"Don't you have faith? Didn't the Sisters teach you anything?"

"What do you know about the Sisters?" Kathleen asked. She grabbed Regis by her starched white apron with a burst of violence; immediately she let go. What had become of her? Could Regis be an angel, sent to her from above? But no; Kathleen looked into her very human gray-blue eyes, and broke down.

"I have no faith," she said, her eyes flooding again. "It's deserted me, along with..." But she couldn't say his name.

Just then, they heard a commotion on the second floor. Kathleen started violently, and Regis hugged her, holding her up. Kathleen struggled, trying to pull Regis into hiding. They had to be quiet, get into one of the wardrobes, keep themselves from being seen.

"How dare you?" Mrs. Wells shouted. "Andrew, Pierce, call the police."

"Out of my way," boomed the Irish voice. It sent chills down Kathleen's spine.

"Up here!" Regis yelled.

"Stop," Kathleen said, clapping her hand over the girl's mouth. But Regis just kept calling. God, Kathleen thought—she's here to help *them*. She was pretending to be an angel, but she was on their side.

Regis shook her off, grabbed Kathleen by the shoulders. As if she knew no surprise could matter anymore, she stared into Kathleen's eyes with strange, incongruous love and reassurance, smiling at her, saying, "It's *him*, it's *Seamus*...."

"Seamus?" Kathleen, shaking uncontrollably, had no idea in the world who she meant.

"The green door," Regis called. "We're in here!"

"No," Kathleen cried. It was all over now...they'd found her. She would never go with them to Palm Beach, so she'd be cast out on the street, with no plan, and nowhere to go, and a baby growing inside. A sob tore from her chest.

Footsteps sounded on the stairs and in the hall. Noises, people scuffling outside—the crack of boards splintering, nails screaming as they were torn out of the wall. Kathleen heard Mrs. Wells shouting for someone to call 911, and then she heard "Out of my way"—that Irish voice again, cruelly echoing every hope and dream she had ever had.

Her heart was pounding. She gripped Regis's hand, holding on for dear life. Was this the end of the world, her life passing before her very eyes, that blessed, beloved voice ringing in her ears? Heavy footsteps on the rough boards of the secret attic's floor, and then, coming around the corner, she saw—it couldn't be . . .

"James!" she gasped.

And then Regis stepped back and away, and he came toward her.

Oh, he was all grown-up, he'd turned into such a beautiful man, the sight of him made her cry: his red hair, and freckles, and laughing blue eyes. But there wasn't any humor in them now; only a lifetime's worth of love and longing, the same that Kathleen had felt for him every day.

"Kathleen," he said, grabbing her, clutching her to him. Their hearts met, beating together as if they were finally one again, as if they had always been two halves of the same whole. She felt as if she had been dead all this time and suddenly she was being brought back to life.

"James, is it you? Is it really?"

"It is," he said. "I found you."

"If only you knew how often I've dreamed," she began, her voice breaking into a sob.

She tipped her head back, and there in the darkness of that secret attic, in all its cold stuffiness, with the ghosts of unacceptable love, she finally felt the sun shining on her face—the beautiful, warm sun that had disappeared that day over ten years ago, on the beach in County Wexford.

"James, oh, James . . ." she said, her eyes open wide, not wanting to even blink, in case he was an apparition, in case he might dissolve or disappear.

"I love you, Kathleen," he whispered fiercely, wiping the tears from her eyes even as his own streamed freely. He clutched her long hair in one hand, kissing her cheeks, her lips, now, even kissing her hair. She saw him looking at it, knew what he was thinking.

"You used to braid my hair," she whispered.

"Let's go, sweetheart," he said, sweeping her right up into his arms. He held her against his chest, carrying her past Regis. Walking through the open doorway—the cracked green door wide open, the rough boards torn off, thrown aside. Nails protruded, and he eased her by so gently.

They went past the Wellses, all clustered together, and James carried her down the attic stairs. Kathleen's arms were around his neck, and she heard the family talking, saying things, but their words were a foreign language.

The only person she could understand was James, whispering in her ear.

"We'll never be apart again," he said. "Never, Kathleen."

He carried her straight down the wide, curving central staircase, past Beth and a girl wearing a black beret, who had to be her sister Mirande, standing with another young woman, grinning and pumping her fist in a gesture of victory. James carried Kathleen right past an older couple, a nun in the habit of Sisters of Notre Dame des Victoires, and the man with blue eyes—James's eyes—that Kathleen had seen yesterday, in his green truck, from the attic window. The nun was crying, reaching out, and instinctively, Kathleen brushed her hand. The contact sent electricity through Kathleen's body, and when she looked over James's shoulder, she saw the nun sobbing against the blue-eyed man's chest.

Kathleen trembled in James's arms, unable to let go, even when he set her down in the front seat of the blue-eyed man's green pickup truck, parked at the curb on Bellevue Avenue. Even then Kathleen kept her arms around his neck, crying softly as he kissed her lips.

Looking into his eyes, she felt that they had lived many lifetimes—yet, in the same moment, as if no time had passed at all. This was the same boy she'd always loved and counted on. They might as well have been gazing at each other through the bars of their cribs.

The thought made her glow, and she started to smile. The smile grew and grew, and it was contagious, lifting James's eyes and the corners of his mouth. They held each other tight, touching each other's faces, making sure this was really real, that it wasn't just another dream, that they weren't going to wake up and find themselves alone, without the other, as they had so many times before.

"Kathleen Murphy," he said.

"James Sullivan," she whispered.

"We're home," he said. And she knew they were: even though they were sitting in a truck on a street she couldn't wait to leave; even though she was pregnant; and even though police cars were pulling up, sirens howling and lights flashing.

Police officers walked over to the truck. The Wellses came rushing out the front door of Oakhurst, Mrs. Wells pointing her finger and screeching like a banshee, saying, "That's him, that's the man who broke into our house...." Andy, still in his pajamas, tried to restrain her, as Pierce and Mr. Wells faded back. Regis and the other girls came running over, and the nun and the man with blue eyes started talking to the police. But some of the officers were still wary, circling Kathleen and James in the truck, two of them with their guns drawn.

"Yes, we're home," Kathleen whispered to James. And she closed her eyes, at complete peace in spite of the cacophony and mad activity all around, because she was with him, with James.

Twenty-Six

The Wellses decided not to press charges, eager to put the whole ugly episode behind them and leave Newport at once. Besides, when questioned, Mrs. Wells admitted that the worst Seamus had done was to run uninvited up to the attic and damage some shabby old boards. She was furious at Kathleen, not so much for her part in the drama, but for deciding not to accompany the family to Palm Beach. Now Mrs. Wells would have to hire a brand-new cook, *and* train her; and at the start of the season, finding someone good would be difficult at best.

So the police signed off on the incident, and everyone decided to head back to Star of the Sea. Seamus was hesitant at first; he hadn't come to America to see his parents—only to get Kathleen. But they had surprised him at the airport, and their help had been invaluable, and he was nothing if not grateful. Besides, Kathleen seemed exhausted, and Bernie said there'd be good food and comfortable beds.

Because the truck was too small for all four of them, it was decided that Tom and Bernie would go ahead, and Seamus and Kathleen would ride with Regis and her friends. Mirande quickly opened up the third seat, in the back of the Volvo wagon, and he and Kathleen climbed in.

With Mirande driving and Regis beside her in front, Juliana and Monica behind them, and Seamus and Kathleen in the far back—plus assorted backpacks, overnight bags, and Kathleen's suitcase—it was a tight fit. But Seamus didn't care. He just held on to Kathleen with all his might, loved the way she rested her head against his shoulder.

"You guys okay back there?" Mirande called.

"We're fine," Seamus said, answering for both of them. Kathleen seemed almost in shock, huddled up beside him, her eyes closed.

"We just have to swing by my house for one minute," Mirande said. "It won't take long."

"Take all the time you need," Seamus said.

He and Kathleen were facing backwards, out the station wagon's rear hatchway, as they sped through Newport. He sensed the sea's closeness, and it made him glad to think of Kathleen in a place surrounded by ocean, like Ireland. When they reached the harbor, he saw the slate surface dotted with whitecaps. The Hibernian Hall stood at the junction of two main roads, Irish flag whipping in the wind. At the sight of it, he squeezed Kathleen and gestured at the flag, and she looked out at it.

"I had them fly that for you," Kathleen said, smiling.

"Did you really?" he asked.

"I would have," she said, "if I'd had any idea that you were coming. How did you find me, James? Or Seamus? What is your name, now?"

"You can call me whatever you want," he said. "I've been using Seamus the last few years."

"Irish for James," she said. "It makes sense, and it suits you. Okay, then—Seamus. How'd you find me?"

"Oh, Kathleen," he said. "I've had every angel, saint, and demon in Ireland looking for you."

"But I haven't been in Ireland for years now," she said sadly.

"I just found that out," Seamus said.

"I wanted to contact you," she said. "So badly. But things kept happening. First, I tried to find you at the Home, but you weren't there.

My parents learned about it, and..." She trailed off, her eyes troubled. "Let's just say they didn't want me in touch with people from the past."

"They thought we weren't good enough for you?" Seamus asked teasingly.

"Oh, it wasn't that," she said. "They had their reasons. What they were, Seamus, was thieves. Always after the prize, and they didn't care how they got it."

"But they came to the Home, to find you," he said, frowning. "Your real parents...you were so happy. They must have loved you, to do that. That's all that matters, right?"

"They wanted me to be a decoy," she said. "So they could score more easily."

"Kathleen, no," he said.

She nodded. "Yes. They had some trouble with the gardai in Dublin, so we moved out of Blackrock...."

"I went there to find you," Seamus said. "After I convinced Sister Anastasia to give me your address."

"You did?" she asked, her eyes flashing.

"Yes, but you'd already left."

"We went to Cork, and from there to Boston," she said. "We lived in a few places there, but they thought there'd be more opportunity in New York. That's where I escaped; I saw an ad for a cook, in the *Irish Echo*, and I answered it."

"The Wellses?" Seamus asked.

"No," she said, shaking her head. "There were other families before them."

"Well," Seamus said, "they were all lucky to have you cooking for them. You were the best in the world; the meals at St. Augustine's were always the best when you were there."

"It's where I learned to cook," she said. "The Sisters always told me that cooking was a way of showing love, and that's what I always tried to do. But Seamus, some of the people I worked for..."

"You've been through a lot," he said, thinking of how wrong he'd been, during the years he'd imagined her in a loving home, and more recently, when he'd pictured her living in one of the Newport grand houses, not cooking for the family.

"Oh, the worst of it was not knowing where you were," she said. "Wondering if I'd ever see you again. How *did* you find me?" she asked.

"Sister Bernadette Ignatius and Tom Kelly," he said. "They brought me the postcard you'd sent Sister Anastasia—of the Cliff Walk. All I knew was that you lived here in Newport, and that I had to come find you."

"And you did find me," she said, smiling, shaking her head in wonder.

Seamus kept his arm around her, stroking her hair, as Mirande pulled into the driveway of a small house. She and Regis jumped out and ran to the front door. They quickly changed out of the black uniforms, into regular clothes. Kathleen kept looking nervously at the door, told Seamus they had a long ride ahead of them and she'd better run inside for a minute. He popped the hatch open, watching her as she hurried up the front walk to the house.

A few minutes later, everyone was back at the car. Mirande's mother walked out to say goodbye. She kissed her daughter, Regis, Monica, and Juliana. Then she shook Seamus's hand, said how incredible it was that he had found Kathleen.

"It's so wonderful when a love story has a happy ending," Mrs. St. Florent said.

"More like a happy beginning," Regis said, smiling.

"That's right," Seamus said, putting his arm around Kathleen. "We have our lives ahead of us. The best is yet to come."

At those words, Kathleen's face crumpled and she began to cry. Everyone was in shock, and the sight of her tears sliced Seamus's heart. What was wrong? What had he said?

"I'm sorry," she said, sobbing. "This is all just such a shock. I'm so happy, completely overjoyed. I just never expected…"

"That's okay," Seamus said, holding her and trying to console her.

"Wait till we get you to Star of the Sea," Regis said. "You'll have the chance to rest, and spend time together, and you'll forget all about that attic." She shivered, reaching for Kathleen's hand. "It was awful up there; living with those people had to be very traumatic."

At that, Seamus felt a terrible quiver go through Kathleen's body. He saw her hold her stomach as if she feared she might be sick. Regis and her friends looked worried, and Mirande's mother stepped forward, looking into Kathleen's eyes.

"Are you all right?" Mrs. St. Florent asked. "Is there something we can do for you?"

"I'm fine," Kathleen said, smiling as she wiped away her tears. "Just emotional, that's all. Everything's good...only...I know it's a long drive, and I might have to stop once or twice. I tend to get a little motion sick..."

"Say the word!" Mirande exclaimed. "I'll pull right over."

Monica and Juliana offered to switch, sit in the rear-facing third seat, and Seamus followed Kathleen into the middle. Mirande kissed her mother again, and then she and Regis climbed in front, and they were under way.

"It seems weird, your first time in Newport," Mirande called back to Seamus, "to not give you a tour. It's so beautiful! I hate to have you thinking it's all like Oakhurst and the Wellses...."

"I don't think that," Seamus said.

"Oh, but there are wild rocky stretches along the Atlantic, and huge castle-like houses towering over secluded coves, one house with more chimneys than you can count, and wild roses everywhere—the last ones are still in bloom—and craggy cliffs above the sea..."

"The Cliff Walk," Seamus said, the words sparking something in him.

"Yes," Mirande said. "The most spectacular path in America...ten miles, all along the wildest coastline. There are palaces along the way, and a tunnel through the rocks, a Chinese teahouse, and Forty Steps, and Rosecliff, the house where they filmed *The Great Gatsby*...." Mirande sounded excited, just listing the things that made the Cliff Walk such an important part of Newport.

They all sounded interesting, but to Seamus, it was important for one reason: because it was on the postcard Kathleen had written, the one that had told him where he could find her.

"Should we go see it?" Mirande asked. "Before we head to Connecticut?"

Seamus's blood beat faster, to think of seeing a place of such symbolism to him and Kathleen. He would've liked to stand on the cliffs, gaze out at the Atlantic, shout back to Ireland that he'd found her. But when he looked across the seat, saw her looking so pale—as if the motion sickness had already started—he shook his head at Mirande, who was watching for his reaction in the rearview mirror.

"I think we'd better get on the road," he said.

"Yes," Regis said, looking over her shoulder at Kathleen, taking note of her pallor and the fact she looked so queasy.

"No problem," Mirande said. "Next stop, Star of the Sea."

Mirande backed out of the driveway; she hadn't driven more than a block before Kathleen let out a small, almost inaudible moan. She looked at Seamus with such helpless misery that he reached for her hand. Even after all these years, he knew her so well. He looked into her eyes and knew that she felt tormented, and it was more than car sickness.

"What is it?" he asked, gripping her hand.

"I can't tell you," she said, her eyes brimming.

"Kathleen, it's me," he whispered. "If you can't tell me, then who can you tell?"

They were in a car filled with young women, but Mirande had the radio going up front, and Monica and Juliana were busily talking in back. Seamus gazed into Kathleen's eyes, and knew they had always been together, even when they'd thought they were alone in the world.

"Oh, Seamus," she whispered. "You'll hate me...."

"I never could," he swore. "No matter what."

"But this... you will, Seamus."

"Never," he said, staring ferociously into her eyes.

"I'm pregnant," she said, her voice breaking with anguish. Her eyes

were wild, and she clapped her hands over her mouth—and Seamus
shouted for Mirande to pull over now, right now, and she did, just in
time for Kathleen to open the car door, and get sick on the side of the
road.

Bernie called ahead to have Sister Ursula prepare two rooms in the
Academy—one for Seamus, the other for Kathleen. Kathleen's was in
the girls' dormitory, and Seamus's was on the guest floor, where visiting priests and male retreatants generally stayed. Although they
were in opposite wings of the building, Bernie knew that they weren't
too far apart. She could only imagine how much Seamus and
Kathleen wanted to spend every moment possible together. Sister
Ursula gave her a quick update on the harvest, which was going very
well, and then they hung up.

"You did it, Tom," she said as they drove along Bellevue Avenue,
through Newport. "You brought Seamus and Kathleen together."

"We did, Bernie," he said.

"No, all the credit goes to you. You're amazing; thank you so much
for letting me be part of today."

"What are you talking about?" Tom asked, hands on the wheel,
glancing across the seat to look at her.

"You could have met him at the airport yourself," she said. "And
taken him to Kathleen . . ."

Tom smiled wryly, shook his head. "You don't get it."

"Yes, I do," she said. "When I think of all the work you must have
done—getting Sixtus to help with his passport, having Chris look
into Immigration over here, to find Kathleen . . . and then to enlist
Regis to help . . . you did it all."

"And what? I should have picked up Seamus on my own, taken all
the credit?"

She shook her head. When he put it like that, he made it sound like
she was thinking in petty terms. But she wasn't. Her heart ached,
because she knew how much she had hurt him. These last few weeks
had been terrible for her—missing him every day, longing to see him as

she walked every inch of the Academy grounds. She could only imagine how they had been for him. "I didn't mean it that way," she said.

"Bernie," he said. "I'll say it again: you don't get it...."

"Then tell me," she said.

"Nothing matters if it's not with you," he said, his voice low.

"Oh, Tom."

"Helping Seamus and Kathleen get together was easy," he said. "I have great cousins, and they helped me a lot. Doing it made me feel alive, Bernie. Helping my son search for the woman he loves, find his way back to her. I did it for him, but I did it for me, too."

"For you?"

Tom nodded. "Because I know how it feels to be that much in love."

"Oh, Tom..."

"Every part of me," he said, "everything I am, has always been in love with you."

Bernie's heart ached at his words. She gazed out the truck window, her eyes flooding. Without Seamus in the truck, the space between them seemed a gulf almost impossible to cross.

"Come back to Star of the Sea," she whispered. "We can work it all out."

"Do you really think that's possible?"

"It has to be," she said.

"Bernie," Tom said, "something has to happen between us."

Bernie closed her eyes. Her thoughts were wild, suddenly turning to what had happened in the grotto that morning. There she had encountered Mary, felt the Blessed Mother's caress, heard her clearly spoken words. *Be ready.* ... As the day had gone by, the message kept assuming new meaning. At first, Bernie had thought the words referred to the surprise of Seamus's arrival, then she realized they encompassed the finding of Kathleen. And now...

Suddenly, Tom turned off Bellevue onto Memorial Boulevard—but heading toward Easton's Beach instead of down the opposite hill, toward the wharves and the bridge home. At first, Bernie thought he must have made a mistake; she started to tell him, but then she saw the purpose in his blue eyes, knew that he was taking her somewhere: *Something has to happen between us....*

At the foot of the big hill, he saw a van of surfers pulling out and took their spot at the curb. Easton's Beach curved between headlands in Newport and Middletown, with long breakers rolling in, white spray blowing off the wave tops. Tom got out of the truck, then held the door for Bernie.

"This is an unexpected stop," she said.

"I know," he said. "Bear with me, will you, Bernie?"

"Tom..." She thought of Seamus, how he and Kathleen and Regis and the girls were on their way to Star of the Sea; she wanted to be there, to greet them when they arrived. But looking into Tom's eyes, she saw the gravity there, could see how important this was to him. He had said that something had to happen, but suddenly those other words became clear again: *Be ready....* Bernie nodded, and climbed out of the truck.

The October air was chilly, and a strong salt breeze blew steadily off the water. They trekked halfway up the hill, across a green lawn, through a gate, and suddenly they were on a narrow gravel path. They were on a cliff. Bernie tingled, and looked up at Tom.

"A cliff?" she said.

He just smiled down at her, leading on.

The land side, on their right, ran past houses and estates, and the enormous, graceful buildings of Salve Regina. The seaward side, to their left, was a sheer drop, down the cliff face, to the ocean. Waves churned and crashed on the rocks below, sending explosions of white water shooting skyward. Bernie looked down and held her breath.

"It's spectacular," she said.

"This is the Cliff Walk," Tom said, stopping her, taking her hands.

"I know," she said. "I've been here...."

"Never with me," he said.

"Tom, it reminds me of Ireland."

"Of that day, Bernie. I know."

A group of tourists walked by. If they thought it strange to see a nun and a man holding hands, they didn't give any indication.

"There are so many things," he continued, "that I want to do with you. It's never been possible, because of our lives. So many nights, I lie awake thinking of places we should go. Paris, Bernie. I want to walk along the Seine with you...and Florence; I know you love art, and I want to take you to the museums there."

"Tom," she murmured.

"New York City!" he said. "I want to take you to a Yankees game, then for a carriage ride in Central Park. I want to go to the top of the Empire State Building, and see how many states we can see. Then out to Ellis Island, so we can look up the ships our families took from Ireland. And I want to take you back to Ireland. Not looking for any-thing this time. Just to be with you."

"Do you know how wonderful that sounds?" she asked.

"I *do* know, Bernie," he said, touching the side of her face with one rough hand.

"But Tom, we've been through this."

"Not like this," he said, shaking his head stubbornly. "Didn't you see the look in his eyes? When he came out of the house, carrying Kathleen? He was wild with love for her, and totally at peace—both at the same time. That's how it's been for me, with you, Bernie. All those years at the Academy..."

She stood still, listening, taking it in. She could see how agitated he felt—Tom, who had been so skillful at hiding his feelings all these years, at getting along and working with Bernie, stifling all of what he was telling her right now—and she tried to keep herself steady, to just let him finish.

"I was just like Seamus," he said. "Crazy about you, but content to at least be with you every day. Working alongside you at the Academy, being your right-hand man."

"You were, and are," she said. "It was so hard this morning, start-ing the harvest without you. And these last weeks, with you gone... I've felt as if part of me was missing."

"Bernie," he said, "I feel that way for you."

She tried to catch her breath. What was she doing here? Talking to him this way, as if they could actually contemplate a life together?

"I wish it were possible," she said, "to have two lives."

"If you can even say that," Tom said, "then you're still thinking about it, about being with me—otherwise you'd tell me to leave you alone. After all we've been through, don't you want to try? See if we can make it together? Give it a chance, Bernie...."

"I took vows, Tom. You were there, at the chapel that day. You know that I can't break them."

"Bernie, please..."

"If I did, if I broke my vows," she began, looking up into his eyes, "what kind of person would I be? How could you ever trust me, to know that I wouldn't break my vows to you? How would you know you could trust me?"

"I'd just know," he said. "Because of who you are."

"But that's because you see me in the light of how I've lived...the vows I took and could never break."

"Do you know why I wanted to come here, to the Cliff Walk?" he asked, trembling.

"Because of the Cliffs of Moher," she whispered.

"Remember, Bernie? I held you there."

She nodded, feeling it all over again.

"It seemed like such a sign," Tom said, "when I saw the postcard Kathleen sent. It showed this place—cliffs, Bernie. Seamus followed her card like a beacon, all the way from Ireland. They love each other so much, but Bernie—you and I have the greatest love this world has ever known. Ever! Don't you know that?"

Bernie felt herself falling apart. She started to cry, her thin sobs swept away by the cold sea wind. Love poured through her body, straight from her heart, all through her veins. She stared at Tom, knowing that if she didn't tell him now, she never would.

"I do know that, Tom," she said.

"Really?"

She nodded. "Yes, of course I do. From the first day I met you, I knew that there could never, ever be another man for me. I followed you all over the grounds at Star of the Sea, at your grandfather's picnic..."

"And then I turned right around and followed you."

"Every step I've taken on earth," Bernie said, holding his hands, "I've felt you right there with me."

He nodded, bowing his head so his forehead touched hers. Her veil fluttered between them in the strong breeze, but his eyes were just inches from her, burning bright blue.

"I've tried to be," he said.

"No one could mean more to me than you do," she said, her voice breaking. "Don't you know how hard it is?"

"You say that, Bernie," he said, "but is it really? You're insulated, in the convent. You have those convictions of yours; you have your vows keeping you locked up and safe."

"It's not safe," she whispered, looking over the sheer, dangerous edge of the cliff—standing so close to it, and knowing that just one step would take her over the side, knowing that this was how she felt every day.

"I felt as if you came so close in Dublin, moving out of the convent; I could feel your doubts—could feel you thinking about it."

"I was," she said. "I pray for guidance every day...."

"Then tell me, Bernie," he said, the words tearing out. "Once and for all, tell me what answers you get back...."

She had to hold herself together, to get this part out. She shivered in the breeze, with the words swirling through her mind, and pictured the Virgin Mary that very morning, when she'd knelt before her, beseeching her for an answer.

"Tom...as much as you say you want me, I've wanted you. Every day I pray to be released from my vows."

"You do?" he asked, looking shocked.

Bernie knew that she had never told him so clearly; she had held this part inside, never wanting him to know exactly how agonizing it was for her. Her face streamed with tears, and her heart ached in her chest.

"I beg for it," she whispered. "In prayer, in chapel, on my knees. I pray with all my heart to be set free...to be with you, Tom. You're the only man I ever loved, the father of my child. I've dreamed of a life with you...."

"Bernie," he gasped, overcome with shock that she would admit it; relief flooded his blue eyes, along with the happiness that had been absent these last few years. He grabbed her hand, pulled it to his chest.

"It's a sacrifice beyond words, beyond imagining," she wept. "I ache for you. When I look up at the stars, I think of us looking at them together. The constellations, moving across the sky. Star of the Sea, Tom...it's the name of our home, yours and mine. But it's also the only place I can be with you...looking up at the sky, I have you in my heart. I suffer so much, being without you....I wish I could marry you, Tom."

"You do?" he asked.

She nodded, weeping, remembering the Blue Grotto. That morning, when the glowing light had filled the small, stone room, Bernie had begged Mary to understand, to let her be a mother to Seamus, and a wife to Tom. But Mary had told Bernie she was still needed in the life she had chosen, that she had to be ready for what would come next.

"Bernie, I didn't know," he said. "Why didn't you tell me?"

"Because I couldn't bear to hurt you one more time," she said.

"Thank you, now," he said.

"For what?"

"For telling me," he said. His blue eyes were so clear, his gaze strong. She saw the old Tom there, her dear, beloved Tom.... "For giving me that. It means everything to me, Bernie."

"Oh, Tom..."

"You've given us back to each other," he said. "That's how it feels. You've taken everything broken, put it back together."

"Even though we still can't be together?"

He nodded. "Just knowing that you want to be with me. That not being able to be together causes you some of the same pain it does me; I never want you to hurt, Bernie. I'd rather take it on myself than think of you suffering. But just to know..." He paused. Still holding her hand to his chest, he kissed her knuckles. His eyes were so wide and clear, such deep blue. They reflected the depth of the sea down below and the sky up above.

"My Bernie," Tom said, his gaze sweeping over the stone-strewn walk, the plummeting rock cliffs. "Seamus brought us here. He knew he'd do anything to get to the Cliff Walk, to find Kathleen. I helped him do that, because I believed I'd lost the chance with his mother. But now I know I've found you...."

"You never lost me," she whispered. "You never, ever could."

"It means everything," he said, his voice so strong and steady. "Just to know that you think about it. That you would have wanted to be my wife... I love you, Bernie."

"I love you, Tom," she whispered, and she heard the words again, so distinct they made her jump: *Be ready.*

The color left his face. He dropped her hand. He kept his own hand clenched, over his heart; she saw him grab at the fabric of his black sweater, and his face suddenly contorted in pain. They were standing on the stony path, on the cliff high over the tumultuous sea. Overhead, the sky was cloudless, so blue. Bernie stepped forward, caught him as he tumbled against her, slumping to the ground.

"Tom, no!" she cried.

He shuddered, then lay so still.

"Help!" she screamed, sliding down beside him. "Someone, please! Oh, Tom... stay with me...."

There was no one in sight, no one to help. They were alone on the cliff, just the two of them under a sky of cool October blue. Bernie clutched him, kissing his forehead as the waves crashed on the rocks below, the salt spray flying so high she felt it on her face, tasted it on his skin. And Bernie's lips moved in constant prayer as she rocked him, holding him close, as Tom Kelly died in her arms.

Twenty-Seven

The funeral was held at Star of the Sea, on a cold and bitter morning. The day started off overcast, with dark clouds billowing in off the Sound. Although it was just October, a Canadian air mass had swept into the region; the temperature had dropped twenty degrees overnight, so when the rain began to fall just after dawn, it came down in tiny, icy needles.

By six a.m., every surface was coated with a thin sheen of ice: the Academy buildings, the steeple, the vineyard, the stone walls criss-crossing the property, the bushes and trees.

Honor had been up for hours. John hadn't been able to sleep since learning of Tom's death. They had been as close as brothers, and the news of it was such a shock. Tom, who had always been so healthy and robust, such a vibrant outdoorsman, had died of a heart attack.

"Why did it have to happen there?" John asked, lying flat on his back in bed, staring at the ceiling as the day's gray light began to filter through the rain-streaked windows. "On that walk with no one around, no one Bernie could have called for help? Why didn't she have a cell phone with her?"

"I don't know," Honor said, lying beside him. "She doesn't always carry one; she must have left it in his truck when they went for that walk."

"If he had gotten medical care right away, maybe…"

"I know."

"He was only forty-seven," John said.

"I can't believe it," Honor said, her eyes filling with tears.

"I keep thinking I'm dreaming; it can't be possible."

"That's how it feels to me, too. I keep thinking I'll look out the window, see him up there on the hill...."

"This is one day I don't want to face," John said.

"I know," Honor said. "I feel the same way." She leaned over to kiss John, then got out of bed. She might as well make coffee, get started. The day would be hard for everyone. All three girls were asleep in their room.

Regis's friends had returned to college. Seamus and Kathleen were staying at the Academy, but the situation was fraught. Honor knew about Kathleen's pregnancy from Regis—and Seamus had seemed shocked and distant since their arrival. Honor could understand; there was so much happening at once: finding out about Tom's death and Kathleen's pregnancy were both such enormous, life-shaking events.

Last night, Honor had spied Seamus walking alone, down to the beach, hands jammed into his pockets. He'd looked so lonely and for-lorn; his posture had radiated anger at the world. Honor had called his name, but he'd just kept walking. Either he'd been totally lost in thought and not heard, or he just hadn't wanted to face her. This wasn't the way she had hoped to welcome her nephew into the fold.

Bernie kept to herself, not wanting to talk at all. She kept herself focused on making the arrangements. Honor watched her friend slip one hundred percent into Sister Bernadette Ignatius mode—the nun who ran everything. When Honor had gone over to the convent yes-terday to check on her, she had found her on the phone to Ireland—making sure Sixtus, Billy, and Niall Kelly and their wives were on the way. Honor had sat across the desk, listening to the conversation. When Bernie hung up, she turned toward Honor.

"I just want to make sure they get here before the ice storm begins."

"When does their flight arrive?" Honor had asked.

"In two hours, according to Sixtus's secretary."

"Do you need John and me to meet them at the airport?"

Bernie had shaken her head, making notes on her yellow pad. "No, the Kellys will take care of that. Chris arranged all the transportation."

"How is Seamus doing?"

"Oh, Seamus…" The mention of his name had made Bernie drop her pen, shake her head.

"How is he?"

"I'm so worried he's going to bolt. The combination of Tom and Kathleen. It's so much for him to handle."

"Did he say that?"

"We can't talk," she had said. "Tom was the one who'd reached out to him. … I feel Seamus can barely stand to look me in the eye."

"Bernie," Honor had said, her heart breaking with her friend's distress, "I can only imagine what mixed feelings you must be having—having Seamus here, but to have Tom…"

"Tom made it possible," Bernie had said. "For him to be here. Him and Kathleen … Oh God, Honor."

"Bernie," Honor had said softly, reaching across the desk for her friend's hand.

Bernie had started to melt, talking about Seamus, but now she pulled back, shaking her head hard. Her hand had felt stiff and wooden in Honor's.

"Please, Bernie, I know how you must feel. Talk to me. …"

Sitting perfectly still, frozen solid, Bernie had seemed unable to move or react. Her eyes had looked so bruised, staring into the middle distance as if seeing Tom die all over again. As Honor had watched, Bernie had winced.

"Oh, Bernie," Honor had said, her own eyes filling with tears.

"Honor, no."

"He was my friend, too," Honor had said. "I loved him like a brother. And you're John's sister; my sister. *Please*, Bernie. Let it out. …"

"If I start," Bernie had said, unable to raise her eyes to meet

Honor's, "I won't be able to get through this. Please, Honor . . . just let me handle these arrangements."

"Okay," Honor had said, backing off after a few minutes. She'd watched Bernie across the desk—her jaw clenched and upper body stiff, her hands trembling, and bright tears glittering in her eyes. Honor had seen anguish there, and it had seemed almost volcanic— like hot lava ready to erupt; holding it in had seemed to take super-human effort, the tension visible in her face and body.

Honor had always known Bernie's capacity for feeling other peo-ple's pain, suffering right along with them in times of grief and loss. But right then, watching her friend try to stifle her own sorrow, Honor had felt so powerless. Her own heart breaking, she'd supposed the best thing she could do for Bernie was to leave her alone, let her get lost in the administrative details of planning the funeral for the man she had always loved so much.

Now, standing at the kitchen sink, Honor ran water into the pot, measured out scoops of coffee, prayed for Bernie to be able to get through the day. She turned up the thermostat, pulled her robe tighter. The weather had turned unseasonably cold so fast, and the day was so dark—almost as if the weather was responding to the dreadful tragedy that had visited their family.

"Hi, Mom," Regis said, walking into the kitchen.

"Good morning, sweetheart," Honor said. "How'd you sleep?"

"Not too well," Regis said. She wore an Ireland sweatshirt over a yellow nightgown; she blinked, her eyes wide, looking so childlike, in need of reassurance. Honor went over, hugged her. "I can't believe it," Regis said. "We were just with him. He was so excited about Seamus and Kathleen . . . about being with Aunt Bernie."

"I know, honey," Honor said.

"How could it have happened?" Regis asked. "*Why* did it happen?"

"We don't know," Honor said. She knew that none of her daugh-ters had ever had to face death like this—of someone their parents' age, so young, alive, and healthy, someone so close to them. Honor's parents had died, and so had John's. The girls' grandparents had been a generation ahead, and somehow that made their deaths more understandable, the grief more bearable. Losing Tom like this was just too confusing and cruel for everyone.

"I don't want anyone to say 'It was his time,' or anything like that," Regis said, wiping her eyes.

"No," Honor said.

"Or 'It's a mystery,' or 'He's with God now.' I swear, I'll kill anyone who says anything like that!"

"You're right," Honor said, blushing at the platitudes that were playing in her mind as she tried to think of things to say to Regis, Agnes, and Cece. How could she explain the unexplainable? Brendan had expressed it well last night; he'd lost his younger brother Paddy to leukemia. Honor had overheard him and Agnes sitting by the fire, talking about Tom. Agnes had said to Brendan, "But how did you make sense of it? What is there to say?" And Brendan had just held her closer, shook his head as he'd stared into the flames. "There's only one thing to say: it's terrible. That's all, Agnes. It's terrible."

Standing with Regis now, Honor knew that Brendan was right. She stared at the coffee dripping into the pot, smelled its aroma, felt glad to have her daughter home from college, even for this reason. She heard the furnace kicking on, sending heat up through the grates. This weather was brutal, but tomorrow it might be sunny. Life would go on—no, she corrected herself: it was already going on. And that, to Honor, was almost too much to bear.

"Morning, Dad," Regis said, wiping her eyes and going to hug her father. John walked into the kitchen, wearing a gray T-shirt and faded jeans, his eyes bleary and short brown-gray hair matted from tossing all night.

"Hi, honey," he said. "How are you?"

"I don't know," Regis said. "How are you?"

John's eyes narrowed. He didn't reply, but walked over to stand in front of the coffeepot. Honor saw his shoulders drooping, as if this was too much for him to carry. Tom had been with John every step of his life. Through their schoolboy summers; into adulthood when John had fallen in love with Honor and Tom with Bernie; Tom had been John's best man at the wedding, godfather to Regis; he and John had discovered family history in the stone wall, and it had led them separately to Ireland, where so much of their lives had changed.

Tom had been instrumental in getting John released from prison early; years earlier, John had helped Tom deal with his devastation over Bernie's desire to join the convent, and just weeks ago, her decision to stay. So Honor knew that Regis asking her father how he was only *seemed* simple, and that the answer, for John, was deep and intense.

"I'll be okay, Regis," he said after a few minutes. "But I'm not right now."

Regis's eyes widened; even at twenty, and knowing the situation, she couldn't bear hearing that her father wasn't all right. Honor hugged her.

"None of us are," Honor said. "I know we will be, but today is hard. We'll get through it together."

"Have you talked to Aunt Bernie?" Regis asked.

"She's been very busy," Honor said quietly, picturing that look in Bernie's eyes yesterday.

"She *won't* talk," John said. "I went over to the convent after it happened, and again yesterday. Both times, she told me to leave, she had things to attend to."

"Like I said," Honor said, "she's busy."

"She's out of her mind," John said.

"What do you mean?"

"Just what I said," John said. "She's beside herself, but she can't admit it. If she stops to think, she'll fall apart. I know my sister. She has all the angels and archangels on her side, and trust me, she needs them. This is bad. For all of us, but especially for Bernie."

"To think of Seamus actually being here at Star of the Sea, after all this time," Honor said. "How happy Tom would have been...oh God."

"Seamus is having a hell of a rough time," John said.

Honor watched Regis; she shivered, as if remembering the scene, how her father had met Mirande's car as it pulled into Star of the Sea. Bernie had called him from Newport with the news about Tom, and

John was waiting. The very first time he met Seamus, he had to tell him his father had just died.

"Poor Seamus," Regis said. "He was wrecked to hear Kathleen was pregnant—I saw the look on his face when she told him. He was silent in the car, almost the whole way here. Then, the second I saw Dad's face, I swear I knew...."

"What are Seamus and Kathleen going to do?" Honor asked.

"Mom, let him get through one crisis at a time. Today we have to bury Tom," Regis said. Then, seeing Honor's face, she hugged her. "I'm sorry for snapping. It's just too much to take. I just...think Seamus is going to leave as soon as the funeral's over...."

"What do you mean?"

"Seamus looked so hollow when I saw him heading down to the beach yesterday," Regis said. "I mean—imagine being in love with someone for so long, and finding out she's pregnant with someone else's child?"

"I saw him, too. Walking alone on the beach yesterday," John said. "I started over to speak to him, but he gave me the darkest look...."

"He's been through so much," Honor said, thinking of what Bernie had told her about Seamus's life. How would he be able to withstand everything? She thought of how much he loved Kathleen, how devastated he must have been to learn she was carrying another man's child. Honor remembered what Bernie had said, about fearing Seamus would bolt; she prayed that if he was going to do that, he'd wait until they got through the funeral. For his sake, as much as Bernie's...

"This ice is horrible," Regis said, sounding furious as she stood at the window looking out. "It's only October—it shouldn't be this cold. Rain would be bad enough, but ice just makes it worse. It's so dark and awful out!"

"It is," Agnes said, coming into the kitchen.

"I can feel this weather in my toes and fingers," Cece said, right behind her. Cece was just twelve, and she started to cry noisily. "Uncle Tom would have hated this day!"

"Why do you say that?" Honor asked, hugging her. "He was a

landscaper, Cece. He loved all different kinds of weather...rain, sun, it didn't matter to Tom. He always said that cold was good for plants, bulbs, bushes....He'd say, 'Sleep cold, under the ground, come back next spring...'" Honor quoted her old friend, felt herself choke up. Tom wouldn't be back, next spring or ever.

"Cece's right, though," John said. "Tom didn't like ice. He always said it was too heavy for branches to withstand. Any time we had an ice storm, he'd worry about trees and bushes giving out under the weight."

"The ice is beautiful, though," Agnes said, standing with her arm around Regis, looking out the window. A thin sheen of silver coated every single thing in sight: every blade of grass, each leaf, each stone in the wall. "It's hard to see something this lovely and know that Uncle Tom can't see it...that he won't, ever again...."

Honor glanced at John, to see how he was taking it. His eyes were dark with grief as he sat down on the bench, pulling on socks and boots. Without asking, she knew what he was going to do: take pictures. The day was too spectacular—in so many ways—for an artist like John to ignore. He pulled on his jacket and a hat, grabbed his camera.

"When will you be back?" she asked.

"In time," he said.

They stared into each other's eyes. She knew that he meant in time for the funeral. Nodding, she kissed and hugged him. He felt so solid in her arms; in a way, she didn't want to let him walk through the door. But she knew that making art was how John would get himself through this; it was her way, too. They stayed alive, even as Tom Kelly, their dearest friend, had died.

Honor held the door as John walked out into the cold. Then she turned around, back to the warmth of her kitchen, and the embrace of her daughters.

As John walked along, he shot pictures. There was something so still and delicate about Star of the Sea in an ice storm—as if it were frozen in time, encased in glass. He went straight to the wall, caught it at every angle, the way the light hit it, the way the ice made every rock glisten. John walked to the section where he and Tom had found the box—hidden there by John and Bernie's ancestor, Cormac Sullivan.

It had contained treasures of the family's Irish past, tokens of their hard work as stonemasons and their desire to build a better life for those they loved. For John, though, it had contained treasures of a different sort: memories, goals, and dreams shared with a man he had come to love as much as if he were his own brother.

Striding along the wall, John felt the icy rain soaking the back of his neck, pelting his face. He raised his camera to shoot, but stopped himself. The weather was art in motion. He could take one beautiful picture after another. But he felt the act of photography pulling him from himself, from the way he felt about his friend.

So he sat down on the wall. As if it were a sunny morning, a seasonably mild October day instead of a driving ice storm. And as if Tom were sitting right there beside him.

John looked down the hill, over the Academy grounds—the vineyard they'd just harvested, the formal gardens laid out in squares, the low hills leading down to the beach, where sand had already drifted over much of the labyrinth he'd built last month. Tom had kept this place running—while John was in prison in Ireland, and before. Tom had loved every inch of this land: because it had belonged to his family, but especially, because of Bernie.

Take care of her.

John swore he heard the words, spoken so clearly.

"Sure I will," John said out loud. "You know how easy *that* is. Trying to take care of my sister is like trying to take care of a nor'easter."

He could almost hear Tom chuckle. They'd talked about it over the years, the frustration Tom felt with Sister Bernadette Ignatius. She was not just strong—she was *headstrong*. Spiritually charged, with the energy of ten people, with a pipeline straight to God via the Virgin Mary, no less.

Hearing a crack overhead, he thought it was thunder, but no, it was a low-hanging pine bough, breaking off a nearby tree. John looked over, saw the fresh wound in the trunk, raw and exposed, as the broken branch dangled precariously. He walked over, knowing that Cece was right: Tom wouldn't like this weather much.

Staring up at the pine tree, at each individual needle encased in ice, John felt himself engulfed by waves of sorrow. Tom had known and loved every single tree here—every pine needle. He had tended this land with pure love and devotion, asking nothing from Bernie except the chance to love her.

Honor was right; Tom would be so happy to know that their son, his and Bernie's, was here at Star of the Sea. That fact struck John as so tragic, he began to cry. Standing right there under the pine tree, thinking of what Tom had missed, John shook his head. Whether it was fate or something else, he knew how unfair this whole thing was: to have Seamus right here, finally, while Tom lay dead in a coffin. When the boy was born in Dublin, Tom had called John from the hospital.

"I have a son!" Tom had said.

"Congratulations!"

"He's fine and healthy, and so is Bernie."

"That's great, man," John had said. He'd paused, hating to ask the question. "Is she still going through with it?"

"She hasn't changed her mind yet," Tom had said. "But I see the way she looks at him, and I think it's going to happen."

"Really? You think she's going to decide to keep him?"

"Yes," Tom had said. "She has to! You have to see her with him, John. The way she holds him, feeds him, looks into his eyes. She says he has my eyes...."

"Poor kid."

"Yeah. But he has her hair, so that makes up for it. The cutest red peach fuzz. God, he's beautiful. I want you to be godfather."

"Tom, wow—"

"I mean, first Bernie has to make it official—tell the hospital and nuns she's changed her mind, that we're going to keep him. But I know that's going to happen. I swear, she won't be able to stand giving him up. You have to see her with him."

Oh, Tom, John thought. Bernie had confounded everyone. Followed her deepest calling. Somehow Tom had stuck with her in friendship, sublimated his love for her, choked it down. He wouldn't ever tell Bernie, but John wondered whether Tom's denial of his strongest needs had killed him in the end.

Suddenly John heard something shattering—the sound was violent yet somehow delicate, coming from down the hill. He looked, saw Bernie standing in her black habit and veil, between two enormous holly trees, holding a long-handled pole, striking each tree once—letting sheets of ice fall from the glossy green leaves and clusters of red berries and tinkle to the ground like broken glass, coming down all around her.

Twenty-Eight

John walked down the hill from the stone wall to the holly grove to meet his sister. She glanced up, saw him coming, didn't speak or greet him at all. She just continued to prod ice down from the tallest branches of the intricately gnarled and twisted old holly trees.

"What are you doing, Bernie?" he asked.

"This ice is going to destroy the holly," she said.

"No, it won't," he said. He saw the way her bare hands gripped the wooden pole—her fingers were red from the cold and looked as if they were frozen in place. "Leave it alone—get inside and warm up."

"You don't understand," she said. "These bushes are very old. They were planted by Tom's great-grandfather. Their branches are so fragile. . . . I have to protect them."

"Bernie," John said gently, alarmed by the look in her eyes. "The ice will turn to rain any minute now. It will all melt, and the holly will be fine."

"Tom always came out in bad weather," she said. "When they were covered with snow, he'd knock the snow off. And during ice storms . . . he tended them personally, as if he knew and loved them. John, did you know that holly is either male or female? There has to be one of each to produce berries. . . . Tom told me that. He knew so much about the land—about every single thing growing here."

"He did know a lot. He loved this place," John said. He held himself back from saying *and you most of all.*

"Francis X. Kelly himself planted these bushes...or had them planted. What would he have thought if he knew his great-grandson was the gardener here?"

"How could he not be proud?" John asked. The words rang in the air; John watched Bernie, her face so full of tension.

"How will we go on without him?" Bernie asked, her eyes red-rimmed. "How will we know what needs to be done as the seasons change?" As if John weren't even there, she raised the pole again, jabbed at a few icy leaves; but her heart had gone out of it.

"He always knew when the roses needed pruning, or when the young boxwood needed to be covered in burlap; he knew how to take care of the oldest plants here, like the holly, and the mountain laurel— the ones planted when Francis X. was still alive; he cherished them so much, because they were a connection to his family."

"We were his family, too."

"But these bushes," Bernie said, frowning, blocking out John's words, "they're so old and rare. What will we do if the storm damages them?"

"Bernie, we can't worry about that right now," John said gently, reaching for the pole.

"But we have to worry about it today," she cried, pulling back. "Because it's icy today! If I don't take care of it now, this holly tree could split and crack—and be destroyed! Oh, John, I can't let that happen! Not after what I did to Tom!"

John tore the pole from his sister's hands, let it clatter to the ground. He pulled her close, let her shudder and sob against his chest.

"Bernie," he said, "you can't do this to yourself."

"I think he died of a broken heart," she howled.

"A *heart attack*," John corrected. "It was sudden and terrible, but it wasn't your fault.... Think, Bernie: he died knowing that he'd brought Seamus to America, helped him find Kathleen. You'd all just been together—that was just as Tom wanted it."

"It was," came an Irish voice from behind them.

Holding Bernie, John turned around. Seamus stood there, under a black umbrella. He stepped forward, holding the umbrella over Bernie's head.

"Seamus," Bernie said, shocked and raw, staring at him.

"Your brother's right," Seamus said. "It was just as Tom wanted it."

Bernie hurried to dry her eyes. She straightened herself up, and John watched her pulling strength out of nowhere, for Seamus. She was still trembling, but her eyes were focused on the young man. As much as John wanted to hold her up, help her back to the convent, he could almost hear his old friend Tom whispering for him to leave them alone.

"Hello, Seamus," he said.

"John," Seamus said.

"Look, Bernie, I'd better go. Honor needs me back at the house."

She nodded, barely glancing at him.

John looked at Seamus shielding Bernie from the ice; his throat tightened, thinking of how often he'd seen Bernie and Tom walking in the rain under a black umbrella. He could almost hear Tom laughing with pleasure over his son's gallantry. And once again, John heard Tom Kelly telling him to get the hell away, leave Bernie and their son alone.

So he did.

"Seamus," Bernie said, "you should go inside. It's icy out here."

"I looked out the window," Seamus said, "and saw you attacking this bush. I wanted to see what you were doing."

"I was just knocking the ice off. It's old, and Tom always took care of it," Bernie said. Staring into Seamus's eyes, she forgot about the holly. It had seemed so important, but it wasn't anymore. "Never mind . . . let's go in."

They walked along the winding path, moving slowly. The ground was slick, and Bernie kept slipping. Seamus held the umbrella over her head; after a few more steps, he moved closer to her and reached for her arm, slid it through his.

"So you won't slip," he said.

"Do you have ice storms like this in Ireland?" she asked.

"No," he said. "The weather is generally more temperate. It's pretty, though, the ice."

"I suppose it is," Bernie said, looking around the campus as if she could see it through Seamus's eyes. Every surface glistened, from the tall blue spruces to the slate rooftops, from the sweeping driveway to the yew hedges. She was shaking inside, but she couldn't let him see. Had he come to tell her he was leaving? They had barely spoken at all. She'd hardly seen him with Kathleen. She imagined his whole world turned upside down, and she didn't know what she could say or do to help him right now.

"Seamus," she began.

"It's hard," he started.

"I know," she said, her heart pounding.

"I heard what your brother said," Seamus said. "Back there, at the holly trees."

"What did he say?"

"About Tom," Seamus said. "That it was as he would have wanted... that last day, when we were all together for a little while."

"Do you think so?" Bernie asked, staring at him. Waiting for his reply, she heard ice hitting the umbrella. He didn't speak for a few seconds, and his eyes looked so guarded.

"You weren't there when he came to see me in Dublin," Seamus said harshly.

"No," Bernie said. "He didn't tell me he was going."

"He told me some things."

"I know there was so much he wanted to say to you."

"He didn't get much chance," Seamus said. "I punched him."

"I know he loved you," Bernie said, gazing up into Seamus's eyes. "And he did from the day you were born. Before, even. He wanted..." She took a deep breath. "Tom wanted to keep you."

"He did?"

Bernie nodded, bowing her head so her veil fell across her face and he couldn't see her eyes. "More than you can imagine," she said.

"And you didn't?"

"It wasn't like that," she whispered. "I had a calling, Seamus."

"A calling to give me up?"

"No. To love and serve God; to become a nun."

Seamus closed his eyes. What was he thinking? Bernie's heart raced as she heard the words she'd just spoken. They came from her heart, but how did they sound to her child?

"Tom and I lived with my choice all these years," she said. "It turned out... well, not to be easy for either of us. We never stopped thinking of you, praying that you were happy and loved."

The storm blew steadily, and gusts of wind nearly turned the umbrella inside out. Seamus got it under control, without saying a word.

"Seamus," Bernie said, "I know that it was terrible for Tom. That's something I have to live with. But more than that, beyond words... I'm just so sorry that you suffered for my choice. I never wanted you to be alone. I thought you'd have a good family...." Her voice trailed off, thinking of what Sister Eleanor Marie had done; she'd gotten a letter from Sister Theodore, saying that Eleanor Marie had been relieved of her duties as Superior, summoned to answer by the order's investigative body.

"Good family?" Seamus asked. Bernie tensed. Was this the moment he would tell her he was leaving? She'd seen such torment in his eyes—even now, fighting the umbrella, he seemed so agitated. She thought of all he had gone through over the years—no mother or father, no happy holidays... She thought of him and Kathleen as babies, toddlers, children together.... The disappointment he must feel in her right now might be fueling him as well.

"Seamus," she whispered.

He gazed at her, and she felt her heart thumping; she wanted to take his hand, make him stay. If he left before his father's funeral, something would always be unresolved. Her blood had pumped through his body; her love for him was so enormous, yet she knew that she had to let him go if he wanted to.

"There are different kinds of good families," Seamus said softly.

"What do you mean?" Bernie asked.

"I had the Sisters," he said.

"And you felt loved by them?" she asked, tears searing her eyes.

He nodded, giving her the greatest gift.

"By them," he said. "And Kathleen."

Bernie swallowed. She wanted so badly to ask him what his plans were about Kathleen, but she wasn't sure she had the right. She had placed them in rooms in separate wings, across the Academy court-yard from each other—just the way Sister Anastasia had back at St. Augustine's Children's Home. She had thought they might wave to each other across the divide, but she was afraid of what Kathleen's announcement about her pregnancy might have done to ruin their relationship even before it had the chance to resume.

"How is Kathleen?" Bernie asked.

"She's beautiful," Seamus said, and Bernie felt startled.

"I haven't seen you together much," Bernie said hesitantly.

"We've been keeping out of the way," he said. "With all that's going on..."

"The times I've glimpsed you, in the refectory and walking the grounds, you've looked so upset...."

"It was a shock," Seamus admitted. "To find out she's going to have a child."

"Yes," Bernie murmured, thinking back to when she'd told Tom.

"It wasn't what I'd expected, but... I'm not sure that matters. We belong to each other."

"Do you mean..." Bernie began. "Will you stay with her anyway?"

"I love her," Seamus said, his eyes fierce and proud. "I want us to stay together forever."

"Oh, Seamus."

"No matter what."

"Have you told her?"

"Of course," Seamus said. "I couldn't have her worrying."

"You're a good man," Bernie said. "Tom would be so proud."

He shrugged; his expression had softened, but his gaze remained steady. Fighting the wind, they had circled around from the seaward side of the Academy to the courtyard. Cobbled with paving stones imported from Belgium by Francis X. Kelly, it glistened under the icy veneer. Cars were starting to arrive for the funeral. Standing apart from everyone with Seamus, Bernie wished she could hide. Stay in the back of the church, follow Tom's coffin to the graveyard, then slip away.

"You had a vision, didn't you?" Seamus asked suddenly.

She nodded. "Yes, I did."

"And Mary told you what to do? To give me up and join the convent?"

"That's what I thought she meant," Bernie said. "Her presence back then echoed what I'd been feeling in my heart. I wanted to love and serve God. But there might have been another meaning...just as there was the day Tom died."

"What do you mean?"

Bernie swallowed. She hadn't told anyone about her latest visitation. She knew from experience how quickly the word could get out, spread, and transform a profoundly personal experience into something the entire church had opinions about. But something about the way Seamus was looking at her—with Tom's blue eyes—made her know she had to tell him.

"Mary appeared to me that morning," she said. "Before Tom picked me up here, to take me to the airport to meet you."

"What did she say?"

"'Be ready,'" Bernie said, gazing into his eyes. She thought of the Cliff Walk; Tom had taken his last breath in a place that had reminded her of where they'd conceived their boy. She'd been so swept away by memory, she'd forgotten to be in the present. "But I wasn't..."

All the Kelly relatives were arriving now. Black Lincolns and Cadillacs streamed into the parking lot, and people dressed in black were walking into the chapel. Chris from Hartford; Sixtus, Niall, and Billy from Dublin. Sixtus spotted Seamus and Bernie; the Dublin brothers all walked over.

"He had the Kelly heart," Sixtus said, his eyes streaming, reaching for Bernie.

"There was never any doubt about that," Bernie said. "He was so strong and brave."

"And it gave out on him," Niall said. "Too soon..."

"Our father died too young," Billy said. "There's no rhyme nor reason. It's a tragedy beyond words."

"Young man," Sixtus said, hugging Seamus, "you have our sympathy. Niall, Billy—this is Seamus. Tom was so proud of him...."

At that, the Kelly cousins all hugged Seamus, telling him that he had family in Dublin, that he always had a home on Merrion Square. Bernie watched him take it all in, his posture erect, holding back, but his eyes glowing with pride. Sixtus shepherded his brothers into the chapel, telling Seamus he would talk to him later.

And Seamus turned to Bernie now, his expression wavering between grief and happiness.

"They're nice," he said.

"They loved Tom," she said. "And they'll love you."

"Their father died of a heart attack?"

"Yes," Bernie said.

"So maybe Tom had the same condition?"

"It's possible," she said. "We always thought that he was so healthy—working outdoors, staying in good shape...but we were wrong. And I should have known. I was warned...."

"You're thinking of your vision?" Seamus asked.

Bernie nodded. She closed her eyes, could see Mary standing beside her, hand on her cheek, whispering with such love....

"Because you thought she meant be ready for Tom's heart attack?"

Bernie nodded, her eyes red, her spirit so tired.

"That wasn't it," Seamus said. "I know you're a nun, and you should know better than me, but I think you have it wrong."

"What, then?"

Suddenly Seamus took her hands. His blue eyes burned, gazing into hers. She could have sworn she was looking straight at Tom, and her knees felt weak.

"Be ready for the gift," he said.

"The gift?"

Seamus nodded his head. "Be ready for the gift you least expect. Every day. It's the only way to live...."

"What do you mean?"

"It's a habit I got into back at St. Augustine's. And it helped me later, when I left and lived...well, when I lived on the streets. It kept me looking for Kathleen."

Bernie tingled, a shiver running down her back. Seamus was talking about faith: belief in light of the absence of proof, enlightenment received through prayer, and that which is seen and unseen.... She thought of the steep trail in Newport, and those other cliffs in Ireland.

"And then you both came along. You and Tom. And I never expected you to help me, or even that I would *let* you help me. But I did. And I let Sixtus help me, too. And because of that..."

"You found her," Bernie said.

Seamus nodded. "It's not perfect. I won't pretend I dreamed that she'd be pregnant, but I don't really care. I love her. People raise other people's children every day. Kathleen and I know that better than anyone."

"Thank you, Seamus," Bernie said. She thought of the Blessed Mother, coming down from the small altar in the Blue Grotto; of course she'd been giving Bernie a gift, reminding her of her deep faith, easing her toward the light in this profound darkness. She pictured Tom's cousins just now, all the way from Dublin, circling around Seamus—leaving Bernie no doubt that they would step in as four wonderful Irish fathers. "Thank you for helping me understand."

"You knew already," he said.

"Maybe I did," she said. "Maybe I just forgot."

He nodded, and they stared at each other for a few seconds, as the moment didn't need words.

"You look nice," Bernie said after a minute of silence. He wore his black suit—the one he'd worn as a driver for the Greencastle Hotel.

"I brought this suit from Ireland," he said, "thinking there might be a reason to wear it, but I never dreamed..."

Just then, the hearse pulled into the courtyard. Bernie's heart caught in her throat as she watched the undertakers climb out, walk through the icy rain to the rear doors. Honor, John, and the girls had arrived, and Bernie could hear her nieces softly weeping. Honor caught her eye, gave her a long look, and then shepherded Regis, Agnes, and Cece into the chapel.

The nuns filed down from the convent and cloister, across the cobblestones. Kathleen was with them, walking beside Sister Gabrielle. She darted over to Seamus, hugged and kissed him, raised her eyes to Bernie.

"I'm so sorry," Kathleen whispered.

"Thank you, Kathleen," Bernie said.

"I'll go in now," Kathleen said, squeezing Seamus's hand. "See you in there."

Seamus nodded, watching her go.

"There," he said, glancing after Kathleen, "that's what I mean. The gift..."

Bernie stood silently, waiting for him to finish as the other pallbearers gathered behind the hearse: John and the Kelly cousins. Sixtus, Niall, and Billy gazed gravely over at Seamus; he met their eyes.

"Kathleen and I being together," he said, "that is a gift from my father."

"Oh, Seamus," Bernie said, eyes flooding. It was the first time she'd heard him call Tom that.

"And from you. My mother..."

Bernie nodded, tears rolling down her cheeks. Seamus reached for her hand. John had been right—the ice had turned to rain. It fell steadily now, a cold drizzle misting their faces. Bernie thought of it sinking into the roots of the plants Tom had so lovingly tended. The rain smelled like salt, blowing off the sea.

"Are you ready?" Seamus asked now.

Be ready....

"I think so," Bernie whispered.

Inside the church, the organ had started to play. The music drifted out the open doors, into the cold rain, drawing everyone together. The pallbearers lifted the coffin. It contained the body of Tom Kelly, and it was all Bernie could do to keep herself standing. Seamus squeezed her hand. Looking down, she saw the Kelly crest ring on his finger. Tears streamed from her eyes.

"He's waiting for us," Seamus said gently. "Let's walk him inside."

Seamus's hand was shaped just like Tom's. Here they were, in the courtyard of Star of the Sea, the place he had always loved so much. John, Chris, and the Dublin Kellys were watching, waiting.

Bernie looked into Seamus's blue eyes. It was as if Tom himself were looking back, gazing at her with all the love he'd always had for her, for their son, for the family they had always been, even when they'd lost sight of each other. Sister Bernadette Ignatius took a deep breath. She linked arms with her son, and together they slowly followed his father's coffin into the chapel.

Epilogue

The baby was four months old. He nestled in his mother's arms as they walked along the narrow path above the ocean, waves crashing and salt spray flying. October had come around again, and today was as brilliant and sunny as the day of Tom Kelly's funeral had been icy and dark.

"We finally made it here, after all this time," Kathleen said, cradling the baby.

"It seemed appropriate," Seamus said, "to come here today."

"I never even got to meet Tom," Kathleen said softly. "I saw him, when you rescued me from Oakhurst. But I never got to thank him...."

"One year ago today," Seamus said. He walked on the outside of the path, protecting Kathleen and Thomas from getting too close to the edge. There had been a wild hurricane in September, and coastal damage had been severe. This narrow path had eroded in spots, with deep gullies slanting down the cliff edge.

"It's hard to believe we haven't gotten here before now," Kathleen said, gazing out over the broad sweep of blue ocean.

"I know," Seamus said. "This is our place, in so many ways."

He pulled the postcard from his pocket. Stained with Tom's blood, it showed the exact scene where they stood right now—grand mansions and craggy cliffs, Atlantic waves breaking on the rocks below.

Seamus had vowed to come here for so long. He thought back to Dublin, all those days he'd stared at the card, feeling the intense, inexorable, tidal pull of Kathleen.

"Why do you think Tom came here that day?" Kathleen asked now.

Seamus didn't reply right away. They walked slowly, feeling the sun on their faces, the salt spray rising on the steady breeze. He thought back to the anniversary, one year ago today; the air had been so chilly, a storm moving in behind the cold front, almost as if the weather had been a portent of what was about to happen.

"Because of us, maybe," he said doubtfully, because something else was tugging at him inside. "Because of your postcard, and what he knew it meant to me."

"Is that why he brought Bernie here that day?"

"I think so," Seamus said. "I think it was his way of being connected with all of us."

"Did she ever tell you what they talked about?" Kathleen asked. "They drove off, came straight here, right? He must have wanted to tell her something, to bring her out on the cliff, such a cold day as it was...."

Seamus stared at the water. He thought of what Bernie had told him, about the vision she'd had the morning of Tom's death. Seamus had given her his word that he would tell no one, and he'd kept it—even with Kathleen. But there were other things Bernie had told him, and he looked at Kathleen now.

"She said that Tom was upset about her decision to stay in the convent...but she felt they came to a sort of peace about it," he said. "For the first time ever."

"I'm glad," Kathleen said, her voice catching, looking into Seamus's eyes. "It's hard when people who love each other aren't getting along."

He nodded, trembling. She was talking about them, partly. The last year hadn't been all easy—nothing like the ease and bliss of what he'd dreamed their reunion would be. As much as he'd wanted to accept the fact she was pregnant, it had been, God help him, a challenge. Over the months, they'd lived at Star of the Sea. Bernie had given Kathleen a room in the convent, and Seamus started out living in Tom's cottage.

Almost immediately, Kathleen began spending every night—she as much as moved in. Although they weren't yet married, and even though it was a Catholic school, no one said anything to them. Bernie just pretended she didn't know what was going on.

Seamus started working on the grounds crew. He found he had a knack for it, and even though he wouldn't want to do it the rest of his life, it was a good way to save up some money for the marriage. He had never felt more right about anything in his life than the day he bought an aquamarine ring in Black Hall and proposed to Kathleen.

She said yes, right away. Even though emotions had been rocky between them, they fell into each other's arms, knowing that this was where they belonged forever. Then, just before Christmas, Seamus and Kathleen got married. Father Quinn, the same priest who'd presided over Tom's funeral, performed the ceremony. Bernie was there, along with John, Honor, their daughters Regis, Agnes, and Cece, as well as Regis's roommates and Brendan McCarthy. Sixtus flew over from Ireland.

Living in Tom's cottage, Seamus had the feeling that Tom was guiding him. John had moved some of his stuff back in; Tom's books were there, and his battered old boots. A whole collection of postcards of Ireland—mainly of the Cliffs of Moher. Seamus had hung them up on the wall, remembering how he'd seen the cliffs from the plane as he'd flown over from Ireland, wondering what they had meant to his father.

And Bernie was always there, acting like a mother to both him and Kathleen. She'd send Cece over with freshly baked bread, hot from the refectory kitchen—or she'd have Agnes and Brendan invite Seamus and Kathleen out to the movies for a double date. When Regis was home from college, she'd stop in with books and CDs, things she thought Kathleen might like. The whole family had tried to make them feel at home.

And most of the time, Seamus did. But sometimes a darkness would open up inside him, deep and cavelike. He'd feel angry and confused, not knowing how to fit into this happy family—and resentful, for the years he'd already missed.

Kathleen helped him through it. They had lost so much time

together, there were some nights they'd stay up until dawn, telling stories and filling in the blanks of their years apart. Or they'd remember someone from St. Augustine's, start reminiscing, and get to laughing so hard they couldn't stop.

As the baby grew inside her, Kathleen got bigger. Sometimes Seamus tried to avert his eyes, or tell himself he didn't care. His wife was carrying the baby of Pierce Wells, idiot playboy of Palm Beach and Newport. There were some nights Seamus lay wide-awake, dreaming of the ways he'd like to kill him. How could some shit just use Kathleen that way? Throw her away night after night?

Seamus would start to sweat, toss and turn in bed until he'd thrown the blankets right down on the floor. He'd climb out, careful not to wake Kathleen up; he'd gently cover her and then go out to the living room to sleep. His mind would race, thinking hateful things about the rich asshole he'd never even met. Kathleen would call for him to come back to bed, and that sometimes made it worse: he'd want to yell at her, ask how she could have let it happen. So he'd storm out of the house, try to walk off the fury he felt inside.

On one of those nights, he stepped outside, sat on a low stone wall outside Tom's back door. Overhead, the stars blazed. He thought of Ireland, knew that he could see the same constellations in Dublin. He could return home. As much as he'd longed for Kathleen all these years, he wasn't sure he could handle these feelings of rage. He couldn't stand how insanely powerless he felt, couldn't bear for Kathleen to see him this way. Homesick for Ireland, for everything that was familiar, he'd gazed up at the sky and prayed to know what to do.

Once last May, a few weeks before the baby was born, Seamus was staring at the sky, intent on his petitions, when he heard a voice.

"It's not easy, is it, kid?"

"Who's there?" he asked, jumping up, turning around, 360 degrees, shocked witless. No one had responded, but he'd sworn someone was there. He'd felt a breeze pick up, where there'd been none before. New leaves rustled on the tree overhead, and the air felt like water moving across his skin.

Had Seamus just dreamed of hearing Tom's voice? God knows he needed an older person's advice and perspective, especially coming from someone who knew a little about the tribulations of complicated love. Jaysus, they'd really done it, Seamus thought: Tom had fallen in love with a nun, and Seamus with a woman carrying someone else's baby.

But after that night, although he'd never audibly heard Tom's voice again, Seamus began to somehow hear it—Tom's voice, thoughts, and advice—not in his ears, but in his heart. Although he'd only met Tom on three separate occasions, Seamus began to feel his presence.

It helped him so much, especially with his love for Kathleen. He stopped trying to fight how upset he was about Pierce Wells, and once he accepted the fact he hated the man and would probably want to kill him on sight, he was able to consign him to a relatively forgotten corner.

Then all Seamus had to do was let himself love Kathleen. And oh, that was easy. Having her lie beside him in bed, smelling her hair, feeling her soft skin, he sometimes felt he was in heaven. Passion would well up in both of them, and they'd reach for each other, so hot with longing and love, and their bodies would find new ways to tell each other secrets that language had long since forgotten how to do.

Seamus knew he had done nothing to deserve such happiness, such an overwhelming feeling of joy and belonging. Emotion flooded through him, his heart and mind, made him want to succeed in everything so he could be a good husband and father to their baby.

For that's how he felt about Thomas.

Sixtus's cousin Chrysogonus "Chris" Kelly had taken care of all the paperwork. Maybe it was his pull with the archdiocese, or just the Kelly way of getting things done come hell or high water, but Seamus's name was on the birth and baptismal certificates. No mention of the nameless creep. Just Kathleen, mother; Seamus, father; and Thomas Sullivan Kelly, their beautiful baby.

Seamus had legally changed his name, in time for the wedding and Thomas's birth. He and Kathleen decided to name the baby after Tom—there was no choice, really. It was just meant to be.

Now, walking along the Cliff Walk on the warm October anniversary of Tom's death, Seamus felt his throat tighten.

"I think this is the spot," he said, looking around. The place Tom had died; Bernie had described it the best she could, and Seamus had taken the details of her description in. He looked down the steep cliff, up at the blue sky, tried to feel his father's spirit.

"Are you okay, love?" Kathleen asked, taking his hand.

Seamus tried to nod, but he wasn't—not really. His father's presence had felt so strong ever since that night in the garden last May. But right now, on this sacred spot, Seamus felt nothing of Tom Kelly; it was as if he had chosen this place of tragedy and grief to desert him. Just then, Thomas woke up. He let out a tiny cry, lifted his head and looked around.

"Hello, sweetheart," Kathleen murmured. "Did you have a good sleep?"

Seamus reached for the baby, held him in his arms. Sunlight sparkled on the water of the wide blue bay, making Thomas blink. Seamus smiled, kissing the baby's head, feeling Kathleen's arm come around him. He felt so bittersweet—happy to be here with his family, but lost and aching without the sense of Tom's presence.

"Maybe we should get going," Kathleen said. "He'll be hungry...."

"Yes, right," Seamus said, looking around.

"I know we came to see the Cliff Walk before we go back to Ireland," Kathleen said, sliding her arm around his neck. "But I have a feeling you were looking for something more."

"Maybe," Seamus admitted, meeting her gaze.

"You wanted to say goodbye to your father, didn't you?"

Seamus nodded, kissing Thomas's head, never taking his eyes off Kathleen. She had always understood him so well, and she still did. Even though he hadn't spoken much about what meeting his parents had meant to him, Kathleen seemed to know exactly.

"You'll never have to say goodbye," Kathleen said fiercely.

"What do you mean?"

"He's with you, Seamus... the way you and I were with each other, all the time we were apart."

Seamus stared into her eyes; he saw such intensity there, and he felt it himself. He knew what she meant, yet still... He had known his father for so short a time, it almost seemed cruel, taunting, to have met him at all.

At that moment, he felt a shiver go down his spine—as if someone had just walked over his grave. He had an Irish respect for ghosts, and as a quick chill rushed through the sunlit air, he felt as if something had stirred the atmosphere.

Seamus turned his head, saw a man wearing an old tweed jacket and walking hat just coming around the bend. He was making his way briskly along the path, and since the way had been narrowed by the storm, it was a tight squeeze. Seamus tensed up, but Kathleen seemed oblivious to the danger. Seamus stepped back, and in that instant, the man came between him and Kathleen.

He stopped on the path. His face was completely shadowed by the hat, but Seamus felt his gaze. Glancing down at the old tweed jacket, he saw that the right sleeve was frayed. He drew in a sharp breath; from this angle he didn't have a good line of sight, but he lunged, trying to see if the jacket's left lapel was stained with blood.

"Tell your mother she's beautiful," the stranger said, his blue eyes shining beneath the brim of his hat. "Tell her to meet me at the cliff path in Doolin."

"Tom," Seamus gasped.

The man stopped, looked Seamus directly in the eye. He seemed to be taking his measure, while trying to absorb every detail about the younger man. Seamus shivered—the man's face was shadowed, but his eyes were unmistakable.

"It's important," Tom Kelly said. "Will you tell her?"

"Doolin?"

"Yes, son," he said. "Our place. Tell her to follow the music. And I'll take her to Tir na Nog, too; she'll know what it means."

Seamus nodded, unable to speak. He had the strongest feeling that Tom meant not the Promised Land of the Saints, but a specific place, here on this earth.

The ghost's expression was urgent with love. Slowly his smile dissolved, and with terrible regret in his eyes, he backed away. Turning, he continued down the other cliff path, walking faster than ever. As he did, a shadow fell over the coastline, then passed along, and the sun was brighter than before. Kathleen didn't turn to watch the man go, or react in any way, and he realized with a jolt that she hadn't seen him at all.

"Why did you just say his name?" she asked with a gentle smile. " 'Tom'? And then 'Doolin'?"

"You didn't just see—" Seamus asked, just to be sure. His heart was racing. He wanted to run after the ghost, but he felt paralyzed.

"All I see," Kathleen said, "are my husband and my son. It's getting late, my love...."

"You didn't just see that man with the hat?"

She shook her head, smiling. "You *are* tired. Come on, let's go now. We can come back next year, when we visit Bernie."

"Bernie..." Seamus said. He had to get to a phone, call her immediately. He kissed Kathleen and, holding the baby, started back along the path, the way they'd come. When they reached a curve in the walk, where it narrowed even more, he saw a few stray threads of wool tweed snagged on sticks protruding from a thicket of bayberry and wild roses: tweed from a jacket.

Slowing down, Seamus reached out his hand. He knew before he touched the yarn what he'd see: brown blood, left from a trip to Ireland, from a fight between father and son.

His own heart nearly stopped. He felt it somersault in his chest. Tom's ghost was gone from sight; all that remained was a light breeze stirring the bushes, blowing across Seamus's skin. It rippled Kathleen's braid and the soft fuzz on the baby's head.

"Are you okay?" Kathleen asked, looking worried.

"Kathleen," he whispered, "I just saw a ghost."

Instead of looking frightened, she began to smile. She looked up and down the path, as if hoping that she would see him, too.

"Was it your father?" she asked.

Seamus nodded. "How do you know?"

"I thought I saw him at Star of the Sea," she whispered. "One morning, when I joined the Sisters for lauds, I looked up in choir, and he was standing right beside Bernie's stall."

"Why didn't you tell me?" Seamus asked.

Kathleen blushed, looking into his eyes. "It was between them," she said. "Such an intimate moment between Bernie and Tom. I...I looked away, not wanting to intrude. I just put it out of my mind."

"What kind of moment between them?"

"Oh, you should have seen the smile on her face...."

"Then..." Seamus began. "Then she knew he was there?"

"Of course," Kathleen whispered.

Seamus held Kathleen tight, the baby snuggled between them. Irish ghosts were a powerful lot. He thought of Sixtus, feeling protected by the ghost of Tadhg Mor O'Kelly rising out of the land beyond the waves every day. And Tom's love for Bernie and—he had to admit this—for Seamus himself, was so strong, he had come back, or maybe never even left.

Holding Kathleen and Thomas, Seamus knew that he had the best family in the world, that he had found real love. Or love had found him...the details of how didn't much matter anymore. He held the bloodstained threads from Tom's jacket as if they were precious treasure, and he thought of what he'd told Bernie about her vision, about the words *be ready*.

He gazed into Kathleen's deep, beautiful eyes, so filled with love, intelligence, and pain, and knew that he would be ready for anything, as long as they were together.

The world was filled with gifts of love, and they had just begun. Waves crashed at the base of the cliff, and Seamus felt overwhelmed with their violence and beauty. His skin prickled, and he knew he had a message to deliver. Bernie was back in Connecticut, at Star of the Sea, and he couldn't wait to tell her that Tom had come to see him as well. But for now, standing on the Cliff Walk, he turned to his wife and child, kissed them both, said, "I love you."

Kathleen whispered it back, and so did the wind.

And then it was time to go home.

PHOTO © GASPER TRINGALE

LUANNE RICE is the author of twenty-eight novels, most recently *The Deep Blue Sea for Beginners*, *The Geometry of Sisters*, *Last Kiss*, *Light of the Moon*, *What Matters Most*, *The Edge of Winter*, *Sandcastles*, *Summer of Roses*, *Summer's Child*, and *Beach Girls*, among many *New York Times* bestsellers. She lives in New York City and Old Lyme, Connecticut.

luannerice.net